Three hundred years ago, it was time.

The world spun as it always had. Men rose and men fell, kings reigned and empires waned, and it was time. Men remembered a Savior Who came, and the world changed for a time. Then men forgot, and the world spun again as it always had.

And it was time.

There was nothing particular about it—some trees, some rocks, and a creek spilling over an unimpressive waterfall into a shallow pool.

Three hundred years ago, it was hidden. An invisible shield cast over an ordinary piece of land where a Tutelo Indian caught a fat trout in the cool stream only the day before. So hidden the Indian would be the last to have looked upon it for centuries to come.

Waiting, aging, growing—untouched, untainted, and unseen

Waiting for him

Waiting for us.

The Glen.

THE GLEN

Carla Coon

To my family,

who put up with a lot.

Prologue

It was a curious wind that blew on that calm, autumn day. No one would notice the lone zephyr or the evil that lay in its wake. It whipped a paper plate off the Martin's splintery picnic table. The plate danced in the air before landing in a pile of torn wrappings and trailing ribbons. The presents were forgotten as fast as Jamie Sanders had chucked the new kickball at Deedee Morgan, declaring a dodge ball war without saying a word. A gaggle of high-pitched screams laced the sleepy Poughkeepsie neighborhood as eight children ran from the swirly colored kickball, enjoying a perfect Indian Summer.

Clarice Martin darted around the corner of the house barely evading a hit. Hugging the wall, she wondered if Em or Dedee had become Jamie's new target. She leaned just enough to peek when her stomach did a nosedive. A whoosh feeling caught her fast like falling on ice. The thought of throwing up cake at her own party flitted across her mind as the scene in front of her waved like a mirage. Her hand flung out to the stucco wall, and Clarice watched everything fade—the bushes, the yellow siding on Snyder's garage, even the other kids. They faded away until all of them looked see-through, as though they were made of Lucite plastic. She squeezed her eyes against the illusion. When she opened them, things seemed even less real, every tree and house replaced with a ghostly image of itself. Ahead, Lizzy and Emma looked translucent too, but they were surrounded by shimmering lights. In fact, all the kids seemed to be wearing these shields of shivering diamonds.

Unaware of anything physical, even the stucco biting her palm, Clarice stood captivated; so absorbed in fact, she had scarcely registered the presence of a thin black cloud slithering overhead when the same blackness swept down toward Emma. It bounced off Em's glistening armor and bounded toward another as if trying to gain entrance. Fascinated, Clarice watched the oily presence swirling from one friend to the next when all at once the thing stopped. It seemed to turn and then face her. Her mouth hung open in a terrified O at the swarm of pulsing filth, beating like a heart and focused directly on her.

Bam!

Something smacked her head, and Jaime's yucking laugh echoed behind her. She watched the blue kickball roll off a foot away, coming to stop by Snyder's garbage cans, which were grey and solid again.

"Yer out, Reece," Jamie yelled, pushing past her to the backyard.

That night lying alone in the dark, Clarice stared out the door of her bedroom to the warm glow on the wallpaper in the hall. A wisp of a girl, Clarice Martin felt tiny in her new pink nightgown in her overly pink room. From the silly poster bed drooling in pink chiffon to the frilly curtains, *Pepto Bismol* walls, and cotton candy throw rugs, her bedroom reeked of pink. Gross! It was her mom who liked pink. The problem was that except for being smaller than most girls, being forced to wear pink and curl her hair, Clarice saw herself as a tomboy. After all, she was the first to shimmy O'Boyle's birch tree, and the only one to take the boy's dare and jump off the garage roof. Which is why as she lay in the dark with her fist unconsciously squeezing the life out of her coverlet, she was irritated at her own fright. She forced her hands to relax. She was no chicken; she was seven now, but what the heck? What was that thing? Defiant, Clarice kicked her leg free of the covers. A chill of icy fingers crept over the exposed foot. She yanked it back under the comforter, wishing she had a sister she could talk to. Of course, her mom never had any more kids. She said, "Lordy, but one was enough!" Clarice had no one to tell.

Nothing to tell, she yelled to her mind. *Quit it, quit thinkin' 'bout it.* She concentrated full force on the hall wallpaper with the gold carriages that looked like Cinderella's coach. Nothing to think about, just carriages, and Cinderella, her new skates, and birthday cake, the new kickball, and carriages, and....

It was still dark when Clarice woke facing the wall. She rolled over looking for the trusty wallpaper, and something on the second-story window caught her eye — a hand, a huge hand, palm side down and splayed against the pane. Her mind froze, unable to process the impossibility of what she was seeing. She blinked, but it was still there. A scream stuck in her throat like peanut butter. She stared at the man's giant hand, bigger than her dad's; it could have been beautiful if it wasn't so scary. *There's no arm. Where is the arm?* Maybe she just couldn't see it. Suddenly it seemed as though the hand knew she was looking at it. Her eyes snapped to the wood floor, and her heart thumped against her ribs under the silky nightgown.

She waited. The house was weirdly quiet—no dripping faucets, moaning pipes, or creaking wood she usually heard when she lay awake. The quiet made a sound all its own as she debated what to do. She pictured the trip down the hall to her dad's room. He'd know what to do. No way would she scream or look at the hand, nor let on how scared she was.

One... she pictured her arms throwing back the pink covers. Two... she saw her feet on the floor. Three! Clarice tore off the covers and ran, keeping her eyes in front. Two seconds later, she stood by her dad's bed tugging his striped pajama shirt.

"Daddy, wake up. C'mon please. You gotta come and see— it." She didn't want to say see the hand, cause if he could see that it was a hand, it would prove she wasn't dreaming. Her father wouldn't budge. She tugged some more and raised her voice a smidgen, careful not to wake her mama. Finally, he gave in and allowed her to lead him down the hall. The hand was still there when they returned, and Clarice tried to decide whether or not that was a relief. Her dad walked over to the window and she stayed behind him.

"It's right there," she pleaded with him.

"Ooookay now, calm down, Reecie," he said after dutifully looking out the window then back at his daughter. He ran a hand through his sandy hair, smacked his lips, and turned her around to bed.

"It's nothing," her dad mumbled gently pushing her little shoulders back on the pillow.

Clarice stared at the hand.

"I see a hand, Daddy. I see it."

"A hand? Out there?" He pulled her sheet and blanket over her giving it a little straightening tug. "Now, Pumpkin." He always called her Pumpkin, and usually the endearment made almost anything bearable — Mama's ridiculous outbreaks, her weird airs, her mean streak, but tonight his tone meant he was putting her off. He kissed her forehead and smiled sleepily. "Maybe it's the hand of God."

She looked back at the window as her dad retreated, thankfully, leaving the hall light on as he passed. The hand had gone. Poof — just gone. Clarice lay wide awake, first concentrating on the windowpane, ready for any stray appendages that might affix themselves to the glass like a Garfield car sucker. Finally satisfied, she scrunched herself tighter, as if her skinny legs could disappear any further under the comforter. She looked out to the welcoming glow in the hallway and studied the gold carriages and footmen.

Hand of God? Well, it was gone now, but one thing was for sure, Clarice Martin thought, she didn't want anything to do with it. No way, nothing!

* * *

March 1991

"You crazy or something?"

Clarice's eyes fluttered, as if light was something new to them. Her head lobbed to one side looking down a row of streetlights, their drooping sunflower heads casting yellow beams like so many stage lights. Huh? She was in the parking lot outside the gym, not

4

in it. Hadn't she been inside cheering, watching the game? Clarice remembered Mrs. Hansen, Dad's hospice nurse, telling her to, "Go, just go and enjoy the game." She never got to go out anymore. It wasn't safe leaving Dad alone with Mom, now that her mom had been diagnosed with Alzheimer's.

"Like whatsa matter with you?" the voice demanded.

She lay on her back feeling the cold sidewalk, the voice somewhere above her, the smell of cigarettes in the air. Two, no three faces came into view — two guys and a girl's staring down, curious but unconcerned. Beyond them rose the looming red brick of the High School, its two Notre-Damish parapets and heavily barred windows staring down at her.

"You drunk?" one of the faces asked.

"Course she's drunk, dim wit. Why else would she pass out on the frickin' sidewalk?"

"Well, help her up already," a girl's voice cried.

"Should we call someone?"

"No! What the frick, we snitches or something?"

Clarice felt a rough hand on her elbow pulling her up, smelling his smoky leather coat in her face. A moment later, she was standing as the girl pushed the boy away.

"Jeesh, Gary let 'er breathe, will ya."

"It's okay," Clarice moaned, embarrassed beyond belief and trying to think of what to say. "I'm okay, I'm... thanks, it's cool." The three parted like the red sea. One of the guys laughed, the snigger catching in his throat ending in a snort sounding almost as bad as one of her laughs. Snow on her backside melted into her jeans and sweater. She walked away—a controlled, even step— then quicker leaving the three smoking Samaritans in front of the gym. She crossed the parking lot, turned on the street heading back to the apartment. There was no debate about getting her coat — the vision of pulsing blackness that drove her outside—screaming she thinks—came back to her. No way was she going back in there. Not a chance.

1

"They Found It"

Low afternoon sun streamed in the tiny bedroom of the Miller's Cape Cod throwing a sabre of white light across the oak floor and ending just in front of a pair of sturdy black oxfords. Mrs. Michelle Nicestrum sat perched on the edge of his bed, a bible in her lap. She'd been keeping vigil by her charge's side ever since he lapsed into another of his catatonic trances.

Michelle noted the hour hoping his parents would not return before the boy came to. These episodes were always more dramatic when they were here. She reached out, placed a hand on Jackson's stiff leg, cold as a corpse, like he stepped out of his shell. Nearly five, the baby fat was gone except for his full cheeks. His rose bud lips were parted, and his green eyes open, staring into space. Michelle glanced up at the picture over his bed comparing Jackson's blond curls and sweet mouth to the print. *Light of the World,* wasn't that the name of the painting? She remembered giving the garage sale find to his mother for the baby's room, pleased with the handsome frame. That was the first time she'd noticed Clarice's aversion to anything religious, though the girl had been too polite to deny the gift. The picture hung first over his crib and now over his bed.

Michelle sighed and shifted her position, short legs pushing the matronly figure on the mattress edge. Even when uncomfortable, Mrs. Nicestrum sat regally. A sturdy five-foot-two practical dresser in tweed skirts and soft sweaters, she had been with the Millers since Jackson was born. Snowy white hair in a dignified upsweep met a pappy face of feathery skin, intelligent eyes, and a compassionate smile. The kind of woman who'll say, "Oh well" and roll up her sleeves when disaster strikes. She owned that quiet, earned authority, given respect not for any great feat but for her daily and personal charity. When people invariably mispronounced her name, she would sweetly correct them saying, "Nice rhymes with ice, and strum sounds like drum."

She'd been sitting so long her joints ached with arthritis, which was bad today. *Well, what can't be helped should be ignored.* Her head bent to the familiar Psalm.

> *Near indeed is salvation for the loyal; prosperity*
> *will fill our land. Love and truth will—*

"They found it."

His clear voice sliced across the verse like a paper cutter. Little Jackson gazed up, vacuous eyes returning to normal.

Mrs. Nicestrum, whose breath caught at the news, managed to level her voice peering over her reading glasses. "They have?"

Jackson sat up nodding, a dampish blond curl falling across his forehead. "Well now,"—she stroked the lock from his eyes—"it won't be too much longer then, will it?"

"Mommy doesn't understand, yet."

Mrs. Nicestrum pulled her glasses from her nose and let them drop on the pearl chain. "I know, dear, but she will."

He was quiet, his eyes cast down. She could never ask his thoughts or what he had seen in his ecstasies. The little boy, who only an hour ago had played with those Legos on the floor, sat alone contemplating a destiny she could but glimpse. Oh, if only she could spare him! Yet, her task called for his protection alone.

"Nicey, when will I go there?"

"Now, now, you know that has not been revealed. The time will be shown to us."

Jackson pushed himself into her arms, almost knocking her off the bed. She sat there comforting the boy wondering just how much he saw in these trances. Such an extraordinary being,

8

intuitive, genius, articulate, graced with compassion and empathy, yet just a boy. She alone understood the complexity of this child and the grandeur of his purpose.

He squirmed in her lap, nuzzling in, unbalancing her. She attempted to lift them both higher on the bed, her bones crying in complaint. At eighty, she felt old and tired. How much longer could she protect him?

Oh my! She choked on a more frightening possibility. *If Clarice and John have found his sanctuary, who else may know of it?* There would be some who would stop at nothing to prevent him from reaching the *silva templum*. Yet, Jackson must wait for the appointed time. She held him closer, thinking of the danger ahead.

* * *

HE

The farmhouse was old and rundown. If it had ever been painted, it would be impossible to say. The hundred-year wood had turned a murky grey, perhaps in quiet sympathy to the neglected yard. Truth was no one in Cobleskill could even remember when the land had last functioned as a farm, and most would be surprised to learn the property was actually in use. To the members of *Ordinatio Triune Orbis*, it was known only as *The Ranch*.

The sun slid further behind the hill, deepening fingerlike shadows that crept across the plank floor, pointing all the way to the ornate desk where *he* sat.

"They found it," He said, opening his eyes looking for his bodyguard.

A brawny, longhaired-Italian named Sergio turned from the front window where he'd been looking out at the barns and bunkhouse. His boss closed his eyes again. Sergio studied him unsure whether or not he had been addressed. *He* always looked the same in one black suit after another. Tall and unnaturally thin from years of self-deprivation, full gray hair swept back with one shocking black streak at the temple. His face was undeniably

9

handsome, even considering his eighty years on earth. He sat stiffly, bony fingers resting on the arms of the red-leather, high-back chair. The chair was gaudy. Everything in the room was garish to Sergio. His eyes roved the once simple parlor — a minute imitation of a king's throne room from the Louis XIV desk on the heavy oriental carpet, to the long gilded mirror reflecting a hundred crystals dangling from the chandelier. Looked like Madame Tussaud threw up. The whole of the room sat in ludicrous contrast to the run-down farmhouse that contained it.

"Found what?" Sergio said, always feeling a little dull in his presence. The compelling black eyes remained closed, so Sergio returned to looking out at the ranch. His mind chicked off a list. He'd checked the barns where Lee and Gage were feeding the girls. Man, it reeked in there. How did they stand the stench? He made a mental note to have the barns hosed again. The gate was locked; he'd seen to that himself, and every inch of the mile of barbed wire cordoning off the private property had been inspected. No one was getting in or out.

"The sanctuary, Judas." He rose, walked over to join Sergio at the window.

Sergio's teeth clenched at the pet name. The master called him Judas because he'd betrayed his own friend for drug money. He renamed Mark too, the other bodyguard. He called him Cain because Mark killed his own brother in cold blood. Both he and Mark were indebted to him. Mark had been seconds away from life in prison while Sergio's own treachery had left him a hair's breadth from being maimed by his former gang. *He'd* given them new lives, fed their every fantasy, given them every privilege as they gleefully fell further and further from any speck of goodness in their pathetic lives. He could care less that they hated him, Sergio thought, so long as they stayed fiercely loyal and obedient, aware of their place under him... and in Hell.

The nickname bugged Sergio all the more since *He* rejected his given name —if he ever had one. His arrogance was bar none, refusing to be called anything by his lessers. Sergio cringed smelling his vile breath so close. He hesitated, unsure of whether he was expected to continue the conversation. "Do, uh, you know where it is?" Sergio said.

"Imbecile," he hissed, "I'm not omniscient." He dragged his S'es like a snake. He fell silent. After a full minute, he spoke again almost as though Sergio were his confidante.

"We must reach the boy before he is led to the sanctuary, Judas. We still have time to find him." One gaunt hand caressed the other, and Sergio stared down at the odd habit, thinking aside from the rapes, it was probably the only human touch he enjoyed.

"The boy's parents are blind to his purpose, and his protector's light grows dim."

Why should they care if some kid lives in the woods, Sergio wondered. What kind of threat could a little boy be? Besides, wasn't it enough they risk being caught kidnapping the girls he requires to impregnate?

SWISH. The old man's hand flew across Sergio's left temple. Blood oozed from the fresh cut.

"Idiot! None of those things are your concern."

Sergio watched him lick blood from the yellow nail that had swiped him. Never sure how to react when his thoughts were read, he swallowed his hatred, made his mind blank, and awaited his next command.

* * *

SIMEON

"They found it."

Father Simeon started at the sound of his own voice breaking the stillness of the chapel on the wooded Hermitage. He hadn't meant to say it aloud, but the vision caused him such joy that he'd broken the rules. The grey-clad monk of a different order two pews in front of him turned to inquire in a respectful whisper, "What's that, Father? Do you need something?"

Simeon shook his head then flicked his hand to make the concerned young monk turn back around. When the young monk seemed in no hurry to obey the flickery, Simeon bent his head back to his beads, more fully ignoring him.

The trouble was the other religious here held him in too high a regard. They saw a tall, sinewy, Merlin-like figure with a long gray beard and eyes that twinkled with suspicious inner knowledge of all their faults. Simeon had become cranky in the winter years of his life, but those who knew him excused the rudeness as impatience for this world and longing for the next. His judgments were true and never minced with false charity. The almost accidental founding of Mount Charbel forty years previous had gained him, he felt, undeserved attention and undue respect. As a young priest, he had come up here to live a solitary life of contemplation and prayer. Eventually though, he was hounded by throngs of people looking for a guru. Mount Saint Charbel, in the hills of Maine, New York was really born of the people, not him. So even though the Marionite Order of the monk two pews ahead now owned the Hermitage, he, a cantankerous old Franciscan, was revered and coddled as its beloved founder.

It was no use. He could barely concentrate after the vision. Simeon gave up on his rosary and re-slung it through the thick rope on his brown habit. Rising, the ancient bones in his knees rebelled with an embarrassing crack. They had the gall to crack again as he held the wooden pew and genuflected in the short aisle. Outside, he reclaimed his walking stick and made his way along wooded paths to a favored bench by the pond. Saint Francis Lake, actually a large dug out pond, was a tranquil spot, its placid grey water completely surrounded by a forest of maples and pines. Brisk air nipped Father Simeon's cheeks as he blessed his woolen cassock. Blue sky seen through a cathedral-like canopy of budding greens was turning that delicious pink azure marking the end of another day. The ducks gathered to beg crumbs the moment he sat. Simeon reached in his robe to find the roll he'd saved for them.

"They found it," he said, tearing tiny pieces of bread, "but the child is not yet delivered." Several ducks fought over a larger chunk. "Squabblers!" he chastised and continued thinking out loud. "I don't know where he is, or who he is. Even the boy's protector remains unknown to me. Oh, but what I have seen! Such mercy! So many souls to be affected by just one." His brow creased, and he directed his speech to one particularly precocious duck.

"It isn't all roses you know. No, my no. Some will see his message of salvation as a threat. There is one at least who won't easily suffer the loss of so many souls." The big brown duck jammed his bill into Father's hand, which in his distraction had ceased tearing crumbs. "Ow! Cheeky aren't you?" The duck's the attack seemed to speak of the boy's imminent peril. Oh, when would he be able to help the child? "Why show me so much," he cried looking up, "when I can do nothing until I meet him?"

But that wasn't true. The bread gone, Father Simeon watched the ducks swim away, freed his wooden beads and prayed.

2

The Glen

The Miller's Gold Blazer grumbled as it climbed the mountainside in Ithaca, New York. Blacktop and yellow lines had disappeared some time ago. The roads were rough and stony, but the scenery more than made up for it. It was the first of June, and the hills were dressed in that bright new green only seen up North when the trees awaken from winter slumber and their leaf buds first open. The air tasted warm and sweet, ripe with the promise of long summer days.

Clarice Miller gripped the armrest on the passenger door looking over at John who was driving. His six-foot frame was firmly planted in his seat while she held on like a kid on a rollercoaster. She was a tiny thing at only 5'2" and 105 pounds. *Easy for him*, she thought. Her husband glanced at her just when another jolt tossed her in the air, her bottom leaving the seat a good six inches behind. When John laughed, she joined him.

"Good," he said.

"What?"

"You, laughing."

He reached a strong hand over and gave her leg a squeeze, leaving his hand on her knee. "Reece, you've been jiggling that leg since we turned up this road. You thinking about Jax?"

Clarice nodded, but immediately justified the fib to herself. After all on some level, wasn't she always thinking about her son Jackson? But her nervous jiggling was something else. She felt all on edge. A curious apprehension tickled her chest, as if something were up there waiting for her. She hated those feelings, and this one was brutal. *C'mon Reece, get a grip*. She placed her hand on John's.

"He'll be fine." Clarice rubbed his big hand admiring the deep tan.

"So does Mrs. Nicestrum know this realtor?"

"Hmm, I don't know," Clarice said, trying to recall the circumstances of Nicey recommending the agency. "I'm not sure she knows anyone there. She did say they handled her house years ago."

"You mean when her husband died?"

"Yeah, I'm guessing it's the same realtor who sold their house when she moved to the apartment."

"Welp, I hope these directions are right." John swerved the car to miss a gorge-sized rut. "This is pretty remote; I haven't seen a house since we left 79."

"Me neither." Stretching her tiny figure in the seat, she forced herself to relax and tapped John's arm. "That bother you, hon? This too far away from where you want your office?"

"Oh, I forgot to tell you," —John gave the wheel a thump— "I found space for rent downtown. It'd be perfect for a satellite office." He looked pleased, that ready to take on the world pleased. "Anyway, I've been clocking this, and if the directions are right, we'll only be about 20, maybe 30 minutes from Ithaca."

Clarice uh-huh'ed as her fingers found the window button. She turned her head toward the fresh air, her right shoulder feeling a little chill making her wonder if the sleeveless shirt might have been a gamble. "Did you bring a jacket?"

"Nope. How many acres did they say were up here?"

"Five," she said, pulling her head back in, ready to talk if he wanted. John leaned over the steering wheel concentrating on the road, looking excited and probably already dreaming about living in a veritable wilderness. She loved that about him, a real man's man, full of adventure and rugged strength. A wavy chestnut-haired Mel Gibson beauty, whose physique fell between that of a linebacker and a quarterback, John was humble, wholesome, and completely unaware of his own charm.

16

She thought for the thousandth time how lucky she was to have him. She'd spent so much of her childhood not fitting in — first fighting for acceptance, then trying just to blend in, and finally content to simply be ignored. She never dreamed someone like him would fall in love with her. Then again, he knew nothing of that ostracized little girl, the one who eventually learned the best way to dodge the taunting kids, avoid the delusional mother, and spare her poor dad was to disappear and withdraw into herself—to become so unimportant she no longer mattered. Clarice shook her head; she was no longer that little girl. To John she was beautiful, loved, and very normal.

John let the conversation drop as he daydreamed. Clarice returned to the window watching the thick, lush woods whiz by. They both loved the woods, loved walking in them, hiking and exploring. Her heart lifted. This might be cool if she could just.... Instead the premonitory sensation vexed her like flies on a pony. She couldn't swat them, but she had a hundred tricks for ignoring them. Her ears caught a string of familiar notes on the radio. She leaned over, turned it up, let the song fill the car.

> *I don't mind spending every day*
> *Out on the corner in the pouring rain...*

It was comfortable like this, not talking. It was never like this with any but John, her son, Jackson and Mrs. Nicestrum. With most she had to put on a face, make conversation, or worse, fight not to see the ugly darks and twinkling lights that accompanied their souls.

> *Look for the girl with the broken smile. Ask her if*
> *she wants to stay a while, and she wiilll be*
> *loved... and she will be lu-uuu-ved.*

The song ended as they pulled up beside a realty sign. John cut the engine, and the quiet of the mountain filled the car. Clarice looked out the window surprised at how flat the land was after the long climb. Sparsely covered with young maples and scrub brush, the five roadside acres stood out, bordered on three sides by dark forest. Across the road, the land dropped back down the hillside.

John leaned over her, pointing out the passenger window. His face was inches from hers, his soft brown hair brushing her cheek and fresh cologne teasing her nose. *Man, she loved this guy.*

"Woo," —he whistled—"look at those giant oaks." Scattered amid the thin, grey trunks of the maples were several stately oaks, their colossal brown trunks sprayed in sage colored moss.

"Whoa, I bet they're at least two hundred years old," she said, visualizing some pioneer planning a homestead, chopping down trees, and sparing these handsome specimens, perhaps to shade his cabin. Whoever it was, apparently never got to build it because, at least according to the realtor, no one had ever settled up here.

"They're perfect, aren't they?" John said, "Made to order." He kissed her head and slid out of the car. They met in the road and turned their attention to the view of Ithaca in the distance where mounds of green hills overlooked the valley below. Clarice tucked herself under John's arm, enjoying the farms and little hamlets that dotted the landscape.

"Check it out," John pointed to the left where a bit of Cornell University could be seen. "What if we get season tickets and see all the home games?"

Despite the view and John's exuberance — both of which she loved — Clarice could barely focus. The feeling had returned, only now the little buggers jumped up and down in her chest like the stars of a flea circus. She heard John's deep voice say something about re-stoning. "What? Re-stone, what's that?"

"I said—" he began then stopped, tilting his head. "You alright, Reece?"

"Yeah, I'm fine. It's... nothing," she lied, taking another gulp of air to smack the skipping, uninvited guests down.

"They use a mixture of tar and stone," John said, turning back to the land. "Road needs more stone, is all. It'll prob'ly be fine after that." A light breeze caught a slice of chestnut hair sending it across his high forehead. "Hey," John said, catching the strand and then shielding his eyes from the waning sun, "what if we build over there?" He did an about face, strode across the road, and looked over the embankment.

It was like this at every property, the measuring, planning and estimating, scoping out the land, weighing every aspect. Of course, her John had a lot more riding on it than most homebuyers since he would build the house himself, or at least his construction company would. She was proud of him, all he'd accomplished, how hard he worked. Nonetheless she watched him pace the distance to the nearest pole with nothing but relief, knowing he would be mentally calculating for a while.

Turning from John, Clarice gazed ahead to the massive timbers bordering the old forest. Before she knew it, she was walking across the lot, crunching over weeds and dodging thickets. Her pace was brisk as she headed for the dark wood. The forward momentum felt right— a sweet release to the pent up sensations. In fact, she thought, finding her way around a giant briar if she stopped walking right now, her spirit might pop out of her body and continue on its own.

Awed, Clarice reached the forest edge and slowed her step. Before her lay a textbook example of ancient woodland from seedlings to fallen giants. Her head fell back, scanning the straight trunks of oaks and hemlocks, stretching a hundred feet above her. Like silent guards to another realm, these regal mammoths with shaggy bark and buttress roots had stood for uncounted centuries. Standing there her heart raced. She pulled her eyes from the lace canopy and moved forward. The ground was covered with leaves, broken branches, lichens, and ferns. She picked her way around a fallen hero, her palm landing on a crop of mushrooms that sprouted from the decaying corpse. Wiping her hand on her jeans, Clarice spied a giant fern. She plucked it and continued walking.

John turned from the electrical wires swooping over the road and caught a glimpse of Clarice's peach shirt disappearing into the forest. *What the heck? Where is she going?* He frowned. He'd wanted to spend more time on the lot; now he'd have to follow her. His work boots pounded easily over the field of bushy weeds, tracing her trail of bent grass. Weaving through slender maples, around bur and briar, John mentally noted which trees would go or stay in their imagined yard. By the time he reached the dark wood, Clarice was nowhere in sight. He followed a crude deer path amazed to find himself in a climax forest, the kind of rare environment where three hundred-year-old trees grow wide and far apart.

John inhaled the spicy pines and rich earth. Yup, this is why they want to live near Ithaca. A couple of years ago, they'd picnicked at Buttermilk Falls and fallen in love with the hiking trails, gorges, and waterfalls. Ever since then, he'd been keeping tabs on Ithaca. His construction company in Binghamton *was* fairly new, still, it could move anywhere there was a market. Ithaca was seeing a resurgence of new homes and Miller Construction intended to tap into it.

Not a trace of her. John doubled back to circle the area. Almost to the forest opening, he stopped, pulled out his new Blackberry. *Crud,* no signal —not one bar. "Reece, Reece!" he yelled, letting out one of his famous whistles. John's whistles were so loud Jackson and Clarice could hear them from the park four blocks from their house. John stood perfectly still for a moment; the old forest stared back at him in stony silence. He ventured off the path, noting a lone sassafras tree. He'd have to start remembering landmarks to keep from getting hopelessly lost. Climbing over the giant cadaver of a rotting fir tree, something green on the dead leaves caught his eye—a fern with its top torn off. Encouraged, John continued looking. Bam, there was another piece. She definitely came this way! He'd seen her pull leaves off like that a hundred times as they hiked.

Far ahead, Clarice stepped around a wide oak, caressing the trunk. As her fingers slipped into the deep ruts, she wondered at not feeling the least bit frightened. After all, she'd seen some pretty scary things in that other world, and this weird call to her spirit reminded her of those feelings. There was no telling what she may encounter, but. . . no, this wasn't like that at all. She felt a hundred percent here. She slapped a fat trunk. *So are you, just as solid and real as you should be.* There was something friendly here, she decided, biting her lip and veering left, as though an arrow were nailed to the tree.

The land curved in a gradual descent, and water gurgled somewhere below. She quickened her step, leaves and twigs snapping underfoot. Whatever it was; it was close. Soon the land leveled off. In the distance, like the backdrop for a stage, rose a short wall of grey shale. Over this spilled a waterfall, filling a small pool and flowing out to a stream. The glen seemed brighter than everything around it. Clarice's steps slowed to a reverent tiptoe.

Framing the Glen, clear waters swept by like liquid glass, trees politely stood apart for dappled sunlight to play on the forest floor, nourishing ferns and undergrowth. A few enormous boulders rose on a carpet of the most lush and healthy moss she'd ever seen. Every rock and twig, every plant, lay in the perfect spot, as if it were meant to be there. . ., as if it must be there.

"What is this place?" she whispered, barely able to take in the Eden-like beauty. Her senses quivered aware of a living presence, something old and powerful. She became conscious of a certain resonance and hum of the place. Bluebirds trilled above her answered by chirrups of tiny sparrows like playful teapots coming to a boil. The sound of leaves rustled by scurrying chipmunks played against the low buzz of insects. Clarice closed her eyes and tilted her head listening to the symphony. A soft wind brushed her cheek, bathing her in pines and flora and wrapping her in curious arms, as though she and the Glen were one.

Long forgotten powers stirred within her. Feelings she'd always shaken off or ignored. Not here. Here they reigned, real, present, and so undeniable.

John continued searching, not exactly pissed, perturbed was more like it. If she couldn't hear him, how would they find each other? *You better keep plucking those leaves, Reece.* He resisted the urge to hurry, afraid he'd miss one. He didn't get it. Why hadn't she stayed on the lot? They only had so much time; what if Jax had another episode?

Until recently, their son's trances had been rare. His condition was a mystery, and doctors were clueless as to the cause. John wondered about Jackson's natural father, whether this problem was in his genes or something. When he met Clarice —God, he fell in love with her fast —she was pretty close-mouthed about the father, who seemed to be totally out of their lives anyway. Jax was barely eight months old then, and Mrs. Nicestrum was already in the picture. He even thought she was Jackson's grandma, she was so devoted. He remembered the first time he met Mrs. Nicestrum, how she stood there holding the baby close while she peered at John, checking him out as if there were an invisible sign with small print on his forehead. Come to think of it, she was like that with anyone new around Jackson.

Shining eyes in a soft pulpy face, intelligent questions in that mellifluous tone, the firm way she held her plump frame. Yet her scrutiny never felt unfair, quite the opposite. One felt justified by her approval and rightly chastised when censured. Nicey warmed pretty quickly to John, and he couldn't have found a bigger fan. All four of them were like family now, and John was Jackson's father, through and through. He'd kill to protect him. But this condition, this illness or whatever it was, if the natural father—

Shoot. John checked his watch. They promised Mrs. Nicestrum they'd be back by seven, and the drive home is at least an hour. Brooding, John continued downward till he reached a flatter area. He heard water gurgling up ahead. Through the trees he caught a glimpse of peach. He approached her quietly admiring his wife.

The sleeveless shirt showed off graceful arms and a long neck. He liked the low riding jeans she said made her look fat. Her figure was real, he thought, not the stuff of Atkins, South Beach, or some Zone Diet; hell, she even drank real coke. His wife had a secret weapon, though —Clarice loved to run (a passion second only to her love of painting). Light brown hair fell to her shoulders in tousled waves that always seemed to do their own thing. It was kissed with gold—a gift of the sun from untold hours outdoors. She wore little make-up, owned few dresses, and way too many flannel shirts. Standing there, as natural as the woods about her, Clarice's petite frame seemed frozen. Her green eyes riveted to the spot, she was entirely too still. All at once, John wanted to get her out of there and back to the open woods.

"So, what do you think?" He stepped forward and broke in on her silent reverie.

Clarice's chin jerked up, her face blank. After a full second, she shook her head, as if to make room for his question. "I think,"— she managed to answer, her eyes still feasting—"it's perfect."

As they walked back to the Blazer, John chatted on and on about the possibilities of the land for their house. Clarice remained oddly quiet coming out of her reticence when they hopped into the SUV.

"I love this place, John."

"So I take it our search is over?"

Clarice nodded and leaned over to kiss him before buckling up.

3

Siren of Screams

Shirtless and barefoot, John stood in the kitchen making up a tray of coffee for Clarice and himself. The linoleum felt cold, but his sweats were keeping the chill off his legs. He'd been up since five thinking about what kind of offer to make on the land in Ithaca. The realtor mentioned a bigger piece available, too. Man, but that land was perfect for their plans! Close enough to Ithaca where he'd already set up a satellite office for *Miller Construction.* And the forest! So un-fricking touched you expect a pterodactyl to fly over. They couldn't meet the asking price though, not that it wasn't worth every penny. He had to consider the cost of building, and even though his own company would do the work, the new house promised to bleed them dry. It wasn't as if the company wasn't healthy. They'd landed the retirement home project, thank God. If he could just keep the costs close to the bid.... When does that ever happen? Still he'd be hung before he'd rip anyone off. Had to look over their finances later and make a fair offer after Mass maybe. Oh yeah, Mike would be calling with names for the crew and the brick order —man, there was a lot of to figure out— but later.

It was Sunday. With Jackson still asleep in his room, he figured Clarice and he could stay in bed this morning, at least till the little guy came looking for them. John gathered two black mugs, the sugar shaker, and spoons, and leaned into the fridge to get the pint of half-and-half. He nosed around for something else to put on the tray. Slim pickings, not a piece of fruit, no bagels, no eggs. *Coffee's it then.* He hoisted the tray, spying the blueprints to their future house on the table. These he tucked under his arm and headed down the short hall to their bedroom, stopping for a second outside Jackson's room.

John grinned at Jackson sleeping like a toddler with his bottom pointed skyward. The clock on his dresser read 6:57. On weekdays Clarice was up by five, well before him, so she could run; Saturdays too sometimes, but not Sundays. On Sunday, Clarice liked to relax, maybe read the paper, and always make a big breakfast for them. He came in seeing her stretch in bed, her elbows bent and her hands behind her neck. He watched delicate fingers push up through her hair and poke out like so many geisha sticks then pull through the waves of brown silk. Two irresistible legs kicked free of the covers. Even in a cut-off gray sweatshirt and shorts, she managed to look appealing. Now he wanted more than coffee... of course, Jax would be up soon.

"Hey," he said quietly, setting the tray on their dresser.

"Ummmm, I'll have mine black, monsieur, with two fluffy croissants and scrambled eggs." She smiled back.

"Sorry, ma'am, just coffee. Kitchen's a little short on extras."

"Ugh, I knew there was something we forgot to do yesterday." Clarice wiggled her fingers in a gim'me here sign, and John passed her a mug of coffee. "Ooo actually," —she took the cup and placed it in on her nightstand—"I gotta go first."

While she was in the bathroom, John snagged a couple of heavy books off his nightstand. He made himself comfortable on the bed, unrolled the blueprints over the covers and placed the books on the edges of the springy paper.

Since they first married four years ago, Clarice and John had been planning their dream house. They envisioned a solid farmhouse with gracious rooms and a welcoming porch that would wrap around their homestead in a warm embrace. Clarice, a lover of sunshine, drew floor to ceiling windows on the many sketches over which they collaborated. John insisted on as many doors as there were sides to the structure, planning labyrinths of stone walkways to connect them. All in all, they pretty much agreed on what they wanted, but this morning when Clarice came out of the bathroom, she knew what he was going to say.

John's head was buried in the plans, his wavy hair a cute mess. "I think we should figure out where we want this laundry room," he called.

"Ssshh, don't shout." Clarice propped her pillows and climbed back in bed. "You'll wake up Jax." She sipped her coffee while thinking of a good argument for having the laundry room upstairs where she wanted it. She thought of a whirring dryer and washer so close to where she wanted to paint. Here she had to work in the cramped, musty basement with the window open and the washer and dryer all of twenty feet away. She only dabbled in painting, but they were planning a studio in the new house somewhere on the first floor. Besides, she reasoned in her mind, the second floor's where all the laundry comes from.

"I still say the best spot's here." John pointed to the narrow hall on the first floor, which joined the East wing to the Great room. "It's out of the way and—"

"Yeah,"—she poked him in the ribs—"out of the way is exactly what I want in a laundry room."

"Hun, I told you about the plumbing problems upstairs. And what if it overflows? I'd have to put in a drain. More pipes, more —"

Ahhhhh! An ear-piercing scream shot through the room as loud and unremitting as any smoke alarm.

"Oh God, Jackson!" John yelled, jumping out of bed. His bulk bounced the mattress, spilling hot coffee all over Clarice's hand. She flung the cup to the nightstand ignoring the sting and tore after John seconds behind.

Jackson stood in the corner of the bedroom, his back to the louvered closet doors, screaming and shaking with fright. His eyes, terror-filled, green saucers, stared into the space in front of him. Poker straight arms at his sides ended in tiny clenched fists like a patient fortifying himself to withstand pain. His shoulders pulled up then fell as his little boy chest pushed out the next roaring sound.

It was too much to take in, the cutting familiarity of his fright. For that split second, she was fourteen again in the high school gym. The evil vision of that night streamed before her with the same paralyzing effect. Clarice gripped the door jamb unable to move, watching the blackness gather slowly from every corner of the gym, beating and thrumming with hatred, joining forces and then... then gushing forward as one, oily barrage, bearing down —

"Reece!" John's frustrated voice broke through releasing her from the memory. Dazed she saw John kneeling before their son, clutching the stiff little arms while Jackson screamed into his face, as if his father were invisible.

"Jackson. Jackson, it's all right," John yelled into the chubby wet cheeks. "Look at me. Wake up."

Pushing from the doorway and stepping closer, Clarice stared at the red and blue trucks on his pajamas, so out of place against the terrifying siren of his screams. *Oh God! Not again.* What's wrong with him? She looked in the direction of his stare, saw nothing—no, ethereal light forms or black menacing shadows. She saw nothing, sensed nothing. Why? If something's there, why couldn't she see it too? She looked back at the red cherub face and the glassy eyes filled with fear.

"Baby!" She reached in front of John, scooped up her son and carried him back to the bed. "Shh, shhh," she soothed as he continued shrieking into thin air.

John followed them and crouched to Jackson's level. "Jackson, look," he demanded, "look at me."

"He can't see us!" She rocked him faster in sync with the piercing cries.

"Why?" John shouted. "Why can't he wake up?"

He sounded accusatory, but she recognized the frustration. This was only the third time that Jax had done this screaming thing and coupled with the catatonic lapses he suffered, she and John were at their wits end. She rocked Jax nervously, studying the bumps of the Berber carpet while John paced the room. *It's my fault. Mine!* She gave this to him, in her genes or something. *Oh baby.* But she'd spent her whole life running from the strange things she saw. Her son had to do the same. Clarice buried her lips against his sweet head and whispered into the mass of blond curls, "You fight it, sweetie. Make it go away."

Jackson screamed, John paced, and Clarice rocked and worried where all this would lead.

Clarice held Jackson closer, nerve-wracking shrieks filling the room when as suddenly as he had begun he stopped. The tiny stiff bundle relaxed in her lap. The shiny pools of his green eyes cleared. His blotchy red face turned up, peeked at her then over to John. The bottom lip turned under in a pitiful frown and quivered out a cascading breath. Finally, he buried his head in her sweatshirt crying softly as John patted his back. It would be an hour before he left her arms.

Later he sat, right as rain, watching some Sunday morning show and eating a bowl of Cheerios.

"We have to take him somewhere you know. Get some professional help," John said at the kitchen table.

She joined him bringing the two mugs she'd retrieved from the breakfast tray, now refilled and nuked in the microwave. She sat blowing a gentle stream of air across her coffee and noticing the worn walnut table could use a little Old English. They sipped silently.

"I wanna call that clinic today," John finally said.

"What? John, it's Sunday. They won't be open. No one makes appointments on a Sunday." She wasn't sure about this new clinic their GP had suggested. No one at work had even heard of it.

"I don't care. It can't hurt to leave a message." His mild hazel eyes pled, "We've got to do something. This is crazy."

Without a word, Clarice went to the junk drawer by the phone wondering if John knew about all of her fruitless visits to specialists as a child if he would still go this route. She saw herself sitting between her mom and dad in Dr. Kinney's waiting room, her mom yelling at her to stop bouncing her leg, then reminding her it was all her fault they had to waste money at the doctors. "Why do you insist on making a spectacle of yourself? Why can't you just be normal?" Even as her mom had said it, her dad had reached out to her thigh with his reassuring touch…. Just like John, but John knew nothing of all that. A fresh wave of guilt washed over her.

The junk drawer was orderly despite its name. She looked at the flowered box trapping the pens, the neat stack of scrap paper, the glass bowl holding paperclips and rubber bands. What was with her and keeping things neat? Anyway, it gave her pleasure while chaos and disorder made her nuts. It probably—no definitely, went back to those feelings of being judged, kids picking on her, finding any excuse, her mom and doctors peering at her like she needed a lobotomy. Neat piles of clothes in her drawers, dresses and shoes lined up like soldiers in her closet, books ascending in towers—Jeesh, they should make two appointments. Dr. Varna's card was on top and on the back was scribbled, *Waterman Health Clinic, Vera Wheaton, MD 607-555-4983*. This woman was supposed to be some guru for hard diagnostic cases.

"Here," she handed the card to John half worried she was ignoring some ominous precognition. "Dr. Varna doesn't know that much about her, but he said the materials that came to his office describing the clinic's psychiatric services seem to fit Jackson's problems to a tee. I don't feel… I dunno—"

"I'll call. It's just another avenue, right? We have to do something."

"I know," she agreed walking over to the kitchen sink, a cocktail of guilt, worry, and frustration brewing in her gut. They fell silent. She gazed out the window at their small lawn where the grass grew faster than John could keep up with it. The tiny tomato plot, tilled and freshly planted, sat in the back like a freshly dug grave. From the sill, she pulled the glass with cut ivy and added water from the tap.

"Needs mowing again," John stated coming up behind her, sliding burly arms around her small waist. She leaned her head back. There was nothing else to say. The matter of fact statement about the uncut grass was enough; the subject was changed. The unanswered questions of Jackson's problems, which had been straining their marriage, would wait, at least for this moment in his arms.

"John," Clarice twisted, looking up, "member the night we met? In that bar, the one with the—"

"Hold on, I know this one." He squinted up at the ceiling. "It was in October, aaaat—"

"*Esprit,*" she said, naming the bar as John gave a cute, no-fair look.

"Hah, remember that guy on the dance floor?"

Who could forget? John and she leaning over a Backgammon table, watching the dance floor, a guy in a spiked doo and retro leather pants dancing....

John let go of her, backing away from the sink and writhing. "If you want my body, and you think I'm sexy, C'mon sugar let me know...."

Clarice's shoulders hiked up with laughter at the falsetto and gyrating antics. Her laugh, letting out a huff followed by a tiny intake of breath, she knew was embarrassingly distinctive, but John loved it, or so he claimed. (Consequently, he loved to make her laugh.) He reached over and pulled her into his lewd dance. She moved with him feeling awkward at first then enjoying herself. A few minutes later, his laugh and her huffs died down. They fell into that comfortable waddle couples do, swaying to some music of love, unheard by any but them. She remembered John the night they met, this strong, honest man smelling of Aqua Velva and sawdust, with earthy humor and a dimpled smile, ordering Gennee in a sea of expensive lagers with an apologetic shrug. Normally shy, somehow she was able to talk to him. When he asked for her number, she knew she had to tell him about her baby. It took courage that night, and Clarice realized she wanted that same courage right now.

She stopped dancing.

"What's wrong?" John said.

Her mind raced. She hid so much from him. Where to begin? Her breaks with reality, the strange things she saw, and... *oh yeah, by the way* our son may have inherited the same problems?

He stood there watching her wrestle with the decision.

"Reece?" he said gently.

She looked in his brown eyes and quickly tucked herself back in his arms for a hug. She couldn't do it, not yet. They don't know what was wrong with him. It might be anything, might have nothing to do with—

He was waiting.

"Uh, don't you have to shower for church?" She smiled sweetly, smoothing his messed hair behind his ears, avoiding his eyes.

John gave her a squeeze and broke away. Her gaze followed him, admiring his strong back before turning to the stove and its four burner covers and other annoying parts that constantly needed the action of a *Brillo* pad. She laid a towel on the counter and scrubbed the pieces one by one, her hands working in the methodical, vigorous movements of a guilty conscience.

The TV in the next room buzzed, and she wondered what Jax was watching. He had odd taste for a boy turning five. Course with such a high IQ, he couldn't be expected to be interested in cartoons, could he? She never thought of herself as excessively bright and guessed his natural father may have passed that on to him. She brought the grates to the sink and ran hot water over the pink slime, thinking of Terry, Jackson's biological father. *What a cocky, self-centered—what's the difference?* It was her own fault. That superior smugness, the way he looked down on everyone like he knew something they didn't know. He was one of those people who search from the moment they meet you for what they think makes you tick. For Terry, making another human being feel uncomfortably inferior was practically an art form. Clarice ran a towel over the pieces and remade the stove. *Terry and his head games.*

She cleared away the coffee mugs and Jackson's plastic bowl, watching the sliver of milk slosh over the picture of the red dinosaur, like her life was in the bowl, a milky white veil barely hiding the monsters in her closet. She loaded the dishwasher as John reappeared in a crisp dress shirt and slacks. He headed for the kooky blue key holder shaped like an old man's face, two hooks for eyes, and a huge wooden peg for the nose—a wedding gift from Mike Barrie, made with his own two bear paw hands.

"You want some pancakes before you go?" Clarice said and closed the dishwasher, cranking the dial. "I can make batter real quick, and I know we have syrup."

"Naw, I can't eat this close to Mass, remember."

She remembered. She just didn't get it.

"John?" She walked over and searched his face, hoping he would see pain in her eyes, *make* her open up.

He kissed her. "You could get dressed,"—he sounded wistful—"and we could all go to church together."

Clarice was silent, not taking his invitation any more seriously than he, hopefully, had made it. John never pushed his Catholic faith on her. She believed in God, she guessed, but she felt mad at him too. Wasn't it his fault she grew up seeing things, lost both her parents before she was 22, and had a son, who—who—

"Don't worry, Reece. God hears us. We'll storm heaven for answers, each our own way, huh?"

She gave no answer, having little or no intention of storming heaven for anything unless it was with two fists demanding "Why?"

"Oh yeah," John called half out the door, "if Mike calls tell him to either bring the bids by, or—" He wagged his hand and smiled. "Naw, tell him I'll call him later." Mike Barrie, John's right hand man, a huge loveable lug, was a fixture in the Miller house, most Sundays anyway especially if there was game on. Calling later meant John would probably blow Mike off for dinner tonight.

After John left for his Mass, she crossed the short kitchen to the living room where Jackson sat Indian style on the floor six inches from the TV watching the Discovery channel. Clarice gave the room a once-over. The heavy leather furniture and cherry bookshelves dwarfed the space, but aside from an out-of-place paisley throw and a fringed pillow on the floor, it was tidy.

"Watcha watchin', honey bear?"

"*Man versus Wild.* They're in the Rockies. Mom, have you been there?" Jackson turned around to look at her. "Mommy, what's wrong?" He untangled himself and darted over. She hoisted him up, and he wrapped his legs around her waist.

"Hey mister, you're getting big, you know that?" She carried him over to the couch, grabbing the pillow and throw on the way. They plopped down sinking in the soft chocolate leather. "Mommy's fine, honey. Let's watch your show."

They watched the man in red flannel hike up the Colorado Mountain. Clarice played with his curls and smelled the baby-shampoo she still used on him, wondering about this morning if his experience was like her own. . . hallucinatory breaks with reality. *That's right; just keep calling them that kiddo.*

"Jax, do you... wanna talk about this morning?"

"No." He stared ahead at the show.

She thought of the first time she'd seen something.

"Cause you can tell me anything. I'll believe you, you know." He nodded an uh-huh and went on watching TV while the memory of a man's hand, a huge palm laying flat against the window of her second story bedroom flashed across her mind. She could still hear her dad's laugh and his words, "The hand of God." Maybe that was when she started blaming God for the things she saw. God never seemed to be there for her, did He? Like when she prayed dad's cancer would be healed or mom's mind would return.

"Honey bear," Clarice brought her head around to Jackson's face breaking the spell of the TV. "Jax, sweetie, whatever you saw you can tell me. I WILL believe you." She waited.

"I know mom, I'm fine."

He sounded so mature. His eyes drifted back to the red-flannelled hiker filling his canteen in a crystal stream. She thought about what he saw, what made him scream like that. He knew she couldn't see it, knew she hadn't seen anything in the bedroom. Maybe that was why he wouldn't tell her anything.

Unconsciously Clarice had been rocking herself back and forth with Jackson in her lap. The rocking increased.

"Mom, stop it. You're makin' me sick."

"Oh Jax, I'm sorry."

"It's alright Mom. You can rock if you need to."

Need to?

"Thanks baby, but I don't need to."

"What I need to do"—she slapped her thighs, moved her son and stood—"is start looking for something to make your father a nice lunch. Just because we missed our big breakfast is no reason to starve."

"Okay Mom. Can I help?"

"Sure can. You're the main course." She dove on him, lifting his shirt for a famous raspberry. He yelped. This is normal. This is what little boys are supposed to be doing! Why can't life be normal? Maybe a doctor can help him. Maybe they'll find something to explain his problems.

These last thoughts were so foreign to her pessimistic nature they actually mocked her. The only avenue left then was the road she often traveled. Ignore it! If things aren't normal, just pretend they are. She squelched her worries, took her son's tiny hand, and skipped off to the kitchen to make lunch.

4

The Waterman Clinic

Oddly enough, they did reach someone at the clinic. The nurse there said Dr. Wheaton often worked on Sundays, and told them they could have an appointment at 4:30. The three of them huddled in Clarice's white Honda Prelude, following the nurse's directions to the clinic a half hour outside Binghamton. The sunroof was open. Jax sat in back stretching his hand as high as he could to catch the air. June had been heating up, and today felt muggy and thick.

"When's the last time you had the oil changed in this thing?" John said from the driver's seat. He liked driving her car. The Blazer was an automatic and he missed using standard.

"I dunno," Clarice said, moving her legs to let air from the vent blow up her skort. "Don't they put a sticker on it or something?"

"Yeah, I was afraid the sticker was right. I'll trade cars sometime this week and get it done for you."

Clarice looked at John then smiled back at Jax, like twin packages in their light khakis and golf shirts. "How much farther?" she said, noticing this far out on Route 12, they'd been seeing fewer and fewer businesses. The last was an Exxon a few miles back. Now they were seeing sporadic houses.

"I think we're nearly there."

On their right, they passed a sunny yellow farmhouse with a barn. Just beyond that, set a ways back from the road was a small, newish looking building of coral brick. They turned at the

Welcome to Waterman Clinic sign and drove up the long paved drive.

"NO!" Jackson screamed from the back seat. "Turn around, turn around! I don't wanna go here. It's bad."

He screamed so loud, John slammed on the brakes. Both of them twisted in their seats to look at their hysterical child.

"No!" he screamed again.

"Jackson, what's wrong?" John said. "There's nothing to worry about."

"No, no, no!" His feet kicked the back of John's seat, and little fists slammed the velour.

"Honey, calm down," Clarice said.

"Stop that." John's deep voice rose. Jackson stopped kicking the seat but furrowed his brow at both of them.

"Tell Mama why. What's wrong?"

"No. This isn't a good place with good people. I want Nicey. Where's Nicey?"

"Nothing's wrong; he's just scared." John continued driving and parked the car in the nearly empty lot while Clarice leaned over the back seat and reasoned with their son.

"Jaxie, it's okay. We're just having a doctor talk to you here. We're going to find out—" She stopped herself from saying *what's wrong with you*, "what's going on."

He continued to plead no and finally John blew up. "Stop it right now Jax. This is for your own good. YOU WILL calm down and act like a gentleman. Now be quiet!"

Jackson obediently piped down, allowed her to unstrap him and take his hand. They walked solemnly to the glass doors and entered a small Formica-clad reception area with a tall nurse's desk. The rush of cool air was welcome, and probably explained the sea green sweater on the lithe, young blond in white pants hurrying toward them. A tiny thing, Clarice thought, even next to her own petite frame.

"Oh you must be the Millers." She approached tossing poker straight locks over her shoulder like a blond Cher. Clarice noticed a delicate silver chain holding a minute black cross round her neck.

"Yeah, I'm John, this is Clarice, and this," John stepped aside to reveal Jax hiding behind his legs, "is Jackson."

The girl shook their hands and reached out to Jackson with a huge smile, "Well, hi there. I'm Tina."

Jackson surprising Clarice refused the hand and instead tucked his fists in his elbows.

"Jackson!" Clarice said, placing an assuring arm on his shoulder. "He's a little scared."

"Oh no worries, I understand — new place, new face." Tina pulled back a bit, re-flicking hair off her thin shoulders. You can fill out paperwork. I'll tell Dr. Wheaton you're here." She went behind the counter and reemerged with papers and a clipboard then disappeared down the hall. Clarice sat next to John and Jax opposite the reception desk. John took out his cell while she filled in the papers. She noticed Jax looking frightened down the hall then pensively back to the front door.

"Let him play a game." She nudged John's elbow. Jackson loved playing on the cell, a privilege he rarely received. John forked his phone over to Jax, who took it eagerly.

A few minutes later, Tiny Tina returned.

"The doctor would like a word with both of you in private. I'll be weighing Jackson and taking his pressure, stuff like that. Then Vera, er, Dr. Wheaton will see Jackson."

* * *

Mrs. Nicestrum stood in line at Walmart, looking past the lavender paisley skirt to her thick tan oxfords. Her feet hurt and the orthopedic stockings felt hot. Oh Well, the store was air-conditioned. What more could one ask? The woman in front of her with three kids was finally finished. A young man behind her in baggy cargo shorts and flip-flops with spiky hair and a scruffy patch of pumpkin beard leaned forward.

"We can pick em, eh? Hard to believe this is the Express line."

Mrs. Nicestrum smiled and only slightly nodded. She didn't want to make the cashier, who looked almost as old as herself, feel bad about the lengthy wait. Price checks were annoying for everyone concerned.

She unloaded her three small items, butterscotch candy to refill the candy dish in her apartment, a can of hairspray, and the white prescription bag. No sooner had she freed her hands than a synthetic tune emitted from her purse.

She was content to ignore it until the young man behind her said, "It's yours."

"Oh, my!" she said, opening her black bag and retrieving the cell phone the Millers had given her for Christmas. She could barely recall the last time she'd heard the contraption go off. That was months ago when John called and asked her to pick up Jackie from preschool. She dutifully kept the phone with her whenever she was out. Jackson kept it charged for her. It was really just for emergencies so the Millers could reach her.

Mrs. Nicestrum opened the lid, said, "Hello," and waited. She pulled the phone away and looked at the glowing screen confused.

"It's a text message," the youth behind her said, tilting his chin of scraggly brush.

"Oh dear, I'm afraid I don't know anything about those."

"Me neither," said the cashier. "My grandson wanted me to have one. I can't even use a computer. What in blazes would I do with it? Comes to $15.97, dearie."

Mrs. Nicestrum placed the phone on the counter, pulled out her change purse, and handed sixteen dollars to the woman.

"I'll help you," the boy said, plopping his six-pack of Gatorade on the conveyor belt. He picked up the phone as Mrs. Nicestrum took three cents and the receipt from the cashier uttering, "Thank you."

"It's a text. You push this button here and scroll down to here. Then..."

He might as well have been speaking Greek.

"Would you mind reading it to me?" She couldn't have seen it without her reading glasses anyway, and they were in her purse.

"No problem," he said, clicking another button. "Nee-see," he began reading then stopped. "Is that Knee-see or Nigh-see?"

"Nice," she said, "My name is Nice-strum rhymes with drum. The boy I watch, he calls me Nicey for short. Says I'm nice, bless his heart."

He nodded and read the message aloud.

> NICEY, AT WATERMAN CLINIC IN CHENANGO IN DANGER. NEED YOU. HURRY.

"That's all it says."

She felt the blood drain from her face. "Oh dear Lord, it's my Jackie," she cried clasping her chest. "I'm his nanny. I have no idea where Waterman Clinic is or why he's there!"

The young man slid his credit card through for his purchase and signed the monitor face. "You can call back the number of the phone that texted you" he said, already punching buttons on her phone and handing the phone back to her.

She held it to her ear and after a couple rings heard John's rumbly voice. "This is John Miller. I'm unavailable, but you can leave a message, and I'll return your call as soon as possible."

"Voice mail, huh?" he said and shoved his card in one of the long cargo pockets. "Your friend mighta turned off his phone. You could ask at Customer Service, maybe find it in a phone book, or they could look up the clinic online."

They both gaped at the queue in front of Customer Service. Two mothers stood at the end of the long line with carts chock full of stuff; one had a stroller, and the other a whining toddler in the cart seat kicking chubby legs into his mom's stomach. Preceding them stood an elderly man holding a box the size of a TV and looking as though he were about to pass out, and before him were at least two more shoppers leaning on carts.

"He needs me right now." She frowned looking from the young man's tatty chin, ochre hairs sticking out like a badly seeded lawn, to his kind eyes. "I simply can't wait in that long line."

The boy grabbed his Gatorade and receipt.

"Right, c'mon." She followed him to the Verizon Counter next to Customer Service where a young girl twirling a curly lock of deep bronze hair looked bored to tears.

"Hey Amy, sup?" The young man sauntered over, swinging the six-pack up and letting it thud on the tall counter. His hand remained on the handle like a crutch while he leaned over grinning at his friend.

"Not much Joey. You? You takin' the summer off or what?"

"Naw, I'm doing Bio again, but this time I got it. Straight up, girl. Hey Amy, you got a computer back there you can google something for my friend? She's in a real hurry."

Mrs. Nicestrum stepped forward hopefully, the top of her soft grey upsweep, nose and eyes barely clearing the counter. "It's important. The little boy I take care of needs me. He's at some place called *Waterman Clinic* in Chenango, and I need directions."

"Hmmm, I'm not supposed to,"—she smiled back at Joey who made a puppy dog face—"We're not supposed to use the internet for personal stuff but I guess for Joey's grandma."

No one corrected her.

"I gotta run Amy. Thanks for helping. You're all right Nicesee. I hope you find your Jackie. Later, Aim."

He took off, a whir of saggy chinos, stick up hair, and florescent Gatorade. In minutes, the copper-haired girl handed Mrs. Nicestrum a sheet of paper from MapQuest. She thanked her and hurried off hearing Amy yell, "You tell Joey he owes me a movie."

***

Jackson sat on the cold steel table feeling vulnerable, wondering when Nicey would get here. Something very black and dark wanted to get him. He could feel it. He studied the nurse, her stethoscope looking like a fat necklace, framing the shiny chain and tiny cross lying on her lime green sweater. She wasn't dark. She had no power. He could feel that too. He was away from Mommy and Daddy and both of their protective auras. He kicked his legs back and forth over the table. She took the stethoscope from her ears and peeled the Velcro from the cuff.

"Now that wasn't so bad, was it?" she said, both her hands scooping long honey-colored hair back over her shoulders. "Your temperature and blood pressure are normal. You'll meet Dr. Wheaton soon. You have nothing to worry about, you'll see." He kept his eyes peeled on her tiny heart shaped face the same shape as his mom's.

"I want my Mommy. I have to be with her now."

"Soon honey. Your parents are talking to the doctor."

In fact, the doctor was alone as yet.

Vera Wheaton sauntered across her office. The kid was here, right here in her building, and she'd engineered it all. Months of planning, gaining permits, financing, building and hiring—all of it—her work. She had even thought to litter local doctor offices with pamphlets and send physicians glossy brochures outlining the clinic's specialties. All crafted to attract the right cases. She had figured if the boy were having the expected trances and visions, then his parents would seek professionals, who of course would find nothing physically or even mentally wrong with him. It took two years to build this place and hire the right help. Although most of the employees were loyal OTO members, a few like Tina were strictly medical professionals.

Ordinatio Triune Orbis, the Order of Three Circles, was a society older by far than all its members combined. The name was a moveable feast adjusting itself to any number of cultures or times but always hidden, deeply secretive, and rarely compromised. It was the power the elders enjoyed. The hold they had over lessers, once they were initiated that is, was complete. Naturally, the power had a price for every member.

Despite all the planning, Vera paced anxiously. She caught herself in the mirror and stopped. Bette Davis eyes stared back at her, still good looking, even pushing 65. A tailored red suit with tiny white piping showed off a trim figure. Her dark hair in a neat bun, she had that sciencey look people trusted.

A firm rap sounded on the door. She whirled around to see a lesser boldly enter the room. The huge man was one of *his* bodyguards and a little too cocky around her, an elder after all. This one always seemed a bit thick.

"Well?" She waited. "M-ust you b-ore me with your in-competence? Speak up." She heard her own staccato speech, her consonants punched, syllables drawn out, delivered in a smoky feminine voice, more than aware of the intimidation it inspired.

"The master has arrived," he said. "I brought him in the back of the building."

She strolled across the room and extracted a cigarette from the gold case on her desk, her action exaggerated. Long red nails held the cigarette to even redder lips, and she waited for him to cross the room with a lighter.

She puffed slowly.

"I seek an au-dience," she said.

"*He* knows. He said to come at once."

Vera nodded once, then ignoring him, she went behind her desk and picked up the phone. Every move had calculated flare, all signature Vera. He left.

Tina answered her phone. "Yes, Doctor?"

"Keep the Mill-ers in my waiting room and in-form them I will be with them shortly."

Vera smashed her cigarette in the tray and slipped out the side door to the hallway.

For all her nervy bravado as her patent leather pumps clicked down the hall, she felt that disquiet always associated with *him*. She'd done it; her work had paid off, and while not a *fait accompli*, the master would have to be pleased with her. She continued to the back of the building with these thoughts.

In Dr. Wheaton's waiting room, Clarice shifted in her seat after Tina left, wondering how much longer until they saw the doctor. John placed a hand over her jiggling knee.

"I don't know, John, shouldn't we be with him?"

"The nurse said he's fine. Just relax. Here read a magazine." He flopped a *Sports Illustrated* in her lap.

"Oh, nice." She laughed, leaning over to switch it for just about anything else. John scooped up the treasured discard, and Clarice flipped *Redbook* pages feeling strange. She popped her head

44

up like a pooch sniffing air, looking about the non-descript waiting room. Something was here in this building; she couldn't put her finger on it. Coupled with Jackson's fussing in the car, she half considered calling off the appointment right now. How would she explain that to John? *Oh John, honey? We have to GO right now. I feel funny, is all — um... no, can't put my finger on it, but something is off. Ugh! You are one crazy broad, that's what's off.* She flipped faster trying to find an article to distract herself.

Meanwhile, Vera entered the conference room at the back of the building, a narrow room holding an expensive table and twelve executives chairs, just enough for a full meeting of elders. *He* stood at the end of the long cherry table; one bony hand played with a silver cufflink on his black shirt—the entire outfit as black as his heart. She felt immediately off-balance—his striking features and polished look, the lone shock of black swept across the full gray hair—his fine looks were impossible to ignore even if his eyes did not draw you in. They drew her in now as a faint but highly interesting scent of rotting flesh greeted her. Envy for what he had become mingled with awe in his presence. She bowed slightly and waited.

"You've done well, Vera, or shall I say Dr. Wheaton. So clever and useful, a credit to the elders, and now you tell me it is all coming to fruition, hmm?"

"It *is* him. I s-aw his light and that of the par-ents as soon as they drove up."

"Most definitely, their lights are unmistakable. They are separated from the boy at present."

It was not a question but a statement of fact. Vera steadied herself with the top of a chair and gave an admiring look.

"Yes," she said, "the child is in an exam-in-ation room at the end of the first hall. His parents are in my outer off-ice waiting for our interview."

"Perfect, you will keep them there while Cain and I secure the boy."

She noted Cain standing in the doorway looking down the corridor. "Do you intend to kill him here or—"

"Tsk, tsk, Vera dear. Curiosity killed the cat. Now we'll go over the layout of your clinic." He waved to the dry erase board behind her back.

Vera went to the board and drew a giant upside down cross, outlining the shape of the building.

"This is the front parking lot leading to the lobby." She indicated the top of the cross and grinned at her own cleverness designing the building as an upside-down cross.

"We are here," she said and drew an X at the opposite end of the cross while glancing out the window behind him. The master's black Cadillac Deville sat in the rear parking lot. "The hall out there,"—she indicated—"pas-ses half a doz-en rooms, most of them doubles. The boy is here." She made another X.

"Any windows?"

"Yes, but all too high for him to reach." She'd purposely designed each of the exam rooms that way. "The boy's par-ents are here." Vera placed a final X on the right arm of the upside down cross.

"Who else is in the building?"

"No one except Tin-a. We couldn't have asked for better timing, it being Sun-day," she said, "I never knew when he might find his way here. I've been here day and night since we o-pened. I—

"Enough" he said, sounding unimpressed and decidedly uninterested. "Send the nurse to her desk. I do not intend to be seen. Go back to your office and interview the parents. Watch the mother carefully. She may have the ability to see you as you are. In that case, you'll have to decide what to do. However messes must be avoided at all costs." He waved. "Go."

Jackson could feel danger mounting, a blackness unseen but closing in on him. He hopped off the steel table and opened the hall door a hair. A clickety-clack of heels passed by, and he thought he saw a glimpse of a hideous hairy mass rounding the corner of the hall out of sight. A shiver raced across his back. He looked the other way down the long, long hallway of yellow walls and closed blue doors. At the very end in an open doorway, stood two men — okay, one huge man and one something else altogether. The something else was all blackness, pulsing and beating. The darkness swam around a tall figure dressed in black, human and yet not. The thing sensed him. Jackson shut the door quick, his chest racing. He turned the lock and faced into the room looking for escape.

They're coming. Jax fled to the side door and twisted the handle. It turned but led to another room, this one an office with a desk and chairs. He looked at the window, dragged a chair over to it, but it was still too high. He couldn't even reach the latch.

Nicey, please come. Come! No time, no time. He tried to control his panic, force his mind to work. The thing coming would get him; he had to get out of this room. He heard doors flinging open down the hall. *They're almost here!* He ran to the door and held the handle. He'd have to make a dash in the hall, the same hall they were walking down. Wait, maybe he could find his mom, sense her light. Jackson stood still a moment, closed his eyes tight. No good, he was too excited, too scared. No choice, he had to run down the hall and turn right or left. He would run to the right since the clickety clack, hairy monster had turned left. He held the door, took a big gulp of air like jumping in the pool, and burst through not even looking back.

He and Cain saw the flash of blond curls exit the room and dash down the hall. Cain made a motion to rush after the child, but the master shot his arm out to stop him.

"The girl is at the front desk, Cain. It will complicate matters if she sees us. We know where the boy is," he said, digging in his filthy nails. "Make no commotion as we pass outside the lobby, Cain." They continued to walk seeing the top of the blonde's head bent over the reception desk. Their steps slowed even more as they rounded the corner slipping down the right arm of the cross.

On the other end of the cross, Vera entered her inner office from the hall. She walked around her desk to the outer office door and smiled at Clarice and John on the couch.

"Mis-ter and Miss-us Miller, won't you come in?"

Clarice noted the neat package of a handsome woman whose stature barely reached her own, but whose presence immediately filled the room.

Seated in chairs opposite the doctor's desk, John answered questions about Jackson —everything from his genius abilities to his trances, and finally his screaming fits.

"And these new ep-isodes of screaming, how long do they last and what does he see, uh what does he say about them?"

"Up to half an hour," John said. "He's frightened alright but doesn't really talk about seeing anything."

Although Clarice heard the doctor ask what Jackson *sees*, and the curious question registered loosely as odd—that prickly odd that sends warning chills down your spine—Clarice was too distracted to notice. John fielded question after question, and Clarice stared at the yellow legal pad on the desk in front of the doctor. Instead of making notes, the sleek silver pen was travelling around and around tracing a tiny pattern. Not an unusual habit, Clarice, a fellow doodler, told herself trying to get a good look at the symbol. It was a triad of circles, but coming up from each circle was a curved whip, like the figure had been spun and the outsides had bled. It mesmerized her for a second. Something was so not right. Her gut tied in a knot—Whooshhh.

Not now, good Lord!

CA-CLANG. A door slammed somewhere in the building, then another. John stopped talking. The doctor's pen flopped to the paper and all three exchanged a quick look.

"Oh," the doctor gave a casual shrug, "That's noth-ing, per-haps another patient. We are a health clinic after all. I should have closed the door, but the air-conditioning doesn't quite reach here."

She's very different, Clarice thought, fighting the flea-circus in her stomach, looking hard at the doctor —one of the tricks she'd devised as a child to thwart the spells. She had so much flare and

48

drama, like a fading star from the old movies. That rough voice punching syllables like a boxer, every mannerism, even her powder makeup, all of it felt as surreal a 1940's movie.

"Now then, you say he's been ha-ving other trances, different from the screaming. How often does he enter these ca-ta-tonic states?"

Clarice felt woozy. Something dark was attached to this woman. She closed her eyes against the feeling to concentrate, but behind her lids, the strange three-circled figure spun.

Down the corridor, Jackson entered the first door he found open and locked it from the inside. It was another examination room with a steel table and a couple of stools. The table was bolted down; otherwise, it would have been tall enough to reach the window. His eyes scanned the room. No phone, nothing.

Help me, God. Nicey hurry!

The file cabinet by the door might be tall enough. He pushed at the metal heaviness of the thing, but it wouldn't budge. He saw a wide air vent above it giving him a neat little idea. Jackson opened the drawers of the file cabinet and stood on the bottom one to test his weight. Looking up at the grate, he saw two screws — the kind with one line. All he needed was a dime, or something skinny— and quick. Stepping off, he went to the metal counter by the tiny sink where jars of cotton balls and such were lined up. Jackson plucked a Popsicle stick, automatically cocking his head and holding it out in front of his glass-covered eyes trying to remember their proper name. *Oh yeah, tongue depressors.*

He opened the next two drawers barely an inch and climbed up the file cabinet. They were drawing closer. Why didn't they run after him when he was in the hall? The screws unwound, he removed the grate. By the door next to him, he saw a fire detector and had another idea. He climbed back down to where he'd seen a matchbook by the jars. If he could start a fire and set that thing off, maybe his mom and dad would find him.

He picked up the metal trashcan and yanked off the lid. It was empty. Everything in this place was new and unused. Over the sink was a paper towel dispenser and stacked on the counter were extra paper towels. He threw the stack in the can and crumpled as many as he could into balls. It took four matches before he got one to light, but it went out. He'd only seen matches struck this way on a few TV shows. Two more strikes, this time he lit the entire book by accident and threw it on the paper towels. Jackson placed the can in front of the door directly under the smoke detector, scrambled up the file cabinet drawers like a ladder, and disappeared in the hole.

Rounding the corner, Cain tried the first door jiggling the locked handle. He was turning sideways to throw his weight into it when the master spoke.

"Don't bother Cain, he isn't in that one," he said, tilting his angular features like a bird of prey. Cain strode to the next door, disappeared in the room, and rustled around in search of the boy.

His chin jerked upward.

"My my, clever aren't you child?" *He* walked a bit then stopped, walked again and stopped.

In the ductwork, Jackson crawled forward, stopped, and crawled forward again. A light ahead meant another vent opening. He reached it and peered into another office type room, unfurnished with another high window. No escape there. He crawled on to the next light turning left. He guessed that meant he was crossing the hallway in the ceiling. He was petrified; something evil was trying to talk to him in his head. He heard the big man trashing a room nearby. It sounded like he was flinging open cabinets and overturning desks.

He stopped again directing his gaze to the hall ceiling. I can see you child wherever you hide. This is pointless, you know.

Jackson froze. Tears brimmed as he whispered, "Mommy, mommy." He looked down toward the blackness below him hearing the words in his head and realized something. "I see you too!" he yelled and scrambled like mad from the dark entity.

Ahead was another light and grate. This time it was a bathroom. Jax smooshed his face into the grid. Over the white sink was another high window with a sink much higher than the chair had been; he could definitely get out that window. Jackson pushed the grate but it didn't budge. He scrunched himself up in a ball and inched his body around in the tin box. After he got all the way turned around, he lay on his bottom, scooched forward as far as he could and pulled his knees up till they hit the aluminum sides. He would need all the force he could muster with his short limbs. Jackson kicked fast. It was hard to tell if it had even moved. He pulled his knees up and kicked again.

He was tempted to scooch around, feel with his hands to tell whether it was loosening at all, but that would waste time. He couldn't evade the men forever. This maze of ducts was confusing them, yet he heard the black heart telling the other which rooms to look in. Jackson whispered a prayer. Holding his arms against the metal sides of the duct for stability, he took a deep breath and reared back, kicking for all he was worth. The grille gave way on one side, flopping down on the remaining screw. He turned over onto his belly and scooted out the hole, the metal sides scraping his shins. Hanging there, he heard them in the next room. Panic welled up, tears sprang to his eyes; he couldn't get down!

He hung from the hole swinging his feet desperate for something to stand on. It was no use; he would have to let go and drop. He thought of Tommy on the monkey bars, dropping casually from the high bar and landing safely on the ground. So far, he hadn't found the courage for that move on the playground. Tommy was taller too. He remembered what he and Nicey read about cats, how they landed on bouncing joints that give when they hit. He just had to make his knees catch him. He'd rather fall than get caught by the dark creature. Jackson braced himself and let go, hitting the floor with a hard thud, but it only hurt a little. He ran to the door, locking it. The sink was easy to climb, and he had the window open in seconds. He hoisted himself up and realized he would be facing the same kind of drop he just made, only higher and on the outside wall. He thought of Nicey and what she would say. She would say, "Well, there's nothing to be done about it, so you best get to it."

He stood outside the Ladies Room. The door was locked.

"Here, Cain," *he* called and stepped out of Cain's way. Cain threw his right shoulder at it three times and the lavatory door popped open. Warm, thick air poured in from the yawning window. And out it, they saw the boy half way across the open field, running like the dickens to a yellow farmhouse.

In the doctor's office, Clarice opened her eyes and gasped. In front of her sat a huge creature, its bristly head, a cross between a hyena and boar. Slime ran down two yellow tusks, its pig nose flared while red, burning eyes gleamed at her. Incredulously from its inhuman mouth, she heard the doctor's voice.

"Miss-us Mil-ler, are you alright?"

Clarice's head snapped downward. Her hand shot to her eyes and rubbed, as if something were in them. Squeezing them shut against the unholy vision, it was eighth grade all over again!

Just then the regal voice of Mrs. Nicestrum, uncharacteristically raised in protest, sounded from somewhere out in the hall. John jumped up, bumping Clarice's arm and turning for the door. As her hand dropped away, she shot a look toward the creature behind the desk but saw only Dr. Wheaton as before. She stood to follow John.

"John, wait up," she called passing out the door. "We have to get Jackson."

"Nicey, what are you doing here? John called his long strides fast approaching the glass door that separated the lobby from the clinic halls. "What's wrong?"

Nicey stood in the doorway with Tiny Tina blocking her way. Her shoulders were back pushing an ample chest against her cotton blouse, clutching her big black purse in front of her. Under the billow of lavender skirt, her chunky shoes stood apart, as though braced for battle. Tina fingering the medal round her neck, her elbows hugging her sweater, shifted her weight and looked to the doctor coming behind them.

"Oh, Doctor Wheaton," Tina called, "I tried to inform this woman that you were seeing the Millers and their son. She absolutely refused to listen."

"It's alright Tin-a, probably a misun-derstanding," Dr. Wheaton said, joining them. She peered down the hall on the other side of them and quickly back at the group.

"Hello, I'm Dr. Whea-ton," she said, "I run this cli-nic."

Mrs. Nicestrum literally snorted and ignored the outstretched hand. The second time, Clarice noted, she'd seen that happen today.

"Where is he, John?" Mrs. Nicestrum said. "Jackie sent me a message, a text message from your phone."

"What? How does he even— He only had the phone for a few minutes while we were waiting. That little dickens. What kind of message?"

"Well, where is he?" she said, sounding extremely irritated and very unlike herself.

Clarice turned to Tina releasing some of her own anxiety. "I thought you were with him. Do you mean to say our four year old son is all alone in some room somewhere?"

"Calm down, Reece. I'm sure he's fine," John said, aiming the last more as much at Nicey as her.

Mrs. Nicestrum piped up again in royal command, "I demand to see the child immediately."

"Tin-a, of course you should have re-turned to the boy," the doctor chastised the girl.

"But you said... I mean you told me—Dr. Wheaton I was just following your—"

"Ne-ver mind, Tin-a!" The doctor cut in. "We'll deal with that la—"

EeeEeeEeeEeeee.... The stabbing scream of a smoke detector went off down the hall.

"Oh my God!" Clarice cried.

"I'll show you where he is." Tina set off with a determined gait, her straight hair swinging over the hood of her green sweater, leading the small troupe and stopping in front of an examination door. She twisted the knob and jiggled it hard.

"Why is it locked?" John's voice bellowed over the screeching alarm. He pulled out his cell. "Does that alarm go to the fire station? I'm calling 9-1-1."

"Oh I'm sure that's unnecessary," the doctor said, "but of course...."

Tina finished scrambling with keys and opened the door. The room was empty, but Clarice noticed the side door to the adjoining office space was wide open.

"He must have gone through here," Tina said, turning to the group sounding nervous. "He was awfully frightened." Her voice was hollering as they all had been to be heard above the alarm.

"Yes," Dr. Wheaton waved her hand. "I see that sort of thing all the time."

John was already speaking to emergency personnel, as the five of them entered the empty room. His deep voice gave the address and cracked adding that his son was missing somewhere in the building. Clarice left and ran from door to door searching rooms and offices. Soon everyone was looking.

After the call, John zeroed in on the whining smoke detector and threw his weight against the locked door not waiting for Tina and her ring of keys. After the door gave, a trash can clanged and rolled away. Clarice righted the can seeing blackened paper towels smoldering but with no flame. All eyes followed the file cabinet drawers hanging out like stairs leading up to the open vent that was missing its grate.

"Jackson," John called. She caught his eye, both of them taking it all in. "Oh my God, Jackson!"

But Jackson was standing in the kitchen of the yellow farmhouse and looking about wildly. To his right were narrow stairs. Across the kitchen to the left lay a dining room. Straight ahead, a hall led to the front door where somewhere a TV buzzed. Outside in the yard, he heard the black voice yell, "Cain, go back and get the car. Pull it around to this driveway. I will fetch the boy. Hurry!"

Jackson locked the kitchen door and ran ahead coming down the wide entry hall. In the room to his left, he saw the glow of the TV beyond which lay a scruffy gold lounge chair sporting the top of a balding head. The head moved, and a heavy man in a red checked flannel shirt stood up and turned around, a remote control in his hand.

"What's this about, now?" The man pointed with the remote, his arms oddly thin while his gut, enormous and round, bulged against the buttons of his shirt. "What in the sam hill are you doin' in my house?"

His light was good. Jackson ran straight up to the man's knees and wrapped his arms about him.

"Help me. Please help me. You gotta call 9-1-1. You gotta help me."

"Son, what are you—" Jackson burst into full-fledged sobs. "Now, now," the man patted his head of curls. "What's the problem here little un? Tell ol Clive all about it."

"If you insist," another voice joined the room.

Jackson looked to the entryway where the tall man in black stood sneering.

"Now just what do you think your doin' comin' in my house like this!" The man named Clive turned his startled face back to Jax. "Is this man tryin' to hurt you boy?"

Jackson nodded and moved farther behind the old man.

"Sir, I'm gonna have to ask you to leave my house. Then I'll call the authorities and we'll just see about all what's goin' on with this here boy." A thin arm wrapped around Jackson's shoulder. "Don't you worry little un, Clive'll—"

"Enough," the dark figure spoke and pointed a long bony digit at the fat man's knees, which smelled of leather, smoke, and Ivory Soap.

Instantly, the old hand dropped the remote. Jackson looked up at the man's contorted face. Both hands flew to his chest gripping his flannel shirt. Clive moaned and his eyes grew wide looking at the dark being whose finger still pointed to his heart. Turning white, the bald man fell away from Jackson.

"No! Stop!" Jackson yelled at the dark figure. "Stop it!"

Clive fell to the floor with a thud. Jackson looked in horror from him to the evil one, who took a step toward him. Jax screamed and ran through the dining room door. He slammed it shut and locked it then zipped into the kitchen. He heard the handle rattle and realized he had only seconds before the dark one would come around to the hall and then the kitchen, which had no door. Jackson looked around in a panic. A tall china cabinet stood to the side of the opening. He chose the highest spot he could reach to make it topple and pushed as hard as he could. It fell, effectively wedging itself between the arched opening and blocking the kitchen entrance. Satisfied, Jackson unlocked the back door and tore out heading to the barn and hearing sirens.

Two squad cars and a fire truck rolled up to the *Waterman Clinic* sirens blaring. Three policemen and four firemen swarmed through the building searching for the missing boy. It sounded like chaos. Clarice stood in the lobby, lights from the trucks whirling around the walls like an eighties disco. Mrs. Nicestrum held a matronly arm around Clarice's waist and looked at her with moist eyes.

"Dear, we'll find him. He's very resourceful."

"Nicey, I don't think he's in the building."

"No?" Mrs. Nicestrum let go of her waist. "Are you sure?"

Clarice nodded, "I think we should check outside."

She and Mrs. Nicestrum headed to the doors. Dr. Wheaton spoke calmly with a police officer holding a notepad. John and the others continued searching and re-searching rooms and ductwork. Tina looked this way and that, her fingers tightly laced and biting her lip.

"Can I come with? I just want to help," she said.

"Sure, of course." Clarice managed half a smile, although she held no animosity toward the girl. If this was anyone's fault, it was hers for bringing him here against her own instincts. "We already checked the cars," she told them standing on the sidewalk. "I want to walk around the building."

The three spread out, Clarice walking faster than the other two around the coral brick building. Her stomach knotted in a trillion ugly thoughts and what-ifs. He didn't want to come here, her mind scolded. He was so scared. *He kicked the seat for Pete's sake.* What had she done? Why didn't she insist on staying with him, and who is this doctor? *What is this place? Nothing is right here.*

As she rounded the left arm of the building, she felt a jolt. It surged through her, making Clarice look across the field and yellow farmhouse. Jackson's light was there. She was too upset to *see* anything more, but she could feel him. A trail of pushed down hay cut a path through the field between the clinic and the farmhouse. Clarice sprinted to the house, her toes trying to grip her tong sandals. She kicked them off feeling crunchy weeds lick her soles and ignoring the rocks and uneven terrain that bit into her feet.

She went straight to the front door, banging madly. No one answered but the handle turned and she let herself in. A TV hummed to her right, and there on the floor lay an old man, his hands clutching his shirt. *What in the world?* Clarice knelt, took his wrist, carefully checking for a pulse—still warm but no life. *Poor man.* She let go slowly, the presence of death sobering.

"Jackson! Jackson!"

Clarice stood, holding still, trying to *feel* her son. He was near but... She walked backed to the entry and down the short hall to the fallen cabinet and smashed china. *Oh, please, oh no, no.* Her panicked eyes swept the kitchen over the top of the downed cabinet. She walked back to the front stairway and gripped the round finial, ordering herself to stay calm. Her head tilted up. No, he wasn't upstairs. Quick she turned for the door and stepping onto the front porch saw Mrs. Nicestrum and Tina making their way across the field toward the barn. Clarice flew after them.

The barn was pitch dark after the brightness outside and smelled of old hay and stray cats.

"Jax," she called out.

"Mommy!" his small voice came from behind the ladder to the hayloft. Her eyes adjusted and saw him peeping out between splintery ladder rungs.

"Oh baby, baby," she cried rushing past Tina, who was whipping a phone from her pocket. Jackson wasn't budging from his hiding place, so she ducked under the ladder to gather him in her arms.

A second later, Mrs. Nicestrum leaned in. Jackson pulled her to the ground with them. She landed in a heap of lavender paisley oblivious of the dirt floor and fairly laughing with relief. Jackson held onto both of them. After a moment, he pushed back, blurting out details in random order.

"The man... he... and the big one kept slamming doors, and I had to run. I hid in the airshafts, a—an, I started a fire. That worked. I had to mom." Jackson turned his head to look at Mrs. Nicestrum. "Nicey, you got my text!"

"Yes, Jackie,"—she caressed his chin—"but what are you—you shouldn't have been... well...." Nicey looked across Jackson's head to Clarice, her normally tranquil face contorted. "He shouldn't be left alone! It's…, well it's not safe for a young boy! He *really* must be watched. You—"

John burst through the barn door followed by a handful of police officers and Dr. Wheaton thanks to Tina's phone call.

A bit of chaos ensued with Jackson still huddled under the ladder. Clarice, unwilling to force her frightened son to move, held him there while various policemen crouched to ask him questions and take notes. A jumble of uniformed figures, coroners, and firemen scurried back and forth between the barn, farmhouse, and clinic, filling out reports, making phone calls and taking statements. Finally, the Millers were allowed to go home. Since Jackson was the only one who claimed to have seen the two men chasing him, officials appeared to be chalking the events up to the strange behavior and possibly the imagination of a savant child with psychological problems. The coroner on the scene said it appeared the man in the farmhouse died of a heart attack. It was unclear how responsible the fallen cabinet may have been, or perhaps it was the excitement or the shock of the intrusion. They said Jackson would have to be questioned again and possibly ordered to undergo psychological testing.

As they were leaving, Dr. Wheaton approached John with her card. "Mr. Miller I will be happy to see your son and help get to the bottom of his er, his condition. Waterman specializes in cases such as these. My work and my personal cell are on the card so please call me day or night. It's no prob—

Mrs. Nicestrum, still picking hay off her voluminous skirt, snatched the card from John's hand. Under Nicey's breath, Clarice was sure she heard, "over my dead body." The two women glared at each other and she swore that smarmy gruff voiced doctor smiled.

When they finally left, Jackson went in Mrs. Nicestrum's gold Buick while John and she drove the Prelude. His nanny would stay the night as she often did, and no doubt, that was for the best. As they drove away from *Waterman Clinic*, Clarice grieved. The attempt to solve Jackson's problems had left them in a quagmire of unresolved questions worse than the ones they'd brought with them.

5

Roxanne

Clarice stared at the computer screen on her small desk, her mind blank. Her eyes wandered around the postage stamp office, which was looking unnaturally neat. Sun behind open blinds cast strips of light on the lone file cabinet revealing the finest layer of dust. Immediately, she pictured dusting under the small terrarium of plants and the photos of John and Jax in handsome silver frames. These were about the only personal items found in her office—no clutter, homey figurines or plaques with clever sayings. Clarice turned back to the screen, refocusing on the ad for a local shoe store wishing she were allowed to do more than neaten the blather written by the owner. She collected a small sketchpad and played. In a moment, a strapped stiletto appeared, juxtaposed with an Italian men's dress shoe. Her hand darted about drawing the straps of the female pump climbing the man's shoe like ivy. It was perfect.

She tore the page off, crumpled it in a ball, held it up like a Nerf toy, and lobbed it across the room for a long shot. Score.

Her mind—without warning or permission—returned to *Waterman Clinic* and the mess there two days ago. Police found no trace of anyone else in the farmhouse. The only one who could have corroborated Jackson's story, one Clive Henkel, was dead. Poor guy's obituary was in the paper today, not a soul in the world listed as a living relative. It can't be Jackson's fault! She threw the sketchpad in the drawer. Jackson doesn't lie, *ever*, no matter what that cop said about children learning to fib at this age. Her son's story was too fantastic, even for a genius. Why couldn't they see that? Then who did chase him? Did it have anything to do with that doctor or—

"Staring at an empty screen is like looking in the refrigerator, you know."

"Huh, how's that?" Clarice looked up, her face as blank as the screensaver.

"Stare all you want, nothin's gonna grow on that screen. You goin' to lunch with me or what?" Roxanne Cassan said and plunked herself on the corner of Clarice's desk. Her wild getup screamed next to Clarice's pencil skirt and white tee.

Roxanne Cassan was a shot of caffeine with her tongue in cheek jokes and crazy looks. Her friend's appearance never ceased to surprise her. She was tall. Next to Clarice's five foot two frame, Roxy's five eleven looked even more ungainly. Olive Oyl thin too, she could eat anything, anywhere without gaining a pound. From the top of her curly red hair to her outlandish shoes, everything about Roxanne Cassan was singular. Clarice gawked at today's ensemble: gold sandals, a silk skirt with greens, golds, and reds, topped with a lime green camisole, gobs of chains and antique jewelry. She trimmed the outfit with the *pièce de résistance* of an outrageous hot-pink scarf with foot-long fringe. The less it all matched, whether color or pattern, the more Roxy seemed drawn to it.

"Yeah, I say we do it,"—Clarice reached in the desk drawer for her wallet—"but something simple for once, Rox. My stomach can't take Thai or Southern Soul food or whatever new spicy torture you've found to entertain your mouth."

"Hmm, that lets out that new Pakistani place on Washington Ave, huh? This will take some creative thought," Roxy swung her stick limbs this way and that over the side of the desk.

"No, it will not either!" Clarice spun her chair sideways and firmly stood up. "We'll go to Denny's or KFC. And you can wipe that shocked look off your face. It won't kill you to be average for one lunch."

"Okay, okay. Geesh, the price I have to pay for an hour of intelligent conversation." The two friends sauntered down the hall, one spindly flamboyance and the other diminutive reserve.

Riding to lunch in Roxy's paper-strewn punch bug, she marveled at their kinship. Only a few such souls enter one's life, and Clarice had found one in the oddest package she could have imagined. On the surface, the two friends could not have seemed more different while deep down, they shared a certain camaraderie. Maybe that was why she was able to tell Roxy the truth about her past and her 'breaks' with reality, yet she still could not find a way to tell her own husband. She hated that, hated lying to him. Well, it's not lying, just not telling. *Yep, you keep telling yourself that. You're a piece of work, Clarice Martin Miller.*

"Breakfast for lunch, that different enough for you?" Clarice said when their Grand Slams arrived.

"Don't pick on me, short-stack. And don't change the subject either. What did the new GP say yesterday about the whole incident? Does he think Jax made up these men, started a fire, and crawled through air vents running from imaginary friends? I mean COME ON!?"

"I kid you not, that's the latest verdict. The doctor calls them self-induced catatonic lapses, claims they're nothing but a phase, and yeah, like an imaginary friend or something." Clarice tucked a fallen lock behind her ear and bent forward for a bite of sausage.

"Honey, all these doctors take everything so casually if you brought Jackson in with a third eye, they'd claim it was a self-induced growth spurt." Clarice laughed. "Reece, Jackson's trances have been going on for like two years. Didn't doctors rule all that stuff out? Let's see physically, fit as a fiddle," Roxy held up her thumb, "no mental abnormalities," another finger went up, "and nothing neurological." The final finger went up in triumph. "Ja ever consider maybe he sees what you think you've seen? If he does, what else can the little guy do but zone out?" Roxy reached for the red-hot Durkee sauce and commenced slathering her hash browns. Clarice fiddled with her napkin, smoothing it over her lap, not answering.

"Umm, member that time," Roxy talked with her mouth full—*God, she loved this woman*— "you were in eighth grade, you told me about buzzing out and seeing your math teacher?"

"Yeah... the doctor did look the same as my teacher, but that could have been my imagination."

"Not likely, sweetie."

"Why not?"

"Cause you ain't got one." Roxy unscrewed the top off the peppershaker, which flakes never came out fast enough for her. "Deny, deny, deny. I swear you shoulda been a politician or something."

That hurt, but truth does. Clarice forgot she'd told Roxy about that day in eighth grade. Trig had been dull and Mr. Evan's voice droned on and on. After a while, she'd felt that roller coaster whoosh and decided to give in to it to see what she'd see—basically out of boredom. She'd let go and boom everyone was transparent and lots of kids had twinkles by them. She remembered looking over at Sue Blaine, seeing a powdery ink cloud over her. She knew something was off with that chick. Up front where Mr. Evans should have been, she saw a misshapen creature on twisted limbs with cloven hoofs, fangs, stubby tusks and a rust colored body, wet with slime. The thing's red eyes glared back at her.

"Helloooo. Earth to Clarice," Roxy snapped her fingers in Clarice's face.

"I, I just believe in the real world," Clarice said.

"Nut-uh, pants on fire, Reece. You *only want* to see the real world. You don't want anything to do with—"

"Oh brother, can we please drop it?" Clarice picked up the hot sauce and slapped some on her eggs.

"Well, well, well, look—at—you!"

"Okay, it is bland," Clarice shrugged, looking from her friend's blast of color back to her yawning choice of khaki and white. She really had to break out of her safe wardrobe one of these days. *At least wear heels more*, she thought, aware she was changing the subject in her own mind.

They chewed silently for a bit.

"Hey guess what?" Roxy plopped a piece of egg on her toast. "I was at that macrobiotic health food store I haunt, and I saw a real live psychic! Now, what do you think of that?"

"Not much."

"No, really, it was cool, listen. The girl ahead of me was taking forever, badgering the cashier to help her friend. I was kind of trapped, you know? Couldn't very well leave without my carrot Slurpee," Roxy grinned, a few strands of her orange-colored coif boinging free from the mass of tight curls. "Anyway, this girl was desperate saying her friend was into witchcraft and had gone too far—whatever that means. She was convinced some sort of spirit had a hold of her. The lady made a few protests, kept denying she could help, but this girl knew some kind of scuttlebutt about her and wouldn't let go."

Roxy's eyes enlarged to Avatar disks, and she leaned forward for emphasis. "Then this Harriet—that's the psychic's name—so Harriet reaches out to touch the girl, just touches her is all, and then she says, 'Cynthia will be fine.'" Roxy paused building the drama. "Only thing is Reece, the girl *never* told Harriet her friend's name!" Rox sat back in her chair triumphant.

Clarice put her coffee down and considered the source of this alien news. Roxanne Cassan had outlandish fashion sense and a hundred other odd but endearing qualities, yet she really was pretty grounded.

"What if," Roxy pointed with her fork, "I mean, why not see if this Harriet could tell you anything about Jackson?"

"What!? A psychic?"

Roxy tipped her head, shrugged one shoulder.

"I don't get what you think a psychic could do for Jackson," Clarice said. "He's not possessed or whatever it is—and neither am I. I can't think about this, Rox. I swear I'll go crazy."

"Whoa, don't get defensive. Whoever said anything about possession? Honey, I just have a gut feeling someone like Harriet might know something about Jackson, his abilities. You know? What harm could come from five minutes with this woman?"

"I don't know Rox, I know you mean well." Clarice leaned back in the booth exhausted.

"It may be Jackson is just—"

"How's everything?" The two friends smiled politely and nodded at the waitress's perfunctory question. Their conversation suspended in mid-air, waiting for the gum-smacking girl to collect the odd dish or two and move on to interrupt someone else's meal.

"Anyway, I don't think he needs a shrink or anything like that," Roxy said. "You know I love Jackson to death. I think he's entirely normal. He's easily the biggest brain I've ever met." Roxy got up. "I'm hitting the ladies room. You?"

Clarice shook her head.

Roxy was right about Jax. People adored her three and a half-foot wonder, whose bright eyes looked at them behind fat glasses that only emphasized his brainy look. Although too young to be tested conclusively, everyone agreed his IQ was genius. He knew the alphabet at two. By three, he could already read first grade primers. Math was still more amazing, already learning long division.

In school, he was as active as any boy his age. The preschool program at BOCES doubled as a class for teens taking Early Childhood Education classes. A wall in the classroom had two-way mirrors so students could observe techniques and behavior firsthand. Parents were encouraged to peek at their child interacting with other kids, or more often, just being cute. How many times had she spied her Jaxie running around as goofy and carefree as the rest of the little monkeys in the room? She wanted all of this stuff to disappear and for them to lead a normal life.

On the way back to the office, Roxy was off and running on some juicy gossip, and Clarice was glad the day was at least half over.

By 6 p.m., Clarice stood at the kitchen counter unpacking the bag of groceries she'd picked up after work, Jax tied to her elbow. She'd shed her shoes and peeled off her stockings feeling a little cooler still in her khaki skirt and blouse.

"What's for dinner, mom?"

"Well, I'm leaning toward spinach wraps?" She pitched it out like a question for Nicey coming in from the hallway. She looked fresh in a crisply ironed housedress that might be older than Clarice.

"That's fine, dear. And do you know I made some lovely chicken salad for lunch. There's plenty left."

"Plenty what?" John burst through the side door from the garage, his jeans splattered with brown and his Tee shirt looking like he'd run a marathon.

"Dad!" Jax shot from her side and leapt at John.

"Good, the gangs all here," Clarice said, already chopping lettuce. She stretched her neck up to accept John's kiss behind her. He smelled of mud and sweat. "Chicken salad," she added patting his sunburned cheek.

"All right by me. How soon?"

"Soon as you shower, big guy."

John returned, smelling soapy and fresh in a pair of shorts and a clean tee shirt. The table was set, thanks to Jax. She and Nicey carried things over. She placed the platter of green burrito wraps and a couple of salad dressings next to Nicey's bowl of chicken salad and plate of fresh greens.

"Soooo," John said as he snagged a beer from the fridge, "I made 'bout fifty calls today looking into septic systems, wells, and oil tanks for the land in Ithaca. Plus, we finished putting up forms for the retirement home. Those babies just slap together. The pour has to wait till next week—"

"Hey, hey back up. What about the phone company?" Clarice said, sipping John's beer almost as soon as he set it down. "Will they continue the line?"

"Didn't get a yes but didn't hear no either."

"Dad, what's a septic for? We don't have one here. Why do we need one if we move there?"

"Oh, that's because—"

Brnggg. Brnggg.

The sound of the old-fashioned doorbell gave everyone a start.

"I'll get it," Nicey said, already up.

John held off on his explanation, and the three of them continued eating in silence listening to see who it was.

"Ma'am, may I speak with Mr. and Mrs. Miller."

Nicey turned around, John and she coming to the door. Clarice recognized one of the State policemen who'd been at the clinic Sunday.

"Officer..." John extended his hand.

"Babicek."

"Right. Come in." John said, moving back to allow him room.

The trooper stepped inside, and Nicey closed the door on the waning sun. The living room was cool, but the shades drawn against the heat made it dark and dreary. Clarice waved the officer to a chair and scurried to the bay window behind the couch, tugging on each of the three shades till they sprang up.

Mrs. Nicestrum was practically glaring at the poor policeman, who stayed put on the little area of slate by the front door. He looked over at Jackson in the kitchen entryway.

"Mrs. Nicestrum," Clarice said, "would you mind taking Jackson for a walk?"

Nicey hesitated. Every stranger is a threat to her, Clarice thought. The old face brightened.

"Yes, of course," she said. "Come on Jackie, we'll see about those tomatoes daddy's growing." Hand in hand, Mrs. Nicestrum led Jackson out through the kitchen. The screen door banged and the man spoke as though on cue.

"I came in person to tell you what's going on," the officer said. "The man who died, er a Clive Henkel, he—"

"Would you like to sit down?" Clarice said and indicated the living room chair, not sure what to offer.

"Oh no, I won't be too long," he said, taking out a small spiral notepad—the kind kids use for homework assignments. He removed his hat and placed it on the tiny console under the mirror. She noticed him glance in the mirror at his cropped hair. He was older compared to John but about John's height if not his girth.

"Clive Henkel, the man in the house, had no relatives, but we did locate several prescriptions—one for blood pressure and another for his heart. His doctor will have to testify to his condition."

"Testify!?" John said.

"First the coroner will have to issue his autopsy report."

"I don't understand," Clarice sidled up to John.

"See, we feel, that is, the captain and I, the most your son will be responsible for is trespassing and possibly vandalism."

"Responsible? But he's only four!" Clarice squeaked in tandem with John's eruption of:

"What the hell are they trying to—?"

"It's not a trial," Officer Babicek said, "I didn't mean to say; I mean it just has to go before a judge. He'll talk to him, that's all." He wrote something on his pad.

"Are they so sure our son is making the whole thing up?" John said.

"Here," Babicek ignored John's question, "June 13, that's the date of the meeting at family court. Judge Harding is one of the best, a real family man, very fair. And you have to understand, we have absolutely nothing to corroborate your son's story. But...well anyhow, I came to tell you in person, you know, about the man and all. I'm still questioning neighbors and looking into that *Waterman Clinic.* I think something smells off there... Well anyway, I just came to tell you."

Clarice took the note with *Monday, June 13; 10:30* printed in chubby letters and thanked him. He seemed genuine, even concerned for them. But what the heck, vandalism, trespassing, for a four year old?

Shortly after they finished eating dinner, Nicey, with a little encouragement from John, left for her apartment. The three of them settled on the couch with Jax between them and watched a little *American Idol.* It didn't take long before Jackson complained.

"They're making fun of people, Dad," Jax said, looking up.

"Yer, right, buddy," John said, raising an approving eyebrow to Clarice. He clicked the remote till he landed on an episode of

Deadliest Catch on the Discovery channel. As they watched raging waters beat against the hull of a crab fishing boat in the Bearing Strait, Clarice could almost feel her tiny family, huddled onboard, rocking in the waves, all helpless and vulnerable. Not only Jackson's condition or this new threat of mystery men chasing him —*and why, why was anyone chasing him?!*—not just police or courts, or strangers dropping dead in farmhouses, but something much deeper and important to her. She wanted to protect them, to spare them. Was it so wrong to want a normal life, to want what everyone else seemed to have?

As a kid, between the insane breaks with reality, the outlandish wardrobe foisted upon her by a delusional mother, the days of missed school ending in botched times tables and addlebrained answers, kids laughing, girls talking, and boys taunting—the extroverted, happy, carefree spirit she had once been was beaten down, day after day, little by little.

Being normal became more than a dream for her; it became a burning desire. By eighth grade, she'd learned to conquer the whoosh feeling, learned to hide play clothes in her book bag so she could dress normal at school, learned to sit in the back of the room, look down a lot, and never, ever ask a question. She studied hard, determined not to be dumb. More than math and science, she studied other kid—how they dressed, how they ate, how they smiled—all to fit in.

Jackson tugged her arm. Clarice realized the show had ended and John had already slipped away to their room.

"Okay honey bear, let's go." She tucked Jax in for the night and joined John in their bedroom. Lying in bed, he watched her undress.

"C'mere," John called softly before she could slip the flannel nightshirt over her head.

Clarice dropped the shirt back in her drawer and walked to his side. John sat up and she stood between his legs. He buried his head on her belly and her fingers passed through his hair.

"It's such a mess John, a stupid mess on top of—"

"I know," he said, lifting his face and pulling her neck down to meet him. He kissed her hard. "We'll get through it, Reece. He'll be alright."

She kissed him back, slow and meaningfully, as she lowered to the bed. Afterward, she lay on her side enfolded by John like a hand in a glove. "We still have our move to Ithaca." His chin moved over her head. "I hope this judge stuff doesn't get in the way."

"Me too. Oh, any word on our offer?"

"So far it looks pretty good. The owner is deciding about the other four hundred acres." John played with her hair. "I hope he sees my offer is fair."

"He will—because it is." She said it with confidence. John was not only fair; John was generous. They fell silent and she thought of the land and of the Glen, closing her eyes to enjoy the delicious feeling it gave her.

"John, did you notice anything about that glen?"

"What do mean?" John said. "It was okay, I guess."

"You didn't feel anything different? I'm talking about where you found me, down that hill by the waterfall?"

"I was just glad to find you. What were you thinking, anyway?" He sounded like her father.

"I wasn't," she said, barely audible. Clarice rolled over, pulled herself up on an elbow to look at his face in what little streetlight seeped through the gauze curtains. "The glen, the boulders, the stream, all that moss, and well. . ., didn't you notice anything special about it?"

His eyes opened and met her gaze in the muted light. "Like what? I mean what are you getting all excited about, Reece?"

She didn't answer, but lay on her back feeling a little lonely. She could never explain it. For a moment lying there, loneliness washing over, she was nine again sitting in Doctor Pool's waiting room, her mother on one side, mad cause they were seeing yet another specialist, her poor dad on the other, looking exhausted facing another layoff and high medical bills.

Heavy silence hung between John and her like a wet laundry sheet on a windless day—her unspoken hurt and isolation clung to the sheet while her secrets caused a rift in the bond between husband and wife.

"It's a climax forest, you know," John mumbled, his sleepy voice reaching out in his own way to answer whatever it was she wasn't saying. "Gotta be like three centuries old. How cool is that?"

She kissed his arm and scooted to her side of the bed.

Clarice dreamt of Jackson in the Glen, bathed in vaporous light. Her little guy squatted by the glass stream, playing with the water, scooping it up in tiny fists and letting the droplets fall before his face, over and over with the most content look. He was healed and whole, no more trances or nightmares. She could feel his wholeness.

Now the vaporous light grew into a thick fog rolling over the entire scene, enfolding him in the Glen. She slid backward, farther away. Her arms flung out to him, trying to reach him. Backward, backward she glided, helpless on an invisible conveyor belt, gliding away from the Glen, away from her son. "Jackson, Jackson!"

* * *

The Elders

"Why are we meeting here?" a stubby Phillip asked, his flabby girth looking weirdly uncomfortable, barely fitting on the conference room chair. Around the long oval table of rich cherry, the twelve leather chairs could hardly be considered skimpy, yet his bottom managed to overflow any seat, Vera observed.

"Quiet, Phillip. Don't question *him;* you'll live longer." Vera pulled a cigarette to her ruby lips with hyper-extended fingers and drama, always with drama. "Besides,"—she looked about the long narrow room at the four elders gathered—"I believe he wishes to discuss the future of the clinic."

"Yes, what a colossal failure for you," Emmett said, getting coffee in the corner and barely containing his glee. Emmett Pierce, a slim man of about 50, was her biggest rival, a real thorn—the dark-haired snappy dresser in the latest Armani cut. She watched him daintily stir his cream.

"Emmett dear, did I miss something?" She mocked a puzzled look. "Just when was it that *you* came that close to delivering the boy?"

"Close but no cigar, Vera." A chunky, Scott Henderson chimed in. She glared at him till he looked down.

She heard a car pull up as Emmett brought his coffee to the table and stood in front of his chair. Everyone else followed with the sound of bodies lifting off leather and heavy chairs pushing back. Sergio, the Italian bodyguard held the door open, and Vera studied his long black hair trying to think of what the master called that one.

"Judas, wait in the car."

Judas, that's it. She watched him exit. The bodyguards lent him an air of importance she rather envied. Of course, she had Worm, her six foot seven adoring tree-trunk of a minion but that was different. Straightening from her bow, she waited till the master signaled them to sit. *He* remained standing at the head of the table; his head gave her an imperceptible nod.

"What is the status of the situation?" His slippery voice slid over the s'es slowly, a style all his own, classy and distinctive, like hers.

"The family is scheduled to go before Judge Har-ding," she said. "He will de-cide if the child must undergo a court-ordered evaluation." Vera's lips pursed, watching her cigarette smolder wastefully in the tray.

"Emmett, we will need your connections now," the master said.

A smug look crossed Emmett's perfect features, and Vera defiantly reached for her cigarette. Lawyers were such a waste of human flesh.

"Of course," Emmett said, "I have no ties to Harding per se, but perhaps—"

"We could arrange to have him re-moved," Vera cut in releasing smoke.

"Don't you think we've had enough of your ideas?" Emmett said.

"Without Vera we wouldn't even know the boy's name even." Phillip piped up, shifting his bulk.

"Stow it Phillip, what are you kissing up to her for?" Scott said.

Amused, the master watched the verbal skirmish, voices raised and battle lines drawn. Finally, he cut them off with a snap of his hand.

"We know the boy's identity. Lessers will track him. You four are to seize any opportunity when he is separated from his protective auras. Meanwhile, the clinic can still play a role."

Vera narrowed her wide eyes at Emmett and imperceptibly grinned.

"Vera, you will keep feelers out to all the local child psychologists. You will also write a personal letter to Judge Harding outlining your concern for the boy's welfare. Mention the fire starting and his bizarre behavior, the parent's statements about his trances too. I'm confident you know what to highlight." He turned to Emmet.

"Emmett, you will keep your pretty ear to the courtroom walls and use every ounce of your power to change the judge. Uh, who do we have there?"

"Several. Richards would be best. He could have the boy—"

"The important thing is to be ready, ready for any opportunity," the master's voice rose slightly. "I want to know every connection the family has where they work, who their friends are, what school he attends. Sooner or later his protector will fail him," he said, and looked across the bestial faces of the elders, "and we *will* be there."

"Now then, let us move on to the business of Ordinatio. There are several financial matters that need attending and at least two sects, one in Tennessee and the one in New Mexico with troublesome reports."

Silence ensued as papers shuffled, pens clicked, and bottoms repositioned to deal with all things *Ordinatio Triune Orbis*.

6

Gabriel Katz

Gabe was enjoying himself. On top of the world, he walked home from school through the Back Bay Fens. He'd aced his exam in Earth Science, although, that was a given; he always did great in science and math. And yesterday for his fourteenth birthday, he'd gotten a neat silver transistor radio. But gym class, now that really made him happy! Today was the first time all year that he didn't feel like a loser in gym. Hard enough being practically the only boy in school wearing the kippah, but to also be the weakest kid in school was unbearable. Today when he conquered the rope, Mr. Tokus' face was perfect. *Ha, take that you fat pig. I did it. You can't say I didn't, and you can't take it away. I did it, and I'm gonna do it again. That ball of pork's gonna eat his words.* His pent up anger and resentment for the gym teacher, who regularly embarrassed him, mixed with his joy, threatening to spoil it. He tucked his hand into the pocket of his brown, corduroy coat from Woolrich's to feel his new radio. Too long to be fashionable, the car coat might have looked smart on a man over thirty. His grandma bought it. Gabe stopped on the bridge and looked about the Fens.

Even in the snow, this place was something special. Guilt stabbed him. His Bubbe didn't want him cutting through here anymore. She said there were rumors of strange men haunting the reedy areas at night—but it wasn't night, and he wasn't scared anyway.

Decades before, the Back Bay Fens, originally a salt marsh had been transformed into parklands that still allowed for water management. Now, paths lined with benches and quaint stone bridges wove throughout the landscaped oasis near the heart of Boston. Rose gardens, ball fields, and tennis courts coexisted without disturbing the natural scenery.

A rich place, the Fens, but still wild in the marshy areas where the uncontrollable reed called Phragmites thrived in the waterways. These reeds were introduced both to hide the unpleasant aspects of the Fens, which naturally filter the city's sewage and serve as a barrier to keep people from the water. The problem with the Fens was that it had suffered from too much naturalization and a lack of funds had led to the wilderness getting out of hand. The reeds created loads of hidden areas where derelicts, delinquents, and social outcasts loomed after dark.

Gabe thought back to his grandmother's warning. "Gevalt!" she had yelled at Gabe and his sister in her thick Yiddish accent.

"Bubbe, it's safe during the day."

"If each one sweeps before his own door, the whole street is clean. No one sweeps the Fens!"

"But Bubbe it's shorter, and there are police around," Gabe half-lied. It was a shorter way home from school, but police rarely made an appearance.

His grandmother shook her head. Her voice softened pleading with them, "Listen to me my little ones. Stay on our street, not in the Fens. Fate is a friend until you tempt her!" Half of these sayings were issued in full Yiddish, but Gabe knew every word.

Bubbe Katz had been raising him and his older sister ever since their mother died nearly ten years ago from breast cancer. Gabe's father, Mr. Katz worked long hours in his delicatessen on Blue Hill Ave. The successful deli kept the Katz family in Roxbury long after most Jews had migrated southward to Dorchester. Harassment of the Jews became commonplace in the 50's. Shops had swastikas painted on them; Jewish boys were beat up on their way home from school, and ugly graffiti was smeared on Jewish homes. The

Jewish exodus left the Katz family swimming against a Gentile crowd—a very tough life for Gabe and his sister.

The reeds poked through the snow everywhere on both sides of the stone bridge. Gabe set down his satchel of books to scoop up some snow. He packed it into a snowball. *Good packing today.* He threw it as hard as he could at the signpost some ten yards away. *Dang, missed!* One foot shy of the mark. Undeterred, he leaned down to make another one.

Below Gabe, three teens stood smoking by the wooden shelter near the bridge. The tall boy shivered in his shiny blue windbreaker. His longish hair blew in the slight wind chilling him more. His friends, the redhead in a heavy bomber jacket and the pudgy kid in a lined jean coat, appeared warmer. All three wore bell-bottom jeans and those half-boots with pointy toes and side zippers.

"Hey!" The tall one punched the redhead's arm. "Hey, look at that," he said, pointing to the Gabe on the bridge, whose pile of black curls was topped with one of those Jewish caps. He could never remember the name of those.

"Don't hit me, jerk!"

"Shut up you big baby. Look at him. Look wouldja?"

"Who, that kid? I know him. His old man runs the deli on Blue Hill. Ha, ha, throws like a patsy, man."

"Stupid Jew. Man, what's he think he's doin?" the pudgy boy stomped out his butt in the snow.

"I dunno. Let's go ask him." The tall one gave a look to the other two. "Catch my drift?"

"I hear ya, man." The redhead zipped up his black jacket.

"Far out." Pudgy followed.

Gabe, tired of missing the sign, reached in his pocket to retrieve his transistor radio. The silver shininess of it still thrilled him. He tuned in a station. *Turn on Your Lovelight* cackled out. Gabe held the sleek radio to his ear enjoying the Grateful Dead. Lifting his head, he spied three guys approaching him on the bridge. They made eye contact, and like a pack of wild dogs threatening to pounce, Gabe knew at once turning to ignore them was not an option.

"Grateful Dead, huh? Not my bag." The leader began real easy.

"He don't know Jack 'bout music, man." Red spit. "Check out the threads." All three laughed at Gabe's uncool duds.

Gabe had no desire to get into it with these guys. Without saying a word, he picked up his satchel and moved to the left, but the fat kid and the tall one-stepped in unison directly in front of him. Gabe moved right; this caused the red head to imitate the others and block him on the other side.

"Hey, back off, wouldja. I don't want any trouble."

"Seems to me you do, Jew. Wearin' that beanie, walkin' in the Fens, like you got any right around here."

"Yeah, seems to us you and your kind is stinking up Boston with that kosher crud your old man serves up at the deli." Pudgy took one look at Gabe's frightened face and emboldened gave him a shove.

Gabe stumbled back off-balance and yelled, "Flake off," trying to sound brave. *Oh Hashem, not another Jew attack, please.* He attempted to pass. This time the tall kid bumped into him with his whole body. Gabe's converse sneakers slipped on the ice, still he managed to stay up.

"Leave me alone."

He burst through the three again, but one of them stuck his foot out and tripped him. Gabe slid, feeling air rush by him falling backward; his arm flew up loosening his grip on the precious Transistor. He landed flat on his back with a fantastic thud. His new radio with an ugly smack ended right by the leader's foot. Its nine-volt battery was hanging out, as if it were sticking its tongue out at Gabe's tormentors.

"You ain't hip kid, you know? You don't deserve a transistor. Like you and your tunes give us a bad vibe." He lifted his foot to stomp on the radio.

"No, you jerk," Gabe yelled, "Stop it!" When his hand went to retrieve his birthday gift one of the boys kicked him in the ribs.

"Stupid, stinking Jew."

Pain shot through his back from the fall, and he reeled from the surge of pressure in his ribs when a second pointy boot slammed into his other side.

"Get outta Boston, Jew-boy."

As he lay there in a pile of pain fighting red-hot tears, Gabriel Katz seethed, suddenly incensed and no longer scared. All these slurs on his faith, all the suffering he and his fellow Jews in Boston endured—so much, most of them had fled to Dorchester! Anger boiled up, a righteous anger that filled him to the brim—an over-filled pot of boiling, splattering, bubbling-over anger till it screamed to be heard. At once a righteous power, very strong and very old surged within him. The power even had a name: *Tzaddik*. A word for his power and his justice: Tzaddik. He *was* Tzaddik!

Gabe's arms flung out like a serpent's tongue to his left and right while two of the boys prepared for another kick. He grabbed their raised feet, and with all his might hurled both boys up and backwards. Their bodies flew through the air doing Saturday morning cartoon back-flips. Gabe leapt to his feet Bruce Lee fashion and stared down the fat one standing before him. Pudgy, twice his size, yelled and charged him.

Gabe raised his hand like a traffic cop, called on the power inside him, and issued a single command.

"STOP!"

"Stop!" Gabe awoke in a sweat, his flannel pajamas sticking to his legs. A dream? It was just a dream, a crummy dream. Another one of those dreams where he had power. Man, they always involved an attack on his faith. Why? He looked at his clock as all three numbers flipped over to 9:00. It was Sunday, yet he'd been allowed to sleep in. His dad would be at the deli already. Where were Bubbe and sis?

Gabe got out of bed, his toes touching the crumpled paint on the wood floor. *Oi yoi yoi*, it was cold! Without taking a step, he reached for the pitcher and basin on the solid maple desk by his bed. He lifted the filled pitcher to begin the ritual hand washing and poured the icy water three times over his hands into the ceramic basin, thanking God for the morning restoration of his soul, which Gabe firmly believed had left him in his sleep. Only now that he had faithfully performed the Netilat Yadayim, could he look for his Bubbe.

He found her in the kitchen of the apartment sipping very strong coffee. Her gray hair was pulled tightly in a bun, and she wore a fading flowered apron over her plain blue housedress. She wasn't too fat for 70, but you wouldn't call her thin either unless of course you meant her arms, which looked drawn and worn from daily chores.

"Ay yay yay, boychik, but you were tired, no?" She stirred from her seat to serve Gabe some breakfast.

"No Bubbe. Sit, please" Gabe placed his hand over his grandma's and pulled out the chrome chair sitting across from her. "I want to ask you something."

His grandma sat, brushing crumbs off the tortoise shell top of the metal table, waiting for a question.

"Bubbe, do you know what Tzaddik means?"

"Tzaddik? But why should you want to know this? Who it is that told you this word, Bubbela?

"I dreamed it, Bubbe. I dreamed I was Tzaddik."

"Oi!" Her hands went to cover her mouth. "Come." She patted her knee for Gabe to sit even closer. She never seemed to get that he was fourteen now and couldn't fit on her feeble lap if he tried. He chose to kneel in front of her and looked into her ample face with love.

She tipped her head back speaking to God, "Adoshem, help me to explain." She gazed into Gabe's eyes as she cradled his cheeks in her palms. "Tzaddik means 'righteous one'—completely righteous, Ga'vriel. It is said that such a one has spiritual and mystical powers. It is from the Chasidic community, but many do not believe this tradition."

"Why don't they believe?" Gabe studied his grandma's serious face, feeling a soreness as her hands cupped his face.

"Perhaps, Bubbela, it is because there ceased to be any completely righteous men; so perhaps also, the power of Tzaddik faded in memory as the presence of good and just men disappeared." The old face looked wistful. "But you my boy, you are so good, so special. Ga'vriel, if Adoshem has given you this word in a dream, He has a reason, no?"

"I dunno, maybe," Gabe said, wincing.

"You are Kohen, a priest, Ga'vriel Katz. That you know. Yes?" Her expression changed, and she pulled her hands from his sore cheeks continuing to hold her palms out and bobbing them up and down pointing to his face. "Aach! Just look at you. You think maybe this was chutzpah? Phooey." She pretended to spit. "I say left, you go right. That is not chutzpah, Ga'vriel; it is meshugeh. Stay out of the Fens. Oi Vai! Just look what those hoodlums did to you."

So he hadn't dreamed it all then. Wow, he thought realizing how well he had blocked the memory of the attack again. The dream flooded back, half real, half fantasy, the crazy part about him having power. In reality, he had been beaten to within an inch of his life before a cop car neared. He remembered the last thing he heard before passing out was the siren and the tall kid shouting: "Bug out!"

Gabe stood, feeling every inch of his injuries, even though it had been almost a week. He looked over at the counter where his father had left the smashed radio he had found in the bloody snow. He wanted to cry and felt his throat close up keeping back the emotions.

* * *

Gabe awoke again, his throat still choked. He rubbed his chin feeling the stubble of today's beard against his fingers. Wow, he hadn't thought about that for years! Those bullies, the beating, Grandma Katz, and even Tzaddik, that strange idea. Why would he dream of that horrible memory? Ha, not the beating—a dream of a dream of the beating! That has to be a new one, even for Dr. Mendelson.

At least this dream was a change. He thought of the one he'd had the night before last. Had that one a few times already—that boy sitting in the forest glade, those fantastic surroundings. What a beautiful and strange child! Why did he keep dreaming of that boy? *Why? Aach!* These dreams were a curse. And now he had one more to dump on his poor psychologist. Great, just great.

7

Thou Win

Gabe continued packing. He knew he should be feeling sad to leave this comfortable home and the people he loved, yet he was excited about going to college. He folded the few things in his tiny closet remembering the last time they moved four years ago. It was only a couple months after the beating, and it was all because of him. His grandma's voice pleading with his dad came back to him.

"Vos iz? You ask me what's wrong, Zun? Your family lives in danger everyday and you make us stay here. For what? For what?"

"Money, ma'me. The store cannot get up and move, can it?" His dad controlled his voice with the same respect he always showed to Bubbe, but Gabe could hear his dad's frustration. The attack on Gabe had caused worry for the whole family, yet his dad was trapped.

"Gelt gait tzu gelt!" Money goes to money, she yelled in Yiddish.

"I have to make a living, don't I? I have to put food on this table and a roof over our heads!"

"Make a living? How do you make a living, Zun?" Her hands flew up and chopped the air. "Me lost nit leban! They don't let you live," she repeated in English then softened her tone, "Money is not a problem, Dovid."

True Gabe's dad was shrewd. He had saved enough for them to begin again in the safety of another town. Bubbe wanted them to settle in Newton where Gabe's mother's family lived. Gabe's uncle, his dad's brother-in-law, had offered to help settle them and to be partners if his dad would agree to open a new deli.

"Hak mir nit in kop!" His dad had yelled, telling his grandma to stop bending his ear. "Gav'riel was just unlucky."

"Feh,"—she spit—"Gav'riel is no shlimazel." The voices got quiet, and Gabe thought his dad was comforting Bubbe.

"Vos gicher, alts besser." The faster the better, his dad agreed. And that was that. They had sold the deli and moved to Newton. In no time, Gabe's Aunt and Uncle with Gabe's dad, invested in another store. They all lived together now, above the new store in a spacious apartment. In two years, it grew to be more successful than the one on Blue Hill had been. Gabe's sister shared a room with Bubbe, and Gabe shared one with his cousin Al, two years younger than him.

Gabe moved to the dresser to pack those clothes and turned to find Al leaning in the doorway.

"Haw, I thought you were down in the store?" Gabe smiled at the lanky figure. Having Al in his life had been a wonderful thing. They were like brothers now, he thought, realizing he would probably miss him more than he would probably miss his own sister, who was a good three years older than him. Ruthie was okay; still he couldn't say they were close. With Al, it was different. He and his cousin had hit it off right away.

"Pop let me take a break to say goodbye," Al peeled himself from the doorframe and landed on Gabe's bed, fingering the old leather suitcase.

"Fraid, I'd skip town without seeing you?"

"Ha," Al leaned back, his gangly legs stretching out, "just memorizing your ugly mug before you go." Gabe shook his head. Al and he did everything together when they were free. Mostly, Gabe would miss their long talks at night, each lying in his bed unloading problems, or sharing philosophies in the dark. Al was the brother he'd never had.

Gabe carried a load of sweaters over to the bed, put them in the suitcase, and shoved it over enough so he could sit beside Al. "Well...."

"Yup."

They sat silent for a full minute—not awkward, just them, each knowing what was ending.

Finally, Al slapped Gabe's back. "Don't be a stranger man, I mean it."

Gabe reached out to meet Al's handshake and pulled Al in for a long hug.

"Gotta get back," Al said and got up. "Write me sometimes and make it sound brilliant, will ya?"

"Hey, twirp," Gabe tossed a pillow at him, "everything I write is brilliant."

Al was gone. Gabe turned to empty the last drawer. Tired of the chore—or ready to move on—he took a lazy man's load this time, scooping the entire pile of clothes and accidentally snagging the drawer liner with it. Something slid by the corner of his eye. Peering down, he saw words etched into the wood on the bottom of the drawer:

Thou Win

He dropped the clothes and knelt running his fingers over the scratched words darkened with age. "Thou Win," he read them again. Those same two words had been there since Gabe turned seven. Who scratched them on the bottom of his drawer? Why? Someone carved them, perhaps his sister, although she had adamantly denied it. Maybe his mother before she died, but that was fanciful. And what did it matter? The words were there, and they always held some kind of meaning for him. He first discovered them following one of those dreams, the ones where he had power and purpose. When he was little, Gabe read them repeatedly until one day Bubbe or mother placed the new flowered liner on top of them, and the secret words were forgotten.

He was always sure those words referred to Hashem. After all, whom else do you call "Thou" these days? Over the years when he would think of them, it was always in the context of his will and Hashem's, as though the two were in a kind of battle. He liked to think his Creator would win. His will winning over Gabe's flawed desires, or rather winning Gabe over—period.

Thou Win.

It was neat to see the old word's again, he thought. Whatever they meant they always comforted him. He would bring those words in his heart to the University of Michigan and beyond. Gabe shut his suitcase, scooped his change and wallet off the top of his dresser, and slowly closed the dresser drawer—another chapter of his life ending, a new one beginning.

8

Sweet Dreams

Jackson giggled streaking up and down the short hallway. Stark naked, he ran from the kitchen table down the hall till he slammed against the footboard of his parents' bed. Boom, he turned around, ran back down the hall to the kitchen table. This was John's brainchild for drying Jax off without towels after a bath.

John lying on the couch, his head on Clarice's lap, laughed so hard he snorted, heightening their amusement to near convulsive levels. They watched the entryway where, every few seconds, Jackson would run down the hall with his arms outstretched to touch the table. He would turn his head toward them to see their delight then comically snap it back just in time to avoid a crash.

"How come you never dry off that way?" John said, wiping a wet eye.

"You wish. C'mon." Clarice tapped the temple she'd been stroking and started to get up, forcing John to lift his head. He mumbled some half-hearted offer to get Jax while rolling over to face the couch.

"Okay, Tarzan," she called to Jax, "ready or not, here I come."

Jackson squealed, expecting his mother to chase him. She played his game running up and down the hall a few times. Finally, she slipped out of sight behind the bathroom door.

"Boo! Gotcha you little monkey." She tickled him. "C'mon, let's put your PJ's on. Did you brush your teeth before your bath?"

"Uh-huh, I flossed too. See."

"Oh, very nice," she agreed, as if she could tell and popped a red pajama shirt over his head. "What do you wanna read, handsome?"

"I don't want to read. I want a story."

"A story? What kind of story?" He loved it when she made up fantastic stories for him. Clarice was good at it too. Princes and dragons were for rank amateurs. Hers were highly creative tales with hot-air balloons or desert islands.

"Flying, I was flying in the hall."

Clarice settled next to him tucking him under her arm, all warm and smelling fresh from his bath. She stared down at her feet tapping together on the blue quilt. Flying... flying? She felt kind of dry tonight. Could tell him a real one? He'd think it was make-believe. What could it hurt?

"Once there was a beautiful girl, a mommy really, only her baby was still inside her tummy."

"Her womb, Mom."

She grinned, nodding. "The mommy was feeling veerry sick."

"Morning sickness?"

"You read too much, you know that?" She squeezed him. "Yes, she was queasy. Someone was cooking eggs next door to her apartment."

"Pregnancy makes the senses bigger, huh Mom? That's why she smelled it."

"Who's telling this story, anyway? And yeesss, she could hear and smell the tiniest things."

It had been the pregnancy with Jax, she thought, that heightened that other sense in her too, the one she couldn't always control. Growing up she would find herself falling out of focus with one world and into focus with that other. She would fight it off like some unwanted lover's advance. She'd been able to avoid any major incidents over the years, and had been so successful she'd convinced herself that they were merely fanciful illusions of her imagination. During pregnancy, however, this incident acutely tested her ability at self-deception.

"It was chilly that morning, and the girl went to her balcony, hoping the fresh air would take the feeling away. She felt a tickle in her tummy, like she was about to throw up."

"Oohhh, I hate that tickle, Viral Gastro... gastro-enter-itis. That's when I had to carry the garbage bag all day, member, Mom?"

"I know you had it once too." She tapped his nose. *God he is cute!* "So the girl stood at the porch rail waiting for the tickle to go away." Even now, Clarice could see the view behind her apartment complex, a strip of blacktop, followed by a wild field that dipped to a gully holding a creek. "All of a sudden the girl felt really funny, not from the tickle either," Clarice's voice lilted with the tale. "Everything around her faded—all the scenery, even the building, and the porch she stood on. Everything was still there but kind of transparent, you know see-through." Jackson's eyes inflated to saucers and she hurried on. "Then she felt a big whoosh in her stomach—like the first hill on the roller coaster. Member at Hershey Park?"

Jackson nodded.

"Her body felt really, really heavy like it was sinking—sinking away, like a lead ball through thick liquid." Clarice's hand moved sluggishly down in front of them. "While her body sank away, she felt her spirit; you know her insides, rising higher and higher." Her hand rose.

"Awesome Mom, her soul? Her insides are her soul? Was she going up to heaven?"

Clarice paused uncomfortable with the terms. Church people talked that way, people who, she supposed, felt close to God. "Well, I guess some people think of the insides as their soul." She patted his leg and continued. "Anyway, she floated up but not to heaven. She just floated there above the balcony. It felt pleasant, you know? After a while, she had this incredible desire to fly, to move forward over that railing and sail down above the tall marsh grass. She wanted to feel the soft air brush across her body."

"Mom," he said, sounding matter-of-fact, "she had no body."

89

"Thennn, how could she feel so many things in all her senses? So free, so alive, the air flowed over her, around and through her. She sailed and sailed, turning this way and that, like a silk ribbon flowing in the wind, bobbing over the weeds with the water trickling below her." Clarice swooped her free arm up and down over the bed covers.

"It was exhilarating but peaceful too. She saw the buildings and the parkway by her apartment. They were transparent too...." Clarice trailed off, seeing the twinkling sparkles of brilliance here and there, the threatening dark blotches. She was about to question her story choice but somehow in the safety of a bedtime story where everything is hidden in make believe, it seemed safe to continue.

"The girl had been up there so long that she panicked. Something was wrong, terribly wrong. She felt danger. What was going on? What could be wrong? Her mind struggled to think clearly, to think of something corporal, you know, physical. Something, someone... someone needed her right away." It wasn't hard to sound dramatic.

"But the girl couldn't return, couldn't let go of such ecstasy. She continued sailing, leaning this way and that, lost in the bliss of flight. Something kept bugging her like a gnat buzzing your face."

"Was it a bug, Mom? They fly. Or was it a feeling?"

"It was a feeling, honey, and the feeling got bigger. She felt like someone needed her right away. Even though she was still enjoying the flight, it just wouldn't let go!"

"What did she do 'bout it?"

"Well, she felt very confused." Clarice's feet waggled back and forth. "She didn't know how to answer it. Finally, she hovered there unable to go on against the pounding doubts. 'Help, help me,' she called out.

"Presently, a light of bright effervescent radiance enveloped her." Clarice brought her arms around Jax wiggling her fingers mimicking a force field. "And do you know what? She felt immediately calm and assured."

"Her angel," Jax said.

"Hmm, I don't know, maybe." Clarice never thought of it as an angel. "Anyway, even in the nice light, the mysterious sense of urgency was still there. The light seemed to turn, and the girl knew she was supposed to turn with it. She trusted the light, felt safe in it, like the light was holding her hand—like when daddy holds your hand in his big strong hand, you feel safe, right?"

He nodded. She was at a crossroads in the story knowing what was next.

"Then the light brought the girl back to her body."

"Why, Mom? What was urgent?"

Clarice climbed out of bed, thinking. She pulled the sheet over him. "Her baby in her tummy needed her; that's all. She needed to come back and be in her body else her baby couldn't be born, right?"

"The baby needed her insides back. I get it. Great story, Mom."

Clarice grinned. That was easy. "Okay, honey bear, time for the sandman." She softly kissed each of his eyelids and his forehead, wanting to hurry off, the memory of the story hanging in her head like heavy cream waiting to be swirled in a cup of coffee.

"Mrs. Nicestrum, I didn't see you there."

The nanny stood in the doorway, her worn chenille bathrobe bobbing above carpet slippers of the same sky-blue. The wire basket she held full of Vo5, a wettish box of Calgon, and some tall purple canister with a fading flower label looked about to lose its toothbrush passenger. Spongy pink curlers peeped from beneath her plastic shower cap, and the humid scent of lilacs and lilies lingered about her in a sweet cloud. Clarice marveled; even in this seemingly undignified attire, Mrs. Nicestrum looked stately.

She'd been with them since June 24, 2000, the day Jackson was born. Mrs. Nicestrum came into her room, wearing a hospital gown and wheeling a metal pushcart loaded with old books and magazines. She had the sweetest face Clarice had ever seen. Her hair of unknown length, a cross between blond and white, worn in an upsweep emphasized her benign look. From the first moment Mrs. Nicestrum held the baby while Clarice visited the ladies room, Jackson and she had bonded. Mrs. Nicestrum seemed nothing less than an angel sent to aid a single mom who needed a second mother herself.

"Oh, I just popped in to say goodnight." Mrs. Nicestrum leaned over to kiss Jax, the toothbrush passenger dangling dangerously over the basket lip. "Sleep tight. Don't let the bedbugs bite." She looked at Clarice across the bed.

Had she heard the story? Why the funny look? Clarice reddened following Mrs. Nicestrum out of the room. In the hall, the sweet pulpy face and erudite blue eyes smiled at her.

"Stories are best when they come from your heart, Clarice. Share them dear, that's the ticket." She slipped into her bedroom calling good night.

From your heart, what's that supposed to mean? Clarice continued down the hall. John's snoring filled their room. Poor guy worked so hard today. She slipped out of her jean shorts and climbed in bed with just a T-shirt. No sooner had she closed her eyes than the heavy cream swirled into the black coffee, and Clarice flew in the light as though it were yesterday....

Up ahead a menacing whirlpool of inky dust circled and circled. *What is it circling?* The question drifted somewhere in her consciousness as she continued to fly. The answer came to her again in her sleep as it had that morning: the baby. The eddy of churning blackness was surrounding her unborn child. In her dream, she flew with purpose and speed, accompanied by the light around her. She drew closer to the porch, seeing a cloud of swirling darkness, in the midst of which, she could barely make out her body standing there, its physical shell surrounded by a maddening black fog racing round and round it.

Swiftly the light flashed forward from her side toward the black cloud, which literally stopped its tornadic twisting, as if to confront the brightness. The two forces met head on, their energy popping and crackling like downed telephone wires. In the confusion typical of dreams, she knew only that she had to return to her body. Ignoring her fear, thinking only of her child, she pushed her way past the sparks of the gladiators of light and dark.

Even asleep, Clarice felt her spirit slide into its sheath as it had that day.

Her relief was minute as her breath caught noting her position —arms outstretched like a tightrope walker and feet balanced on the precarious perch of the wrought iron rail. Her gasp caused a dangerous teeter—Ahhhh!

She dropped fast, her chest in a nosedive.

Baby!

The scream stuck in her throat. She woke with her hand clasping her stomach. Clarice lay still, allowing her heart to slow. She moved planting herself against John's bulk, feeling the rhythm of his breathing. She hadn't fallen that day, she reminded herself. She had balanced her weight before leaping backward to the safety of the deck. Drifting off again, she remembered how she had gripped the metal stiles and laughed in some sort of absurd comic relief, huffing-out and hawing-in, thinking that at least her nausea was gone.

9

Introspection

June 10, 2005

Clarice awoke after a fitful sleep, bright sun hiding the time on the nightstand clock. Shoot! darn it! She missed her run and was late to boot. That dream last night kept her up, that and the looming judge interview in family court on Monday.

She hurried to the closet and eyed the limited selection. It was sunny, so she'd dress sunny. A flowered rayon skirt and mustard sandals joined a yellow v-neck tee from the dresser. Everything landed on the bed, and she ran to take a quick shower.

She was blow-drying her hair in front of the dresser mirror when Mrs. Nicestrum peeped in the door. Clarice turned the dryer off to hear the lilting voice.

"Good morning, dear. Don't you look like sunshine!" she said. "Would you like me to make you breakfast? Have it ready in a jiffy. There's time I think."

"Oh thanks Nicey, I'll just have toast and coffee. Be out in a minute."

Clarice ran the brush through light brown hair that flipped this way and that just as it pleased. The yellow tee was a good choice– the skirt...was it too short, too clingy, emphasizing her hips? Ug! Too late to change. Her eyes squinted a second, looking for any resemblance to Jennifer Garner that Roxy swore was there. Emerald eyes gazed back, demanding eyes, full of questions and hurt. The story, the dream, it was always there, this other part of her. John, John if only he knew, how would he react? Clarice turned away quickly.

A few minutes later, she was sitting at the table with Jax. He'd made her breakfast himself and proudly pushed his handiwork under her nose: two pieces of wheat toast, smeared in peanut butter with smiley faces made out of Cheerios and raisins.

"Oh wow, look at that! Look at that Nicey."

Mrs. Nicestrum turned from the sink to look over apologetically. Clarice magnanimously took a big bite of the toast, and a gulp of coffee. "Did Daddy leave yet?" she asked, pretty sure he had. Jax nodded his head stuck in a big glass of orange juice. "So what are you two planning today?" She smoothed the ever wayward curl on Jackson's head.

"Actually," Mrs. Nicestrum said, placing a frying pan in the dishwasher, "I have some errands to do downtown this afternoon. I'm hoping to bring Jackie to the park on Chenango Street. Oh, what's it called? You know the one."

"Ots-in-engo," Jax pronounced it slowly.

"Oh exactly, pumpkin. That's it exactly." She closed the dishwasher, and dried her hands on the kitchen towel hanging over the handle. "I was wondering—that is, if it wouldn't be too much trouble—if you or John could pick Jackie up from there?"

"I'm sure we can work that out."

"Maybe around 5:30, then. We'll just wait for you at the park."

"Sounds fine. Mommy's gotta go now, honey. Fridays, we have a staff meeting," she said, more in conversation with Mrs. Nicestrum. "They're so lame, but there's no way out. I could strangle the department head, Hannah—" Clarice stopped herself noting Jackson's eyes wide with interest. "Hannah Banana, they should call her." Hannah Mueller was mental, foisting her mindless charts and time-wasting graphs on everyone. Today she would nail Clarice to the wall for her missing sales projections. Clarice's right leg bobbed nervously under the table. She threw back the rest of her coffee, kissed Jax, and left for the day.

In the car she thought of Terry. Terry could have sliced Hannah up and had her for lunch. He knew how to deal with her kind. She felt a quick stab thinking of Jackson's natural father. She was only 22 when she started at the *Binghamton Journal*, fresh out of college. Their affair would have ended after the first encounter, had it not been for her fascination with the mind games.

Clarice could still see him, sauntering over to a group, identifying the weakest link, and then neatly disposing of the lesser mind—usually some poor guy who'd have a passionate but hopelessly inarticulate argument on some subject he knew little about. She had admired the quickness of Terry's mind. What sick allure it held, watching him do that to someone! And when he played the games on her, it was like a tennis match or tournament of minds that caused her actual titillation.

She knew his type, no strings, no expectations. Back then, she had no desire to marry or have children. Then she discovered her pregnancy—the result of a failed diaphragm and a tilted uterus. The argument when she told him had been typical Terry.

"I can't believe you! This doesn't make any sense," he'd screamed at her.

"I'm not doing it Terry. I won't have an abortion."

"So you just want a baby all of a sudden? You see yourself, all mommy and diapers, formula and daycare? Do you?" Terry had yelled, getting in her face. Pulling back, he visibly calmed himself and put on that smug *I-soooo-know-you* look. "Clarice, can't you see what you're doing here? You're just trying to fill that empty space your parents left you."

This had been low, even for Terry. Her father had died in her senior year of high school, and after that her mother's dementia progressed at a frightening rate. Barely 21, she had to sign the commitment papers herself. Clarice had faithfully visited her every night until her death—just two months before her pregnancy.

Terry had argued, played every mental and intellectual game on her, but what he said last stuck with her and haunted her to this day.

"What kind of mother will you make? You're so screwed up mentally. You know it! And you'll pass your messed-up crap to the kid, too. You don't have to do this; it's not like you don't have a choice these days."

But it was exactly like that. She could no more have harmed the life within her, than murder a puppy with her bare hands. It was impossible. So was the idea of adoption she'd toyed with. She remembered feeling a connection to the baby before she even felt its butterfly movements in her womb. In truth, she'd been relieved that Terry wanted nothing to do with her or the baby. He quit *The Journal* to move out West for a job in a California ad agency, and that was that.

Pulling into the lot at the *Journal*, Clarice wondered for the hundredth time why she ever got involved with him. Had she been that needy? When she'd turned sixteen, boys were suddenly interested in her but being an only child with two sick parents... High school had been torture. She remembered the last day she ever had a friend over to the house.

Unlocking the kitchen door with Amy behind her, they saw her mom half dressed at the table. She wore a slip that barely stayed on her emaciated body; her hair was half in curlers, and what wasn't trapped messily in a curler, stuck out in a tangled web. She fairly jumped out of her seat and ran at Amy.

"Who are you?" She yelled waving a hairbrush in Amy's face.

"Mom, it's Amy, you know Amy." Clarice stepped between them, but her mother moved even closer to the cowering girl.

"We don't want you comin' round here," the brush waved, "you been stealing my jewelry."

The accused shook her head. "No, Mrs. Martin, I never..."

"I know it was you. It was you. All my stuff is disappearing. You tell me that, huh? Tell me that."

Every word got louder. Amy ducked as Mrs. Martin's arm came down on her with the hairbrush. She ran out of the house, and Clarice knew that was the absolute last friend she would dare have over.

She recalled leading her mom to the second bedroom, the one she had to share with her.

"The missionaries are taking over." Her mom's eyes flashed; then the light disappeared replaced with a sad confusion. "Aren't they?"

"I don't know, Mom." Clarice sat her on the twin bed opposite her own, and bent to take off her mom's slippers, the silky ones she'd bought for Mother's Day the year before, before the Alzheimers. Mom had been so grateful.

"It's them witnesses. They go around telling you 'bout Jesus, comin' to the door, letting themselves in. Oh yes, don't I know it." Clarice lowered her down, pulling the comforter over her. "And they're not the only ones either."

"Okay mom, you rest."

"Wait! Wait." Her mom reached for her shirt to hold her there, and Clarice had known it was best to let her finish spinning her conspiracy theories. It was as if all the spy novels her mom used to read were floating around in her mind, a mind that could no longer process or organize a mind that could no longer distinguish.

"The lawn people," she'd yelled. She seemed to yell everything then. "They're taking over too. They walk around the yards spray, spray, spray...."

As her mom babbled, she left the room, about to get some dinner when she wanted to see her dad. He stayed in the room across the hall because her mom said that she couldn't "stand the stink o' that man anymore." It did reek. The melanoma had been eating her dad from the inside out. Clarice alone had changed the bandages and treated him with dignity.

"Dad, you awake?" There'd been no answer, but she'd crept to his side. In the last stages of his cancer, he had slept a great deal with all the pain meds. They'd blown past Vicodin, Percocet, you name it. He needed straight morphine at the end. She'd knelt by his bed and cried for him, cried for her mom, and cried for herself.

Clarice found herself crying now over the wheel when a loud tapping noise jarred her. She jerked her head up; saw a familiar face peeping in the window. It was Jenkins, a copywriter at *The Journal*. He bent to look at her, his gut hanging over his belt like so much dough ready for kneading. Under a receding hairline, thick wooly caterpillars of black and spiky gray crawled across his brow obnoxiously overshadowing the tiniest eyes Clarice had ever seen on a man's face. An equally shaggy and unkempt mustache matched the bushy brows, the likes of which seemed laughable in proportion to the scant amount of hair on his skull.

Lou Jenkins was a nosy gossip, the kind of guy who'll hunt you down for the story if anything about you seems new or out of place. Jenkins hounded Roxy for a week before she stopped toying with him and admitted that the Porsche she was driving was a loaner while her car was in the shop. Of course, then he had to pry her for details about the nature of the repairs to her Bug, and go on to endless commentary on how unreliable foreign cars are. Such was the nature of Lou Jenkins who had an expert opinion on every—absolutely every—topic.

"You all right, Miller?" He smiled as if he couldn't hide his pleasure at finding her and another juicy story ready for spreading. It was almost hard to hate him though as his brand of gossip was the type meant only to force people, who would otherwise ignore him into some form of communication.

"I'm fine. I … it's nothing really." He stood there rudely waiting for an explanation. "My, uh, cat died; that's all."

Feigned empathy seared his face, making the caterpillars one unit, but still not hiding that I-got-you-now grin. Jenkins nodded like a bobble head, "Oh, I had a dog, Samson … lived fourteen years." He waited for reciprocal sympathy. Clarice nodded conscious of her wet eyes. Why had she said her cat died? "Yup, golden retriever, too!" he said, as if the loss of that particular breed was somehow more of a loss. "They're the most loyal you know." Her face was blank. "Well cats aren't even in the running for that," he snorted. After a moment longer of her non-reaction, his face changed, probably realizing the callousness of the comparison he'd just made to someone who had just lost their pet.

Clarice used the opportunity to give a shocked look that she hoped would dissuade him from prodding her with questions about the fake cat she never owned.

Uh, I know what it's like." His head bobbled, straightening up from leaning into her window, then he hiked his slacks higher over the pile of hanging dough and added, "So anyway, like I said, sorry 'bout your cat." He turned to leave, finally allowing Clarice to exit her car.

Roxanne Cassan stood in the lobby a purply *muumuu* number sticking out under a lime bolero and a dozen Mardi Gras beads that only Rox could get away with.

"Sorry kiddo, saw Jenkins had you cornered when I drove in and saved myself. Figured why should we both go down?" She laughed as the two fell in step, wondering if she should slip into the ladies room, splash some cold water on her eyes before the meeting.

"Saw her again." Roxy said.

"Who?"

"That psychiiiic." Her voice trilled.

"Oh." Clarice opened the door to the stairs.

"So, I can ask her anytime you're ready."

"Ready for what?" Clarice said.

"For Harriet to read Jax or feel him or whatever it is."

"Rox, I may never be ready for that." Clarice said, as they passed Roxy's office.

"Sec," Roxy said, slipping inside. From the doorway Clarice looked around an office as haphazard as Roxy's car. Rox grabbed a file and hurried out.

"Hey, you want me to go with you on Monday for that judge thing?"

"No thanks. Both John and I are going, and Nicey insists on being there too. It's already shaping up to a three-ring circus. The whole Miller family united against one poor judge. Just can't imagine what he'll think when he hears Jackson's story."

"Maybe, he'll get more out of him than you do." Roxy jabbed an elbow into Clarice's shoulder. "Don't worry about it Reece. It'll all work out."

They reached the break room where the sales department held meetings each Friday.

"Ready for Hot-flash Hannah?" Roxy spoke out of the side of her mouth.

Clarice shrugged, "Is anyone?"

10

The Park

His fingers slid over the safe deposit box before lifting the long lid. The velvet bag stuck out amongst manila envelopes, papers, and cash. *Just throw the new money in the box and snap the lid shut.* Too late, his hand already caressed the blue velvet, feeling the jewels inside. He pulled the silk ribbon fast and dumped the crystals into his palm. Held up to the light, the rainbow colors sending an involuntary thrill to the remotest corner of his heart, a corner so tiny and unused the thrill was more pain than pleasure.

The memories of his mom, flashes really, flooded him: she at the vanity, he standing behind her looking in the giant round mirror, her smiling face and her voice asking her little gentleman to latch the gold clasp, her dainty fingers touching the Austrian crystals handed down from her grandma, her smile, her—

NO!

His fist closed on the jewels so hard they nearly broke his thin skin. He shoved them back in the bag, threw it into the safe-deposit box, slapped the new envelope on top, and dropped the metal lid twisting the key. He handed the box back to the bank official just outside the door.

Driving alone from Albany to the clinic, he thought what a shame that neither Sergio nor Mark—*Judas and Cain* he corrected himself, grinning. It was delicious the way they resented their given names. Loyal workers christened in blood, he had given them new names for new beings. *One must be named at one's christening; one simply must.* In any case, it was a shame that neither Judas or Cain could have been trusted to drive him to Albany, but the coven's holdings, deeds, all its accounts, everything was in that box. It has to be protected. Not even the elders may know its location. Cain and Judas were window dressing, useful of course for a hundred biddings... then too, an elder might attempt a coup, though that was unlikely with his power.

He thought of his meeting with Vera. *Quite the little vixen—* exquisite, so capable, and what a little cutthroat with Emmett. He smirked. Why she has as much ambition as myself, and such magnetism, so—

Shocking warmth spread over him.

What in hell's inferno was that!? He never allowed himself the pleasures that lessers enjoyed. It was, he was convinced, one of the reasons he was able to absorb and carry such higher powers. He would punish his body for that slip; just see if he wouldn't.

From the passing lane, the exit for Chenango Bridge flashed by him. *Drat!* His slip had already cost him. He'd have to merge onto 81 and double back bit. Annoying but—

A sharp twinge stabbed him. *What's this? What have we here?* It was a light, a lone light and nearby. He slowed the car on the highway thinking what could be emitting such light near this section of route 88. There were no hospitals nearby. A local college, but... if anything a school would emit many separate weaker lights. No, this light was strong and different, almost arch-angelic... the protector! It had to be. He commanded his mind to think of the area. The only thing around here was a park, Onenengo or some such, an Indian name. An angry beep whizzed past his car, which had slowed to 35 in a 55. The exit for Front Street lay ahead. He took it and followed the road to the park and the light.

He pulled the Deville in just outside the entrance so as not to tip his hand. The protector was somewhere in this very park, alone with the boy *and vulnerable.* Now it was a bigger shame his bodyguards were not along. He could have engaged the protector while his guards simply kidnapped the boy.

Ultimately, killing the child before he reached sanctuary was all that was necessary, yet if he captured the child, sacrificed him properly, *he* would be the one—the one who brought the prodigy to the master. *He* would be immortalized through the sacrifice, and he intended for it to be done right.

Pride, was it just his pride? After all, killing the boy outright would be the safest, easiest way to go. Well, he wasn't ruling that out, was he? He's just... Anyway, the sacrifice of such a being would pass its power into him. That was the consensus among elders; it is what they all believed. That power would make him—well, it was beyond saying.

From his car outside the gated entrance, he could *see* the child on a swing set. His knowledge of the park was limited, but he thought there were several such playgrounds scattered among the three miles or so of—He looked at the sign: Otsiningo Park. Under it, green blobs and color-coded walkways showed the park's layout. Pity he couldn't be closer, yet there was no sense alerting the protector to his presence. His plan was simple. He would spiritually engage the protector, whose power was fading. He could feel that even more being this close in an unprotected area. While overpowering her, he would gain entry to the boy mentally. Parlor tricks and child's play really. Then he would lead him to the car, a pied piper calling the most coveted prophet of the last two millennia to a black Cadillac outside an everyday park. It was almost too easy; he would simply open the door and the boy would climb in—simple.

Simple, he repeated then closed his eyes to concentrate every ounce of his power, sending its swirling pulsing, beautiful blackness out in search of the unsuspecting enemy.

* * *

Clarice pulled into the park through the open gate, past the black caddy with the dark figure inside. John was tied up on the retirement site, and Clarice had been looking forward to picking up Jax all day. And what a day! Sapphire blue sky spotted with pink-rimmed billows. A cool breeze off the unseen river carried a heady scent of yew as she got out of the car. Otsiningo sat on the shores of the Chenango River with shaded walkways winding around playgrounds, volleyball fields, and tennis courts. Those who weren't walking or jogging rolled by her on bikes, boards or skates, enjoying two miles of smooth pathways and pleasant landscape.

Clarice passed the first playground area, which was empty and continued along, confident that Nicey and Jax would be in the one with the sandpit at the end of the park. She stretched her legs resisting a natural urge to jog, glad for the gorgeous day and sweet greenery. Course, the strapped wedge sandals would hardly do for a run. So she strolled enjoying every fresh, clean-air sunny minute of it. A Scotch Pine seemed to stick out its branch in a welcoming handshake, and Clarice helped herself to a score of long pine needles. A brave hearted sparrow hoping for crumbs flew down to the path in front of her safely out of reach. Clarice stopped to admire him when out of that amazing sapphire sky a strange sensation of déjà vu overtook her.

Clarice took off in a run.

The urgency of the feeling was unmistakable. There was no analysis, no reasoning—only a pressing need to reach her son. Leaving the walkway, she cut a diagonal to the right through the long grass.

Her muscles kicked into practiced motion—powerful quads lifting and pounding, well-defined calves flexing and extending—one trained foot followed another as she sprinted like an Olympic runner. For all the effort she pumped into her arms and legs, not moments after leaving the path, she noticed awkwardness in her limbs. They felt heavier and heavier, like running in a nightmare—her worst nightmare—even as the urgency to reach her son compounded. She was moving—could feel the feet, even in the unlikely wedges, land and then lift to strike again—but she was getting nowhere. So confused was Clarice in this state of inexplicable urgency versus her uncooperative extremities that she nearly missed the oncoming rush of her altering condition.

Whoosh!

The old dropping sensation, down the unseen rabbit hole, flood waters seeping in, her spirit rushing out. *Are you kidding? Now?* It was too late to stop it—the park faded, the scenery receded to background, and objects turned translucent. *No!* She had to stay in control. She had to reach him. All of her. She concentrated willing her spirit to move with her body and vice versa.

It was hard to tell at first since even before she skidded down the rabbit hole the scenery was barely moving. Like the knight in Monty *Python's Search for the Holy Grail* furiously galloping over an unchanging landscape, she appeared to be moving but gained no ground. Now though, with some relief, she realized she was indeed moving forward, albeit scant inches, furthermore that her body continued to move even while disconnected from her spirit. Was she doing that? She'd never been able to do that before.

Over all these realizations, she knew something else, too. She had no idea how she knew this, but as sure as there was a sun and a moon, she knew where Jax was. No doubt, it was due to some psychic tie—one she wouldn't have admitted. The same one they had shared since her son first formed in the womb. Clarice *felt* Jackson and his unknown plight; she HAD to reach him.

Rabbit hole or no rabbit hole, connected or not, it felt like running in water or more like trudging through thick Jell-O. Her weighted legs lifted, pushing against an invisible thickness, a living thickness that pushed back. Clarice groaned and shoved, feeling heavy and so tired, the incredible effort sapping something far beyond her physical strength. Her mind sagged under the heavy weight of it. Like a sopping wet blanket of despair, it threatened to crush her will.

Suddenly a sense of utter futility flooded her.

WHY? Clarice wondered why. Why was she pushing? Why work so hard? Why should she have to move when all her body wanted was to—*What? Why is it?*...

Her mind became as gel-like as the mystical resistance trying to immobilize her legs. She realized she couldn't focus as she had been able to only a moment ago when she thought she knew why she was pushing against the ethereal rubber. Now all this work seemed pointless. *Why?*

The reasons for her struggle slipped by her consciousness just out of reach, and a new emotion crystallized in their place—

loathing. Loathing for being in this state. Loathing for fading backgrounds and other realities that kidnapped her from everyday life and tossed her into some insane place where bodies felt like afterthoughts and minds swam in terrifying circles of fear and joy. She hated this! Hated all of it!

QUIT.

The word came at her from somewhere outside herself.

"Quit!" it spoke to her.

Yes, why not? I could just quit. Clarice agreed with the word and the unknown tempter but continued to press forward as doubts spilled in on her. Why should she have to fight this thing? She didn't sign up for this.

"So quit," the tempter taunted.

Yes, she could quit. Quit right now Reece. Just shake it off. *Snap out it, Reece. Wake up or something.* She just needed to come to, return to normal. Something else wanted her to as well, for every thought of hers coupled with some invading thought from outside herself.

"Quit, quit," it demanded.

Plodding like a harnessed ox working in mud, the more Clarice doubted the harder the work of moving became. Yet her confused mind could not connect the two. Instead, it drifted slowly toward the only clear direction it was receiving.

"Quit!" It yelled.

Oh God! I can't—

M-O-M-M-Y!

She heard Jackson's spirit call for help as clearly as a baby screams for his bottle. Her son's fear, his profound and absolute terror raced through her every vein. At once, Clarice's doubts evaporated, pure will propelled her and the rubber barrier parted as butter before a hot knife.

"J-A-C-K-S-O-N, I'm here! I'm coming."

Ahead a furious jet-black cloud hovered—a throbbing version of twinkling lights, each dot of which beat with such hatred, its evil could not be mistaken. This entity raced around Jackson, who appeared as a ghostly figure of beautiful colors. Between him and the blackness, lay a waning but beautiful light. It reminded her of driving in a snowstorm at night, these lighted snowflakes hitting a windshield. They swept outward pushing, or trying to push, the black away. It looked only a matter of time before the blackness would overcome the shielding light source.

Jackson, or rather his wraithlike color, held onto something… was it a bench? With all his little might, he held, as the sucking force pulled him body and spirit. She could have painted what she saw more easily than describe it, for the vaporous colors and substance of her son, her baby, were being stretched out like so much silly putty. He continued to scream as she charged forward to rescue him from the swirling blackness.

Just looking at the blackness, more an absence of light than any color, proved torturous. Abruptly it turned an invisible eye toward her. It would be hard to say if she froze right then or after the black octopi arms stretched out from the cloud, slithering forward in mesmerizing waves.

Cold, so cold. Icy tentacles stroked her and even as she wondered how a spirit could shiver, the tentacles laughed and oozed a stench of burning hair or sulfur, bringing her back to chemistry class. One of the cloudy arms shot directly up her nose and exited her mouth and ears. The smell grew to a thousand heads of burning hair; her mouth, her tongue, every taste bud swam in the same vile flavor. Again, she questioned how her spirit could smell or taste when a new torture rang. Incredulously, a literal phone rang and an icy tentacle held it to her ear:

"Hello. Is Clarice there? This is Hell."

Now a maelstrom of cries and groaning met her ears. On the phone with Hell, she heard the voices of the damned lamenting every vice for which they were condemned, a shocking cacophony shrieking at her soul. Guttural sounds, hateful slurs and sorrowing moans swam about her sucking her into a whirlpool of lost souls and burning flesh.

Whether she did or only thought she did, Clarice clasped hands to her ears and hunched forward swaying in pain. As her senses reeled in the hellish assault, the tiniest morsel of light broke through, a pinprick on a black sheet of construction paper. Conscious of its being some basal instinct of motherly love, Clarice clung to it: Love for her child—the only force on earth that could have moved her any closer to that thing ahead of her. Jackson's terror stabbed her heart, releasing a swell of protective love, blotting out her own fear and ending that phone call from Hell.

"Hello Hell. This is Clarice. We don't take phone solicitations." CLICK.

She watched the swell of her own love materialize into a ball of light. It flew full force toward Jackson's rainbow aura with such intensity that for a split second, she flew, body and soul. The two lights, hers and the one still feebly defending her son, fused into one and together grew brighter, forming a sheath of pulsating rings orbiting Jackson. A familiar sweetness permeated the other light— Mrs. Nicestrum's unmistakable aura. A second later, Clarice's entire being united to her son's spirit, and Jackson's fear released.

The blackness receded, a short distance at first, then farther. All three spirits in the light relaxed in a sigh of relief as real as any audible sigh on earth. The farther the black retreated, the safer they all felt. United like this, they shared every emotion as a unit. As their fear lessened, Clarice experienced a wonderful closeness to Jackson and Nicey.

No sooner did they relax than the retreating ink turned and gathered itself up. Without warning, it threw itself forward hurtling down, closing the distance, which now seemed to have been nothing more than a running start. The terror of the trio returned as quickly as the thing rushing down on them.

UNITE!

A word (*was it a word?*) broke in their mist, its meaning clear. Clarice threw herself into the idea of uniting and felt Nicey and Jax do the same. Their light exploded with new brightness and power; this time however, Saturn-like rings in rainbow colors spun on the outermost limits. The absence of light met the rings head on, slamming as it were into an immoveable wall. The entity's retreat was immediate. It swirled upward in a backward tornado and disappeared leaving the rings pulsing as softly as a baby's breath.

In the Cadillac, *He* picked his head up from the steering wheel, shaking with anger and covered in sweaty blood. He felt weak, disgustingly weak. His hand fumbled for the door handle. He wrenched it open, jerked his head out, and spewed a putrid, worm-filled vomit out of his mouth. He swiped his black sleeve across a drained face, sat back in his seat, and slammed the door.

This could never have worked, the moment the boy's mother showed up. As strong as he was, he couldn't deal with all three auras, not once they were united.

Arrogance? No, he had come damned close, damned close! Exhausted, he cranked the key, threw the car in gear, and sped away from the painful trio of light.

Clarice returned to normal, hearing a car screech its tires in the distance. She found herself on a bench with Jackson and Mrs. Nicestrum. Both women had their arms wrapped about Jax and each other.

"I was too far from home," said Mrs. Nicestrum visibly shaken. She spoke more to herself than to Jackson or Clarice while pulling away from the huddle. "My fault, not enough protection. My fault."

Equally dazed, Clarice continued to hold a crying Jackson.

Then as if it never happened, Mrs. Nicestrum made some excuse about a swarm of hornets frightening Jackson. She hurriedly accompanied them back to their car excusing herself and saying it had been a long day. Incredulously, Clarice watched her elderly friend make her way across the parking lot, practically hobbling and looking unusually spent, even for her 80 plus years.

11

Sol Mendleson

Rabbi Katz adjusted his kippah and stifled a cough so as not to disturb Dr. Mendleson, who was on the phone. The doctor's chair was faced the picture window overlooking Boston Harbor, pretty much blocking his view, which left Gabe to look about the room. Sol's love of sailing was plastered all over the office walls in vivid blues and sleek sails on modern looking, unframed boards. In fact, Gabe thought, this weekend they're supposed to sail to Cape Cod, a three-day trip ending at Martha's Vineyard. Nice of Sol—nice they'd become such friends. Certainly, he'd been seeing him professionally for... how long now, two years? He started coming to him now and again to discuss the dreams. Really, who didn't have a psychologist these days? He told himself, aware of a self-conscious twinge.

"So Gabe," Sol twisted around in his chair and hung up the phone. "Sorry 'bout that. You know how Jerry is. Oh and he's not coming on Saturday; says he has some golf thing with his firm."

"No problem, Jerry drinks all the good stuff anyway."

"Yeah, usually before we leave the Harbor," Sol added. "Look at you Gabe"—he pointed with his palm—"you're so blessed. You could be a poster boy for Jewish rabbis. If I had an inch of your good looks."

Gabe shook his head smiling. Sol was always saying stuff like that.

Sol was about his age with frizzy orange hair; what was left of it stuck on the two sides of his head a little like a clown. The bulbous Durante nose dominating his face didn't help. Nonetheless, Sol was smart, intuitive, and easy to talk to. They couldn't look more different Gabe agreed with Sol. If anyone could look Jewish, he guessed people would say it was himself with his classic hooked nose, olive skin, and thick eyebrows over slightly droopy eyes. He'd be the last to admit he was handsome yet the first to claim for his 52 years, he was in excellent condition.

"So where were we?" Mendleson asked.

"It's the same really except the dream with the black tornado is more intense," Gabe said. "I feel like I'm suffocating. Oy, I can't even stand elevators anymore. Feel all closed in. By the way," Gabe jerked his chin, "have I thanked you for being on the tenth floor?"

"Really, you walked up? I can get you a prescription if it's as bad as all that."

"No, thanks, besides that dream is rare." Drugs weren't the answer. He'd take over-the-counter stuff, something for migraines, but that was it. How could you function?

"Well," Mendleson said, "let me know." He rocked back in his chair. "Now, the dream of a dream is not as unusual as you might think. But in all of these dreams, the fact that you awaken and remember so vividly... well, it's likely you aren't getting the rest you need. Your REM sleep is disturbed. Let me tell you something, you don't want your REM sleep interrupted too many nights." Sol pointed with the gold pen he was holding. "Difficulty concentrating, irritability, hallucinations, and now don't misunderstand me, even signs of psychosis after only three days. Well that's what they found in tests anyhow." He made big circles with his pen in the air. "That can lead to stress, and that can lead to more stress, which may lead to more restless dreaming. You see where I'm going?"

"Yeah, I get it, but Sol," Gabe leaned forward for emphasis, "I swear there's no stress in my life right now."

The dreams were anomalies of a sort—different from normal dreams, more intense and lifelike. He dreamt of a young boy, serene, sitting among the trees in a veritable paradise. He dreamt of others too, the woman, the ancient bent man. The dreams were repetitive and real, as though he were right there experiencing the joys and the horrors. He thought of his favorite: the one with the spirit woman flying. That one always ended badly, the black cloud enveloping her and crushing the life within her.

"What about work?" Sol said. "You're leaving for Israel again aren't you?"

"Yeah, after our sail. But my work could hardly be called stressful," Gabe got up and paced a bit, sensing Sol was off track. "Do you know what a privilege, an honor it was when the Director of the Boston Museum of Fine Arts asked me to join the team?"

Sol turned his chair, "Tell me about the project?" He sounded doctor-y, like he was fishing for stress.

"What can I tell you? The museum wants to create a special collection of artifacts," Gabe landed by the window, looked out at the harbor. "The idea is to represent the cultural history of the Jewish race in the Fertile Crescent; you know, tell the story of the Hebrews archeologically. Most of the pieces will come from three museums: The Jewish Museum in NYC, the Oriental Museum of Chicago, and the Israel Museum of Jerusalem. That's the one that houses the *Shrine of the Book* holding the Dead Sea Scrolls. I'm on board as both an archeologist and a rabbi."

"I suppose your credentials didn't hurt," Sol said, "hundreds of articles and half a dozen books, your interpretive work on the Scrolls. Didn't you even work with the teams excavating Tell Beit She'an and the City of David?"

"In '86," Gabe said, touched at Sol's interest. "And you've obviously read too much of my boring work to remember that."

The truth was Gabe had tooled around Israel after gaining his degrees, volunteering, excavating, and learning firsthand what he'd studied ad nauseam in books working toward his Ph.D. in Anthropology and Archeology. After that, he felt called to something more and decided to study for semicha to become a rabbi. His degrees helped there and he had a good head start in languages when he entered Yeshiva University in NYC. By the time

115

all was said and done, Gabe had another masters in Hebrew Letters, a Doctor of Divinity, and a second Ph.D. in Jewish Studies.

"I'm flying to Jerusalem after we get back next week," Gabe said, still by the window spying a particularly handsome yacht. "The whole project is expected to take over a year to put together, and for the time being, it means a lot of travel, but no stress, I swear."

"What about your brother Al? He on your mind again?"

"My cousin," Gabe corrected turning back to his chair. "Al's on the whole family's mind, isn't he? I mean, who becomes a Messianic Jew? It's crazy, he needs—" He stopped himself; you don't call a shrink a shrink to a shrink. Bad form.

"You know Gabe, despite the fact that you or I don't get their reasoning, Messianic Jews see themselves as still being Jewish, faithful to scripture and the prophets. I have a patient who's one. He believes that Yeshua was that Messiah our ancestors expected. He says he will return and offer the Jewish people, still the chosen ones, a chance to accept him as Lord and savior. Who's to say?" Sol shrugged his shoulders. "But what do I know. The man is my patient after all. I listen; I don't judge."

"I know," Gabe said, "Al's in New York; he writes me these long letters explaining his so called conversion." He had to write, Gabe thought. His cousin had tried phoning, but the conversations always became overheated. Was it his fault the Jewish religion meant so much to him? Gabe was certain his cousin was becoming a kook, and he knew it was painful for his aunt and uncle, who felt Al had rejected their teaching and heritage.

"Look," Gabe said and sat in the chair, "Al and I were close and all, but the stress involved in his, his weird ideas—anyway it's not causing these dreams; I know it."

The session ended with Sol mentioning hypnosis as an option and Gabe knowing he was nowhere near that desperate. They solidified plans for Saturday's sail and Gabe, as usual left without making an appointment. He only called for those once in awhile usually after a new dream or a particularly bad one.

***

Saturday morning rolled in with perfect sailing weather. Gabe headed toward *The Constitution Marina where* Sol kept his 30-foot sailboat, *The Dreamer*. With its teak trim inside and out, brass fittings, head, galley, and four sails, she was yar. Roomy too, sleeping six with so much headroom below, Jerry at six foot two could stand upright. With Jerry cancelling, Sol had invited another friend to keep the crew at four. These trips, about 60 nautical miles, took more planning and teamwork than simply deciding what beer to bring.

The engine was running when Gabe hopped on board. Morning chill swept his cheek, and he half rethought the skimpy windbreaker, but by the time they got her out, he knew the sun would warm them up fast.

Sol was rigging the mainsail, attaching the halyard to the head. He pulled the slack and called to Gabe.

"Hey rabbi, if that's really you under that ball cap, undo those sail straps for me, will ya."

"A covering's a covering," Gabe said, coming forward. "Besides how many kippahs can a man give to the ocean?" He gave his plain white cap a tug. Sol rarely wore a kippah, neither did most of his friends, but even though he ribbed Gabe, he was pretty accepting of his orthodoxy.

After freeing the sail on the boom, Gabe was winching it up when he saw a young man in a Red Sox hat hoisting a cooler aboard.

"Gabe, this is my son-in-law, Dan Kellar, he's taking Jerry's place."

"Hey," the young man put down the cooler to shake hands. "Gotta warn you I'm green, only been out a couple times with Debbie."

"My daughter," Sol said. "Don't let him fool you; Dan's a quick study."

"Well, if you're filling in for Jerry, you'll have to get busy emptying that cooler," Gabe said, cleating the line.

"Never mind that, Dan," Sol laughed at the inside joke. "Just put it in the galley while we cast off. We'll all help empty it."

Sol slid *The Dreamer* from her slip and inched her out of *Constitution Marina* to the open harbor. Gabe eyed the cacophony of mega-yachts, sailboats, and motor boards, white riggings, and masts dominating the sky. He pulled up the fenders keeping below the boom. He kept one hand for himself as they say and one for the boat, which meant he held onto something as he walked around the moving boat, leaning over the side to retrieve the foamy bumpers. He remembered the first time he forgot that rule and was summarily tossed off a sailboat.

"Prepare to jibe," Barry yelled by the jib or outer sail.

"Hello to you too, Barry," Gabe called to him, pulling the mainsail to the middle. The warning and the one following of "Jibe-ho" were essential for all the crew to remain clear of the boom, which can move with incredible speed and lethal force as the boat's stern is turned through the wind. Barry looked great, youngish at 45 compared to Sol and him, a little paunchy in the middle but basically sporting the beer belly he deserved. He worked in Sol's practice and came out sailing every chance he could.

The crew got busy with the business of sailing, catching the wind, moving the lines in and out, yelling directions, and working as a team. Gabe loved this. He held onto a guide wire and looked out over the bow when the engine was cut and the wind caught the wrinkled sail, hearing the snap as that first push flowed over the wrinkles like an iron on a sheet. Feeling that first yank forward always gave him a rush, the kind of rush that makes you feel you could do this forever. *The Dreamer* cut through the sparkling steel blue water at a good clip, a seagull swooped low, and Gabe breathed deep the intoxicating freedom.

In no time, the small harbor islands slid by as the Boston skyline shrank in the distance. They traveled South East as they left Boston Harbor. The wind was SE too, so they would be running with it most of the way. A perfect breeze, Gabe noted. They'd barely touch the motor the whole day if it stayed like this. The boat's GPS was easy to use; still, Sol reveled in charting and mapping the old-fashioned way. Gabe programmed it just the same as a backup, loading coordinates for a buoy near the marina, another at Wellfleet, and one just outside Martha's Vineyard.

With the lines cleated off and the boat a sweet 45 degrees away from the wind, the four relaxed, and the jokes flew, as did the beers and grilled steaks. Barry was getting a major kick out of Dan's stories as a med surge nurse in the psych ward. Sol looked uncomfortable, as though he'd never gotten used to the fact that his son-in-law was a nurse.

"So what did you do?" Barry said on the edge of his seat.

"Like I said this guy was about 300 pounds, barreling straight at me with a half ton of crash cart. I had nowhere to go at the end of the hall. So I yell to him, 'Fred, what are you doing?' and he yells back, 'I don't know.' So I scream at him, 'Well, turn around!'" Dan was really enjoying the audience leaning forward as he talked. "And he did. Did a 180 and barreled down the hall the other way."

"Oh man, that's rich—"

"Prepare to come about!" Sol yelled and the guys ducked instinctively then scurried to their jobs, pulling the mainsail to the middle, and adjusting the jib. They distributed their weight accordingly. *The Dreamer* began a nice turn, 90 degrees starboard turning into Provincetown Harbor after a long and perfect day of sailing.

"What happened to the plan for Wellfleet?" Barry asked Sol at the wheel. They'd initially planned to use a slip in Wellfleet Saturday night, a good 17 miles further South East.

"It's almost six. We're at least four hours from Wellfleet, so I called Flyers Rental in Provincetown and reserved a mooring in their sea field for the night."

"Great, I love Province," Barry raised his Molson.

"Barry, we shove off at the crack—scratch that—before the crack of dawn. Most we should do is a few sober hours of touring."

Gabe listened and decided right then he was sticking with his plan to eat on the boat, although, he'd tool around with them if they headed out. He'd just do it on a stomach full of kosher food.

It was tough being orthodox and a rabbi, although technically they were all Jewish. He wasn't sure about Dan, actually, but he knew Sol and Barry weren't all that concerned with kosher laws. Still, Sol was decent about his needs; even kept two sets of pans in the galley, one for meat and one for dairy. He'd do the best he could this trip. It was always difficult, but for the Almighty, what was too much?

Later that night, Gabe rolled into the rack opposite Barry by the Galley. Sol finished his bottle of water and disappeared into the bedroom where he was bunking with Dan. Turned out all four of them were exhausted from their first day sailing. They'd walked around Provincetown, past cabarets, sideshows, and nightlife about to heat up, then stopped in a bar, had a round and headed back to the boat. Gabe listened to the tiny waves lap the hull and thought of how these trips made for instant bonding, the working as a team, the camaraderie, the long hours of shooting the breeze, sharing their stories. It was like boy's camp for men. He said his evening prayers, thanked Hashem for their safety, and let *The Dreamer* rock him to sleep.

Sol kept his word; Gabe checked his watch, which read 4:45 AM, hearing a good racket topside. He took exactly two steps to the sink, used a bottle of water to perform Netilat Yadayim, donned his ball cap, and hit the head. He and Sol eased the boat out of the harbor. By the time they hoisted the sails, Barry and Dan were on board offering coffee and a hand.

From the school of dolphins that joined them, jumping happily alongside the boat at ten in the morning, to the great green swells that threatened to swallow them at two, to the pelican that used the mast as a resting place at six, the day could not have been better. They anchored offshore, cooked a nice dinner of pasta and kosher wine, and played a few hands of cards. Everyone hit the sack pretty well satisfied.

By late Monday afternoon, *The Dreamer* was tacking, heading into the West dock of Tisbury Wharf on Martha's Vineyard. They were just south of Vineyard Haven, where the Ferry drops off tourists and cars, and just in time to enjoy dinner and some touring. Sol had secured a slip for a mere $120.00 where they'd be good till checkout at eleven on Tuesday morning. It was preferable to using a dinghy, which last time had resulted in some wet sailors.

Sol turned into the wind making the boat practically stop. Then he commenced gliding her carefully through the crowded wharf. Gabe and Dan stood in the bow enjoying the scene dominated by old-fashioned wooden schooners and tall ships. The whole wharf felt old-fashioned, a charming throw back in time thanks to the restoration work of dedicated shipwrights and preservationists.

"If you're not bored, you're going too fast," Sol called to Dan. True enough, even in his two years of sailing, he'd seen his share of accidents as boats maneuvered in and out of busy ports and narrow slips.

Once everything was secure and the stuff they cared about stowed, the four men headed out to the Black Dog Tavern. Vineyard Haven was a dry town, so they were packing, or rather Dan was. He had graciously volunteered to carry a couple bottles of Kosher Chardonnay in his backpack. Gabe gratefully stretched his legs on the walk after the long sail. In no time, the familiar black dog on the signpost in front of the gray clapboard restaurant appeared. Sol stopped on the red brick walkway outside and turned to Gabe.

"You sure you're okay with the Black Dog? I know your kasrut standards are pretty strict."

"Sol, it's not as if there are any kosher restaurants on the Vineyard. With all the travel I do, I've had to learn to compromise, haven't I? Or maybe I should starve?" Gabe laughed, hearing his Bubbe's Yiddish inflection on the last word. "Tomorrow, I'm heading to Cronig's to restock a kosher galley for the sail home." Cronig's in Vineyard Haven had been a mainstay on the island since 1917 and carried the full line of Hebrew National foods.

"Agreed," Sol said and followed the others through the door. "I don't know if it counts, Rabbi, but at least when I'm with you I'm a better Jew, eh." Sol slapped his arm on Gabe's shoulder and left it there while they walked in.

Inside they saw plenty of ocean views, rich woods, dark beamed ceilings, and a fireplace that looked cozy despite the warm night. The conversation was lively, and even the hour wait at the restaurant didn't dampen the high spirits. Everyone had the fresh tuna except Barry, who'd thrown a couple beers in the backpack and had them with his prime rib and potato.

"Hey rabbi," Dan jerked his head and swerved his eyes left toward a lone diner in the corner. "She's hot for you."

Gabe shot a look at the woman, a girl really. He looked down embarrassed as her eyes met his with a bold stare. "She's half my age!" he said.

"Don't sweat it, Gabe." Barry spoke with a chunk of rare beef in his mouth. "She's probably checking me out, not you."

"Yeah, right, she'd have to be nearsighted," Sol said.

"Seriously," Barry said, looking again, "that kid is staring at you."

Gabe took another quick peek himself. In a man's black "wife-beater" undershirt, she was thin and pale with long—very long — jet black hair, half a dozen piercings, and a pile of silver chains. Goth, thought Gabe, isn't that what they call it?

"If looks could kill, eh?" Dan said.

"Yeah," Barry lifted a fork with a speared potato wedge and waved it pointing, "that glare is pure hatred, Gabe, hardly idol worship. Chick gives me the creeps."

"Well for Pete's sake, ignore her," Sol said, dividing the rest of the second bottle of wine among the three glasses. "Believe me; you don't want to antagonize certain types. Still, it's odd Gabe; do you know her, maybe a friend's daughter?"

"No, never saw her before."

No one questioned it further, and as unsettling as the girl was for Gabe, he soon forgot her and went on with his meal. The waitress came over and took their orders for dessert. Gabe and Sol both opted for cheesecake. Dan declined while Barry ordered Tiramisu and coffee. While waiting for their desserts, Gabe wiped his mouth and announced his intention to hit the head. As he rose, the woman in the corner stood too. He came around from the table and took three steps when a flash of steel caught his eye. In that instant, he saw her tearing across the restaurant wielding a butcher knife and screaming.

"Die Tzaddik! Die Tzaddik!"

Gabe barely had time to register what was happening: the raised knife in the thin arm, the tall body in black miniskirt and fishnet hose, the piercings and tattoos. However, the flashes of steel blade coming full speed ahead registered loud and clear.

Without any forethought whatsoever, Gabe's hand flew up, his palm pushed outward.

"Stop!"

He yelled so loud his body shook. Something went out of him—straight out of his palm. He watched the invisible something, or rather the result of it, slam into the knife wielder's gut. A whir of black hair flew forward as her body slammed backward against the table behind her. She fell in a heap, upending a table and two chairs. In seconds a cook from the kitchen appeared and snatched the weapon from her hand. He held her shoulder down, even though she lay unconscious.

Gabe lowered his hand and looked from the girl to Sol, whose expression could not have been more shocked. Barry went to her side and ordered Dan to call 9-1-1. The cook passed the knife to the waitress, who looked confused as to just what she was supposed to do with the knife that had clearly come from their own kitchen. The cook continued to hold her as Barry took her pulse. Good thing too, for as the girl came to, she kicked her long legs and screamed while the brute size cook held her down.

"No, I'll kill him, I will," she screamed. "No, no, leave me alone!"

She was still screaming, even as the police arrived at the Black Dog, tasers and all. After two verbal warnings, they subdued her the easy way and within minutes, she was carried outside.

One of the officers asked them not to leave so they returned to their table. A few minutes later, the waitress approached Gabe.

"I am so sorry. She's crazy. You know? I mean really nuts. I know her; I went to school with her." The tiny young blond barely took a breath. "I used to think she was just into Goth, then we all thought she was like into witchcraft. Lots, I mean lots of kids are doing that, it's a fad, you know? But then I learned she's messed up with Satanism. She's a Satanist; I know it for a fact. That sick bunch of

"Mindy, shut up and give the guy an inch of space, wouldja? Holy moly, he was just attacked, and you wanna be in his face with your mouth." The manager pulled the girl away.

One of the policemen came back in to talk to Gabe and the others.

"So, you have no idea why she would attack you?"

"None, we're only visiting, a sailing trip. We're from Boston. She alright?"

"Probably, buzzed out on coke, or worse. At least two witnesses out front recognized her, couple of college kids."

"Three," Sol pointed to the waitress standing in the kitchen doorway, watching everything as she talked to her manager.

"Yeah, I'll get to everyone. You boys staying in town tonight?"

"We're bunking on the boat," Sol said. "Have the slip till 11 tomorrow. It's *The Dreamer*, parked in the West Dock at Tisbury Wharf."

The officer took what information he could think to take and said he'd stop by the boat before they left if he thought of anything else.

"It's probably random that she chose you. Anyway we have plenty of local witnesses."

Barry stepped forward.

"Mr. Katz has business out of the country this week. You won't ask him to postpone that? We have a friend who's an attorney—"

"No problem," the cop waved Barry down like an excited puppy, "Rabbi Katz, we have all your information. I'm sure things can be handled long distance depending on what charges you want brought against the girl."

"I—I, uh... I only want to see her get help."

"Best help for a crack addict ain't in jail, but anyway, we'll see. At any rate, it's not your problem. Sorry about all this spoiling your visit."

The officer asked them how often they came to the Vineyard and how they like it. They exchanged a few more niceties, and he left after wishing them a safe sail back.

They finished their dessert, which Mindy brought with a smile, biting her lip against more juicy gossip, and for which Gabe had lost his appetite. She'd called him Tzaddik, which was plain freakish; the whole incident was freakish. He didn't even want to think about what he thought happened when he held up his hand and felt what he thought he felt coming out of it like a shot of power, like a superhero or something, like Spiderman throwing his first web. *Hashem, what in the name of all that's good is going on?*

The four attempted to pay the bill, but the manager insisted after what happened that their meal be on the house. Each of them threw a five on the table for Mindy and left.

"Well what now? We still up for a little touring?" Sol looked at Gabe as though it were all up to him.

"It's okay by me, but there's not much to do here in Vineyard Haven at night. We should catch a shuttle to Oaks Bluff."

Nods went round, and they set a peppy stride, walking two and two toward the bus stop by the Ferry. Barry was telling Dan about the Gingerbread Houses they would see in town and filling him in on a bit of the history.

"Yeah they were built in the nineteenth century; they go around in a circle and in the center is this open air church, Tabernacle something or other, built for all these Methodist revivals they used to have. You're Catholic aren't you Dan? By law they wouldn't even let you own one of those houses all the way up until—"

Barry's voice faded to where Gabe couldn't really make out what he was saying. He and Sol had dropped back enough to talk privately. The slowing was Sol's doing.

"That Zadique thing, that name she called you, that's the same one from your dream as a kid, isn't it?"

"It is," Gabe almost choked hearing it said aloud again, Sol's repeating it confirming the reality of what he'd heard in the restaurant. They walked not talking.

"There has to be an explanation for what happened, for what we saw." Sol said.

"What *did* you see, Sol?"

"I uh, I think I saw your hand stop that knife-wielding girl like a full-blown traffic cop."

"That's what I thought." The two walked in silence, hearing Barry's voice still talking Dan's ear off against their own steps on the sidewalk. Gabe looked up to see the sign for the bus ahead.

"She could have fallen backward," Gabe proffered, hearing his voice sound as unconvinced as he felt. "She might have been frightened, thought I was going to hurt her or something and stepped back losing her balance. She *was* high on drugs they said."

Sol paused so as not to catch up to Dan and Barry.

"Shame on me." He slapped Gabe's back. "Who is the level headed psychologist here? And you're the one offering logical explanations."

They reached the bus and dropped the confidential conversation, Gabe hoped for the rest of the trip. He had too much to sort out. It sure as hell better not turn into a new nightmare.

Surprising himself Gabe more than managed to enjoy Oaks Bluff—the quiet streets, warm salt breeze, gingerbread houses and elegant Trinity Park Tabernacle, quaint shops and strolling islanders. His mind left the deeper questions of why a perfect stranger would call him that name and try to murder him for another day. Martha's Vineyard, *The Dreamer*, sailing, it was too nice to be spoiled for long.

He'd go on his trip to Jerusalem. When he returned, he'd call and ask after the girl. Until then he'd forget the whole thing. Hell, he'd probably wake up and find out he had dreamed it.

12

Judge Harding

All weekend Clarice felt different, different about Nicey, about Jax even, and different about herself. The park, the whirling evil, trudging through invisible barriers, in and out of her body, uniting with Jax and Nicey... *Well, that was cool*—No, it was more of the problem. It was NOT normal, none of it made any sense. And somehow, she was being sucked into it all like someone who wandered on stage in the middle of a scene expected to deliver lines on cue. No script, no direction, and no clue what was going on. What was she supposed to do?

Get a grip, that's what.

Nicey called it a swarm of bees—oh please. But what's the alternative? All that stuff was real and she hadn't imagined it? Bees will do—bees from hell, but whatever.

Nicey had called twice on Saturday, once in the morning speaking with John and again in the afternoon to Clarice. She asked what they were doing, what their plans were, whether they were leaving the house, which they weren't.

Dwelling on it was getting her nowhere, so Clarice decided to throw herself into good old-fashioned spring cleaning. Okay, one season behind. She told John and Jax she wasn't going to the GI party alone and issued the kind of invitation only a wife and mom can issue—the kind that can't be refused. At least John laughed when they were washing the siding and she called it "family time," instead of throwing a bucket at her. He was being a good sport. Of course, now they had a date for closing on the land in Ithaca, they had to get ready to sell. Their first open house was scheduled for next weekend—nothing like the thought of persnickety strangers roaming around your house, peeping in closets, opening cabinets, to set a Mister Clean fire under your tush.

Jax was a doll, helping her take screens and storms down and scrubbing them in the backyard, washing all the windows. And while Clarice freshened the sills with paint, on his own he went down the basement and organized all his toys and books. John knocked at least three repairs off the "Ya-can't-sell-a-house-like-this list." Clarice's brush kept swiping long after the male crewmembers jumped ship. While doing the sills and sashes, she had to take down the curtains, which gave her a good excuse to wash them all. Then she hit the doors and the baseboards since they were the same color and the paint was already open. Although, that didn't explain the can of butter cream she opened and the new brush she wet for the kitchen cupboards. Nope that was just plain workaholic Reece. The fumes would have killed a lab rat, but there was a good breeze, and John had every window and door wide open.

Thanks to the work, she'd actually been able to sleep Saturday night. On Sunday, Clarice made them a huge breakfast of scrambled eggs, French toast, bacon, and hash browns. After John's Mass, they played monopoly, ate junk food, and watched two movies. And all weekend no one, no one mentioned the hearing with Judge Harding, even though that was what was on everyone's mind.

Monday morning dawned with grey skies and sober faces for the Millers at the Binghamton Courthouse on Hawley Street. Quarter after ten they sat, fifteen minutes early, crammed on a bench outside Judge Harding's chambers. Clarice glanced at Jax in the adorable blue suit he wore to be ring bearer at her brother-in-law's wedding in April. Even John donned his one, grey suit. Heck, all three of them wore one, she realized, looking embarrassed at her powder blue number. It was the most dignified thing she could find; it was that or her little black evening dress.

Jackson sprang up, and Clarice looked over to see Nicey coming off the elevator. *Whoops*, there goes another suit, hmm...

peach linen. How soft Nicey looked in that color. Even so, a firm set jaw and worried eyes betrayed her true disposition. As Jax held Mrs. Nicestrum's hand, John stood to offer his seat, but she shook her head while rubbing Jackson's hand.

"There's someone, something I have to tell you. I do hope you'll not mind. I've asked a friend to join us, umm, to help actually." Mrs. Nicestrum looked to the elevator. "He's parking the car, you see he drove me. He's a lawyer, Mr. Alan Katz. His group meets at our church. I spoke with—"

The elevator opened again.

"Here he is now."

Clarice stood with the others and watched as a lean man wearing a rumpled tan suit, paisley tie, worn loafers, and a fat smile stepped off the elevator.

"Hi, Al Katz," the lawyer shifted his briefcase to shake hands with John. "Mrs. Nicestrum filled me in and asked if I'd come by."

"John Miller, this is—"

"Clarice," she said as she met his hand, already liking his quirky appearance, "and this is Jackson." Clarice placed a hand on Jackson's shoulder, hoping he would not refuse the lawyer's clasp. No problem this time, she thought, as Jax returned a hearty shake.

"I'm not sure we need..." Clarice stumbled for words. "I mean really we were told it was only—"

"Oh, I should explain, I'm not here as paid representation, just as a friend," the man said, and Clarice heard a hint of Boston. "A favor to Mrs. Nicestrum. Short notice, I know, but I have a good idea of what occurred June fifth at the Waterman Clinic and at Mr. Henkel's residence, at least as much as Mrs. Nicestrum was able to tell me, and I've a copy of the police report, but I have a few questions if you don't mind."

John asked one instead. "Just how do you know Mrs. Nicestrum?"

"We met at my church, dear," Mrs. Nicestrum said. "Mr. Katz was searching for a place for his group to meet."

"We're Messianic Jews," the lawyer said. "We, uh, tend to be somewhat misunderstood and rejected by both religions, Jewish and Christian. We're kind of like Jesus with no place to lay His head. You know, birds have nests, foxes have dens, but the son of man..." He looked at their two blank faces. "Oh well, the thing is Mrs. Nicestrum's pastor allowed us to use their church basement. Her prayer group meets right before our group, so we got to know each other. This is a favor for her, but if you're uncomfortable—"

"Oh, uh, not really, I—from what we understand, this is an informal hearing."

"Yes, but it never, I mean never hurts to protect your interests. The last thing in the world any parent wants is the state or, the Almighty forbid it, CPS unnecessarily involved in their child's life."

"CPS?" Clarice asked.

"Child Protective Services."

Just then, a uniformed guard, a bailiff Clarice supposed, came out of the judge's chambers.

"Judge Harding would like you to go on to courtroom 213 around the corner." The bailiff pointed down the hall. "He said it looked like there may be too many of you for his chambers."

Clarice held Jackson's hand and followed the tiny Miller circus of suits to the courtroom.

"Great," she whispered to John, "a real courtroom, just what our nerves need."

"I know; I haven't stopped saying Our Fathers."

Yeah, that will help, Clarice thought. Isn't God the one who made this big mess? The stab of guilt was immediate, but dangit that's how she felt.

Clarice and Mrs. Nicestrum sat on the bench behind the defendant's table on either side of Jackson. John sat with Al Katz at the defendant's table. The lawyer plopped a heavy looking overstuffed brown satchel on the table. Seconds after they sat, the courtroom door swung open and a slick looking middle-aged man in a handsome dark suit seemed to glide down the aisle. He did a double take and stopped in front of Mr. Katz.

"Al," his voice was cold, "surprised to see you here."

"Ditto, Emmett. This isn't your usual territory, is it?"

Clarice couldn't help but note the stark differences between the two men. The hunched unkempt, almost poor but congenial look of Al Katz with mussed black hair in need of a good cut, slacks that looked like he pulled them damp from a dryer, and a simple chain holding a cross and the star of David. Next to him stood a suave, Fifth Avenue, perfectly coifed man in a pinstriped suit, ruby cufflinks, and a tie that probably cost more than John's suit. *Wow.*

The judge's door opened before Clarice could ask Mr. Katz if the man was a prosecutor or a DA. The two men sat down.

All was quiet as the judge took his seat, opened a file folder, and read. A robust looking man with a short gray beard, his high forehead continued to a bald patch atop his head, which looked all red, like he had high blood pressure or a sun burn. After a minute that felt like five, he scratched his scruffy beard and looked up over his black reading glasses.

"Hmm, looks like a bit of a mess here, but I'm sure it will all be worked out." He smiled directly at Clarice, and she realized her leg was jiggling. "This is only a preliminary examination of the incident that occurred on June 5. Don't think of it as a trial or even a hearing. It's more of an inquiry." He looked at the slick man. "Pierce, you making a move I don't know about?"

The man named Emmett cleared his throat, straightened his already straight red tie. "Michael Craighton asked me to step in for the DA's office."

"Since when? There some shortage of prosecutors in the department? Highly unusual, Emmett." He looked to the other side of the room. "How you doin' Al?"

"Fine, Judge Harding."

"This a case already? I couldn't be more confused by the interest in this, this incident." He did look confused, Clarice thought, but he also looked like someone who could unravel Watergate in a day. He reminded her of the old guy in the *Grape Nut's* commercial.

"Now let's start easy," Judge Harding said. "Mr. and Mrs. Miller, why were you visiting the Waterman Clinic last week?"

John hesitated. "He... we made the appointment after—"

"Your honor the child has a sleep disorder of sorts and wakes screaming," Mr. Katz said. "The Millers were seeking—"

"I have a statement here," the judge cut in, "from the director of Waterman Clinic, a Doctor Vera Wheaton. Says here her talk with the Miller's—"

"Judge isn't that confidential?" Mr. Katz's voice squeaked.

"Al, keep your socks on. Dr. Wheaton sounds genuinely concerned for the child," Harding said, his eyes still perusing the two-page letter. "She'd like to examine the boy and I think since Mr. and Mrs. Miller came to see her—"

"No, never!" Mrs. Nicestrum stood in a huff of peach indignation.

"Who is this? What's your business here?" the judge bristled making Clarice's stomach lurch. All they needed was an angry judge. Mrs. Nicestrum sat down and placed an arm around Jackson.

"This is Michelle Nicestrum, Judge Harding, the nanny. What she and the Millers adamantly feel is that the Waterman facility failed to watch or protect their child and having anyone associated with the Waterman Clinic involved in any way with a possible evaluation of Jackson Miller is out of the question."

"I'll decide what's out of the question," Harding said harrumphing. He looked past them. Clarice followed his gaze up the aisle where a very short and plump lady with maroon cropped hair was making quick steps to the prosecutor's table. Her stunted arms were stuffed with a messy array of manila files and papers, which she noisily unloaded the moment she reached the DA's table. A bad imitation of a blue-jean Prada bag, also overflowing with loose papers, was flung from her shoulder and plopped by the sloppy stack of paperwork. Perhaps the total silence of every other being in the courtroom made this newcomer's every move seem off-the-wall loud, or perhaps she was just loud. She finally sat, as noisily as her baggage, with an audible exhale that doubled as an obvious sigh of relief.

"So CPS did make it." The judge nodded, "Catherine." She half waved back and continued shuffling the top dozen or so files. She pulled a thin one out and waved it at the bailiff, who collected it and brought it to the judge. Clarice's skin crawled. Harding read the papers and aside from a few coughs, Jackson's swinging feet tapping the bench riser, and lawyers shuffling papers, nothing was heard.

"Okay, let me see if I've got this," the judge looked up. "Firemen and police arrived at the Waterman Clinic. They found no fire but did find the missing child in the barn of the late Mr. Henkel. Aaand... CPS was contacted by whom?"

"Waterman Clinic, your honor," the round woman answered.

"No sir, that's not... the District Attorney feels—that is to say, Mr. Henkel's rights were violated, his property trespassed, his house vandalized—"

"Emmett, do make a point. Does the DA have reason to believe the child is a danger to himself or others?"

"We do, judge, unquestionably. Jackson Miller needs immediate evaluation and the state on behalf of Mr. Henkel's wrongful death—"

"Are you serious, Emmett?" Al Katz yelled. "I think you forgot the kitchen sink in there. Firstly, he's four, four years old your honor. So any charges of vandalism or trespassing—now, come on! And for what purpose? Furthermore, wrongful death? I mean, the man had heart conditions and those complications are what he died from. There's absolutely no proof a fallen cabinet or a little boy in the house is responsible for his heart failing."

"The child was exhibiting bizarre behavior," Emmett said. "Caused no less than four state vehicles to respond to Waterman, set a fire in—"

"Let's stop right there a moment," Judge Harding smiled at Jackson. "Son, would you like to go out in the hall and have a little treat with your, uh, nanny?"

"Joe,"—he turned to the bailiff—"Get that box of Salt Water Taffy Ellen brought me from Atlantic City, would you? And take the nanny and Jackson into the hall until I call for them. That okay with you folks?" He looked at John and her.

They nodded. Jackson and Mrs. Nicestrum followed the bailiff.

"I don't want him tainted by anything we say here. I'll probably have a word with him alone." The judge got out a hanky, gave a loud honk, and waggled it around his nose. "Damnable summer cold outliving my energizer battery. Now then, we were discussing the odd behavior of the child. He actually crawled through duct work?"

"He's very advanced, your honor," John piped up then looked at Al. "Is it alright for me to answer?"

"I'd prefer it," Judge Harding said. "Got more people involved here than a Saturday night vice bust."

"He's tested genius your honor, and he's never once lied to us. He says—"

"Judge Harding the wild fancies of the child only make it more apparent he is deeply disturbed—"

"Judge," Al spoke over Emmett's voice, "this entire inquiry into the unfortunate heart attack of Mr. Henkel is based on the complete doubt and utter dismissal of the little boy's explanation of his own behavior."

"Well counselor," Harding said, "that seems reasonable or do you know of any other four year olds who crawl through ceilings, start trash can fires, run helter-skelter into strange houses and upend china closets?"

"Exactly," Al coolly played with his pen. "Except the boy's claim of being chased has never been fully investigated. It would be different if there were proof."

"Proof!?" Emmett yelled.

"Look Al," the judge said, scratching his beard, "is there something you've uncovered we ought to know about?"

Clarice watched feeling surprised at how competent Mr. Katz was and thinking how well he seemed to play this game, especially considering the look of him. She half worried that he may expect some compensation, favor or not. John and she would have to discuss that. He could use the money by the look of it. Then again, he seemed unmaterialistic, and perhaps that was why his suit was dated and his shoes were worn.

"I'd like more time, your Honor, to investigate the boy's claim."

"Al, really, I can't see what's to be accomp—"

"Please Mitch." Katz locked eyes with Harding, and some kind of mutual respect passed between them.

"Fine, we'll adjourn till..." the judge flipped a page on his desk, "tomorrow at 9:00 AM. That's the only opening all week, and that's how much time you have. Pointless to drag such a small decision out anyway. I'll talk to the boy, er Jackson Miller." The judge got up, everyone scrambled to stand. He exited with a nod to both attorneys and not one further word.

Clarice felt a mixture of relief and angst. On the one hand, it would be better to get this over with, but on the other hand, Jackson was safe for now. *Safe? Why say safe?*

The CPS lady came over to their table. She had a sausage stuffed figure, youngish face and burgundy hair in one of those boyish cuts that you see in old hairstyle magazines at beauty parlors. She looked uncomfortable in tight navy slacks and a tucked in flowered blouse she was bursting out of.

"Hi, Catherine Hall. I'm sorry about all this, but really, CPS is not the monster you've read about. We're here to protect the child, see that he gets whatever he needs."

"We're his parents," John said. "We'll see he gets whatever he needs. It's not like we're abusers or—"

"Oh there's no abuse suspected," the lady said, adjusting her baggy purse, "but negligence is also a serious issue. Sometimes the parent's aren't aware of—"

"Negligence!" Clarice practically shrieked.

"Certainly these claims have to be investigated based on any accusations."

"Who's accusing us of being negligent? We have a right to know." Clarice was feeling angrier by the second.

"I'm sorry but that information would always be confidential and really there's no need to—"

"Shout?" Clarice said. "Do you have any children Ms. Hall?"

"I, well no I—"

"Well I'd like to see how you would handle being falsely accused of negligence." Clarice spun on her heel, brushed past the others, and stormed down the aisle. Fuming, she burst though the courtroom door, seeing Nicey and Jax on the bench. Nicey held the box of taffy and Jax was unwrapping one, which he immediately held out to her. She sat down by Nicey, waving the candy back with a forced smile for Jax.

"Everything alright dear?" Nicey said.

"A ghoul from Child Protective Services just accused us of negligence that's all. Where's John?" She looked back to the door. He should have been right behind her, she thought, but he was either talking to Mr. Katz or apologizing for her rudeness to the CPS lady. It better not be the latter.

Nicey said nothing but patted her leg. Clarice heard Jax on the other side of Mrs. Nicestrum whisper, "He's here." She figured he meant John and she stood to face the courtroom door. Then she heard Nicey answer in equally low tones and realized they both thought she couldn't really hear them and that they were speaking only to each other.

"I know. I feel him too. He can't hurt us. We're all together," Nicey whispered.

"What?" Clarice said, turning back to face them.

"Nothing dear, nothing to worry about. Do you want to tell us what happened?"

"Oh we're adjourned; I guess they call it, till tomorrow. I think your Mr. Katz is buying us time."

Emmett Pierce swung out of the courtroom after the appropriate cordial nod to Mr. Miller and Al Katz. Catherine Hall had already left, but she had enough paperwork to keep the Millers sufficiently occupied when the time came.

He headed for the elevator, pressed the down button. He could feel the old woman watching. When he got on, he turned around, met her glare, and watched her protectively shield the child's light from his view, *or die trying*, he grinned, satisfied. No doubt about it, she can see elders. The doors closed and Emmett looked up waiting for the number one to light. He was surprised when the thing went up instead, past three, past four, finally stopping on the fifth floor.

Emmett sensed *him* before the door even opened. He stepped back while the master stepped on turning his back to him. The doors closed. The elevator sank for half a second when the master waved his hand, and the elevator jerked to a stop. Between the fourth and fifth floor, Emmett decided as those numbers stayed lit and blinking.

"It wasn't my fault." Emmett spoke to the master's back, studying the wide black streak in the gray hair from the temple to the nape of his neck. He cut a good suit, even if perpetually black; this one had the soft sheen of silk. "There wasn't time to get Harding removed, so I've involved CPS. If all goes well there'll be plenty of opportun—"

"Silence," his low voice held the "s" and the "c" unnaturally long. "I will show you how little time is needed to accomplish so small a task. You said Richards was our best man. See that he is available tomorrow morning to take over for Harding." He waved his hand again and the elevator started up.

"Fires of Hades, this place stinks!" His profile spit a wad on the floor. "Too much light! Never would have guessed that in a government building." Emmett spied a maggot crawling out of the slime. The elevator door opened on the first floor. He followed his master across the lobby, past security, and out the double doors.

***

Tuesday morning dawned with roads still wet from last night's rain. On the way to the Courthouse, the Blazer sat at a red light. Clarice had her visor down against the sun's glare and caught a glimpse of Jackson's keen interest in the school bus ahead of them. They'd discussed school but had no clear solution yet. Nicey was pushing for some kind of homeschooling where Jax could stay at home with an advanced curriculum allowing him to move at an accelerated pace. Clarice frowned. It *would* be convenient seeing they were moving to Ithaca, though Jax needs friends too....

One problem at a time, Reece. She picked a piece of lint from her navy skirt deciding the simple white blouse and skirt were a good choice for court—light, comfortable, conservative and best of all, not a suit. Nicey had spent the night, and John was driving them all in the Blazer. Mr. Katz assured them he'd be there again —that was a big fat comfort. John opted for a dress shirt and tie, skipping the jacket; still, they put the little suit back on Jax. He liked it; they liked it—what's not to like? Nicey looked comfortable in a cotton paisley skirt and cream sweater, officially ending the circus of suits.

"Mrs. Nicestrum," Clarice turned and leaned over the seat to look at her. "I wanted to thank you for asking your friend to help us."

"You're welcome, dear. Al is good people, Clarice. God is with him, he'll fix everything."

"Anyway," Clarice ignored the heavenly honorable mention, "John and I were talking, and we want to compensate Mr. Katz for—"

"Sshh!" John tapped her knee, turned up the radio.

> *. . . the judge found yesterday afternoon in his chambers. Authorities believe Harding suffered a fatal heart attack sometime between 11 AM and 2 PM. Initial reports indicated there were some signs of a struggle in the office when Mrs. Ellen Snell found the judge on the floor of his chambers surrounded by books from a fallen case behind his desk. Snell, the judge's assistant, described the scene to several coworkers. Official's preliminary investigation indicated the judge himself might have pulled the bookcase over while suffering the fatal heart trauma.*
>
> *In other news, this morning at 4:45 a minor traffic accident sent one man to Binghamton General for...*

"That's our judge, Judge Harding," John said as he turned down the radio. "Should we call the courthouse?"

"Oh my God!" Clarice said. She thought of the grey bearded face, the tough, no-nonsense court manner that she suspected covered a warm, honest even funny personality. Gone, gone just like that. A heart attack like Mr. Henkel.

"I can't believe it," she said then remembered John's question. "We're almost there... I think we should go. No one called to say we shouldn't, and they have your cell, mine too." She wrestled to free hers from the small purse prison, finally springing it from its cell, a too-tight compartment supposedly designed to hold it. Slightly annoyed, she flipped the lid checking for missed calls, then popped the recently sprung inmate into her skirt pocket. Clarice turned to check on Jax, who looked serenely out his window. Mrs. Nicestrum shrugged. *Guess he wasn't listening.* Good, no questions from him meant no answers from them.

At the courthouse, they had to stop at security to be scanned while the guard checked for their names on the list of what cases were on the docket in each courtroom. John went through first, retrieved his shoes, keys and cell, and then spoke to the guard. She slipped on her shoes and reattached her watch watching him. John looked important, standing before the guard's desk as one of those men who commanded attention—deep, rumbly voice, authoritative demeanor, a born leader yet never bossy.

"Can you tell me what's happening with Judge Harding's hearings today?"

"Shame," his head wagged, "It's a shame isn't it? You just never know when your ticket will expire. Great man he was, a truly great judge, solid, fair, always decent to everyone. He'll be missed, that's what—a real shame." The officer ran one thick finger down a page and tapped his shabby gray mustache with another. He looked back up at John. "Yup, yup. Seems Judge Richards is stepping in, at least for this morning's 9:00 AM, not sure about this afternoon. You Millers are all set."

John frowned, "But will a new judge... I mean we started the hearing yesterday—"

"I'm sure Judge Richards was briefed. He's ah, well, it'll be fine. Let's see..." He commenced tapping his stache and finger-surfing. "Yup, your lawyer already went up."

Hearing him call Mr. Katz their lawyer felt odd but good too, Clarice thought. They'd have been lost yesterday without his help. With no idea what to expect of this new judge, Clarice held Jacksons's hand and they all made their way upstairs. They filed in, sitting precisely as they had almost 24 hours ago when the seat in front of them had been filled with such a respected presence. A life gone, just plink, gone, and the world spins just the same.

8:57 and everyone was here except the judge. Al twisted in his chair to face them. "Judge Richards is taking over."

His face was puffy, his eyes red. Clarice remembered the looks that had passed between him and Judge Harding, and it dawned on her they may have been close. She reached out to his hand searching his eyes.

"I'm sorry about Judge Harding; he seemed like a good man."

"*Was*, and thanks, I ah..." His eyes met hers reading a genuine concern and opened up. "He really loved life. He was going on vacation—Maine, next week. Wife, three teens, his oldest gave him a grandson about six months ago, I think. Beautiful family. I stopped over to see Joan, his wife, she... well everyone is in shock. He—he didn't even have a bad ticker. I just don't understand."

"Oh Alan," Mrs. Nicestrum leaned forward and across Jackson to place an arm of sympathetic support around his shoulder. "Life is full of mystery."

Ten minutes after nine, the side door opened, and a stunning young man entered in a judge's robe. He flashed an engaging smile of unnaturally white teeth at them and especially Jackson. His demeanor spoke more of a politician (or a male model) than a judge. Full head of blond hair, a side-part swooped up and back like a weatherman's, bright blue eyes in a baby face. He was a good height and a trim figure, which even under the robe showed a hint of toned muscle. *Looks like a schmoozer and waaay too young to be a judge.* Clarice sized him up with immediate prejudice, and just as quickly chastised herself for it. But darn if he didn't remind her of

Joel Cramer, her first date in high school, a guy only out for one thing and would say anything to get it.

"Now then, I'm Judge Richards. I've been assigned here this morning. As you probably know, Judge Harding suffered a heart attack just beyond those doors. I trust we'll all make the best of a bad situation. Got a full docket, but I'm sure we can get your son the help he needs without too much ado."

John turned, gave her a look, which mirrored her own over Richard's choice of words, as if the hearing was all decided. Mrs. Nicestrum stiffened next to her.

"Mr. Pierce, would you care to begin?"

"Your honor the child is clearly disturbed, a savant of sorts. His parent's have already admitted his need of psychiatric evaluation by seeking Dr. Wheaton's help last—."

"Objection! Judge Richards, seeing a doctor for possible sleep disruptions is hardly an admission that their child is—" Al bit it back. "It's hardly a reason to hand the care of one's child over to the discretion of the state or CPS or Ms. Hall here, no matter how well intentioned."

"Mr. Katz," the judge said, scooping a small pile of papers up and tapping them into an orderly pile, "we're not talking anything beyond an examination by a state psychiatrist, probably up at state hospital. Is that right Ms. Hall? You've set that up I understand."

"Yes your honor, CPS will transfer the child directly from here. We also require an investigation of the parents."

"What?" Clarice burst out turning to the CPS ghoul. "What gives you the right to—"

"Mrs. Miller, you will not speak out of turn in *my* court," the young judge said. "Aaaand, *I* ask all the questions."

Clarice's inside dropped in a ball hot embarrassment and fear, even as the words petulant hall monitor popped into her head. John reached back; Clarice placed her hand in his and he gave her a squeeze.

"Now then Ms. Hall, investigate the parents for what?" Judge Richards drew a hand lightly over the top of his GQ hair.

"It's standard procedure in any neglect case," Catherine Hall said, glancing to Clarice.

What in the world had this woman been told and by whom? How could this be happening? The whole thing was spiraling, Clarice thought.

"Excuse me, your honor, when did this simple inquiry turn into a case of neglect?" Mr. Katz piped up in loudish, but respectful tone.

"There are reports," Ms. Hall said, "to our office and coupled with the unexplained behavior of the child—"

"Not to mention that same behavior causing the death of a man," Pierce said.

"Course you can't *mention* it Emmett," Al sneered. "It would be ludicrous to *mention* it, wouldn't it? When it didn't happen that way! There's positively no proof whatsoever—"

"Counselor calm down," Judge Richards said. "All we're talking about here is a temporary removal of the child for evaluation purposes. If his behavior can be explained, the Millers should be happy to accept the help of the court, and if nothing turns up in the neglect charge..." Richards' voice trailed off, his eyes looking toward the door.

Clarice turned in her seat. Officer Babicek, the same policeman that came to the house, walked toward them. He hunched beside Al Katz and whispered something. The two went back and forth when Judge Richards issued a loud "Ahem."

"Officer is there something you want to say to the court?"

Al scooted out from behind the table and approached the bench. After a short exchange, the smarmy judge looked at the policeman then said to Al, "Fine, fine, but I'd like to hear it for myself. Will Officer... " He wagged his fingers.

"Babicek," the policeman took a step forward.

"Officer Babicek, will you tell us all exactly what you found?"

Babicek coughed, coming forward. "You want me to take the stand?"

"That's not necessary. This isn't a trial. Just share what you know."

"Well," Babicek said, "I was questioning neighbors about Mr. Henkel, you know his heart problems, and a Mrs. Tapernaum... " He snapped out his trusty notebook, "lives at PO 3654 Route 12, Chenango, basically across the street from Henkel. So she said she saw a black Cadillac Deville speed away from Henkel's' place shortly after five PM—that was around the same time our squad and the fire engines arrived at Waterman. Mrs. Tapernaum says she was putting her cat out—puts him out same time every night —so she puts him out and sees the car back out of Henkel's driveway and speed off. Says she thought it was odd since Clive Henkel only owns an Accord and I quote, 'Clive hasn't got a soul in the world who visits.' Said she saw two men in the car. Thought it was 'them Jehovah's Witnesses', and she wondered why they skipped her house." Officer Babicek stopped talking and slipped his little red notebook in his back pocket.

John gave Clarice's hand an I-knew-it tug. She knew it too, and now the law had to admit the truth. The thought of two men after her son was suddenly more real. Why? Why and who?

"Your honor, this changes everything," Al said. "This information corroborates the boy's story."

"Judge Richards," Emmett practically screamed sounding panicked. "May I have a word with you in chambers?" He glared at the judge. A look exchanged between the two, but Clarice couldn't decide what it meant. John turned around to Clarice lifting his brow. After a long moment, the judge made a pretense of checking his watch.

"We'll have a short recess. Give everyone a chance to stretch, digest this new information." He stood banged the desk with his hand instead of a gavel, announced, "Fifteen minutes," and exited the side door.

Two seconds later, Emmett crossed in front of them and hastened out the same door.

"Hope that helped," Officer Babicek said, stopping by Clarice on the bench.

"It's great news," John said. "I knew it! I knew my little man wasn't making anything up. My God, two guys really chased you. It's so crazy." He put his arms out for Jax to climb in.

"Scary is what it is," Clarice wrapped her arms around them both tight, as if she could glue the three of them safely together.

The two men, both suave, one young, one middle aged, walked down the hall in silence till they reached Richards' chambers, a typical judge's office with bookshelves, leather furniture, huge desk. Richards went straight to a corner cabinet, pulled down two tumblers, and poured brandy without a word. He offered one to Emmett, who refused to take it. The young judge plopped it down and shrugged.

"You know how this has to go here," Richards twirled the brandy, took a swig. "Don't even pretend it can go any other way."

"Oh it will," Emmett fumed, "and you'll see it does too."

"There's a witness now. The boy's claim of being chased is corroborated. There's no cause now, no reason not to believe the child."

"Nevertheless, you will continue as we planned and order the boy taken by CPS."

"What? Impossible. Katz would have a field day with me. And if the Millers go to the Press... I'm not ending my career over this?"

"Aren't you? Have you any idea who you're dealing with?" Emmett glared at Richards, who leaned against his desk swirling the amber liquid. "You would be nowhere without us, without *him*. Do you realize you're the youngest prosecutor to make judge in this state? You're going places, and you must know why."

"I know you and a few others pulled strings. I know there's something I owe, of course, but—"

"Damn straight you window-dressed little snot. You're going to make this happen," Emmett stepped to the window and looked over the view, the view he'd practically provided. Neither spoke; a few footsteps clapped by in the hall.

"You listen to me Mis-ter Pierce, I didn't get this far to just slide down making backroom deals with the likes of you over two cent cases involving witnesses for God's sake. There's a witness now," Richards slammed his drink down and got off the corner of the desk. "I'm going back in there and doing whatever makes sense —Not the right thing, not the wrong thing, but the thing that makes sense. I'm building my reputation with or without you and your friends."

Emmett swung around incensed at the arrogance of this smarmy lifeguard looking kid. He glared at him. He'd thought Richards was a lot like himself, had big plans for him, too, been moving him along nicely. Hell, political office was next.

Richards grew uncomfortable under his gaze and looked down at his Italian shoes. "Look I—I'm not unreasonable. I understand debt, I do. But it has to be when it makes sense when there'd at least be a legal question that could logically go either way. Another time—"

"This is the time, Richards." Emmett pushed past the judge, stalked to the door, then turned back on him. "The sooner you realize who you owe the better. Rule in my favor, put that kid in the control of the state, or you'll regret it."

Clarice, Jax, and Nicey returned with waters from the machine. Jax seemed pleased once he understood that Officer Babicek had found a witness who had also seen the two men. Nicey changed her tune about Officer Babicek altogether singing his praises.

Clarice handed a water to John, who pointed to the back corner of the courtroom where Catherine Hall was in animated conversation with Officer Babicek.

"They've been at it since you guys left the room," John said.

"They fighting?"

"No, I don't get that impression. It seems more like CPS is questioning him."

"Oh," she said. "Where's Mr. Katz?"

"Bathroom."

She nodded and swigged her water. John got his cell out, turning a game on for Jax.

"No thanks, Dad. Nicey and I started a Sudoku."

John shook his head, smiling. Nicey pulled the dollar-store puzzle book from her purse and a pen. The back door opened, Al Katz and Emmett Pierce walked down the aisle splitting to their separate sides. Al gave them a friendly smile then glanced to the back where Officer Babicek and Catherine Hall broke up and returned to their seats. The princely judge returned, straightening his robe. He sat, loosened his tie a hair, and cleared his throat.

"Ahem, the Officerrr... ah, Babicek has taken a statement from a certain neighbor who saw a, uh, an unidentified vehicle with two unidentified men. All of that is, or may be pointing to some corroboration of Jackson Miller's story. I'd like to hear a little more though. Jackson, would you come up here and talk to me like a big boy?"

Al whispered, "If you feel comfortable, I won't object." John shrugged and Clarice gave Jax a small encouraging push.

"Excuse me Your Honor," Catherine Hall spoke up. Clarice reached out to hold Jax back for a second. "CPS is moving to close their investigation. I made several calls after speaking with Officer Babicek here. There seems to be no reason to doubt the child's claim of being chased, and under the circumstances—"

"But—but" Emmett Pierce spluttered, "What about the neglect? Your Honor!"

"Forgive me Judge," Ms. Hall shook her head, not a plastered maroon hair moving as she did so. "As of this morning our office has found the charge of neglect to be as phony as press-on nails. Turned out to be a phantom charge. We get those sometimes. It's complicated, but the best scenario really has happened. I mean we *were* able to follow through on the claims and found them a fabrication. There's no way I'm afraid to determine who is responsible,"—she shot an apologetic look across to their table— "We don't have that kind of manpower. Anyway, the only other concern CPS had was that there seemed to be no explanation for Jackson Miller's bizarre behavior, which now appears to have been sound reasoning and quick thinking in a threatening situation."

With that, Catherine Hall shuffled her leaning tower of Pisa, shoving and pushing the papers into a workable pile. She scooped them into dimpled arms, slung her jean bag over her shoulder, and stood. "If you'll excuse me your honor, I received a page about another case." The judge nodded looking a bit dazed.

Within minutes Judge Richards declared an end to the inquiry, ruling there was no reason to hold a four year old accountable for the actions he took while likely being pursued by two men who apparently intended kidnap or harm.

They invited AL Katz back to the house for a celebratory lunch of KFC and lemonade. They sat outside on the Miller's pint-sized patio in Briarwood, a comfortable breeze rustling the neighbor's trees. Jax was swinging with the little boy next door. Feeling relaxed, Clarice wiggled her toes freshly freed from the pointy navy pumps she'd been wearing.

"So tell us about yourself, Mr. Katz," Clarice said with half an eye on Jax and Tommy Murray.

"Call me Al," he said with a smile. "So what's to tell? I'm pretty simple. Grew up in Boston."

"I thought I heard a little Boston," Clarice said, "But it's so slight."

"Well I've lived away since I was a kid and I actually worked to pronounce my r's—found I got on better in college. Believe me when I get worked up I can Pahk yuh cahr in hahvuhd yahd with the best of them." They all laughed. "Yup we lived in Brookline. I worked in my dad and Uncle's deli, shared a room with my cousin Gabe—"

"That's the rabbi, isn't it?" Mrs. Nicestrum asked, refilling lemonades. He nodded and sipped.

"A rabbi!" John reached for another piece of chicken. "What does he think of your conversion to Christianity?"

"Uh, first off, we don't call it a conversion. We accept the promised Messiah, that he came and that he's Jesus. We retain all our Jewish faith. We see it—"

Clarice stopped listening, watching the boys disappear around the side of the house. She knew they were probably just getting a drink from the hose, but she used the excuse to leave the conversation. *Conversion, Christian or Jewish... religious people get talking and look out.* She got up, calling the boy's names, and yes, running away from any talk of God. Mad at him? Let's see, he would be the one who gave her weird abilities (make that afflictions), took both her parents, and—and what about Jax?

What about him, she asked herself, holding the hose for the boys. Jackson was alright. Whoever those men were, he had escaped them. Then they'd all escaped CPS, thanks to Babicek, or... was it God. Did he—

She pulled the hose further from Tommy's open mouth. "Careful Tommy." The boys still weren't great about only drinking from the stream and not letting the metal touch their mouth.

"Thanks Mrs. Miller."

Jax kissed her cheek, and he and Tommy darted out back.

That sweet Tommy Murray thanking her for something so small, she thought, turning off the hose. Only five and so polite. Clarice had never begrudged anyone a thank you before. Well she wasn't going to start now.

Clarice Martin Miller looked up to heaven. "If you're out there, and you did it," she said, feeling weirdly choked up, "thank you. Thanks for that." She wound up the hose, and rejoined the others on the back patio.

13

Wednesday Afternoon

It was John's turn to bring Jackson to preschool, first picking him up from home, and then taking him to BOCES. Cars filled the always-full parking lot. John pulled around the sprawling complex of BOCES. A behemoth cooperative, BOCES ran dozens of programs for children of all ages, even adults. One branch of the school was for occupational training while another provided programs for children with disabilities. Half the building contained interesting classrooms from hair salons, masonry, and auto shops, to a tiny but real grocery store. For John, the half that cared for the special children was even more winning.

John unbuckled Jax from the car seat, grateful they were still coming here, even though Jackson had long since completed the morning preschool program. During the school year, John had brought him three mornings a week, dropping him off on his way to work. When they'd come early enough to have breakfast in the cafeteria, special children would invariably join them, fawning over Jackson, as though he were a toy. Gentle souls who looked at John's burly frame and rather than being intimidated, seemed drawn to him. He wondered how anyone could doubt what a special and rare gift each of these children was—perpetually innocent and happy, put here, not for us to love, but to teach us *how to love*, unconditionally, as only they can.

John and Jax walked into the back entrance passing the daycare area then the hairstylist classroom with a dozen barber chairs and students in blue smocks.

"Dad, where are the other kids who were in my class? How come I never see them anymore?"

"Well buddy,"—he tousled his son's curly top—"they finished preschool in May, like you, but you're still coming so you can help Kate."

"Oh," Jackson said, both of them peeping into the masonry shop where a student in a black rubber apron pushed a wheelbarrow piled with sloppy cement.

"You like helping and visiting don't you, bud?" John asked of the current arrangement they enjoyed. After preschool ended, Nicey had requested Wednesday afternoons off for her church work. Clarice suggested daycare, but Mrs. Nicestrum had been dead set against it, saying something about BOCES being safe. As it turned out, John's friend Kate Walker, a Special Ed teacher, called. During the year of preschool, they had often dropped in to visit Kate and her beautiful students. Kate explained that Jax was such a hit she hoped he'd still visit. It was a perfect solution.

John thought of the first time he met Kate at SUNY. He was finishing his degree, and Kate had returned to get one after raising her kids. Two decades older than him, she looked like penny nail in a box of brads with peppered grey hair she refused to dye, wearing long skirts and bobby socks. Still what began as a polite acquaintance grew into a warm friendship when each recognized in the other a common spirit.

John and Jax stood in the doorway of Kate's classroom. Not wanting to disturb the class, John peeked in first, but she sat alone at her desk with her head buried in paperwork, probably government red tape. Ashen hair in a long bob on a delicate face was topped with dark-rimmed glasses too big for her tiny features. Short and thin, she forever dressed comfortably in penny loafers and any one of a dozen cotton skirts that fell almost to her ankle. Chilly as usual, she wore the long knit cardigan she got from her trip to Ireland.

He and Jax stepped quietly into the room. Sun streamed in on two long tables, walls lined with messy shelves of art and learning supplies, and two big easels ready for smock-clad artists. In the corner, a large crate held balls, ropes, and hula-hoops used for coordination and motor skills. The reams of paperwork covering Kate's desk paled in importance to the actual human beings struggling to learn what comes easily to others. The whole room looked untidy and hopelessly disorganized. Learning here was different and couldn't be approached with the attitude of a regular classroom. The children thrived, too. Kate's patience, in fact the patience of all the workers at BOCES, never ceased to amaze John.

Kate looked up. "Well hi there," she said. "Oh my goodness, what time is it?"

"It's 12:10. In fact," John added, "we're even a little late. Where is everybody?"

"Oh, they must still be at lunch," Kate said. She looked at Jackson, her whole face changing to that mien which fondness for children causes in women. "How's my biggest helper ever? You wanna come with me to find those naughty aides who obviously kidnapped my class."

"Uh-huh," Jackson nodded. "Is anybody absent today?" One of Jackson's jobs was taking attendance for Kate, a task done several times a day.

"I'll let you check when we get those guys back here. Okay? Tell you what though; let's give 'em a few more minutes. You think you could set up the finger paints and give each chair a giant paper?" Jax nodded and turned eagerly to the art shelves.

"You've had quite a week, eh?" she said and got up, coming around the desk to give John a hug.

"I'll say, but hopefully it's all behind us now."

"So you said last night, you think those two men are out there looking for children to kidnap or, oh boy, I don't even want to think... "

"At least it wasn't in our area or neighborhood."

"How did the men know a child was in the clinic?" Kate said, shoving papers in a folder and plopping it on a pile that looked like a game of Jenga.

"One theory is that the men were robbing the place, maybe looking for drugs, after all it was a Sunday. Place should have been empty. Maybe they just stumbled on Jax, chased him to silence the only witness. Anyway, the police want Jax to describe them for an artist."

"All done!" Jackson announced waving his hand like Vanna White over the tables where each colored seat had a paper and a jar of finger paints.

"Okay, let's go find the kids," Kate's voice bounced up.

The trio exited and walked the halls heading to the cafeteria. Jackson walked ahead while Kate talked quietly to John.

"I can't thank you enough for bringing him each week. Honest you have no idea the impact he has on my kids. You should see him sitting at those tables involving himself in their activities. It's heartwarming, John, your little guy next to some giant, lovable teenager who's mentally five or six. It's ironic, the connection, you know? Neither appears to fit in their own skin; here's Jackie, a savant in a child's body, bonding with one of my guys in an adult one."

"I know what you mean. It's as if he can under—"

Loud commotion around the corner cut John off mid-sentence. He and Kate hurried their steps. They came upon a frightened group of aides and teachers huddled in the safety of the hall. Half a dozen cowering adults stood about looking into a classroom like bees buzzing outside their own hive where a hornet had taken up residence.

"What is going on here?" Kate demanded over the noisy excitement.

"It's Gordy," reported an oriental aide in big glasses and a busy flowered smock that made her look like MAD TV's Miss Swan. "He's got a desk, and he's swinging it over his head. He's gone nuts!"

Kate and John had gotten close enough to see inside. John recognized Gordon, a 16-year-old, 200-pound boy with autism, violently swinging a student desk over his head as easily as a cowboy slings his rope. Kate questioned onlookers while John stood there figuring out what he could do to disarm the huge boy.

Without warning, Jackson tore past his father into the classroom, ran straight up to Gordy, and flung himself against Gordy's huge legs. John watched horrified as his little boy wrapped tiny arms around the young man's knees. Jax called out Gordy's name.

"It's all right Gordy. I love you. I understand."

For a heartbeat, the desk arcing down looked as if it would land square on Jackson's tiny head of blond sympathy. Then Gordon stopped mid-swing, holding the desk in the air. John was a breath away from intervening when the huge child lowered the desk to his side. Finally, Gordon let go of it altogether so that his giant arms could return Jackson's embrace.

John, unsure, tentatively placed one work boot over the classroom threshold. Gordon was a particularly volatile child whose moods flipped as easily as a light switch. John had experienced his Jekyll and Hyde temper one day when Gordon and he were sitting in the cafeteria enjoying French toast and a good laugh. John reached for the syrup, maybe too fast, too unexpectedly, clumsily, or maybe laughing too loud, John never knew, but it set Gordy off. He grabbed the syrup, yanking it from John's hands. The huge boy in a man' body, in overalls and a Big Bird Tee-shirt, yelled "No!" and hurled Aunt Jemima across the room, missing poor Patty Scott by a hair. A chubby Patty with Down syndrome, all smiles a moment before, had looked confused at the wall behind her where exploding streaks of amber goo oozed downward like a hundred worms inching to the ground. With no idea what set Gordy off then or now, John hesitated, afraid his very presence would cause Gordy's mood to swing like a saloon door.

Huge tears rolled down Gordon's face as a smile and look of relief slowly spread over it.

"Jackie knows G-ordy is g-g-good," he stammered, "good."

"I know, Gordy." Jackson continued to soothe him. "I know you are good. I *know* you."

And he did, John thought standing there watching his son hold the mammoth legs and coo soothingly. There was something in the way Jackson said *know*... he sees people, really sees them for who they are. John stepped slowly, like he was sneaking out of a baby's room at midnight, till he was close enough to gingerly lift the desk-weapon away. He caught Kate's eye as he set it down safely out of Gordon's reach. In one smile, he could tell she was thinking the same thing. He knows... he knows good, and he probably knows bad—John thought of the clinic. Jackson knows people.

* * *

MICHELLE

Michelle Nicestrum was surprised when her church group cancelled this Wednesday's visit to the Nursing Home. She didn't see why at least a few of them couldn't have gone. Just because Pastor Vann was sick, they had cancelled. Michelle tsked. Well, there was nothing to be done about it; John had already come to pick up Jackson. She sat at the Miller's small kitchen table in Briarwood, sipping her afternoon tea and wondering what to do.

No use wasting the day. Think, Michelle, think. A sing-songy voice played in her head. *What to do? What to do?* She was having more trouble focusing these days. *How bout it Lord, what do you say I should do with this extra time?* She took a sip of tea, looked out the open window. A light breeze rustled the cut ivy in the glass of water on the sill and continued across the room. The sunflower clock on the wall ticked loudly against the quiet.

No? No answer? How 'bout you, angel, you have any ideas? Michelle Nicestrum believed unequivocally that her angel was there, indeed, that everyone has one. Nothing was too small to share with her heavenly friend.

The buzzer to the Miller's dryer went off; Michelle's head popped up from her tea. *Well that's constructive.* She got up from the walnut table, gathered her tea things to a neat pile, and carried them to the sink, then crossed the kitchen to the basement door. The Miller's one story house, a typical cape cod with oak floors and creamy woodwork, had a pleasing array of rooms, thanks to Clarice. Even with so little space, they had generously made the third bedroom into a guest room for her. Nonetheless, she maintained her independence in an apartment in town. The arrangement suited everyone allowing her to feel part of the family without feeling intrusive.

Michelle's knees creaked on the painted basement steps. Lordy, how the arthritis hurt, getting worse and worse. The basement was dry and a pleasant scent of laundry detergent hung in the air. Her oxfords clacked over the bare concrete floor. She circled around Clarice's art shelves, dodged two ride-on toys, passed John's workbench, and finally landed in the laundry area. The narrow window shed a goodish amount of daylight; still she reached for the dangling string over the laundry table. The lone bulb spread a skimpy yellow glow.

The clothes felt warm. She pulled one item out at a time, folded and placed it on one of five different piles. Michelle peeled a dryer sheet off John's jeans, flattened it out, then meticulously placed it in a tissue box. She never wasted anything. These little sheets would be used to dust furniture, or scrub a sink with cleanser, maybe even out in the garage for John to wipe his greasy hands.

Michelle Nicestrum was a child, actually a teen, of World War II. During the war, she remembered using ration stamps for just about everything. Stamps for gas barely got her to her job and back at the local Methodist church where she worked as a secretary after school. They used stamps for sugar, meat, coffee, and butter to name a few. The shortage of real butter saw the birth of oleomargarine, and a hundred recipes for cakes and goodies, which used precious dairy frugally. Recycling too was an invention of WWII, done cheerily for the boys overseas. So complete were their efforts that even tiny foil gum wrappers were mindfully saved for collection. Such early lessons of deprivation and sacrifice made Michelle forever careful and never wasteful.

John's chinos went on John and Clarice's pile to be carried to their room when the piles were high enough to bother. Michelle leaned over to reach the last item and smiled folding Jackson's overall dungarees. He always looked funny in those silly pants. The overalls were simply the wrong package for Jackie's Poindexter looks.

Oh Jackie, Jackie! Not long, little one.

But how long, Lord? That narrow escape in the park last Friday, surely that meant there would have to be a new protector soon. Michelle shivered. So much power! How long could she have held out if Clarice's aura had not joined their? *Wrong park!* How stupid of her! Not a church within miles. No, nor any hospitals or nursing homes where the strength of good souls abound.

I don't know why I'm even allowed this great task. Not that I'm complaining Lord; I'm in your hands. You know I'll do my best for You, but surely, You have someone else in mind for what's to come. The plan for Jackson was not hers. She only knew her part in his protection and the small glimpse she'd been given of his future. She was careful too, never to discuss with him what he saw in his trances. Idle curiosity must not be allowed to taint God's plans.

Michelle shut the dryer door, wound her way around workbench, toys, and easels, and began the painful ascent back up the basement stairs. Her thoughts sang again. *What to do? What to do?* A flake of chipped gray paint on the third step reminded her of the basement stairs in her old house. She paused enjoying the memory. How often Matthew had painted those steps for her! He'd sweep them and their porch steps nearly every day, maintaining everything around her, knowing it pleased her—his cherished "I love you." Oh, how she missed him, gone these twenty years now. He never understood her though.

"I bet you do now, eh, Matt." She tossed the comment heavenward. "We had a good run though, didn't we, dear? Forty-one years!" She shook her head in awe. Yet in all those years, he never understood her gifts from God, her dreams and premonitions. No wonder Clarice kept her visions to herself. Maybe she was right, for her Matthew had treated it all judgmentally. He'd acted like his wife was imagining the things she shared with him. In the end, she stopped sharing. No, she tried. Whether he ever believed her or not, she never hid from him as Clarice does from her husband.

Poor thing! Oh what that girl could see if only she'd open herself up to God. And what a gift in her aura! Yet there is nothing to be done for her. Clearly, the girl is in deep denial. It would be too risky to explain things to her when everything indicates she would reject the truth. She shut out the spiritual world so completely that any attempt might cause her to reject herself as the boy's protector... that can NOT be allowed. Besides his mom's aura was obviously enough. Clarice had definitely participated in repelling the evil in the park. Her heart was good; God would lead her.

Back in the sunny kitchen, it occurred to Michelle that it was the perfect day to visit Matthew's grave at Riverside Cemetery and work on his flowers. She had to thin those red Geraniums, which ought to make room nicely for the new Impatiens. Michelle tilted her head up, squinting her eyes. Just where had she put those new flowers she bought with Jackson last Saturday?

Outside Mrs. Nicestrum followed the planting beds lined with neat boxwoods and burgeoning Hydrangea, to the side of the house. She found the plants and then fiddled around in the garage for a bucket, gloves, and a few hand-tools. Her heavy cotton skirt and white blouse seemed a bit impractical but changing would waste too much more of the glorious afternoon. She decided instead to bring a brown grocery bag on which to kneel. *That's the ticket... but now, where are the keys?* She checked her dresser fist, then the key hook in the kitchen, then rifled through her big black handbag. *No? That's strange.* She went to the gold LeSabre to deposit the bucket and plants. Sure enough, the keys dangled from the wheel. Tsk, tsk, tsk, *Michelle, you can't keep doing these dotty things. All ready then.* She fired up the car and carefully backed down the driveway.

It was odd. For no good reason, Harriet Mansfield decided to cut through Briarwood on her way back to work at *Macromania*. She'd run home for lunch today instead of eating at the health food store. She felt in no hurry to return to work. She'd had her fill of carrot stained smocks, soy everything, bags of beans, rice, and dried fruit. Had her fill of cardboard tasting candy, chalky carob treats, and worst of all the customers. Oh, don't forget the customers with every mad craze of magnets, centering and eye-popping, New Age, save yourself and the planet fad that could be dreamed up by man. And they all find their way into her line.

But why complain?

Macromania brought her clients—her clients, the people she helped.... And even if she wasn't quite sure how, Harriet knew things about them and their loved ones. She helped them. Yes indeed, that made Harriet someone, someone more than just a clerk who sold tofu fudge and carrot slurpees. That made Harriet special.

She turned up her CD, Ella Fitzgerald singing *That Old Black Magic*, humming along.

> *That old black magic has me in its spell*
> *That old black magic that you weave so well*

Going through this neighborhood could hardly be considered a shortcut, but her red Toyota Corolla took the right instead of staying straight on Hooper Road—like it had a mind of its own. So here, she was driving up the winding knoll as Michelle Nicestrum backed down the Miller's drive.

> *Icy fingers up*
> *And down my spine*
> *The same ol' witchcraft when your eyes meet*
> *mine.*

Harriet hoisted her short pudgy frame higher in the seat to peek in the mirror and erase the last trace of Big Mac from her face. Her platinum hair needed dye by the look of those black roots seeping out from her thinning hairline. The pile of cerulean blue eye shadow looked shocking over her tiny eyes as did the bright pink lipstick. She needed to go tanning, Harriet decided settling her heavy bottom back in place.

Vrooooom.

Her car shot forward, the engine making an incredible roar. A foot not her own lay on the gas as heavy, as if it was made of lead and the pedal of marshmallow fluff. The Toyota blast off at an absurd speed reaching seventy in eight seconds.

> *Down and down I go,*
> *round and round I go*
> *Like a leaf that's*
> *Caught in the tide....*

Harriet had no control over the car and NO idea why she was barreling toward the back end of the Buick LeSabre and the little old lady driving it.

"Oh my stars!" Michelle yelled pressing the break. "The bag!" What in heaven's name would she kneel on? She threw the car into forward.

Harriet screamed and slammed on the brakes. The Buick moved barely an inch when Harriet's Toyota whizzed past her rear bumper, a paper's width apart.

A millisecond from impact, the tires spun, smearing black hot rubber on the road as the Corolla skid a good fifty feet past the Miller's house.

"Saints in heaven!" Mrs. Nicestrum yelled, her hand flying to her mouth, her foot firmly holding the brake. She could hardly process the near miss. *How fast was that car going anyway?* Michelle slipped the Buick in PARK and turned over her shoulder to see what happened.

A huge jet-black entity hovered above the red Corolla with Ella Fitzgerald's voice spilling out the window. All at once, gaping at the menacing black mass as it swirled and tossed over the vehicle, Michelle realized that the Toyota had meant to slam into her. The driver of the red car sat stunned in the middle of the road, staring straight ahead, her hands gripping the steering wheel, music blaring.

> *Baby down and down I go,*
> *All around I go*
> *In a spin, loving the spin that I'm in*
> *Under that old black magic called love*

Michelle watched. The lady twisted backward in her seat and waved at Michelle, the innocent person she'd nearly killed. The woman's shoulders shrugged up. She lifted her palms in an exaggerated way, owning up to the nearly fatal faux pas.

It was in that moment, with the woman shrugging and the blackness swirling above her vehicle, that Michelle realized the stranger had no idea of the evil force obviously hard at work in her life. The red Corolla drove off with Ella's voice trailing in the distance. A shaky Michelle Nicestrum returned to the garage for the brown paper garbage bag, thanking God and his angels for her safety. She prayed for the woman while firing the Buick and inching her way out to the road and continued to pray all along her very careful drive to the cemetery.

* * *

Alone, sitting on his throne at the ranch, *He* smiled thinking of Harriet Mansfield. True she had missed the protector, he saw that much, but she had shown herself useful, pliable. *He'd* have to work on her, certainly, she was not yet one of them. Such an unsuspecting fool, prideful, arrogant, enjoying her glory, basking in borrowed powers, and strength. His hands slowly passed one over the other.

Yes, Harriet, you'll do. Waterman Clinic was fast looking like a dead end, a long shot at best, now that both Vera and Emmett had failed. And the mother's best friend had already made contact with Mansfield. Yes, this will work, she will do—Harriet, a self-made psychic, who smeared false charity and fake humility over her pride like a kid smears jelly on toast.

"That old black magic has me in its spell," he sang, "that old black magic that she knew so well. Icy fingers—"

Aaaaaha!... The scream was followed by an eruption of noise in the entryway.

"Silence!" he bawled coming out from behind his desk. "Enter Cain! Explain this insolence." No one would dare make noise on the first floor of the farmhouse, so what impertinence was this?

Mark's huge girth contrasted with the sheepish way he entered the room. His bodyguard looked ready to soil his pants, and well he should for allowing the disturbance.

"It's a new girl; it's not my fault. I had no idea she would scream," Mark whined.

His bodyguard's fear, although a sign of his own power, all the same disgusted him. *He* came to the doorway to view the impudent wench. What wasn't trapped—mainly her skinny legs— kicked and flailed as best they could. Sergio held one massive hand clamped over her mouth while he laced his other arm through her scrawny elbows, making an arm-bar behind her back. Eyes wide with fright, her wild struggle stopped the moment she saw *him.*

"That's more like it." His voice became silky. He drew up to her horrified face. "Now then, why are you insulting my hospitality, hmm?"

Standing behind *him*, Mark blurted, "She's new, I mean brand new. We picked her up yesterday. This morning she took the test like everyone else, only, she musta been pregnant when we found her."

"I see, I see." *He* said, never taking his eyes off the girl. She would remain calm as long as *he* willed it so. His eyes bore into hers, "You are indeed blessed, my dear. Others taste hell before they reach the comfort of those upper rooms." His bony digit pointed upstairs. Tears wet her eyes, but she continued to hold them open looking at him, as *he* willed. Slowly Sergio released his clasp of her mouth, testing the water.

"You needn't worry, little whore. You and the life within you will be cherished in those rooms. It's nothing like the barn where you left the others. Oh, they would gladly trade places with you, I assure you. But you have the golden ticket." He reached out to pat her abdomen. She looked about ready to faint at his touch.

Wanting to return to his dark contemplation, he dismissed them with instructions. "Take her up. Tie her for now. Tomorrow, bring her to visit the barns, and the grounds. Be sure she meets the dogs. She'll soon enough see the wisdom of accepting my hospitality. Be gone!" With that, he turned releasing his gaze on the girl.

He heard her begin anew. A second later when it muffled, he guessed Serge—Judas' hand had returned to her mouth. Cain shut the parlor door, and *he* resumed his throne.

* * *

Riverside Cemetery was handsome property with its Old World iron gates, large brick walls, and expertly trimmed hedges. Michelle drove past a row of spirey cedars, around the four pinkish mausoleums stacked two high, and past the saddest section of baby angels, pinwheels, and loose teddy bears. It was here she parked.

Walking to Matthew's grave, she held the paper bag in one hand and the bucket of tools and Impatiens in the other. The bag waved as she walked. *A bag*! She couldn't believe a garbage bag had saved her. Wait until she told Matthew! Reaching the gravesite, she took a deep breath, set her things down on the grass, and touched the brown marble tombstone that bore an etching of Matthew as he looked at their wedding. Michelle brushed debris off the top of the handsome stone confronting the words as she had some thousand times since his death. One thousand and forty to be exact.

> *Devoted Husband*
> *Matthew Nicestrum, 1921 — 1985.*
> *Until We Meet Again.*

Her heart ached. Oh, Love! Oh, my dearest love!

"No," she said, forcing the wad of pain back down her throat, "I brought you flowers and news, so I won't stand here feeling sorry for myself and making you ashamed of me." She spoke aloud and as usual, the other residents did not seem to mind.

Michelle dropped to her knees and began pulling the tiny weeds that had dared to invade the miniature garden in front of her husband's grave. She dug some of the soil around the Geraniums, loosening them, talking to her husband as if he were right there. She replaced the soil after tucking the new white Impatiens in the center of the bed and finished catching him up on all the news. Still on her knees, she leaned back admiring the new look.

"What do you think, love? Quite attractive, wouldn't you say?"

Rising proved difficult, so she allowed her bottom to plop on the bag, one arm holding her up, and her legs bent to the side. She sat there offering a few prayers for her husband's soul. She dwelled for a moment on her Jackson and his destiny, happily thinking of what she knew of God's plan. What a merciful plan it was! Like so many of His works, however He expected the cooperation and trust of His children.

"I don't know, Matty. What's to happen? I feel so tired and weak. What good can I be? I nearly got myself killed today." The admission caught in her throat. At times over the years, the weight of her task or perhaps the loneliness of it, the fear of being able to accomplish it, could feel overpowering and this was one of those moments. She cried for herself, for her husband, for the world, and even for the sad state of that woman so unaware of her demise.

A warm breeze slipped across the otherwise still June day, gently kissing the line of tears on her face.

"Michelle."

"Matt?" she said, hearing his voice on the breeze. Did she really hear him? It was clearly his voice, yet how could that be? The things she saw and heard were here, in this world, never from the next. The instructions she received came as inner locutions, never to her physical ears. Never ever had she heard Matthew's voice—not in the twenty years since he passed.

"Michelle, Michelle," her husband's familiar voice called softly a part of the gentle zephyr itself. "Don't be afraid, dear. We will be together very soon. I am so delighted by you. You have been so faithful. I have completed my perfection through your prayers. Thank you. I await you, very soon dear."

It ended. Even the mysterious wind died. Soon, soon, she thought wiping a teary line from her fleshy cheek. Another protector was coming. She would pray for that and strength for all of them. Thank God! How marvelous! *Soon, soon! Give us strength!*

She had energy now to stand, almost springing up. Mrs. Michelle Nicestrum gathered her things and would have skipped on those arthritic knees if possible back to her car.

14

Their Land!

A rush of cool air met her face as John held the glass door to the office building for Clarice. Her heels clicked at full volume crossing the expanse of marble floor. Thankfully, she avoided a full-fledged wobble in the four-inch heels. The lobby of the ten-story building, shining with glass, marble, and mirrors said one thing: money. Perfect building for a lawyer's office, Clarice thought. Not likely clients will forget how much it's costing while the clock ticks dollar signs around them.

"Did you have any trouble getting time off?" John asked, leading the way to a stone bench between two huge palms in the circular lobby.

"Nope, did *you*?" she said and immediately regretted her emphasis—a cheap shot at the number of hours John put into his company. He shook his head, looking hurt.

"I took two days off for the hearing and a half a day today."

"You're right, you're right. My bad?" Clarice pulled him in for a quick kiss on the cheek. "You've been great. Have I thanked you for all the last minute repairs?" John had managed to check the big items off their list before the open house, which had been a hit and landed them an offer.

"Hmm," John pulled her back in, "I have a feeling you can thank me later. Now sit tight, I'll see what's what over there."

The stone felt nice and cold under her skirt, especially with the sun beating on her back through the window. She was hot, wearing her baby-blue suit again. *Brilliant choice.* She fussed with the fluted skirt then made herself stop. They'd come to sign papers and close on their land. Their land! Hard to believe their dreams were but a few pen-strokes and hammer swings away. She watched John talk to the guard at the information desk. He was so unaware of his incredible magnetism: firm, broad-shouldered, wearing his quiet strength like a well-cut suit. Hair needed a trim, but she liked it when he got too busy for a cut when you could see the chestnut waves. He had thrown a striped dress shirt and olive suit coat over jeans and loafers, a casual, dressy look few men can carry off.

He came back to her.

"The guard called up for me. Schrader's secretary said he's still in with another client. She said he apologized, but since the seller's lawyer was late, he's spending some extra time with this guy."

"How late? We still closing today?"

"Oh yeah, only about a half-hour. She said we could wait upstairs, or leave and come back. We could take a walk?"

"In this heat, I'll melt. Sides." She pointed to her shoes.

"Oh yeah,"—he took her hand, helping her up—"Personally, I like my women with a little wobble."

She slapped him laughing. "Careful what you wish for big guy, I bought champagne for later."

"Good." He held his arm out like an escort. "My Lady."

On the seventh floor, the elevator doors opened to a sumptuous space, huge floor to ceiling windows, a sweeping view of Binghamton and the hills beyond, red mahogany, rich brown leather and enough black lacquer for a modern flair. The receptionist or the top of her head, sat behind a quarter-round desk attached to one of those high privacy counters. She stood—all blond chignon, fresh out of college, 120 pounds of her—acknowledged them with a smile and turned back to her work.

"Impressive," John said as he studied the architectural elements.

He always did that. In his blood, she supposed. Although an engineer, John's father never missed an opportunity to work with wood, always pounding away or sawing something in his garage. His mother, who had taste beyond their means and a designer flair that left her forever yearning for better things, pored over magazines, pining after the homes of the more than fortunate. It was she who got John interested in Architectural Digest, discussing everything from moldings and friezes to layout and landscaping. It was no wonder John went into construction.

"We have the party tomorrow at six," Clarice said as they both chose the couch and sat close.

"I know, the big five, going on twenty. He's smarter than me."

"Ya think." Clarice dodged his fake punch. "Oh, I almost forgot. I can't get off early. There's a few things I need you to pick up for the party." She pulled the list from her purse and unfolded the 8 1/2 by 11 sheet.

"Few things?" he gasped.

"Don't be a baby. Look, really, it's not that bad. Cake from Wegman's—I already ordered it. Ice cream from Pat Mitchell's—they're the only ones who have his favorite kind. And... um, the rest of this stuff is from Maines. It's all spelled out."

And it was, she thought embarrassed, typed in fact. Such a methodical planner, but birthdays are a big deal. Every family event was. She raised her brows to make sure he was complying.

"Ok. Okay," he put the list in his pocket.

The elevator dinged. A sixtyish balding man, in gray Dockers and a checked shirt stepped off and went directly to the receptionist.

"Hi, Jed Niles. I'm meeting my lawyer, Ellen Sanders for an appointment with Mr. Schrader at 3:00."

"Oh, Mr. Niles, Mrs. Sanders called to say she was running 30 minutes late. She asked you to please wait here for her."

"So I guess my being late wasn't so bad then." He rapped the counter twice with his knuckles and turned to find a seat.

Clarice recognized the name. She remained seated while John half stood to shake hands.

"I'm John Miller," they shook, "my wife, Clarice. Guess we're the lucky ones buying your beautiful land."

"Oh, you're the lucky couple alright. I'm Jedediah. Call me Jed." He pumped Clarice's hand too while he sat down in the armchair next to them. "See, I almost didn't sell it to ya. Least ways not the big piece." John and Clarice exchanged a look of surprise. "When the Realty lady said you wanted the other 400 acres, I got mad as a hornet. I didn' cuss her out, er nothin' like that," he snorted a chuckle. "It's just I never gave her permission to go and offer that piece to jes anybody."

"I don't understand," John said.

Clarice's senses tingled, something about that land, the Glen. Unconsciously and ever so slightly, her leg jiggled up and down.

"It's kinda complicated. But when I heard you knew a Prey. Well, that just changed everything." Niles fell silent as if done.

"I'm still not following. Was there a problem with the land?" John sounded concerned.

"Oh no, no, nothin like that." His hand waved. "No, ya see that land was meant for a Prey, or at least only a Prey should decide what comes of it. Near a hundred years ago, Preys owned that land. Well, their family got mixed up with my family, and my grandpa ended up acquiring it. Preys were losin' it to taxes or some such. I'm not real clear on the details."

Again, he paused an unnatural length. John shifted in his seat. Like a jumpstart, Niles continued.

"My grandpa told me that land was to go to the Preys if ever they wanted it. I did tell the realty lady I was sellin' the five-acre plot by the road, but only that I *might* be thinkin' a selling the other."

The elevator door binged, and a woman stepped off. Ellen Sanders, Clarice guessed. A moment later, Schrader showed his client out and ushered all four of them into a conference room.

Clarice wracked her brain trying to think where she'd heard the name Prey before. John gave her a blank look.

"Mr. Niles," John caught his arm, "I'm not sure we're the right people for your land. You see we don't know any Preys or anything of the family. I'm afraid you may have been misled."

"Now, don't you worry none about it. A Prey knows you, and they want you to have it. Let's get her done; I got things to do."

It was June 23, 2005, only three weeks after finding the land. They left the lawyer's office with the deeds in hand, so euphoric they could barely contain themselves till they reached home. Jackson had been dropped off at Mrs. Nicestrum's before their appointment. They were celebrating two victories since they had also received an offer on their Briarwood home.

"Knew we asked too little," John said, hanging his keys on the hook as they entered the kitchen from the garage.

"No, it's perfect. The Steeles said they could wait up to six months to close, so we'll have time to build our home without needing to hurry out of here. Besides we got what we wanted for it." She kicked off her heels reaching down to rub a sore toe.

John headed straight for the fridge where cold champagne waited, twisting the stopper as he walked. Clarice heard the pop as she collected the two crystal flutes from their wedding she'd chilled and followed him to the living room. John poured the cabernet'; Clarice stopped him before he could clink her glass and swung her arm inside of his. The height difference was a disaster. Champagne dribbled down the glass, down her chin and her arm. John didn't fare much better. They both exploded in laughter, her huffs and haws, she knew making him laugh more. Her laugh was awful and the fact that he loved it...

Pulling out of the cliché position, he gave her a look over his glass. She knew that look. Clarice slugged what hadn't spilt, kept her eyes on him while she took both glasses, and lowered the flutes to the coffee table. Their kiss was full of passion, triumph, and hope. This land, this house meant a new start, hope for the future. Her hands rubbed his muscled back and slipped down the length of his powerful arm to his giant hardworking hands. She brought his fingers to her lips and met his gaze. He would always be her hero, always be the best part of her. She would give him as much of herself as she could, push that part of her, those hidden secrets, far away from both of them. Someday, someday it would be right to tell him, but this moment, she felt only their love and closeness.

Later they lay on the living room floor where they'd landed, late afternoon sun warming them.

"Umm, this is heaven," Clarice mumbled, her hand on John's chest, her fingers tracing circles on his belly. "I could lie here forever,"

"Jax might miss us," John said.

"Oh my gosh, Jackson!" Clarice said, lifting herself off John.

"Relax, I told Mrs. Nicestrum we'd pick him up around seven."

"Good, you drive, I'll fly." Clarice sat up, her back against the couch. She reached for the champagne bottle, feeling slightly self-conscious of her nakedness. She poured John a second glass. "How soon do you think the guys will have the frame up? I'm dying to see our plans take shape."

"Foundation takes longer than the frame. You know I'm going to have to be there night and day." John watched her casually slipping into his shirt. "Aw, don't cover up on my account."

"I'm cold," she demurred. "Anyway, I expect we'll both be there every chance we get. Believe me; I know all the things that can go wrong if you're not watching those guys."

"You happy with the plans?" She nodded her mouth full of champagne. "Once we break ground and get going I don't want any major changes. I hate when clients do that to me. It kills the momentum and almost always adds to the cost." John wrapped his free arm back around Clarice and she settled in gingerly balancing her champagne glass.

"Well, Mr. Contractor, I hope you don't try to get your way with other clients by plying them with champagne and—"

"No, ma'am, only the most difficult ones."

15

Unfinished Business

John awoke thinking of the date, June 24...Jackson's birthday. It was also the feast day of his patron, Saint John the Baptist. He had a list of to-do's a mile long, but somewhere on that list, he vowed to squeeze in a quick visit to church in honor of his patron. It was Friday, so at least he wasn't going into the office or expected at the work site. Fridays, he worked from home, as much as possible anyway. He was a second from popping out of bed when Jackson came tearing down the hall and fairly leapt onto his dad's bare chest.

"Whoa there, buddy. One of these days you're gonna thump on the wrong part, put your old man in the hospital."

Jax straddled his chest. "Naw," he laughed, a lilting giggle that betrayed his excitement. "Know what day it is, Dad?"

"Hmm," John played dumb, "let me see. Um... yes, I do know,"—he snapped his fingers—"It's Friday."

"Aw, that's not all. What's to-day?" He bent his cute face right down to his father's nose.

Nose to nose, John could hardly talk for laughing, "Well, I'll be darned. You're right. I almost forgot!"

"Yeahhhh?"

"It's Mrs. Nicestrum's day at the beauty parlor."

"No,"—Jax sat up still on his chest—"think, Dad." He was enjoying the charade. They both were.

"I know. It's Saint John's feast day. He's my patron."

"What's a feast day, Dad?"

"Oh, hmm... let's just say when a holy person—a really good person," John clarified, "dies, that day is called their feast day. It's their first day in heaven, see?"

Jax thought for a moment, but apparently, his train of thought brought him right back to the more important matter. "Oh a feast day is like a birthday—the person's birthday in heaven!" Once again, he leaned in nose to nose. "Know anybody having a birthday, today?"

Score, game over! John shoved his hands under Jackson's armpits and hoisted him in the air, swinging him side to side like a flying superhero. "Yes, I know someone who's having a birthday, and he's five today!" John flipped him on his back. He climbed out of bed and hovered over him. "If there's any five year old boys left in this room in five seconds, the birthday monster is going to have to give them five birthday spanks and a pinch to grow an inch." John growled and held up Frankenstein arms. Jax shrieked and scooted off the opposite side of the bed while his zombie dad chased him from the room.

Later, showered and shaved, clad only in a towel, John ran downstairs to the basement looking for his pile of laundry. Mrs. Nicestrum was loading a basket to be carried upstairs.

"I'm sorry, dear. I was just bringing these up to you."

"Hey Nicey, no apologies; not your job anyway." Today, she didn't bother to remind him for the thousandth time that she liked doing laundry for the family. "I'm on the hunt for my dark jeans. Have you seen 'em?"

"These?" She indicated with a nod, her hands full of the basket handles.

"Perfect, Nicey. You're a gem." John leaned down to kiss her cheek, a stretch for his six-foot-two height. He bounded up the stairs then took two steps back down leaning over the thin wooden rail. "Oh, I'm running out to get some things for the birthday party tonight, but I'll be back in plenty of time for your hair appointment. Okay?"

"Fine, dear." She was still smiling from the kiss.

Before leaving, John had a few quick words with Jax telling him why he couldn't come. "I'll be back soon, Bud. You don't wanna spoil your surprises, do you?" John patted his pocket for the list and headed out the door.

While out, he chicked off the things on Clarice's very specific list in a relatively short time. He placed the Maines' grocery bags carefully next to the half sheetcake and bucket of Honey Pot ice cream then took a circuitous route home pulling into Saint Michael's Church for a quick visit.

Walking across the lot, he thought of his reawakening in the faith over three years ago. Tony Fucelli was responsible for that. Coincidentally, Tony was also the one who'd set John on the right track for a career back then.

The second youngest of five children, John had to pay for the bulk of his college education. His dad hooked him up with a construction job right after high school. The first thing he learned was dry walling. While slapping it up and taping seams wasn't much of a challenge, mudding, as they called the plastering work, was an art of sorts. The dirty work of sanding between coats was one of the unpleasant jobs reserved for new workers, and John had his fill of it from house to house. He found plenty of opportunities to learn all the skills involved in house building. His boss, a good friend of his dad's, made it clear to John from the start. "Miller, the biggest problem in the construction business is finding a crew that shows up. If you're reliable and hard working, there's no limit to how far you can go here."

John didn't mind the dirty work, so long as he could admire the finished product when he was through. A quick understudy, he was much in demand by senior carpenters, siders, and even plumbers. E&S Builders had a myriad of craftsmen working for them, building homes, apartments, and commercial properties. Workers either reported to the job site or the office to get their assignments or pick up materials. He remembered meeting Anthony Fucelli, an E&S project designer.

John had been glancing at some blueprints left unrolled on the front counter.

"Any bright ideas, or do you merely look like you know what you're looking at?" Anthony had smiled at John. Wearing slacks and a sports coat, he was one of those clean cut men, the type that make good news casters because someone that nice looking must know what they're talking about.

"Uh, I wouldn't say I've any ideas about it. Why?" John had said. "What's wrong with it?"

"Oh, I'm just having one of those mornings. I'm Tony Fucelli, by the way. You're John Miller aren't you?" John nodded and Tony extended his hand for a firm shake. "Your name's tossed around quite a bit. Someone's always asking for you on his crew. That speaks volumes here."

"Oh," John managed. Disarmed he turned his attention back to the blueprint. "I like this layout. It'll be a nice addition to this house."

"I guess I'm disappointed," Anthony said. "It feels a little less open than I hoped."

John continued to study the drawing feeling shy.

"Go ahead take a stab. What would you change?"

John hesitated. "Maybe you could sacrifice a little space up here,"—he moved his fingers over the paper sketching his ideas— "and push back this room, kinda extend the stairway across here,"—he indicated—"Make this part into a sort of loft up here, instead of a whole second floor."

"Not a bad idea. Are you in school John?"

"Yeah, I'm finishing my Associates in Business."

"Hmm, business degree is handy, but if you get a civil or mechanical, with all you're learning firsthand about the business, you could really make something of yourself in construction." Anthony Fucelli had no idea what a seed he'd planted that day. John spent the next three years gaining his degree in Mechanical Engineering while working at E&S. Within a year after graduation, other guys in the business were calling him to build houses. By 2000, he'd saved enough and learned enough to found *Miller*

Construction. Two years later, he collaborated with Anthony on a development project where so many problems crept up that Tony, a Catholic, suggested they pray together. He'd treated it matter of factly saying, "You're Catholic too, aren't you John?"

John, a cradle Catholic, had grown cold in his faith, neither attending Mass nor praying to any degree. It wasn't as though he had ever ceased believing in God or the church, but religion didn't seem a factor in his life. Anthony and a couple of his workers called themselves "born again Catholics." They studied their faith, went to Mass daily and confession often. John grew to respect them and soon followed their path falling in love with the faith of his birth.

Saint Michael's wasn't his regular church, but he knew they had a side altar dedicated to Saint John the Baptist. Entering he admired the architecture, his hollow footsteps echoing in the empty worship space. So many churches these days were locked to walk-in adorers, he felt grateful to find it open in the middle of the day.

He genuflected toward the tabernacle box holding the Blessed Sacrament, the consecrated Hosts used for Holy Communion. For John, Jesus was right in that box. Kneeling on the hard marble step before the statue of John the Baptist, he looked up at the image of his patron saint. "Hey Saint John, just wanted to visit and wish you a happy Feast day. It's my son's birthday, too. Quite a coincidence, huh?" He offered an Our Father in the saint's honor then closed his eyes lost in prayer.

SLAM! A sudden flash of light zapped across John's mental view blinding him. In the next moment, he saw a picture of Jax, standing on a board, suspended over an abyss. Confused, John realized his eyes were closed and forced them open to erase the figment, yet even with them open it lingered with Jackson a hair away from falling to his death. The sharpness of the image stunned him. He gasped and the flash was over.

What the heck was that?

He knelt there, but the inexplicable flash, so short-lived, was completely gone. Everything quickly returned to normal. He

175

decided he was probably working too hard lately—selling the house, closing on the land, ten-hour days on the construction site—it had to add up at some point and make a guy see things. He neatly passed it off and prayed a minute longer, filing the incident away as no more than his imagination.

John returned home in time to relieve Nicey for her hair appointment. She stayed long enough for John to unload and hide all the party supplies. He made lunch, and Jax munched a PB & J at the table when Clarice called.

"Hey, you get everything? Any problems?"

"Yes, mommy," John's voice squeaked.

"Funny," she said. "Anyway, I didn't call to ask that. I wanted to let you knooowww, the bounce house is coming at five o'clock. They set it up and everything. They'll remove it too, tomorrow morning."

"Who's they? What?" John walked out of Jackson's earshot. "Bounce house? Did I know about a bounce house?" he whispered from the hall bathroom.

"Well,"—she sounded like Samantha Stevens—"I just thought of it this morning. Actually, I was doing an ad for that new camping store, and they rent them. I mentioned Jax's birthday, and well. . ., I couldn't turn him down. He's letting us have it for the night for only seventy-five dollars."

"Seventy-five!" John managed to keep his voice down while his tone said everything.

"But honey, that's how much they charge per hour, see?" She pleaded for understanding. "We get it overnight."

Hanging up the phone, John looked out the kitchen window for Jax. He found him busy in the backyard looking for bugs, a favorite pastime. Looking at him, the bounce house did seem like a good idea. Jax needed more opportunities for rough and tumble with boys his age. On his way out the back garage door, John's Blackberry rang.

"Yeah?" John answered in his no nonsense work voice, watching Jax, who sat on his haunches by the dime-size tomato plot peering at some tiny creature. Mike Barrie, his right-hand man described a crisis while Jax cupped the insect of interest in his hand. Mike Barrie had been with John for the last six years and was as trustworthy and capable as they come. A giant of a man, everyone called him Bear. Like a cross between a Grizzly and favorite Teddy bear, he was equally feared and loved. Mike helped John with hiring and had a knack for picking honest, hardworking men. Without a doubt, Mike's emergency was urgent.

John yelled, "He what?" Jax looked up as his father's voice reverberated across the yard. Once again, John slipped out of Jackson's earshot and stood in the garage. "That son of a B! He can't do that! It's not true. I checked those specs myself. Kazmark couldn't inspect his own arse for a hemorrhoid."

No question, John had to get to the worksite and handle this himself. The five-story apartment complex that *Miller Construction* was building for a retirement community just outside of Binghamton was too big to ignore. After the heated phone call, John called Clarice, but she wasn't at her desk and apparently had left her cell off. Next, he called Nicey's beautician, who told him that Mrs. Nicestrum was in the middle of her perm. John looked at his son. Could be fun for him. Just get Mike to watch him maybe show him around, keep him out of sight while he tore that sorry excuse for an inspector to shreds.

In the car on the way over, Jax was full of questions about the construction business.

"Guess what, sport, I was only a little older than you when I built my first building." He had let Jax sit up front with him, and a fascinated smile had not left his little face. "Yep, I was only ten when we moved here. Member, I showed you our old house where Grandma and Grandpa lived before they moved to Florida? Anyway, there were new homes going up all around that neighborhood. We'd hang out at all the construction sites, watch the men work, ask a lot of questions. They'd always give us something for our time—nails, leftover plywood or scraps. We'd drag it out to this spot in the woods across the street."

"What for, Dad?" Jax asked, straining his neck to look out the front window. His skinny legs ending in red Nikes did an animated paddle.

"Oh, only the tallest, best, tree house you ever saw, that's all! Three-stories high, built between four trees. The first two floors had walls and framed windows. Not glass windows, but you know, holes." John laughed. "I remember Randy Boyer, cut himself so bad with his dad's saw. Instead of getting sympathy, he got spanked for taking the saw without permission."

John continued talking to Jax about his childhood memories. He told him of the tragic day when a neighbor sadly informed the boys, the lot on which they had built their dream fort had been sold. They had to dismantle a summer's feat of hard labor—still every scrap of wood was reused. First came the go-cart, a regular hotrod, or it would have been, had the boys scored Mr. Benton's old lawnmower engine. Even so, everyone agreed it was an awesome go-cart, mostly due to John's perfectionism.

His passion and perfectionist nature led to his young success. Of course, customers admired his artistic ability most about his work. John was familiar with every aspect of building a home, from the excavation and framing, to the electric and plumbing, to the finishing touches of paint and hardware.

It was impossible for John to build something he knew to be substandard. If it needed more strength and that took more money, so be it. If the wood was warped and had to be wasted, so be it. And above all, if the design was inferior, John found himself unable to contain his ideas. If homeowners had trouble visualizing his ideas, John would go the extra mile and knock up a model out of scrap wood. He once did this for a homeowner, who was so delighted with the makeshift model he painted it and gave it to his granddaughters for a dollhouse.

Whether John worked for or with someone, he was adamant about the hired help. They were well paid, but in return, John expected an honest work ethic. He had a three-strikes-you're-out policy. If they showed up late, slacked off, or did shoddy work, they would not be allowed to return.

That's why as they neared the commercial site, John was ready to boil. He knew every specification had been met for this stage of the work. He also knew if the inspector said it wasn't, all the wheels would stop. The project would be late and might cost his fledgling company more than just profits—might cost its reputation.

Jax stared at the fascinating work before him. The red steel structure must have looked like one of his erector set builds. The wall-less steel frame rose five stories high. All around them men in hard hats passed, trucks of every kind beeped chugging backward and forward moving piles of steel, rebar, sheet piling, and concrete blocks. Jax with an impressive Hot Wheels collection had seen some of the trucks before in miniature but never for real. He held his dad's hand, and his free arm pointed to each piece of equipment, expertly naming them, and surprising John. "Fork lift, dump truck, front-end loader. Awesome, a hydraulic boom!"

John spied Mike Barrie and two of his managers in a huddle. Off to the side by a Subaru wagon, was the inspector, Alan Kazmark that weasel. John had gone to high school with Alan, who had never been popular or well liked. Whereas John had played football and any other sport for which he could find time. Friends admired John's sense of humor and fair play. Sure, he had a temper, especially when he saw an injustice underway. He could rabble-rouse with the rest of them, but his intentions were always good. Even when they partied—and John could hold his own—he made one of those pleasant drunks, the kind you don't mind tucking in while they pat your face and splutter about how much they love you.

John had been popular in a good way and was well liked. Which is why Alan Kazmark stood out, as one at least who never cared for John. John always suspected it was jealousy, plain and simple, then and now.

He and Jax approached the huddle. "What's the word Mike?" John asked, "He budge yet?"

"Nope, says the bolts aren't uniform. Also citing some crap about safety provisions."

"Son of a—" John looked at Mike who nodded toward Jax. "gun, son of a gun. Uh, Mike, you know Jax has never seen a commercial site. How 'bout giving him a li'l tour?"

Mike took Jax over to a table of hardhats while John engaged Kazmark. Men smiled at the boss' son as Mike showed him equipment and talked about beams, welding and scaffolds. One worker in particular paid close attention to Jackson's every move. The guy was skinny, not a regular hire but a temp, sent by an agency. Mike thought he looked a lot like David Spade. He followed them, barely noticed, except when Jax caught his eye once. The temp gave a friendly wave to him.

Jax gawked at the huge red skeleton of a building all around him. Mike pointed out the aerial lift. "What say I give you a ride on that in a bit?"

"The articulated hydraulic boom? Yeah!" Jax beamed and Mike laughed. The long arm of this machine had several jointed sections, which could be controlled to extend the lift platform in a number of different directions. It was used to reach work on the top floors and transport materials. One man could operate the lift alone.

John's voice suddenly erupted in a full-fledged roar.

"You've got some nerve. You know damn well those meet spec. I oughta string you upside down from that beam so you can take an honest look at them." Mike must have worried John might do it, or maybe he feared a lawsuit more than the weasel's safety. Either way he decided he better get back and step between John and Kazmark.

Mike plopped Jax on an overturned five-gallon bucket. "Jackie, you stay here a minute. I'll just be out front... ahem, helping your dad deal with something."

Mike shot off in the direction of the rising voices on the opposite side of the structure, leaving Jax by the aerial lift. In fact, out of curiosity or concern, all the workers headed that same way.

"Hey superman. Now you look real fine in that hardhat."

Jax looked at the small set, blond-haired man approaching. If he had a funny feeling, a premonition or any bad portent, what the man said next made him forget it.

"You know what kid? Mike and your dad are gonna be tied up till you leave here." The strange man made an exaggerated frown under his pointy nose and wiped a limp strand of his blond hair behind his ear. "Didn't Mike promise you a ride on the boom?"

"Yeah," Jax said, excited looking at the platform of the boom lift a few feet from them.

"I tell you what. Mike would want you to have that ride, I betcha. He'd feel real bad if you didn't get it too. You know I happen to be the engineer who runs that lift every day. So I woulda probably been the one to take you and good ol' Mike up there, anyway." He let this info soak in. "How 'bout I give you that ride while Mike's busy?"

Jax looked about ready to say yes then said, "Mike told me to stay here."

"Oh I know that," the man pshawed with his hand. "But he'd feel so bad if you didn't get your ride on account a him? We wouldn't want Mike to feel bad, now would we?"

Jax shook his head.

"Okay then, let's get this puppy in the air." Jax got off the bucket and followed the man onto the lift.

"I'll even let ya push the buttons."

As Jax rose into the sky, Mike reasoned with John. "Cool down, I mean it. C'mon, man, look at me! He's not worth it."

"He's got us by the pants, Bear. We can't let him get away with this."

"I know. I know." Mike had positioned himself directly between the two, now placing his huge arms on John's. "John, you know we're gonna get this thing resolved with or without this squirrel." Then under his breath, "You're makin it worse, big guy."

That did the trick, John's better nature kicked in. They decided to get a cup of coffee in the trailer office, turning their backs on Alan Kazmark like so much garbage. Kazmark feeling every inch of their dismissal, made a show of tearing off the carbon copy of his inspection report and followed them, no doubt intending to ceremoniously hand it to John. They heard the paper tear; Bear turned and in two steps was in the scrawny man's face. "You better git, little man." He snatched the yellow sheet while staring down at Kazmark, who managed to stick his pointy chin an inch higher before turning toward his car.

They weren't sipping coffee for more than a minute, watching the weasel drive off when John thought of Jax.

"Mike, who's got Jax?"

"Oh Jeeze," Mike gave a hearty laugh. "I almost forgot. He's still sittin' on a bucket by the lift."

The flash from this morning's visit to Saint Michael's lying just beneath the surface of his consciousness came back to him. His heart took a nosedive, and John knocked his stool over lunging for the trailer door.

"Bear, you shouldn't have left him," he called storming out.

"John, buddy, calm down. He's fine," Mike followed sounding confused.

They hastened around the structure, weaving in and out of trucks and piles of supplies. Yet, it was easier to go around the mess than through it. Barrie clumsily knocked into a skid of PVC pipes, sending a dozen rolling off clunking and bouncing to the ground.

John's apprehension grew every second until it exploded in reality. "Where, where?" He turned to Mike, a frantic look in his eyes, yelling, "Where'd you leave him?"

"Right here, right here. Jeeze, John take 'er easy. He's around here somewhere. Jackson, Jackson," Mike called.

John joined him calling his son's name while both men gingerly, and not so gingerly, stepped around palettes of brick, over giant spools of wire and cables, and on pieces of scrap metal searching the ground floor of the steel exoskeleton.

John's heart continued to feel constricted, the terror of losing a child sweeping over him in waves of regret. Why did he leave him? Why did Mike? *Oh my God*, what was that image in church? Was he showing him something? This made John think about the circumstances of the flash. He was up high!

"Up, I gotta go up. Where's the lift?" It wasn't till that moment that he noticed the platform of the lift raised all the way to the top. "Bear, was the lift down here or up there when you left?"

Mike looked confused, "Down here, no one's working up there today."

John and Mike both set themselves under the lift, peering up, trying to see if they could spot Jackson. "You think he's in it?" Bear asked. Then both men yelled in unison, "Jackson!"

No answer.

Mike and John went over to the lift's ground controls. The ignition switch was off, and the master key removed, making the lift unusable from the ground.

"Aw, for cryin' out loud, what is going on around here?" Mike thundered.

John's gut told him he had to reach the upper floors and quick. He ran to one of two open spaces planned for a stairwell where the workers had been using telescope ladders. He reached the first stairwell gap with Mike a second behind. No ladder. He saw it, pulled up from inside, lying across the steel beams of the second floor—unreachable. They couldn't see the other stairwell space beyond a tarp-covered pile of supplies and skids of bricks. Even as Mike headed that way to check it out, John knew there would be no ladder. Some *thing* was after Jax. Some diabolical force had cut off access to the upper floors.

John wasted no time, scaling the red steel beams as fast as he could, calling for Jackson the whole time. "Jackson, Jackson. Answer me, son!" The columns were too vertical to keep a good footing, so John moved over to the outside wall where diagonal steel bracing crisscrossed between floors. He worked his way up each truss like a kid going the wrong way up a slide. Zig-zagging, he reached one floor after another, not seeing or hearing Jackson, fear mounting with every step.

By this time, other workers had caught on to the commotion. Mike ordered the crane be brought around, so he could use it to lift one of the guys up to search the boom platform. Some men stood back from the boom, shading their eyes from the noon sun with their hands. They peered up at the lift, looking to see if the little boy was on it. Others searched the work site, in and around all the trucks, supplies, and equipment.

The crane operator brought the crane around the structure. All well trained, no one would dare to swing dangerously from the hook on the arm, however, most of the guys, albeit against regulations, sometimes rode up with the loads. A pack of steel sheets lay ready for transport. Mike shouted orders to hook up the wires to the load, intending to ride up with it himself.

John continued to call and climbed, almost to the top floor. His head was coming over the fifth floor girder when he spied Jackson wedged between the space of a corner column with his index finger over his mouth, his eyes wide with fear.

FUMP!

A work boot landed straight across John's face. He saw it too late to stop the blow but soon enough to grip the I-beam near him and brace himself from falling.

"No!" Jackson screamed giving his position away. "Leave my Daddy alone."

"Aha, there you are you!" The temp yelled. "You shouldn't a gone and yelled now should ya?"

"Leave me alone," Jax cried, but seeing the man coming for him on the beam, he left the safety of the column. The steel frame had vertical columns every 18 feet connected by horizontal girder beams about eight inches wide. Narrow joists ran perpendicular to the girders and were little more than two inches wide. Jax was trapped with the man between him and his dad. His only choice was to swing around the other side of the I-beam column he had been hiding in and walk across the girder on the perimeter.

"I see youuuu." The man's voice sang. "I'm cooooming."

John heard Jackson scream. With a heave, he pulled himself the rest of the way up onto the girder.

Down below, a worker yelled, "There he is. I see him."

Others pointed and yelled while they held their breath watching Jackson walk across the beam, though they couldn't tell why he was doing it. Shouts of: "Stop!" "Stand still!" "Sit down," and a few more confusing directions sailed upward.

John shook his head still recovering from the blow and climbed the rest of the way up. Balancing deftly, his left cheek and eye already swelling, he worked his way toward Jackson. He saw the scraggly haired man, who was closer to his son by a whole girder length and would reach him first.

"Why are you doing this?" John demanded. "Is this some sort of vendetta?"

The longhaired temp turned for a second to engage his present boss. "Ha! Vain much? It's about the kid, boss-man, not you." On the eight-inch wide girder, he continued to step, Jackson continued to step, and John continued to step.

"Touch him, and I'll kill you." John summoned his deepest commanding voice.

"Not before I kill hi-immmm." He sang it, making John sure he was deranged. The man's movements however were calculated and cool while he worked his way to an ever-retreating Jackson, who had nearly reached the next column.

Below him many of the workers followed Jackson's progress on the ground, stepping over building debris but keeping their eyes glued to the boy. Some of the crew, copying John's ascent, climbed the cross beams to get to the top. Two others scrounged for a ladder. Several stepped some fifty feet back in order to get a look at the scene on top of the building. These saw the bizarre chase going on there. One recognized the man he had been working with all morning. "Holy hammer, that's Derek."

"Who the hell is Derek, and what's he chasin' the kid for? He nuts?"

"I don't know him. Just his name's Derek. *Manpower* sent him. Been here all week." That's all they knew. That's all anyone would know.

Jackson made a change at this point. A smart one for him too, as the man drew closer. He struck out on one of the floor joists, beams decidedly narrower than the girders, a good foot and a half narrower. Even Jackson's little feet had to balance on this bare two inches. But for the grown men in their huge work boots, the inches of steel might as well have been a tightrope. John had enough of watching this. Seeing his son forced to cross a bar joist in terror was all he could stand. Determined, he took two long, daring steps to lessen the distance between him and the man.

"Tut tut, you might fall and not see the big shoooow. I can do tricks too. Want to see me run on a floor joist, hmm?"

"You're insane!"

"Just following orders, Mr. Miller. Your *son* is the *one*; he can't get away. I knew it the moment I saw his little halo head." At these words, the man ran as expertly as any circus performer, grabbing Jackson's arm just as Jackson reached a support beam.

"Let go, let go!" Jackson squealed, "Dad, Dad!" Jax hugged the beam with his free arm while he shook the other violently, trying to free himself from the man's grasp. His action caused the man so much imbalance he was unable to dash Jackson from the beam. Instead, it was all he could do to hold onto the boy while his body swayed and jerked, trying to regain equilibrium.

"No" John yelled, and with the same daring the attacker had shown —even more so as his eye clouded over—John leapt the last few feet separating him from the maniac holding his son's arm. He grabbed the man's arm and held it while trying to swing a punch. The punch whiffed the air making no contact. The effort nearly caused John to lose his footing. It also forced the temp to let go of Jackson's arm in order to catch the support beam and keep himself from falling.

"Go Jax," John ordered him away while holding the man's arm. "Son, go as fast as you can back to the edge."

No way was that psychopath following his son, John thought. He held the arm fast and braced his knees to keep his balance as the man wriggled to free himself. The temp turned, striking out at John with his free arm. John caught the arm, but both men lost their balance. They each reached for the support column near them. Their feet followed their arms until both of them, one on each side, stood hugging the column. The man reached around the post and caught John's hair. For a bizarre second, he questioned why he hadn't gotten his hair cut this week. Using a fistful of John's hair, the temp bashed John's head into the steel beam.

John jerked his neck back and reached up to fling the guy's arm away. The temp's grip loosened on John's hair. He was going nuts watching Jax get away.

"No, he can't. He can't!" He lunged forward in Jackson's direction. Jax screamed, still inching his way on a two-inch bar joist. John seized the man's shirt. With a horrible shout, the man turned on John and threw himself at him. At the same moment, John, still holding the beam with one arm, steadied, brought his other powerful arm back, and let it fly full force in the man's face. The temp's body flew back, and if John hadn't caught him by his arm, he would have fallen.

By this time, several workers headed for Jax on the girder. The crane had landed Mike opposite them. He jumped off the stack of steel approaching Jackson as well. All four of them watched the tussle between John and the temp.

John saw with relief that Jax was now safe. He had no desire to see the man fall, nor did he wish to continue to fight him.

"It's over," John said. "Give it up, man."

The temp looked at John with such a mixture of hatred and confusion. "It's over for me. I blew it. *He* knows. *He'll* see I pay. *He'll* make me pay." John saw the look in his eyes, one of pure unadulterated desperation. He would never forget that look. "I won't. I won't pay."

Then the man did something that everyone on the top of that steel structure saw. He deliberately threw himself forward. John reached out, "No!" His arms flailed the air out of reach. The body sailed down, splattered five stories below. His head hit a concrete cinderblock on the ground. So even if the broken back hadn't killed him, the broken neck surely did.

After getting Jax down safely and calling the police, John took him into the trailer office to call Clarice. When the police arrived everyone was detained for lengthy questions and detailed statements. Lucky for John, the final moment of Derek Haines life was well witnessed, but the fact that he essentially committed suicide didn't answer any of the other questions surrounding the fight on the roof, nor his motives for attempting to kill the boss' son.

When Clarice arrived, she argued that she should at least be allowed to take Jax home and leave John to continue with the questioning at the police station, but police were intent on questioning Jax ad nauseum, too.

It was 8:30 by the time John, Jax, and Clarice got home. Mrs. Nicestrum greeted them at the door, looking slightly disheveled with her blouse untucked and wisps of grey hair straying out from her upsweep like escaped prisoners. Clarice held a sleeping Jackson in her arms. Mrs. Nicestrum spoke in a soft whisper while her eyes remained fixed on the boy.

"I reached all of the children's parents on the guest list. I told them you would call them when things settle down."

"Things may not settle down for a while," John brooded, stepping in behind Clarice and closing the front door behind him. "The news crews showed up before the body was cold. They'll make a scandal for the Retirement Home... and our company."

"Let's get him to bed," Mrs. Nicestrum said, stroking Jackson's cheek. "He'll need to sleep as much as possible, I suspect." Clarice still holding Jax agreed. Without another word, the two of them headed to Jackson's room.

John walked to the kitchen to hang up his keys and stopped dead in his tracks. Out the kitchen window stood the giant, blue and yellow, blown-up, bounce house, looking so ridiculously large in their tiny backyard. He walked to the sink and looked out at the toy. His fifth birthday—how close they came to losing him! *Why? Why?* He slammed his fist on the edge of the sink in frustration over the unfamiliar feeling in his throat—a feeling, he was pretty sure, meant he was about to cry.

16

Jackson

Swinging back and forth on the swing set it was hard to tell at first, but now he was sure. It was happening again. Jackson could feel it happening sometimes, sometimes not, just plunk—gone. He was buzzing out more slowly this time. Would it be scary? He hated scary. Sometimes it was so bad that he just screamed and screamed, waiting for *them* to go away. He knew they couldn't hurt him, so long as part of him stayed attached, inside his skin where he belonged.

He wondered if there would be a helper. He liked when there was a helper. He was coming through on the other side. At least it always felt like the other side. Other side of what? Jackson was never sure.

Clarice was working at the kitchen sink, glancing at Jax out the window, remembering his birthday two months ago. Jackson barely got to play in that bounce house before the tent company came to take it down. Since then, they'd been incredibly busy with the new house in Ithaca. The foundation went in, and after considerable headaches getting equipment up the hill, John's crew was framing it this week.

Clarice washed the dishes, enjoying the warm sudsy water, thinking of all the windows and doors she had to order soon. Hopefully for the doors, she could score something antique. Jackson was still swinging happily when she looked again. Nothing so great as a kid on a swing, not a care in the world except watching those feet go higher and higher above his head. Clarice smiled.

Jackson saw his mother in the kitchen window looking directly at him. She was going to be upset again. He wished he could help her. He held on to this world a moment longer, thinking maybe he could reach the glider and sort of buzz out there without her noticing. It was useless. A part of him slid out of his body with the same sensation of sliding down the big slide at the park. Not the little one in his yard, he thought, looking to the slide on his left. The slide blurred till it looked kinda see-through. Not everything looked that way. The young boy next to the slide appeared very fleshy and bright. He looked friendly, too. *Oh good,* Jax thought, *there's a helper!*

"C'mon," the boy called.

Jackson knew he could follow the helper even though he felt a part of him still attached to the swing.

"It's alright, come with me." His eyes, fun and inviting, smiled at Jax. "Race ya!"

With almost no hesitation, Jackson took off after the beautiful helper. They ran and ran. At first, it seemed Jax was still in his yard, but then the scene changed. They ran on a leaf path in the woods now, even though there were no woods in his whole neighborhood. *That's strange.* He ran after the laughing, brightness ahead of him. Skyscraper trees soared above him, and the air smacked of a crisp, musky scent, unrecognizable chirrups, and gurgling water.

They stopped running; Jackson turned this way and that trying to take it all in—the waterfall and pool ahead of him, the huge boulders, and the cushy moss beneath his feet.

"Where are we?" he asked, no longer able to see the boy of light.

"This is where I desire to teach you," a beautiful voice echoed in his head.

Putting down the cleanser, Clarice looked up from the sink.

"Oh my God, not again."

She threw the sponge and tore outside to the swing where Jackson's stiff frame had slid to the ground. She bent to pick him up chilled by his eyes, glassy, unseeing orbs that stared up and past her. She carried the almost unbending body to the tiny seat on the glider. She sat on the mini bench, arranging him on her lap as best she could, his stiff legs sticking out over the plastic arm.

It had been so long since he'd had an episode, she'd almost begun to think he'd grown out of them or that he knew how to fight them. Her heart tightened like a fist on a sponge full of tears. She gazed at her young son. Nothing could stop it from spilling out now. Clarice allowed the grief she so often denied herself to wash over her. Sobs wracked her body causing the glider to glide. Back and forth, back and forth, she was vaguely aware of the tempo meeting her mind's effort to lull her thoughts.

"What are you seeing baby? What do you see?" Over and over, she repeated the question. The repetition, like the rocking, had a Band-Aid effect, calming her down. A tear slid off her nose onto Jackson's forehead. Her hand wiped it then moved to his chest where a normal heartbeat offered at least some comfort. The minutes dragged on and the afternoon sun piercing the treetops sank lower in the sky.

"How long you gonna be like this sweetie?" She spoke aloud, snuffling air past her running nose, wondering if he could hear her. "You gonna wake up before Daddy comes home?" John was in Ithaca using every free hour to get the house framed and roofed before winter. He should be spared, poor John.

Clarice hunched her right shoulder up to wipe a drip from her nose on her shirtsleeve when she felt Jackson's limbs relax and saw his eyes come into focus.

"Mom?" he said, his arms went up, wrapped around his mother's neck, "Oh, Mom!" He hugged her then released his grip and squirmed out of her arms.

Well, this is different, Clarice thought a little bowled over. Usually he woke up scared and crying. Jackson stood, making the plastic swing wiggle under their feet. He faced his mom and sat down in the seat across from her.

"It was beautiful, mommy. He showed me it; you know the place you found."

"Whaddaya mean, honey bear? Who showed you, showed you what?"

Jackson cocked his head and gave her a *you-know* look. A haunting giggle escaped him. "He's gonna teach me!" he said and knelt backward on the seat, looking toward the house. "I'm hungry, Mom. Can we have dinner?"

Jackson was up and off the glider before she could object, running into the house. She sat there dazed. Clarice wished she had a tissue. She also wished she knew why she had no desire to ask her son any more questions.

17

SIMEON

Whaam. Whaam. One ax followed the other, the sound of the blows chopping into the afternoon quiet of the Mount. Simeon worked alongside Ed Holmes, their tools swinging, taking turns. It was nice of the Doc, Simeon thought. He was a good friend, lending a hand with anything the priest happened to be doing at the Hermitage. It wasn't regular, wasn't planned, but sweet as Pete he'd show up at the right time and pitch in, no questions asked, no uncomfortable *can-I-help-you*'s, nothing but a silent work partner for the day.

This morning Simeon had been chopping when he heard a second ax echo his blows. Looking behind him, he found Ed Holmes, short, balding, robust, and despite his heavier frame, strong as an ox. They were working to replenish the woodpile, which had to be topped off now and again—not so much to heat his modest cabin as for the chapel and the morning Mass lot. Hard to believe people would drive out here in the wilderness, freeze their bottoms off on logs masquerading as pews, and kneel on hard planks to hear Mass by an odd-ball Franciscan turned hermit, but there you go. Everyday more people discovered Mount Charbel, 600 acres in the hills of the little town of Maine, NY.

Simeon took another whack at the tree in front of him, let go of his ax and stepped over to the water bucket. He slurped noisily off the ladle, letting water roll off his scruffy beard.

"You believe it, Ed? Twelve years ago there was nothing here but woods and ponds."

"Yeah and you living in an army pup tent saying Mass for the squirrels and deer."

"Aaannd," Simeon winked, "they were as grateful and attentive as the fishes who heard Saint Francis."

Ed stopped and came over, joining him for a slurp. "Now now, Father, you can't tell me you're not glad to be housed in a proper cabin after three years in that tent and then that thing you called a hut." Ed wiped his mouth on his sleeve.

True enough, Simeon admitted, but only to himself. To Ed, he merely harrumphed. It was best not to overly encourage these do-gooders. They'd have him eating bon-bons in a chalet one day if he let them. The log cabin wasn't the only sign of progress since he first came here. Today visitors found a rustic chapel next to the sturdy cabin, paths galore, two outhouses, and a huge donated statue of Our Lady of Peace. She stood in a clearing on the highest hill overlooking the surrounding valleys and towns praying for the world. Magnificent! And they were beginning giant crosses for the fourteen outdoor Stations of the Cross.

The priest watched Ed arch his back, shoving his fists into thick hips until he heard a crack. *We're both pushing sixty*, Simeon thought taking up his ax, *only I intend to push it right back where it belongs*. He could do it too, at six foot three, two hundred pounds with a strong chest and muscled arms. Simeon took a healthy bite of air, swung his ax a little higher and came down a little harder.

Ed was still by the bucket. "You ah... doing okay since those fevers and chills few weeks ago? You suffering any joint pains or fatigue recently?"

"Do I look tired?" Simeon barely broke stride, but in truth, the Doc had touched a chord. He'd been feeling positively old for weeks. Bah, old age was for sissies, the trick is to keep busy. Those who sit still too much and wallow, those are the ones who curl up and let age overtake them. Ed followed Father's lead and went back to splitting logs.

As he worked, Simeon pictured himself when he first came here. He was only about forty-five then when he'd begged his Order to allow him to live as a hermit on his family's land. His superiors acquiesced, concluding time alone would be helpful to the priest, who lately seemed bent on avoiding the communal life of the Franciscans.

At first Simeon lived in an army pup tent, alone day in and day out, spending himself in almost constant prayer. For his body as well as his spirit, the new hermit worked. He cleared areas, gathering the rocks to build stonewalls, here and there, anyplace really, and for no apparent reason—creating nothing aside from a great outdoor altar to say Mass. Then one day he heard the Holy Spirit whisper on the wind. Wouldn't it be wise to build a chapel? And so began his first building, elegant in its rustic simplicity, log after log, built the old-fashioned way. That's when Ed first showed up. Came at his family's request to check his health and pitched in that very day. Later the Doc's wife, Marge started bringing food and supplies.

Eventually word spread as word does when curious behavior is afoot. Inquisitive Christians made their way to visit him, pick his brain, or hear him preach. Most often, they came to talk about their life or why God put them here.

"You hot?" Ed stopped, leaned on his ax.

"As blazes," Simeon said.

"I'm losing mine, Padre. Try not to get distracted."

"Not to worry, Doc." Simeon laughed lifting his arms to free himself of his wet tee shirt.

Ed's practiced eye squinted at him. "Father, raise your right arm again. Let me see something."

"Oh, you're impressed with my youthful physique," the priest said and raised both arms, flexing some fairly impressive muscle.

"Simeon, this is serious. What is that?" Doctor Holmes reached out to examine the questionable area of a three-inch patch of rashy skin underneath his armpit, a red-ring in a bulls-eye pattern.

"Doc, you're off today." Simeon reclaimed his arm, taking up his ax again. "You don't have to look for patients among these peaceful trees. It's nothing, a bug bite or something."

They finished chopping, drank and doused themselves with water from the creek, then commenced carrying the wood, load after load, stacking it on the pile between the chapel and the cabin. After the last load, Simeon conveyed thanks in the form of a single thump on Ed's thick back. Anything more, anything said would only embarrass his friend.

"Father I can't tell you how much I envy you up here, living this solitude, working, praying," Ed said, brushing bark off his jeans. "I just feel like it's easier on the Mount, easier to hear God, you know?"

"That it is, Ed. That it is." Simeon wiped his brow and looked about wistfully. "But even I'm no island, not alone anymore. God sends more souls every day, doesn't he? I could have gone on in solitude in that tent. Prayer was the only thing I needed; still is.... I hear Him whisper on the wind." Feeling pretty tired, Simeon sat on the edge of the pile of wood and looked at the ground. "You have to be real quiet to listen to the Holy Spirit, Ed, quiet on the inside, the kind that spills to the outside."

"I know what you mean, Father. I, um... I've had that spilling over thing happen at work." Simeon's eyebrow lifted. "Yeah, hard to believe for a busy doctor, but once in awhile, I'll be so united to prayer, my work so focused, my spirit real quiet like you said, my patients all become... I don't know brothers and sisters, even Jesus in disguise, or," Ed gave an embarrassed look. "Or maybe it's...uh, as if I'm healing them and they're healing me. I don't know how to say it, but I *do* get it."

Simeon scratched his tangled whiskers and looked at his treasured friend thanking God for the gift of him—all five foot five, good, honest ball of muscle of him. The way he'd close his practice for a day and just show up, or the way he'd work right next to you and not *need* to talk. Ed got it, he did. He understood how to meditate and pray while expending himself in physical labor, that effort at continual union with the Creator.

Simeon felt flushed, as Doc Holmes bid him farewell for the day. He noted the worried look on Ed's face. He'd been telling him to slow down, and Simeon had been faithfully ignoring him. *Bah! Doctors are like mothers, nags, and worrywarts.*

Dinner was easy. Someone had dropped off a bag of canned goods day before last. Simeon pulled a can off the lone shelf. Still no electricity, but those meddling devotees were all a-buzz with talk of how to make it happen on the hill. He had no control over that merry bunch of faithful followers. At the sink, Simeon pumped some water from the well into a glass. With no ice in the icebox, and in the summer no way to keep milk cold, he had to rely on powdered milk. He reluctantly stirred some of the stuff into his glass. Ed's wife Marge was probably right about him needing calcium. He felt kind of achy lately and bone tired. Simeon swigged the concoction and followed it with the beans eating them straight from the can.

From a hook on the wall, he plucked his cassock and a small towel and headed to Sacred Heart Lake. It was the furthest pond, very private, surrounded by drooping pines, invigorating on a hot day, but murderously cold when the weather turned. Today the black water was exquisite. Simeon returned to the cabin refreshed. He hung his wet things on the rope line and headed for the chapel. The crooked screen door banged behind him. He entered pausing a second to decide if there would be enough daylight left to read his Divine Office prayers or if he would have to light candles. The space was simple, not much longer than it was wide and that a mere sixteen feet. It had one aisle flanked by three short rows of log benches ending in a simple hand-carved altar. A cool scent of evergreens and cut lumber wafted through the open window. No statues as yet, but there was talk, he thought grinning.

Simeon genuflected and retrieved his breviary and reading glasses from a small table. Kneeling in front of the altar, the waning sun cast a glow on the shiny tabernacle. He recited the Liturgy of the Hours, joining his prayers to those of his brother priests and millions of faithful around the world, all praying the same evening prayer. After the final song of praise, which Simeon actually sang in handsome Irish tenor, he fell quickly into a meditative state. In time, he could feel the Spirit take over, sharing his thoughts, guiding, and enveloping him in pure love. Simeon floated pleasantly on the good and perfect Will of his Creator.

In point of fact, Simeon did float some twelve inches off the floor. A phenomena he guessed was happening but would not have confirmed till witnessed one day by a little Vietnamese sister.

Transported in this state, Simeon steadily became aware he was looking at a hand. The hand lay flattened against the pane of a window. The sight was so out of place in his meditation, it made no sense, yet he was conscious of being outside with the hand. It was huge and beautiful. Simeon looked down—bushes, a sidewalk, it was an apartment building, and the window with the hand plastered on it was on the second story. He looked inside—he and the hand a pair of peeping Toms—seeing a bedroom, a girl's bedroom with everything covered in pink. The little girl too wore a frilly pink nightgown and couldn't have been more than six or seven. The little one rolled over looking toward the window. Her eyes widened in fear. At once, the tiny head of golden waves snapped away. Clearly, the hand, splayed palm side down against the pane, had frightened her.

Poor thing! Was it his? Simeon pulled his own hand away, waved it in front of his face, aware he was in the chapel, even somewhat aware he was floating, but floating in two places, outside the little one's bedroom and here in the chapel. Bilocation? His hand was his own, he decided, not the handsome dismembered one on the pane, which ended as naturally at the wrist, as if no forearm had ever been designed for it.

He looked back inside. Where was she? The frilly pink bed was empty. She wasn't by the white painted dresser or closet door. A doll lay on the bed, a white bow stuck to its head, a few boxes and bows with trailing ribbons were piled on the dresser. Was it the little one's birthday?

She returned, coming in the door leading a man by the hand to the window. Her father?

"Dad, can't you see it?" Simeon heard her say.

The dad answered, yet no sound met Simeon's ear. Still it was obvious he didn't see the hand. He led his daughter back to bed and tucked her under the covers. She looked horrified, poor child. Why wouldn't he stay with her? The father kissed her and left. The little girl lay stone still with big green eyes squeezed shut against the image of the hand. Simeon didn't want to scare her, but she wasn't looking at him, she'd only seen the hand.

He watched her while trying to process something. She was... chosen. She was being chosen to bear *him* one day! The revelation barely sank in when a surge of power emanated from the hand and sailed to the figure in the little pink bed. A bright glow of light shone from the girl even as her beautiful eyes remained tightly shut against the hand and its power. She had received it; he could feel it, see it. She was too young to reject it, too pure, really, and too new to understand it.

Was he, Simeon, choosing her, he wondered, or was he merely being shown that she was chosen? He wasn't sure. Did it matter? What did matter? He struggled to think. No, no, no, he was doing it wrong, trying to capture thoughts. He had to let go in this state, empty his mind to understand the Spirit.

He saw it now. She would bear a son one day... on the twenty-fourth day of the sixth month. . . But what year? Not clear, or not being shown that? Again, he told himself to let go. Let the spirit guide him. It came again.

Her son, the son she would bear would need Simeon, need this girl, his mom, just as surely as the world needed her son. This little girl in pink, eyes tight and arms clasping her doll, would bear a great gift, a gift to the world.

"Thank God, praise the Father and Son and Spirit," Simeon released his breath in snippets of praise.

Abruptly, the hand, the pane, the pink room, and the girl vanished. Simeon was jolted away and floated on a blank canvas until the empty white darkened, gradually opening to a new scene.

The first thing he noticed was the man's gray hair with the unexpected streak of black slicked back against angular bird-like features. The man dressed in all black, but he was no priest. Eyes closed, thin lips chanting as his body swayed. Behind him, hooded figures held long black candles, their bodies too waved in unison. The flames of the candles burned in an odd manner, seeming to shed darkness instead of light—none of that brightness or peace of the candles at church. Beyond the robed ones, he could make out the walls, dripping water into frozen calcite popsicles. It's a cave.

Simeon returned to the chiseled countenance of the leader, whose back faced the worshippers. Yes, they were all worshipping something powerful, but nothing worthy of praise. He stared into the undeniably handsome face when the eyes popped open, black and soulless. They flickered for a second, and in that instant, Simeon realized the man was aware of his presence. The look of surprise faded. The comely face glowered back with the mile-deep black of his eyes boring into Simeon's.

Here, he concluded, was his rival and the worst kind of enemy for her child-to-be. Determined to end the magnetic glare, but compelled to study those soulless eyes once more, Simeon forced himself to steel up and look a moment longer.

He must have been meant to do just that. For an instant, deep down in the pools of black, he saw the man as a little boy on a swing. A pretty middle-aged mother smiled and dutifully pushed her little boy. His jet black hair was neat and trim, his scrawny legs pumping as hard as they could, joy all over his face. He turned to look at his mom with love.

"Aaarrggg!"

The scream caught Simeon completely unawares, cutting through him like a sword. A second before the chilling screech made him look away (and slip away), Simeon managed a smile. He sent that knowing smile straight to the evil heart of his newly discovered archenemy.

"I know you," he whispered.

***

Ed Holmes held Margie's hand as they trudged up the steep path to the chapel of the Mount. Quarter after six and fifteen minutes early for morning Mass, but both of them liked time to prepare. Marge was always slightly out of breath at the top. They paused on the tiny stoned area by the front door to let her breath catch up to her short legs. His wife smiled sweetly, always grateful for his attentiveness. She was even shorter and heavier than Ed. After ten children, her worn heart didn't allow for exercise beyond the daily chores of raising their large family. Still Margie worked harder and longer for others than she ever would for herself, Ed thought. Her charity extended far beyond their home and unconditionally embraced everyone who came in her path.

"Oh Eddy, look at that,"—she looked to the clothesline and tsked—"he didn't use the clothespins I gave him. I told him, they'd be wrinkled."

"Well, I tell you, Margie," Ed leaned in, using his most gossipy tone, "it's all the squirrels talk about, his wrinkled work clothes."

"Ed!" She slapped his arm and laughed.

Inside they found nothing lit but the sanctuary light, which was odd since Father was usually there by six to say his morning office before Mass.

"I'll light the candles," Ed whispered to Marge as she settled on the front bench. He lit two candles in back on the wall, two freestanding ones in front, plus the two on the altar. Afterward, he slipped into the tiny side room, which served as a sacristy for the vestments and communion items. Ed counted six hosts from the small plastic bag to be consecrated at this morning's Mass. If one or two more showed up Father could simply break some in two. He placed the wafers in the ciborium, topped it with the paten and linen, and then poured a small amount of wine. These he carried out to the altar.

Still, no Father Simeon. Ed knelt by Marge and both of them turned hearing the screen door. It was Joe Hand and behind him, Anita Perez. Only one more, Joy Webker would probably show up. The five of them were the usuals this summer, although once in while they saw a new face. Come the hot busy months, only a handful came to morning Mass here, although more and more were hearing about Father Simeon and learning of the Mount, so you never know.

Ed checked his watch, 6:22. Marge put her hand on Ed's wrist to see for herself and shrugged. By 6:26, Joy came in and Marge leaned over.

"Eddy, maybe we should check on him."

Ed nodded and held Margie's hand as she genuflected.

Outside Father's cabin door, Ed knocked loudly and waited then knocked again. He called out, "Father?" heard nothing, knocked again, called out several more times then looked at Marge because he was about to invade the privacy of a priest.

"Go ahead," she said with a flick of her hand.

Ed continued to call stepping inside. A second later, he yelled to his wife who had stayed by the door.

"Margie, come quick!"

"Sweet Mother of God!" she shouted, seeing the priest laid out flat on the plank floor.

Ed was already taking his pulse. "He's flushed with fever, unconscious."

"Should I stay with him while you go for help? You're faster than me." Marge said, already recovering. A nurse in The Big One, she was great in a crisis, never fell apart in the four decades he'd known her.

"Yes, remove his sandals. Wet towels and cool him down. Start with his head—"

"Eddy, it may have been forty years ago, but I think I remember how to deal with a feverish patient." She smiled but allowed one worried look to pass her sweet features, "Ed, do hurry."

"I will dear, but we may see this is a blessing, his being unconscious I mean. You know he never would have allowed us to take him to a hospital. I've been telling him for months then last month that drop-dead flu that wouldn't let go, and yesterday—"

"Later dear, tell me later."

Ed took off.

It took the ambulance a full thirty-five minutes to get there and then find the road. Even with Joe, Anita, and Joy standing in the road trying to flag it down, it whizzed by and missed them (or almost hit them, depending on how you looked at it, what with Joy jumping back two feet to spare her toes). On the second pass, they managed to catch the driver's attention, and ten minutes later, the ambulance was racing Father Simeon to *Ideal Hospital* in Endicott.

18

It has Begun

JUNE 24, 2000

The diagnosis for Lyme disease came later. Not until the late 1970's did researchers begin describing the symptoms of Lyme disease to help physicians diagnose the disease. And only in 1982, that the deer tick was identified as the cause. neurological symptoms indicated Father Simeon was in the late stages of the disease. The priest suffered months of numbness in his limbs, disorientation, dizziness, and confusion as the spirochete attacked his nervous system. Aggressive antibiotic therapy began, halting the progress of neurologic damage. Unfortunately for him, the delayed diagnosis meant a much longer recovery period. It took more than a decade for complete recuperation.

Simeon continued on his way from the auditorium to the tiny outdoor garden of the Sister Servants of Mary in the Bronx. It was the feast day of their patron, Saint John the Baptist; he'd just finished the final day of a three-day retreat for the twenty-one white-clad sisters. His long convalescence at the Motherhouse was responsible for that. Too weak to do any physical labor, he gained special permission to spend his time studying the ancient craft of exorcism, ever mindful of the evil he would one-day face. His pastime, (obsession as his peers called it) of demonology and the occult, vials of oils and holy water, mounds of salt and collections of crucifixes, alongside dusty historical books and transcripts of exorcisms overtaking his small cell was more than troubling to his many of his peers. After many a complaints, he was made—under the vow of obedience—to spend his time instead writing of his experience as a hermit. The Franciscan's published his memoirs as a book. Although the book never circulated to any degree beyond religious houses, he found bishops, priests, and heads of orders inviting him to speak or give retreats on the Holy Spirit. This business was a far cry from the quiet solitude he hungered for, Simeon thought walking the spotless halls of the convent.

"Hard to argue with omnipotence," he said, ignoring the tiny Vietnamese sister passing by, who looked startled to see him talking to himself. "Still I should like to repeat my request, Lord, to be allowed to return to my life on the Mount... er, whenever you say," he threw in, as the little sister's white habit whisked by him in the other direction.

Fact was his painful and lengthy recovery had almost closed his beloved Hermitage. While he battled Lyme disease, the Franciscans had difficulty manning Mount Charbel. Without a hermit on the Hermitage, and no daily service, patrons stopped coming, and the Mount was all but closed. The talk of closing in 1990 brought droves of old supporters, who prayed for a way to keep it open. Their prayers were heard when cloistered Marionites from Connecticut, who had the unique and enviable "vocation crisis" of having too many postulants, offered to buy the property. Bishops were consulted, permissions granted, papers signed, and the Mount successfully changed hands.

"Yes," the old priest spoke aloud entering the simple garden space and wishing he'd worn his brown habit instead of the black pants and tight-collared shirt of a priest. "The Marionite monks are perfect for your holy mountain."

Full of burgeoning pear and peach trees, the convent's garden in the center of the Bronx was inviting and deserted this time of day as the sisters prepared to make their house calls. Tonight, as they did every night, each one of the Sisters in this tiny order would sit with a terminally ill patient. Throughout the Bronx, family members would find rest leaving their loved ones under the care of these good women, whose order was dedicated to this limited and specific need.

Simeon found a poor looking bench, as run down as the rest of the sister's leaking convent. These religious, whose very work and living conditions would depress the average person, instead went about with young cheerful faces. Amid peeling plaster and leaking roofs, stepping over puddly floors when it rains, the sisters who rely entirely on donations wait for God to provide a new roof as they focus on the sick and dying. They bear all, withstand all, and live all for Him and his mother. With that thought, Simeon sat straighter, counted the beads of his fifteen-decade rosary, and soon fell into a deep meditative state.

Transported and still holding his rosary, he saw her. She was a grown woman now and so very lovely. The golden waves had turned to soft brown, and instead of the pink nightgown, she wore one of white cotton. She lay in a white hospital bed holding a blue bundle, her radiant face cooing into the blanket, gently touching the pink face. He watched her unwrap the bottom of the cocoon and play with the tiny new toes, as though she couldn't quite believe their perfection. For a split second, she looked to the corner where he knew he stood. For a split second, he thought she saw him. Her head flew down to the blue bundle; her pretty young eyes squeezed shut.

"So he is born!" Simeon rejoiced. "It has begun."

In a flash, he was transported again back to the garden. Barely a moment and the small fruit trees in front of him changed—their green leaves spilled and morphed, no longer confining themselves to just the trees. In front of him, a sheet of water burst forth over the tan bricks, fast being replaced by jagged grey slate. Father's eyes followed the streaming water, crashing in a pile of dancing bubbles and ending in a stream of liquid diamonds.

Simeon realized he was not actually present, at least not as he had been in the hospital room moments ago. This was pure vision, not any kind of bi-location. He took in the trees, enormous and ancient, the green moss and flora almost pre-historic—Eden in a simple forest glen. He saw a blond boy kneeling in obvious rapture, arms open wide, face upturned. Simeon joined the child in ecstasy, but not for long. The boy and forest faded and something enormous materialized in its place.

The face of purest peach was framed by long waves of silken hair blowing gently behind him. The powerful body beneath the smoothest tunic of a shimmering material narrowed to a waist cinched by a gilded cord. Most magnificent of all, the gossamer wings of the being spread as long and wide as the angel himself, emanating light from each perfect downy feather.

Yet, he knew this messenger was pure spirit, and for all the angel's splendor, its form was taken only for Simeon's earthly benefit. The breathtaking image represented well the vast disparity between Simeon's mortal nature and the angel's phenomenal intelligence and power. It was akin to the evolutionary ocean separating an ant from a human being.

Despite the grandeur and magnificence of the being before him, its message was simple:

> *"The child you have seen has the spirit of the Preparer, a second voice crying in the wilderness."*

Had it not been for some Divine assistance at his elbow, which he suspected was his own unseen guardian, Simeon would have fainted dead away. The heavenly voice spoke again assuring Simeon that he would behold the child before his death.

> *"For this you were named, and for this you were chosen. Too, you shall aid in the protection of this child in a way that will be revealed to you, for his enemies are your enemies and mine. Indeed they are the enemies of all who serve God."*

Unknown to Simeon, Sister A'hn, the same little Vietnamese sister, carrying a tray of food for his dinner, had come to look for him in the garden. The Sisters were about to leave for their work and would not return until morning from their keeping vigil with the nearly dead. At first, all Sister A'hn could see behind the evergreen bush was the face and creamy beard of the tall priest, looking even taller than she remembered. She hurried around the path, balancing the full tray while squeezing her red prayer book between her elbow and hip. And there was the priest, not one or two feet taller than her, but at least three. She stared at his black oxfords hovering a full foot above the brick path.

Shocked, Sister's fingers let go of the tray of food, which crashed to the ground splashing noodles and liquids in ten directions. Sister A'hn caught the book just before it joined the tray, her hands gripping it tight. She stared at the suspended priest. A second later, her tiny mouth and full lips cried out in a thick accent.

"Sacred Heart of Jesus, have mercy!"

Father immediately fell from his paranormal loft, barely catching his balance and collapsing on the splintered bench.

"What... where am—" he sputtered then saw the nun. "What's wrong child?"

"Father, you, you were floating, right there, right in front of me." Tears christened her eyes with a mix of wonder and fear. "Father? Forgive me but —"

"Ohhh," he said, understanding her look, and (even if unconsciously) feeling a morsel of relief that someone had finally seen what he had only suspected all these years. He sensed that it occasionally happened, on rare occasion actually, but never had it been confirmed. He knew the levitation meant nothing. Certainly not that he was holy or any better than those he served, like this lovely teary-eyed soul before him.

"It's a miracle, Father Simeon!"

"Sister, sit here." He pointed to the end of the bench and pulled himself up to a more dignified position at the farther end. "We mustn't make more of this than God would intend."

But I saw... I saw you. Oh Father it was miraculous and I know what I saw!"

Her excitement was a warning to him. Simeon paused, immediately settling upon a different tack. "Sister, such a manifestation can occur for many reasons, an outward sign from

God to mimic our hearts rising to Him in prayer, a sign given to show pleasure with the retreat or his little Servants of Mary and their work, even a sign given just to you Sister, uh..."

"A'hn, Father, Sister A'hn Nguyen." She pronounced it *Awn New-wing*, her eyes still wider than usual.

"Sister A'hn you really should keep this incident to yourself. People always jump to conclusions about such demonstrations of God's power. And who is to say,"—he sounded light—"we are not both imagining things."

"My confessor, Father,"—she looked worried—"may I tell him?"

"Oh, yes of course," Simeon agreed without choice, hoping her confessor would disbelieve her. "I suggest you pray first. If you still feel you must share what you *think* you saw with him, leave my name out unless..."—Simeon frowned—"he requires it."

"I will, Father. I promise." He followed her gaze to the overturned tray. Spilled coffee pooled on the brick walk, tuna casserole noodles splayed out from under the metal tray, a few strings decorated the bush like pasta tinsel. She got up, but before she could bend over, Simeon reached for her arm.

"Leave it Sister A'hn, I wish to clean it myself. I will not be responsible for any one of you being late to your work helping those families." She looked about to argue when he raised his brow and tapped his watch. "I wish to be alone Sister. I'm perfectly capable of cleaning a little mess."

She left him then, giving a quick bow, clutching her red prayer book. He watched her snow-white habit billow as she hurried away to her angelic work. Angelic, thought Simeon. What a vision, what a message! It would take time to understand all he had heard, but one thing he knew—it had begun this 24th of June, the year of Our Lord 2000. Her child was born. God's plan had begun.

19

Hide & Seek

Behind the storm door, Jackson waved goodbye to his mom. The school bus next door made a loud beep-beep sound as it backed up. He pressed his nose to the glass for a peek at the bus he wished he were riding. Nicey came around the corner pinning her hair, trapping a wayward wisp neatly in the French twist. She watched Jackson run from the front door to the small bay window, catching one last glimpse before the yellow bus disappeared down the street on its way to a school Jackie could not safely attend. Of course, there were other reasons he could not attend regular school, and it was these Michelle had discussed with the Millers long before September's enrollment.

Jackson finished the preschool program at BOCES in the spring. He should have been enrolled in Kindergarten, except academically, Kindergarten would have been absurd. So she had suggested that Jackson be homeschooled. She showed John and Clarice an accredited program, which provided a challenging curriculum where Jackie could move at his own pace. Clarice voiced a concern about his missing out on the social aspect of school, but Mrs. Nicestrum pointed out several home school groups in the area. The one the Millers joined was well organized with emails to members, newsletters and countless activities, even joint art and gym classes.

Twice a week Jackie spent the day at BOCES where he worked alone for several hours in a quiet corner of Kate's classroom, filling in workbook pages. Afterward he would happily involve himself with the special needs children. The rest of the week Jackie spent almost exclusively with Mrs. Nicestrum or Clarice. He needed little direction, sailing through the curriculum. He excelled in all of his subjects but particularly in reading and comprehension. Little Jackie had an extraordinary gift of communication, simple, strong and succinct. To listeners his words were as clear as their own thoughts.

"C'mon love, let's get you to your studies. Do you have any questions from yesterday?"

"Not really. Nicey, may I do my math on Mom's bed with the TV on?"

"Oh dear, I don't know if that's wise. Do you think you can concentrate with a TV program on?"

"In math it's easy. I wanna watch the news while I do problems."

"Why the news, Jackie?"

"The news is very important, Nicey. People all over the world have problems, and they need someone to help them. They're lost and lonely. A lot of the news is sad, but I'm supposed to know about it."

Supposed to?

"Well, hmm, I suppose we can try it, but when we check your lesson if any problems are wrong then we'll have to go back to no TV. Fair enough?"

While Jackson worked, she went to her room to say her morning prayers. Later when he came out of his parent's room to look for her, she was cleaning up after popping a batch of oatmeal cookies in the oven.

"Nicey, I've been wondering about what all these sayings are in my books. Like this one." He held up his English book, pointed to a blue shaded box.

"Oh, what does it say?" She said, a little distracted, putting the timer on the oatmeal cookies.

"And he brought them to the border of his sanctuary," Jackson read slowly, "even to this mountain, which his right hand had won."

"Oh my!" He had her attention now. "Well, that's from Psalm 78, I believe."

His schoolbooks had a Christian based curriculum. Although Clarice had declined to sign him up for the religion course, much of the other subjects interjected Bible passages within the lessons. Mrs. Nicestrum wiped her hands on the little white apron covering her smart tweed skirt and soft gray sweater. She walked into the adjacent family room, sat on a nearby chair, and patted her lap inviting Jackie to climb aboard.

"I wondered when it might be time for that," she said as she stroked that errant curl and Jackson fondled the pearl chain holding her eyeglasses.

"Whaddaya mean, Nicey?"

"Let's see, you know how your daddy sometimes sits in the morning and reads his book?" She repositioned the boy off her arthritic knee. "That book is the Holy Bible and it is very, very old. Many people read it, just as your daddy does. Nicey reads it too, every night."

"Oh, it sounds very important, but why don't people ever finish it?"

She laughed; for Jackson, you read a book once then moved on to new material. "Oh it's not that they don't finish it Jackie, it's that it holds many, many ancient secrets, truths that one must study and study in order to find happiness and meaning in life."

"What's it about, Nicey? May I read it too?" His aqua green eyes shone with anticipation.

"It is about God, and about why He made us, and why we are here. It also tells about God's Son." She paused for a moment sending a silent prayer for direction in her words. Anything of this nature, she knew, was to be handled by Him alone. He would teach the child, Him alone.

After a brief moment, Jackie stretched up, holding her soft old cheeks in his tiny youthful palms. "It's alright Nicey. I think I can read it by myself."

"Fine, love, you read anything you like out of your dad's big brown Bible. There will be things you won't understand, Jackson. You can ask me or your father about anything that confuses you."

He kissed her and scrambled down from her lap.

"Nicey, will Mom be home by lunchtime? Are you coming with us to see the new house?"

"Yes and no, dear,"—she tapped his button nose—"Yes, Mommy will be here by 11:30, and no, I'm not going with you. I've got my prayer group tonight. I can't chance we won't be home in time. Besides, I want to see it when it's even closer to being done. You can show me then, okay?"

The buzzer went off on the cookies, and Jackie ran to the kitchen to get milk.

When Clarice came home as promised, she and Jackson set out for Ithaca. John was working on the retirement home in Binghamton still inching its way to completion.

The Prelude's front wheel drive easily climbed the hill in Ithaca. How different the road was since that first time they came here! The Town had resurfaced the road with tar and stone. Not a full-fledged paving, but it was more level. Still, she could see her sporty, religiously maintained, and immaculate white car taking a mud bath as she drove. It was late November. The light snow from last night was melting with temperatures hovering around forty.

Clarice was excited as they neared the top. Regular excitement, she thought, none of those strange sensations of that first trip. This was the pure anticipation of seeing the outside of the house completed.

"How you doing back there, honey bear; you cold?" Clarice looked in the rear-view mirror at Jackson.

"No, I'm real warm." His eyes peeped from between the huge blue scarf and thick skullcap. He did look hot, poor guy. She'd overdressed him. The new house had no heat yet, and she had worried Jax would get cold while she made sketches of it.

"How much longer, Mom?"

"We're almost to the top sweetie." He fell silent and looked out the window, the forest whizzing by.

They'd come a long way since the summer. By the end of October, all the outside work was complete, from the siding and roof to the elaborate stonework on the chimneys and porches. Few things had changed from their original plans, just as Clarice had promised.

"There it is!" she sang.

Between the old-fashioned design and the regal oaks, spared a second time, the Miller's new homestead looked as if it had stood for a hundred years. The long driveway, which would eventually be covered in white crushed stone, wound around in a sweeping curve past the front entrance to the side of the house and the detached garage. The garage, which had been cleverly disguised to look like an old carriage house, connected to the house via a breezeway.

"Wow," exclaimed Jackson seeing the house for the first time. They'd kept him away from the site. After the terror of the ordeal on his birthday, John wouldn't let him near any construction.

"Mom, it's huge!"

Gracious *was* the best word to describe their new home, she thought. Built in three sections, six magnificent stone pillars framed an extra wide front porch. Two one-story wings flanked the two-story middle section that had three dormer windows across the top. Each section had its own entrance and steps ascending to the front porch, with the middle steps wider and more prominent. Floor-to-ceiling windows stood on each side of the double oak doors, which Clarice had found while antiquing. John had rescued the long shutters from a demolition project, and Clarice finished them in the same rich walnut color of the doors.

She parked the car on the circular drive in front of the center stairs. Jackson freed himself without waiting for the usual permission and ran excitedly up the rightmost stairs, peeping in the French door to the east wing. That sunny, empty space with soaring ceilings and skylights must have proved uninteresting for he ran along the porch to the main entry and jiggled the brass handle on the solid oak door.

"It's locked, Mom," he yelled down to Clarice still standing behind the car enjoying the whole view.

"I know," she yelled reaching in the car for her sketchpad and pencil. "I'm coming with the keys, but you can't go inside the house without me. There's a lot of tools and nails and stuff around."

Jax looked in the window by the front door at the curving wood staircase leading to somewhere yet to be explored then continued along the porch to the French door of the west wing. Same cathedral ceiling as the other wing, but this side was clearly the kitchen. Some of the cherry cabinetry had been hung on both sides of the long room, and a huge porcelain farm sink, a coup from an estate sale, stood ready to install under the kitchen window.

"C'mon Mom, hurry!" Jax called, his nose still pressed to a windowpane on the kitchen door.

Clarice opened the front door and stood in the generous foyer. The house smelled of sawdust. "It's open," she yelled. In seconds, he tore past her up the stairs.

"Hey, slow down. I told you it's not safe. Wait for me." He obeyed standing at the top of the stairs looking down at her.

"Which one's mine?" he asked when she reached the top step. She took his hand, walked toward the room on the right of the squarish hall. Jackson ran to the dormer window at the end of the bedroom and knelt on the cute window seat, looking out at the front yard.

"Hey, there's a neat secret right underneath you," she told him.

"Huh? What?" He noted the hinges on the seat, jumped off to open the lid. "What's that for?"

"Your toys."

Jax peeped out the octagon window that looked over the roof of the west wing, took one look in the empty closet, then zipped out the door. Clarice followed him, their feet echoing on the plywood floor. He made quick work of the space for the bathroom and landed in the smallest room at the back.

"Whose room is this, Mom?" he asked, standing by the long picture window that overlooked the woods beyond.

"Oh, your father and I figured we would use it for lots of things: the treadmill, dad's weights, my sewing and ironing, and maybe even some of your toys. Jax stared out the window at the forest. Clarice joined him, her thoughts wandering back to the Glen and that first day on the land. The woods looked bare this time of year with only a layer of snow to clothe the naked limbs. What would that magical place look like now? A chill shot up her arms as she noticed Jackson, still as night, staring out the window. Her heart skipped a beat. He hadn't had an incident for months that she knew of. Unless... Nicey hid episodes from her, the way she had shielded John last time.

"Jax," she said and put her hands on his shoulders holding an unconscious breath. He broke his stare to look up at her. "C'mon champ," she said in an exhale, "let's check out the rest of the house."

Plenty of afternoon sun filled the master bedroom. It was identical to Jackson's room, but the space was much longer and included a large walk-in closet and a master bath with tub and shower. Instead of the oh-so required whirlpool, they'd installed the largest antique claw foot tub they could find.

"Look Mom, a window in the roof!" Clarice looked up at the skylight, a feature both John and she wanted despite its undesirable appearance.

"Guess what?" She knelt and placed her arm around his waist giving him a hug. "At night we'll be able to see the stars and moon like in the planetarium at Kopernick."

Downstairs they turned left, walked through the tiny dining room then out to the Great Room—the huge area at the back of the main house that would become their family room. Piles of colorful fieldstone lay in the corner next to the half-constructed floor to ceiling fireplace. It would be magnificent when complete. In the short hall to the east wing, they passed the laundry room.

John had won that one, she thought, but he put in a neat laundry chute so it wouldn't be bad here. They took in the long, empty space that would hold her art studio and John's office then headed back, passing through the Great Room to the kitchen. Jax picked up a heavy staple gun turning it over in his hands.

"Oh my gosh, put that down!"

"Aw, Mom it's not plugged in."

"Look here, mister, it has a battery pack, see." She took it from him. Clarice looked about the kitchen strewn with power tools: a table saw, two drills, a circulating saw, a saws-all, and at least three nail guns, and two tools she couldn't name. "Well, this isn't going to work. Let's go outside, so Mommy can make a sketch or two."

Outdoors sketchpad in hand, Clarice stood a good distance back from the house while Jackson walked along the dirt drive, checking out the garage. Ignoring the chill, her pencil flew expertly over the paper. Without a doubt, the most outstanding feature of this noble residence was the stonework, giving the house a retreat like character. Stone clad were the six massive pillars, the two chimneys, and the base of the porch; Clarice drew a fortress of enduring strength.

The stones they used were actually harvested from the dig. John called them his spoils. Mike had another name for them since he and the guys had to spend umpteen hours pulling them from the excavated soil. Although John hired a local stone artisan to oversee the work, Mike, Clarice, and he took pride in choosing and organizing the stones. John used the leftovers to line some crude paths from the house to the garage and shed. So plentiful was the stone that he had even begun a path toward the thick woods beyond.

Clarice became lost in the joy of her work. After a bit, the sketch of the house came alive and was soon done. She held the pad out from her, satisfied with the product.

"Jax, Jax," she called. No answer. He was probably around back and couldn't hear. Clarice walked to the car, threw the sketchpad and pencil in the backseat, then followed the driveway around to the garage. "Jackson!" Still no answer. This wasn't like him. Maybe he was in the garage. He wasn't. From inside the garage, she followed the breezeway back to the mudroom leading to the kitchen. Clarice jiggled the door handle. It was locked, so he hadn't come this way. Still he might be in the house. She fumbled for house keys, sticking one after another in the keyhole. *Good Lord!* Why did we put so many doors on this house? Her nervousness grew. "Jackson, Jackson."

At last, one of the keys worked. Clarice called again and again flying through the empty rooms, checking the upstairs last. Finally, she ran out the front door, across the porch and leapt off the side, dispensing with steps. Straight ahead at a right angle to the garage, stood the unfinished shed about 100 meters away. It had no door and looked empty; still she sped to check it out.

On the floor of the shed lay the workings of the garage door opener ready to be installed. Clarice stared at the pieces, the control box, a giant spring, and heavy metal bar. A cold tremor ran through her, seeing a sort of blackness about the parts for a moment; then it was gone. *That was weird,* she thought, shaking the feeling and checking behind the uninstalled garage door leaning against the wall. Jackson was nowhere in sight.

Clarice followed the stone paths John had begun searching for his footprints in the muddy ground. *None.* If he came this way, he had stayed out of the mud. *Oh God,* she warned him about getting muddy. What if he was being so careful he wasn't leaving any prints? She remembered the way he'd stared out of the upstairs window at the woods. What if the Glen called to him the way it had to her? He could be out there... all alone. She found the path of stones John had begun. This time she saw his prints right off. Jax had gone to the woods after all.

Clarice cursed herself for not thinking to forbid him. He wouldn't have gone if she had only said not to wander. Terry's ugly words haunted her; she *was* too messed up to be a good mom. She *knew* that forest might have the same effect on Jax. What kind of mother is so lost in her work, she would forget to watch her only child? She beat herself up with every step, tears making it difficult to see his footprints. John's stones had run out and she continued toward the thicker woods over the field reeds and crunchy snow.

"Jackson, Jacksonnnnn," Clarice screamed, her heart racing with fear. Stopping to listen, she heard a tiny voice on the wind and on the ground saw little prints this way. A bit further, she paused to yell again.

"Mom?"

Clarice heard him a ways off but definitely up ahead. Sure of her direction, she ran oblivious of the rough terrain and tripped on a rock. Her nose broke her fall, and blood trickled out. Clarice got up wet with snow and continued calling. This time she was rewarded with the sight of her son. He stood in front of an enormous oak with a stone in his hand, carving something into the tree.

"Sorry, Mom," he said, dropping the stone. Clarice was too relieved even to look at what he'd carved in the tree.

"Oh my God," she cried. "I was scared to death. Don't ever, ever—" She fell to her knees and hugged him to herself. After a moment, he pulled away.

"Mom, you're bleeding!"

"Oh," Clarice reached a hand up to her face then examined her blood-streaked fingers. She held her nose pinching her septum. "I'm all right," the words sounded strange. "Any chance you have a tissue?" Without a word, he left her side heading back toward the woods. "Hey, hey, where you going? Come back here."

Jax turned back, "It's okay, Mom. This tree has some leaves you can wipe your nose with." He headed to a tree not ten feet from them with big yellow leaves still hanging from it and brought her back a surprisingly supple leaf.

"Thank you, sweetie."

"You sound funny, Mom."

She looked at her son in no mood for silliness. "You scared mommy," she said softly, not sounding accusatory but matter of fact, still feeling the brunt of her guilt in not watching him properly.

"I didn't go too far, and I didn't get muddy. See." Jax showed her his wet sneaks, indeed relatively mud free.

"I know honey bear, that's good, but you shouldn't go off alone. The woods are dangerous."

"No they're not!" He sounded sure. He turned away from her and stared at the dark forest. "Can't you feel it Mom? It's safe."

"I was worried about you."

"It's alright, Mom. It's not time yet."

These words should have elicited the most obvious question. Instead, as Clarice looked at him, her conscious mind registered but one fact: he was safe! That was all that mattered—not the involuntary shudder that ran down her spine at his words: *It's not time yet.*

She let the comment lie there where he had spoken it—in the woods with all the other secrets that ancient forest held.

20

Saint Elizabeth's

March 2006

John lay on the cold wood floor getting his bearings. Man, was he sore. Last night had been one of those fevered efforts to finish a job that probably could have waited except for his excitement. It was close to done, or so he thought when the guys left at six. They had been putting in the cherry wood floors, a beautiful but damnable wood to work with. Could have chosen Pergo—easy, durable, and clean—but the mill had all this cherry for a steal, and he preferred the real deal anyway.

Rolling over John felt every bone in his body. He'd crashed on the dining room floor exhausted from mitering into the wee hours. The plastic on top of him had been a good idea—Mike's huge rolled up work coat, not so much. He rubbed the indents on his face from the buttons. Dang, was it cold. Outside as a March wind blew snow against the window, he kicked the plastic off and rose to turn up the new thermostat.

Then it hit him, CHURCH! It was Sunday; he had to get to Mass. He should have driven home last night. He had no idea where to find a Catholic Church, let alone Mass times. He dialed home praying for reception on his cell. Hit and miss up here, they'd made little progress in getting the phone company to continue the line. It was ringing. He waited for Clarice to pick up and thought of how easy this would have been three years ago. Before his conversion, he would have missed Mass with little or no compunction, telling himself he had a perfectly legitimate excuse. Now, a born-again Catholic, he devoutly followed every precept of his faith—not as a rule but out of love.

Clarice answered.

"John, for Pete's sake," Clarice said, "why didn't you just come home?"

"Honey, wait till you see these floors! I finished the last board about three AM. They're ready for stain."

"You didn't even call—"

"I know, I know, I'm sorry. It was so late, and then I couldn't stop." He heard Jackson in the background asking if it was daddy. "Listen, Reece, I need a Mass, a Catholic Church in Ithaca. Can you look online for me?" He heard her breathe, detecting a slight exasperation, as her fingers clicked on the laptop in their kitchen.

"Did he forget, mom? Did he?"

"What's Jax saying?"

"Well,..." She laughed. "You tell me."

Silence.

"John, really?"

"What? What are we talking about?"

"You're sumpin big guy. It's only your 35th birthday, that's all."

"Oh man, I totally forgot!" Jax said, "Dad" in the background and he guessed he was sitting on the counter top as his mom googled. "Do we have... uh, plans?"

"I'm not telling," she lilted. "Just be home by six; wait, make that five. Okay, you ready?"

John found a pencil stub and scrawled the address on the instruction sheet from a light fixture box.

Clarice had found a ten AM Mass at a church called Saint Elizabeth's not too far from the satellite office in town.

Easy to find, Saint Elizabeth's of monstrous pink sandstone in classic gothic style, sat atop a small hill outside Ithaca. After pulling into the lot, he ascended cascading steps to the huge bronze doors with five minutes to spare before Mass. Inside the church was equally traditional. John's gaze followed the flying buttresses on the vaulted ceiling ending in a ribbed dome over the nave. In front of him three aisles parted, a sea of dark pews ending at the marble altar. John knelt in a center pew, feeling conspicuous in his saw-dusty work clothes, wishing he'd chosen one of the tiny side pews.

He searched for the tabernacle to pray, seeing nothing in the center but a giant chair for the priest and no telltale sanctuary light. He noticed people genuflecting before entering their pew—out of habit, he guessed since the Real Presence was nowhere to be found. Perhaps the tabernacle is in a separate chapel somewhere. He frowned.

The Mass was great and especially the young priest's sermon. He listened to the words of the slightly overweight priest with the boy-scout looks. Rich in theology, the homily held the same ardent zeal John had experienced in his conversion. The closing hymn played, and the priest, who looked like a chubby Fox Mulder, processed to the back of the church and stood in the doorway.

John got stuck in the line of parishioners waiting to shake hands with the young priest. Self-conscious in his work clothes, he planned to escape as soon as he reached that point in the crowd where he could slip out to the side door. He was about to scoot across the empty pews when a middle-aged man in a camel overcoat stuck out his hand.

"You're new here aren't you?" he said as John reluctantly met the grip with his calloused, none-too clean hand.

"Um, yeah, actually I was working on our new house." John reclaimed his hand and brushed his work coat. "Sorry, I'm covered in sawdust. I'm John Miller, Miller Construction. We're moving here soon."

"Collin Banks. Construction, huh? Good business to be in right now. You got kids?"

"One."

"You're gonna love this new pastor, Father Tom O'Donell, fresh out of the seminary. He's a Steubenville boy. You know that college?" John's face was vacant. "Well, he's on fire, let's just say that. Anyway, he loves kids. Just look at him." Closer to the door now, John saw the priest pull the ponytail of a little girl and deliver a fake punch to her brother's abdomen.

John still managed to slip out the side door as planned. Getting in the car, he decided Saint Elizabeth's would be his new church when they moved. Not only was it relatively close, but with this Father Tom there, it seemed the best place to go each Sunday. Leaving the lot with nothing but a hot shower on his mind, two words jumped out of nowhere: paperwork and answering machine. He banged the steering wheel and turned back downtown toward the office.

On the sidewalk outside Miller Construction's new home base, John wrestled with his key, feeling exhausted from last night's marathon and wishing like mad he'd taken care of this business on Saturday. He let himself in through the glass door to the overpriced space. *High rent, low square footage, good location on a busy side street—one out of three ain't bad.*

John looked about, satisfied. The office was much neater than he'd left it. Not only did his pretty little wife organize the files, but she'd already added a few touches, too. Two sturdy metal desks stood on each side of the room, one his and the other for whomever they hired to answer phones and fill out paperwork. Two plastic lawn chairs sat in front of his desk for visitors. Have to replace those ASAP when they officially open. Clarice had added plants and a few paintings. *Things were shaping up.*

Fiddling with the answering machine, he heard a tapping on the glass. Outside stood a tall, graying man with the archetypal ponytail and tie-dye shirt of a middle-aged hippie. John opened the door to the friendly face.

"So I saw you inside and figured I'd say hey," the man said, his hands in his pockets. "I guess we're neighbors. I'm Ken Willis; I own the coffee shop next door."

"Bookworm Joe's?" John asked.

"That's the one. Mostly we sell coffee and sandwiches, but there's this book and art thing going on too. So you up and running?"

"Not exactly, we've got a foot in both worlds, finishing a couple projects in Binghamton..." John trailed off noticing Ken admiring the painting over his desk, the one of a gauzy spirit sailing over a meadow stream with outstretched arms.

"Totally unique. You know the artist?" Ken asked.

"Only in the biblical sense," John said. "My wife gave it to me on our first anniversary; said our love was like flying."

"Whoa, so like that's her soul high on love or something?" Ken leaned in closer examining paint strokes then slowly withdrew a few steps, still gazing. "Does she have a studio? I would loooove to see more."

John showed Ken two small paintings on the opposite wall. "Fresh," Ken said then cocked his head, "Say would your wife be interested in showing her work in Bookworm's? We like to encourage local artists." Ken was intense, a close talker when he wasn't admiring the art. Slightly taller than John, he leaned in to him like John was the last soul on earth. It was a little disconcerting—but the guy was so sincere.

"John, it's like this. I joined a small group of art lovers, and we founded IPAS, Ithaca Promotion of Art Society. We, ah, pass our love of art along. Witty, huh?" John had to step back, the closeness too awkward. "We get local businesses to promote new talent by displaying their art. It's a beautiful thing, John. The artists get exposure, and the public get to see art in all these unexpected venues." He stopped, nodding his head like he was listening to music.

"Nice," John moved back another half inch. "I'm pretty sure Clarice would be interested."

"We'll have room for say... twenty of your wife's works first week of May. IPAS requires at least three weeks commitment, but I prefer four. See, the only reason I have an opening is on account of a cancellation," Ken said and thankfully allowed John to keep a polite distance. "Young guy moving to Boston, can't blame him. Name's Seth Edwards. His drawings are like primitive with a purpose, kind of hard to describe. I kid him about it. Call 'em cave drawings."

Ken moved back across the room to view the flying spirit painting again. John let out a stifled yawn and studied the grey ponytail deciding the guy was likeable, despite or maybe because of his intensity. Ken turned back around and continued, "I've shown his stuff before.... Annny-whooo, Seth got an incredible scholarship to complete his masters at the Boston Museum of Fine Arts School. I guess the Masters will come through Tufts University. Part of his scholarship involves actual work at the museum. So, like I said, can't really fault the guy for pullin' out on me."

John eventually learned a few more details about the proposed art show and promised to have Clarice call Ken. After his visitor left, John looked at Ken's card with its logo of an open book propped in front of a steaming mug of coffee, like the mug was reading the book. It was cool but humorous, interesting like Ken. The date on the back of the card in Ken's writing said Sunday, May 7. John rapped the card twice on the desk. Hitting the lights and locking up, he thought of the news he had for Clarice. He jumped in the Blazer certainly looking forward to dinner and the expected homemade cheesecake, but just as certain, he looked forward to bringing home a surprise of his own: *Reece's first art show!*

21

Rude Awakenings

It took nine months to build the house and finish the inside. That fall and winter went like a whirlwind with John spending more than half his time in Ithaca, and Clarice working on the house, buying fixtures, and helping with the Binghamton Office. She gave her notice at work and trained a replacement. She was relieved when The Journal offered her freelance work. Now she could work from home, pursue her painting, and enjoy more time with Jackson. It was the end of March. They were moving in two weeks.

Despite his intellect, Jackson was still a boy, not even six, yet. He seemed oblivious to the sadness of leaving the only home he had ever known, oblivious to leaving his neighborhood, his little friends, and even BOCES where he loved to help, but standing in the kitchen doorway still bundled in his snowsuit and mittens after sleigh-riding at Highland Park with his dad, her little boy was devastated.

"Nicey's my protector. You can't take me away from her." Jackson remained in the doorway. Clarice turned from the counter where she was pouring hot chocolate mix into mugs, a reward, which followed sleigh riding in the Miller household as day follows night. Squatting by Jackson, she searched John's face, but John merely shrugged and upheld his palms in defeat.

"Daddy and you were talking about the move?"Jackson could only nod before he threw himself into his mother's arms sobbing. "C'mon, honey bear; let's get you out of this suit. We'll talk about it while we drink our hot chocolate."

Clarice tossed the wet things in the dryer, swiped a towel over the wet spot by the backdoor, then joined John and Jax sitting at the table. Jackson's head was down, and his red hands cradled his cup for warmth. He looked up at them through teary eyes.

"Aw, honey bear,"—Clarice slung the dishtowel over her shoulder and rubbed his arm—"you've known we're moving. We've been up to see the new house being built. You even helped Mommy pick out your curtains and the light for your new bedroom. Didn't you ever think about leaving Mrs. Nice—"

"No! No, she's apposed to come with us. She would never leave me." Jackson's lower lip quivered while he struggled to hold back more tears. "But Dad says she's not." He shot his father a look.

"He asked about where her new house would be," John said, "and I had to set him straight. Bud, she can come visit, and we'll be able to visit her too. It's only 45 minutes to Ithaca."

"NO, she has to watch over me, not just visit. She has to keep me safe!" He spoke with a calm firmness, as if he were teaching a preschooler about road safety. "She knows me and *them*. She never lets them near me."

John gave Clarice a puzzled look. She felt uncomfortable as some nagging ball rolled in the pit of her stomach. Staring at her son's golden curls, she knew who he meant. *Them, Them!*... She pictured the gym in senior high, the biggest game of the year. Mrs. Hanson, the hospice nurse, had come to check on her dad. The nurse knew the situation with Clarice's mom, knew about the big basketball game too. She practically forced Clarice out of the apartment for the night. She remembered enjoying the game, laughing, feeling free and gloriously normal when she... saw... *Them*. She'd been having such a good time, she hadn't even noticed the swoosh feeling or felt herself slip to the other side. Everything dark in the gym came to life, and each fiendish organism knew she could see... *them*... *Them* flying towards her, bearing down, her-- running, screaming to escape *Them*, ...*Them*! *Oh Baby*, Clarice cried in her mind, *Mommy knows what you mean.*

But it's all in your mind, sweetie. You have to fight it. Fight with your mind. Fight Them!

Jackson's head snapped up, his wet eyes searched hers for a moment when John physically turned Jackson's chair to face him.

"Whadda ya mean them?," John asked him. "Jackie, has someone tried to hurt you?" Jackson's chair squeaked as John turned it to face him and looked Jax in the eye.

Clarice thought she'd throw up if John dug too deep. She stood abruptly. "John, I think we should wait. Talk to Mrs. Nicestrum about this." She tilted her head toward the living room and walked. John patted Jackson's curls and followed her leaving him at the table with his hot cocoa.

Clarice walked till she reached the front door and stopped. "It's probably nothing," Clarice said, pulling the rag off her shoulder. "Just a feeling he has that Nicey's the only one who can watch him. We should explain it to Mrs. Nicestrum, and she can probably ease the transition. You know she has a way with him."

"Don't you think we should ask him why he's using words like protect or save?"

No, I don't, Clarice thought but said, "He's five, John, he doesn't know —"

"He's a genius, Reece; He knows exactly what he's saying, and I want to know why he said it."

"No, John, he's upset; he's really hurt. I think Nicey should talk to him first." Clarice swiped the top of the console table with the towel, hoping she looked nonchalant. The last thing in the world she wanted to happen was for Jackson to explain himself to John. What if John changed toward him, the way her mom had towards her? It was bad enough with the trance—those couldn't be hidden—but if Jackson admitted to seeing things, things that weren't really there, things normal people don't see....

She looked down at the table not speaking, aware John was watching her.

"Fine, okay," he said, giving in to her silence.

John called Jax into the living room to pick out a movie, and Clarice returned to the kitchen to make popcorn. They liked it when she made it the old-fashioned way, the way her dad taught her. She busied herself getting out oil, popcorn, butter, and a pot. She tore the top half off of a brown grocery bag, snapping it open to accept the hot kernels. All the while, her mind was preoccupied with Jackson's words.

Really, the only time he was away from them was when he was at BOCES. Clarice vaguely remembered something odd about their decision to send him to BOCES. Before they chose a preschool, she had asked a few co-workers at The Journal if they knew of any programs appropriate for a gifted child. Brookhaven stood out. Her boss among others had highly recommended it. She pushed the popcorn pot back and forth over the gas flame, remembering how Mrs. Nicestrum had shaken her head, vehemently questioning the choice.

"No. It's no good. He won't be safe there."

"What's wrong with Brookhaven?" Clarice had asked.

"Dear, Jackson will be safe at BOCES surrounded by good people."

Clarice remembered thinking at the time that she had meant safe from Mensa-types fouling up his natural development, or maybe safe from New Age or experimental programs, or whatever, but not physically safe. Now, she wondered. The incident at Otsiningo Park last summer jumped to her mind. He wasn't safe then, and she knew it. *It wasn't real,* she told herself, *the swarm of bees that was all. Oh come ON!,* an alter ego played devil's advocate in her head. What about *Waterman Clinic* and then his birthday, and that bizarre attack? Why would anyone want to harm him? Were these crazy men connected to the black swarm? Do she and Nicey protect him somehow, and from—

"Reece, what are you doing?" John yelled, grabbing the handle of the pot from Clarice's hand. "Man, can't you smell it?"

"What? I—I didn't . . ." She watched as John held the pot over the bag and dumped the burnt contents. A layer of black kernels stuck to the bottom of the pot. John used a wooden spoon to try and loosen them. Smelling the charred kernels, her mind took note of the waste. "I'm sorry. I don't know what's wrong with—"

"Well this pot is history. I don't see how that stuff'll ever come off of there!" He sounded annoyed.

"Dad, why don't we make the microwave kind? Mom keeps it up there." Jackson pointed. "S'okay, Mom. The butter's not burnt."

Clarice looked at the glass bowl of melted butter with no memory of melting it, let alone taking it out of the microwave. *Crazy woman! I'm a crazy woman,* she thought and sighed. "I guess I'll lose my license to pop corn, huh?"

John put a bag in the microwave, threw the burnt corn, pot and all, in the brown bag, then lifted the window over the sink. "Open the door, Jax. We'll air the house out." Clarice hadn't moved or lifted a finger. John slid his hand across her back, turning her from the stove and pointing her in the direction of the hall. "You're not fired, but you need a sabbatical. Go take a hot bath. You've been working too hard."

No argument there, she thought. She'd been working incredible hours to get things ready for the move. In the tub, running the hot water, Clarice forced herself to occupy her mind with nit-picky details of the move only weeks away.

* * *

It was the day before the big move, and everyone was busy all morning. Mrs. Nicestrum had done her best to prepare Jackson for the separation, and whatever magic she used was at least effective in calming his fears. He seemed more at ease knowing that his mom would be staying home with him from now on instead of going to the office to work every day. Mrs. Nicestrum, who'd been helping with a hundred and one things, was in the living room alone with Jackson so they could say their goodbyes.

It was meant to be a very private moment, and Clarice and John left the living room in deference to that. John was out in the garage puttering on some last minute cleaning there. He'd swept the floor and hosed it down, and was busy removing as many oil stains as possible. He wanted the Steeles to move into a clean house, and that included the garage floor.

Clarice finished the laundry in the basement and carried the folded load upstairs to pack. She did not intend to listen in, but standing at the top of the basement stairs, laundry basket in hand, she heard Nicey speaking to Jax. The basement door, which opened into the kitchen, blocked Clarice from their view. She still worried how hard her baby would take this last goodbye. So she stood there quietly eavesdropping on the touching scene.

"You know I love you very much Jackie."

"I know it, but..."

"I know you are afraid, but you must believe me when I tell you my time with you is at an end. I have done what was intended. Since you were born, I have watched over you, and we have kept you safe. You must believe you will continue to be watched over. A plan will unfold. Meanwhile you know you are safe with Mommy and Daddy. They have been given very strong auras, even if they do not understand their part yet." Mrs. Nicestrum's voice rose and became very firm. "You need to remain with one, or the other until another guardian is sent for you. Promise me. Promise."

"Uh, I will, I will, but... I love you."

Clarice imagined them in an embrace. She heard the regal voice, "There, there, Luv. I know, I know."

Auras, guardians? Had she heard right? Somehow, she knew it was all too real. She'd always felt as though a part of herself were protecting Jackson. So many times there had been an inexplicable feeling of something threatening them, something bad,... no, evil. Exhausted, Clarice lay her head against the basement door, dwelling on Mrs. Nicestrum's words. *What guardian? Who*? The smell of chlorine and laundry detergent tickled her nose. The fresh laundry reminded her of dozens of tasks still to accomplish, and Clarice in typical fashion shook her head to order it to quit thinking. "Later, think about that later," she whispered in the dark taking the last step and continuing down the hall to pack for the move.

22

Miracle

A wispy cotton streak inched its way across the skylight above Clarice. It still felt unreal waking up in this huge house. High ceilings, tons of new furniture, spacious rooms, their dream come true! Not that they hadn't worked their fannies off to finish it! She had slaved like a madwoman, painting every room, every doorway and sash, staining and polyurethaning all the woodwork. Made your head spin just thinking how much they had accomplished. A lot of changes, a lot...

"C'mon Mom, we're hungry." Jax yelled, his feet tapping down the oak staircase.

"Okay, okay," she said, stretching and leaned to slap John's backside over the covers. "Hey sleepy, scrambled eggs or waffles?"

"Umm, both" John mumbled from his cave under the down comforter.

Clarice slid out of bed and headed to the shower wishing she could loll in the claw foot tub. She'd been working double-time getting pieces ready for her first show, but the excitement over showing them was more than making up for the stress. She donned her favorite jeans and the new shirt from Express. High was only going to be fifty—unseasonably cold, even for May. The chunky Aran cardigan with big brown buttons Roxie had brought back from Ireland was appealing. A little kitschy but... She resisted the urge to re-think the casual choices. It was a college town, and she didn't want to look old or prissy at the coffeehouse slash bookstore. Plus from what John said, the owner Ken Willis was something of a hippie.

After a huge Sunday breakfast, to which she'd added bacon and biscuits, John helped her clear the table and pile the dishes in the sink.

"I'm bringing Jax to ten o'clock Mass with me at Saint Elizabeth's," he said. "We'll meet you at the bookstore around noon for lunch."

"Oh... um, I—" she said, turning on the water.

"Reece, we already decided Jax'll be too bored to stay with you while you set up for the show."

"Oh, I know... I just thought he'd stay at home with you."

He reached over her already wet hands to flip the water off. "I'll get these; we need to get your car loaded or you'll be late." He handed her a dishtowel. She left the kitchen walking around to the dining room where they had carefully placed her paintings— seventeen in all, most 16x20's the rest smaller and one large one like the spirit woman. They worked carefully placing the canvas bag covers she'd made over the pieces and carrying them out to the Prelude parked out front. Clarice thought about church the whole time.

Jackson hadn't been to a church since he was baptized in a Presbyterian one and again at their wedding—not that she had a problem with religion per se... *well maybe I do*. Raised Presbyterian, she had basic Christian beliefs, Baptism, Jesus, sin, heaven and hell, but the Martins never practiced any formal religion beyond services on Christmas and Easter Sunday. What little she knew of religion, or God for that matter, made no sense to her. Religion was kind of a non-subject for her. She watched John fold down the backseat and fit the wooden contraption he'd made for her to separate the paintings. His strange conversion three years ago and his new obsession with everything Catholic was a real mystery.

"Do you have to go to church *every* Sunday? Why can't you just skip it and stay home with Jax?"

"What's the big deal Reece?"

"He's too young to understand all that sitting, standing and kneeling stuff." She moved in front of him to slip a painting into the car. John slid strong arms around her waist and kissed her neck.

"Jax can have some dad time, and I promise not to allow any men in black abduct him. *Here come the men in black....*" He launched into his famous falsetto then crucified Will Smith's rap.

> *"The good guys dress in black, remember that.*
> *Just in case we ever face to face and make contact*
> *The title held by me —M.I.B."*

Clarice huffed and wheezed, twisted around in his arms. "Uncle! Uncle. Anything you say."

"You sure? Cause I got more—"

She held her finger to his lips. "No, it's fine, I promise. You're right; I'm being stupid. I'm going to set up my art show, and you take Jackson with you. You can even pray for me; you know, 'God forgive my heathen wife, she knows not what she is missing.'"

After Clarice drove off, John called Jackson. They washed and dried the breakfast dishes together then headed upstairs to get ready for Church. John chose an outfit of khakis with a pullover sweater for Jackson and helped him get dressed. Then they crossed the hall to the master bedroom. Jackson watched while his father laid out navy dress slacks and a blue oxford shirt on the bed. Then he took off without a word as John headed for the shower. John was looping his belt when Jax returned dressed in his own little blue oxford shirt and dark pants. He roared, scooped his little man up, and spun him around.

Pulling into Saint Elizabeth's lot next to a budding crabapple tree, John spoke solemnly, "We don't talk in Church."

Jax mimicked John's serious tone, "What DO we do?"

"You can unbuckle, wise-guy. Just do what I do."

The twosome climbed the cascading steps and fell in line with other parishioners filing in through the heavy bronze doors. Jackson's hand slipped out of his, darting forward forcing his little body through an elderly couple ahead of them, and around a small family. He stood awestruck in the center aisle. John quickly caught up to him, reclaimed his tiny hand, and led him to his usual side pew in the back of the church.

Jackson imitated him kneeling in the two-man pew. After a brief prayer, John sank back waiting for the organ to signal the beginning of Mass. No sooner had he sat, than Jackson abruptly popped out of his seat and tore down the side aisle. He sailed past the first pew and plopped himself at the foot of the side altar. The small marble altar (and its complement on the other side of the church) rested in an arched, recessed niche. In the wall above each was a gold door to an old-fashioned tabernacle. Jackson sat on the stoop holding himself as close as he could to the marble structure, pressing his curly head and soft cheek against it.

John watched momentarily stunned. Embarrassed, he got out of the pew, walked with slow— he hoped dignified —steps to the front of the church. Faces of amusement and pity met John's eyes. Looking at Jackson's frozen smile, he thought a few of them might be thinking his son was special. Everyone looked at least sympathetic. Everyone that is, except the priest, Father Tom, who had been placing the cruets of water and wine on a small side table in preparation for Mass.

Father's dumbfounded look confused John. Was he really that shocked by the behavior of a child—inappropriate or not? He loves kids. His expression made no sense. Uncomfortable John approached his son while the priest stared, motionless, the water and wine vessels poised in front of him.

John crouched in front of Jackson, whose green were eyes open but not seeing. His heart skipped a beat. This could be another episode. John placed his hand on Jackson's shoulder and whispered his name. Jackson's eyes came to focus on John's, and his small voice cried.

"It's him; it's the helper! He's in here, Dad."

John released an unconscious breath, relieved it wasn't a trance. His relief washed over his son's words, effectively blanking them out.

"Jax, we have to sit down. You have to come with Daddy back to our pew. You can't come up here. This area is for the priest and altar servers." John knew he only had to say so once, for Jackson was nothing if not obedient. In fact, his obedience was so immediate and complete they sometimes took it for granted without noticing how unusual it was compared to other children.

Back in the pew, Jackson sat dutifully but stared to the front at the old side altar. Mass proceeded as usual, except that Father Tom seemed distracted. At Communion, John held Jackson's hand, and they walked in line toward the priest, who held the chalice of hosts, uttering, "The Body of Christ," over and over to each communicant, who answered, "Amen" as the priest placed a host in their cupped hands. One after another received while the organist played the familiar old tune, "Lord, Who at Thy First Eucharist."

> ". . . *With longing heart and soul, Thy will be done.*
>
> *O may we all one bread, one bod-y be,*
> *Through this blest Sa-crament of U-ni-ty.*"

John's anticipation mounted as they processed so that he barely noticed the antics of his mesmerized son.

Father Tom however did notice the odd behavior. As they neared the head of the Communion line, he had been aware that this was the father and child who so stunned him before Mass. While the little one kept his hand respectfully in his dad's grasp, Father saw him leaning as far to the right of the line as possible. Amused Father Tom watched the boy stretching his neck out ever farther, looking to the front. To the priest, the bright, round-cheeked child with the big glasses was in obvious expectation of something. When the boy's father's turn to receive neared, he genuflected, (as some do) then rose and stepped forward, his eyes fixed on the Host held before him.

"Body of Christ," Father Tom repeated.

"Amen," came the response.

Tom proceeded to place the Host on the big man's extended tongue. Occupied in that moment with the execution of the man's communion, Father Tom didn't actually see another host rise from the chalice. In the next moment—that split second after placing the Blessed Sacrament on the father's tongue—he saw a single host floating in the air. It glided past his peripheral vision and gently placed itself on the tiny pink and extended tongue of the curious boy.

Just as Father Tom's point of vision followed the floating phenomenon and came to rest on Jackson, John opened his eyes and followed the priests gaze. John looked down in alarmed confusion seeing his young son ingest a host. He assumed Father Tom had accidentally communicated Jackson, who probably opened his mouth imitating John.

John tugged his son's little fist to step out of line, but Jackson stood immobile, eyes closed, as still as an ice sculpture. Embarrassed a second time, John swept his unresponsive son up in his arms and hurried to their pew. At least he wasn't stiff. He knelt holding Jax, who seemed to have fallen asleep, on his shoulder.

The accidental Communion troubled him. No idea what the rules say about that. He would have to stay after to explain what happened to the priest. Other children receive the sacrament at seven or eight... but only after religion classes, and only after the sacrament of Penance, *and only when you're Catholic for Pete's sake.* His conscience would bother him until he knew what the Church taught in such a matter as a non-Catholic accidentally receiving Communion. Still, Jesus was with Jax right at this moment, Body, Blood, Soul, and Divinity, John found it hard to believe God would mind.

After the closing hymn, John remained in the pew, still holding a sleeping Jackson. While waiting for the long line of parishioners to greet the priest, he fell into a slight meditative state of prayer. Fifteen minutes later John was startled by a tap on his shoulder.

"Excuse me," Father Tom whispered. "Sorry to disturb your prayer."

"Oh... not at all, Father." John shifted Jax, feeling hot where he'd been stuck to him. "Actually I, uh... stayed after to speak with you." He rose, careful not to wake his son.

"Is the little guy alright?"

"Oh, yeah, he's been sleeping like a baby since Communion."

An indecipherable look crossed the priest's face. He motioned for John to follow him. Father, he knew, wouldn't speak in the nave while even one parishioner still prayed, and he often preached against such indiscretions. John followed the priest, Jax over his shoulder, taking a right turn before the very altar Jax had run to earlier. John studied the priest from behind, straight brown clean-cut hair, a peppy determined stride. Father Tom was shorter than he'd thought, maybe five foot eight and only a bit fleshy— probably not much chance for physical activity in the life of a parish priest. A mini corridor led to the sacristy where the priest and altar servers dressed for Mass. A door led them to the chapel. John was sure they were headed for Father Tom's office in the next room. He was therefore surprised when Father halted and unceremoniously sat down in the first row of chapel chairs in front of the carved wooden altar and tabernacle. John hesitated.

"Oh don't be alarmed," Father Tom said and stretched his arm out over a chair. "We can talk here. The Blessed Sacrament has been temporarily removed." Below a high forehead, the squinty Irish eyes in a full face looked kind and welcoming. "I'm sorry to say we've never met, although I have seen you at Mass. Even some daily Masses if I'm not mistaken."

"Yeah, I'm John Miller. This is Jackson. We, uh, moved here recently. Sorry I never introduced myself. So many seem to hang around you after Mass, I... well it never seemed as important as whatever they all needed." Even now he sped, afraid to take up the time of a busy parish priest. "Anyway I stayed to apologize for what happened. You see my son's never been to Church and—"

"Where are we, Dad?" Jackson stirred in his arms.

"We're still in church, Bud. You fell asleep. This is Father Tom." He placed Jackson on his feet.

"Pleased to meet you, sir." Father offered a fleshy hand. The moment they touched, Jackson's expression turned to a mix of admiration and wonder.

"*Sacerdos*," he said, "you belong to Him. Do you live here with Him?"

Father Tom cocked his head. The silence was awkward. John had no clue what the word meant.

"Father lives in the rectory through those doors, Jax."

The priest stood then leaned down, "Would you like to see my office? I have a Lego project in there that could use an expert's touch."

Against old leather furniture and a heavy mahogany desk, the children's Lego table in the corner of Father's office stuck out like a sore thumb. At present, the table held a large structure of red, blue, and yellow Legos. Father Tom explained he'd been fiddling with the thousand or so pieces, recreating his version of the church basement.

"I'm trying to see where the best spot will be to fit a new elevator for the handicapped. Maryann and Mrs. Murphy, do you know them?" He waited for only a second then waved his hand as if to say why should John know them. "My secretary and the housekeeper, they don't believe my motives. They say I like to play with Legos, plain and simple." He laughed and John guessed they were right. He really liked this young, open priest.

Father Tom left Jackson to play with the Legos, not the least bit concerned in how the alleged replica would be destroyed. He led John back to the chapel to talk. John prepared to begin again his explanation of the accidental First Communion, except it was Father who began in earnest.

"You see I was cleaning the chapel late last night," the priest indicated the carved piece in front of them. John recognized the scent of Tung oil and admired the gleam of the dark wood as Father continued, "and I had to remove the reserved Hosts to a temporary tabernacle, but the huge one in the sacristy has a broken lock. I didn't feel right about leaving Eucharistic Hosts in an unlocked tabernacle, so I searched all the old key rings we keep in the sacristy drawers." He shifted and crossed his legs, folding his hands over the top knee. John wondered why the priest was bothering with details about moving the Eucharist. Did he think John was still questioning their talking in the chapel?

"I tried dozens of old keys; then I found one that unlocks the side tabernacle." The priest paused and then emphasized, "You see, this was like 11:30 at night. No one was here when I relocated the Blessed Sacrament to the right side altar. I'm afraid that's why I froze when your little boy practically hugged the altar where he did; it was as if he knew Our Lord were in there."

John sat trying to take in what the priest was suggesting. The altar Jax ran to held the Eucharist, and somehow Jax knew it? A thought jumped out at him that maybe the communion was no accident, and he blurted, "Is that why you gave my son communion?"

It was at that moment that Father Tom realized John had not seen the miraculous floating host. Yet John Miller's question did confirm that he knew Jackson had received communion. Tom had begun to delude himself into thinking that he hadn't seen what he saw but only imagined it—the result of staying up too late, breathing funky chemicals, or reading too many saint's stories. He had just about convinced himself that he had only invented it because of the child's antics in front of the tabernacle where Jesus secretly lay. He knew one thing; he didn't put that host in the child's mouth as John Miller clearly thought he had.

"You see Father, Jax has never been to Church. He was imitating me when he opened his mouth to receive. You couldn't have known he wasn't Catholic or how young he was."

The priest looked at John and realized it might be best to keep quiet about what he'd seen. His own thoughts were confused anyway about how the Host had arrived on Jackson Miller's tongue of its own accord. He wanted to speak to his old spiritual advisor, Father Simeon and tell him about the incident and about the child who knew Latin and called him *sacerdos*, the sacrificer. The old monk would know what to do.

Father left it with John Miller that no harm had been done. He quizzed him a bit learning about his construction company, Clarice's artwork, and the couple's new house. John opened up sharing his background as Jackson's foster father, talking about his own conversion, and about his wife and son not practicing any formal religion.

From his office window, Father Tom watched John and little Jackson Miller cross the empty lot to a gold Blazer hoping he'd made the right choice in keeping what he'd seen to himself.

Strapping his very somber looking son into the car seat, John figured he was hungry.

"Sorry that took so long, buddy. We'll stop at McDonald's for lunch on our way to see Mommy's art show."

"Dad, he wants me to come back. Can I? Can I come with you on Sundays?"

Why would the priest go behind his back asking Jackson to return with him? ... But when had the priest asked him? He had been with them the whole time and couldn't for the life of him recall the request.

"We'll see what Mommy says, alright Bud?"

Jackson was silent the rest of the ride while John chewed over not only how he would make the request for Jackson to join him on Sundays but how Clarice would take it.

23

Dogs of Hell

It was chilly. The house was quiet except for the low dull saw of John's breathing. Lying in bed looking up at a lone star in the skylight, Jackson's words came back to Clarice. "*It's safe at His house, Mom. I'm safe there.*" The art show had been exhilarating. She had been so engrossed in conversation with visitors she'd barely noticed how late Jackson and John were. Her son's unexpected question about going to church on Sunday had thrown her, but she'd been too busy with appreciative onlookers to give his words much thought. Instead, she'd gently pushed her little boy to the side with, "Not now Jackson, Mommy is really busy with the show."

She hated that she'd brushed him off. Why did her conscience always bother her after the fact? After she had been lost in work or absorbed in some task or creative project—after she had ignored him—always after. She lay in the dark, listening to John's soft snore, wondering whether she should agree to let him begin taking Jax to the Catholic Church on Sundays.

Clarice rolled over to her side and squished her pillow under her neck. Her thoughts wandered. She needed to buy more green for the mural on Jackson's bedroom wall. She was painting the woods, the Glen. Why did she always think of that place? Clarice shivered, tugged the covers higher, and twisted her head to the skylight. The lone star looked back at her, reminding her of how early she had to get up. She gave herself permission to fall asleep, promising to remember the green paint in the morning.

On waking, her first thoughts landed instead on Mrs. Nicestrum. They hadn't seen her in well over a month. Usually she called Jackson every week or so to chat with him, but even the last phone call was about three weeks back. Here she was practically a mother to her, all alone in the world with no relatives they knew of, not many friends either, beyond some church people.

The clock glowed 5:45 AM. She smooshed her nose deeper into the pillow, trying to enjoy one further moment of rest. *Uummm, okay, okay, okay, I'm up, I'm up.* Had to get up to get her jog in before John left for the office. If she missed a few days in a row, she felt like a zombie on Thorazine. Saturday and Sunday, she'd skipped—too busy with the art show. Clarice forced her legs to the floor and headed to the bathroom, glancing at the digital thermometer: 52, already warmer than yesterday's high. She threw on a black jogging bra, tee shirt, and Capri running shorts and ran down the stairs.

Sitting on the wicker settee on the porch, she laced up her sneakers keeping one eye on the magnificent fog rolling over their front yard. It promised to be a spectacular day when that fog burned off. The chilly May air was fast dressing her in a sheet of goose pimples; Clarice sprang down the porch steps anxious to work up a little sweat.

The road felt good under her feet, every step lighter and lighter, down the drive and out to the open dirt road. Her mind went back to Mrs. Nicestrum, all by herself in that apartment, no Jackie to fill her day. Gotta call Nicey as soon as she got home. Running... running, free and light on her feet. She thought of Roxy, feeling a little guilty there, too. She wanted her to come up and see the new house, but Roxy's last message mentioned that Harriet woman again. Rox still wanted to arrange a meeting for Jackson. That so-called psychic gave her the creeps. Clarice's arms pumped back and forth in the familiar motion, her legs warmed enjoying the exercise. Though, what was the harm? Maybe this woman could help if Jackson's problems were paranormal. Who knows why these things are happening? And what about all this

Catholic stuff? John's a good person; why should she care if their son followed his dad's spiritual—

Her chest suddenly tingled, the sensation spilling over her. Something changed. The air felt different—not the fog burning off, or the air warming to the rising day, something else... something... coming. Clarice snapped her neck over her shoulder looking behind as her feet continued to hit the stony tar. Seeing nothing, she upped her pace, hoping to blot out the sensation and focus instead on the rhythmic repetition of her footfalls. Clip-clip, Clip-clip, Clip-clip...

Still it drew closer.

Pay attention to your feet. Clip-clip, Clip-clip... But thick fog swallowed her steps; foreign air prickled her skin... and something was coming—coming for her.

Stupid, paranoid feeling, that's all. Knock it off, Reece. She concentrated on her legs and the comfortable movement. Clip-clip, Clip-clip...

Still it came.

It's nonsense! NOTHING is there.

But something was. And every tingly sensation and madly beating heart thump said it was too.

Clip-clip, Clip-clip, Clip—

Closer...

Clip-clip, Clip—

...and closer.

"What!" Clarice screamed in the fog coming to a dead stop. "What are you?" Standing there, as if giving the thing permission to take form, Clarice thought of dogs. Every jogger has a real and legitimate fear of dogs. She carried no stick or bat like some do. Why would she, never so much as heard a dog bark out—

All at once, her ears pricked; the unmistakable sound of dogs in pursuit filled the air. Clarice stole a terrified look in the distance behind her. Just over the hill, tiny black specks at first, then too fast for belief, three black Rottweilers appeared bearing down on her.

Clarice whipped around; willed her feet to run. How far away were they? She twisted looking back at them, meeting the fiery red eyes of the beast in the center. This was no pack of wild dogs; the sounds as they barked were surreal and maybe 100 feet away from ripping her apart. She ran with all her might off the road toward the thick forest. Her feet bounded to the nearest deer path, running neatly over branches, stones, and roots. The trio followed with such vile noises, her heart melted like wax, shrinking before the evil trying to swallow her up.

"Oh God, God!" she cried to the One everyone cries to in crisis, saint or pagan. The ground sloped every which way over thick leaves, twigs, and branches. With eyes peeled for exposed roots, Clarice ran deftly, ignoring the real possibility of breaking her neck at this speed on rough terrain, so fleet, her lightning steps barely hit the uneven earth. The ground flew beneath her skating by so fast she was flying. The Rottweilers grew louder, their angry snarls closer.

Rip!

Pain shot across her face as the snag of a dead tree ripped into her cheek. A chunk of torn flesh flapped against her chin. She swore at the searing pain, even as more branches reached out of the dark wood scratching her limbs. Sweat ran down every inch of her body, her feet sliding in the stuff as it pooled in her sneaks. This dread, the fear! It would be easier to collapse and succumb.

Quit.

Are you kidding? The park all over again, that invading force trying to break through her psyche.

Just quit.

Overwhelming sensations attacked her mind. This was too much. Too much! The physical exertion, the panic, and now a mental assault!

"Screw this!" Clarice yelled at the pulsing force. "Screw you!"

The dogs drew closer, getting louder and louder. No way could she dare another look, dodging and weaving odd branches. Her cheek was killing her, burning and literally flopping wet blood on her chin. "Oh God, I feel their breath."

A foul odor rose behind her, the dogs literally on her heels, snapping and snarling. Her feet hitting rocks and roots, twisted;

248

she continued running willing her ankles to perform over this terrain. One miss, just one... she was barely keeping a hair's breadth ahead of their jaws. A slop of hot, foamy spittle hit her calf and she shrieked.

"Oh my God, they're real, they're real" she cried, this time very much to her Creator. "Please save me! Save me!"

Suddenly, she felt a pull forward—something familiar, deep in the forest. Its sucking power drew her adding to her own Gazelle leaps. Still feeling the dog's hot breath on her heels, barely but perceptibly, Clarice gained a precious inch. Hope swelled and she gave a bigger mad push even as the vacuum suctioned her forward. She gained a foot of distance and recognized the curving descent of the land.

She was very close; she knew it. Ahead, the sound of the water crashed over the falls, and behind were the terrifying snarls of the dogs from hell. The ground leveled out, and like a child being swept to protective arms, her terror lifted. Clarice fell forward, embraced by the invisible borders of the ancient Glen.

The rabid fiends let out an ear-piercing yelp. She turned around, but nothing was there, no fearsome Rottweilers, nothing but woods. She was safe. Holding her pounding side, she collapsed on a huge flat rock close to the running stream. She squeezed her knees up and buried her head, holding herself tight in a ball. A shaking, shivering, scared little girl, Clarice Martin Miller cried in waves of grateful relief.

Time slid by, minutes... hours... she had no concept. Soft wind caressed her body as sweetly as a mother calming her frightened child. Clarice loosened her grip and shyly lifted her head. She felt a bit like an intruder trespassing on something sacred. Everything looked as it had before—waterfall, crystal pool, rich moss and dappled sunlight. Her eyes drank in the beauty of the spot that she had only dreamed of since that first day on the mountain.

Clarice got down from the rock, pain searing her gouged face. Gingerly, her fingers explored the wound and exposed cheekbone. The hanging flap of skin stuck to her chin with gelled blood. She peeled it upward and laid it back over the gaping hole pressing it there with her hand. It felt like fire as she moved to the edge of the brook. On the moss-laden ground, she removed sneakers and socks with her free hand and stepped into the cool water. Liquid energy flowed around her feet. Clarice captured some and dribbled it on her ripped cheek. It tingled, but the water felt good. She let go slowly; the skin seemed to be staying in place. She used both hands to hold water to the wound then splashed a little on her sweat-ridden body.

A sudden urge to get in the water all the way, found her stripping her tee shirt and capris and wading to the stream's center, thinking of one of those adult baptisms. She cupped her hands and splashed herself with the crystal elixir, laughing, uninhibited, scooping the water over and over, feeling free and happy.

Exhausted and oddly not shivering, she lay on the thick moss to dry off. After awhile, she sat up, examining her calves. Not a scratch on them! Her hand shyly explored her right cheek. Her fingers ran over and over the smooth flesh, even around to the other cheek incase she had gotten mixed up. Smooth as any baby's. Impossible!

As Clarice dressed, her earlier confusion and recent fright replaced by a blessed peace and understanding. So much so, the thought of leaving the protective enclosure of the Glen didn't bother her in the least. The Glen was a safe place, but ultimately, she understood, not meant for her. With that simple acknowledgement, and one more appreciative glance at the unmistakable beauty of the place, Clarice turned for home, down the same path she'd found over a year ago.

At the house, John was hanging up the phone as she came through the mudroom door. He looked miffed, giving a nod toward the kitchen clock.

"Took your time today; it's seven thirty," he said, then seeing her wet hair added, "Man Reece, how hard did you run?" He was out the door a minute later (skipping the kiss, who could blame him) and grumbling about being late for Monday's meeting with Mike and the guys.

Clarice turned from watching John disappear through the mudroom door and smiled at Jackson seated at the black walnut table in the breakfast nook. He hadn't touched the half-eaten banana and cereal in front of him since she'd come in. His eyes shimmered.

"*Many dogs surround me; a pack of evildoers closes in on me. So wasted are my hands and feet that I can count all my bones.*"

Jolted, Clarice gripped the chair in front of her for support, not taking her eyes off her son, "What in the—what are you saying? Where did you hear such a thing?"

Jackson looked back at his cereal reaching for the spoon in an attempt to look casual. "It's from the Bible, Mom, Psalm 22. I read it this morning." She knew he frequently read the Bible, but that could hardly explain the coincidence of these words. She pulled the chair out and sat facing Jackson. Placing her hand on his, she studied his eyes.

"Do you know something? Is there something you want to tell me, Jax?"

"It's okay, Mom. It also said that the Lord did not stay far off and would come quickly to help you. "*Deliver me from the sword, my forlorn life from the teeth of the dog.*"

Her face went cold; the blood drained like seeping sand in an hourglass. He hopped out of his seat, wrapped his arms around her, and hugged her tight, burying his face in her side.

"It's alright, Mom; you're stronger. You'll know more too; you'll see."

She wanted to pull out of her child's embrace, to hold him away from her and literally shake answers from him. In reality she was afraid to ask the questions and deathly afraid of what the answers might be. Weirdly her mind grasped for something to do, dishes, laundry, anything to run from that world. Jackson pulled away from her.

"You can take your shower now, Mom. I'll start my lessons."

24

Keeping in Touch

She slid down against the porcelain, sinking under the hot water till her head was completely immersed. At first, the heaviness of the water felt good closing around her. Then the blackness swirled, pressing her down—holding her under. Her eyes popped open looking through the water at the wavy ceiling. In a violent heave, she thrust upward, gasping for air as a bucket's worth of water sloshed all over the floor.

"Dang it!" *Like this morning wasn't enough.* Way to go Reece, spook *yourself* why dontcha? She grabbed a stack of towels and threw them on the floor, sopping up the puddle. Then she wrapped herself in the one still hanging on the door. She combed her hair, crimped it with her fingers to let it dry naturally, and got dressed.

Making the bed, Clarice found a certain satisfaction in the room: the ceiling she'd painted in shades of blue and subtle clouds, the same blues in the spread and pillows, John's signature woodwork. If only life could be made as perfect as easily.

Holding the basket of wet towels, she headed across the open hallway to check Jackson's room. The sidewall where she was passionately recreating every inch of the magical glen jumped out at her. She sat on the edge of his bed surveying the half-finished mural. What is it for? Why was she drawn there? *Acch, not now!* Jackson's jama pants were crammed in the basket and she sprinted downstairs remembering her promise to check on Mrs. Nicestrum and call Roxy.

Jax sat busily scratching out answers in his workbooks at the dining room table, exactly where she thought he'd be. After throwing the load in the washer, Clarice went to the kitchen to hit the coffeepot. Popping a mug of cold black brew in the microwave, she hoisted herself on the island to dial Mrs. Nicestrum as her eyes roamed the new kitchen: balled feet of the cherry cabinetry, favored pieces of china and crystal stemware behind glass doors, the cook top grill and shiny copper pots hanging above. How great was this house!

No answer at Mrs. Nicestrum's. That was odd. She should have been home this early in the morning. Maybe she was doing laundry, taking a bath or something. Clarice left a quick message on her machine saying she was only checking in with her and asked her to call back. Then she rescued her coffee and dialed Roxy.

"Hey what's up?"

"Hey yourself!" Clarice settled on the island and swung her legs.

"Nice timing, Reece! I'm just putting my purse down. Long time no hear, honey. I left you like three messages," Roxy said.

"I know, sorry Rox. I miss you. I'd kill for one of our crazy lunches." Without explaining her previous avoidance, Clarice chatted briefly about the art show and shared how she'd been out of touch with Mrs. Nicestrum.

"Hmm... can you call her landlord or some friend of hers to check on her?"

"I guess I could call Kate Walker. She goes to the same church."

"Well, I hope you reach her, and hey, if worse comes to worst call me; I'll drive over there."

"Ooo, sugar, I have a client due at nine AM," Roxy said, "think we could get together tonight for dinner to catch up?"

"I could ask John to be home by five."

"Great! Meet me out front of the *Louisiana Purchase* on Old Vestal Road at six." She was gone in a click. Clarice shrugged and dialed.

She reached Kate at BOCES, hearing chaos in the background of Kate's classroom. "Kate, so sorry to call you during school."

"Perfectly alright," Kate said. "The kids are a little excited about a new puppet I brought in today. How's Jackson? I can't tell you how much we all miss him."

"He misses everyone there too, Kate. I promise I'll bring him by some afternoon when I'm in town. I called to ask if you've been in touch with Mrs. Nicestrum lately." Happy loud voices in the background erupted anew.

"Michelle? *Guys stop it, wouldja?*" her voice left the phone then returned. "Sorry Reece. Um, I usually see her at service, but she must be going to a different church cuz I haven't seen her in a few weeks, not even at Bible Study."

That caught Clarice by surprise. She couldn't imagine Mrs. Nicestrum changing her routine, let alone her church. "Kate, any chance you could make a few calls to some friends?"

"No problem. *Hey, get him! Come back here.*" Clarice heard a commotion and a door bang. "Jimminy! Reece I gotta go. I'll call you back."

Clarice hung up, nuked a second cup of day old coffee, and called Jackson over to the kitchen table. After math, Jax read aloud from his eighth grade history book while she munched on a bagel. Such a strong, clear voice and so much comprehension! Her mind returned to the dogs, their snarls, their breath on her calf, the torn cheek; her hand went to her face. Jax looked up and asked if he could watch TV, which for Jackson usually meant the Discovery Channel.

"Sure you can, honey bear. Mommy wants to paint anyway."

He ran off and she slipped away to the East Wing.

Filled with light, the studio was a great space for her work. Shaped exactly like the long kitchen, the room lent itself to their duo needs. John's huge chestnut desk dominated one end, and behind it, a picture window offered a living landscape of the woods in their yard. Two high back tapestry chairs, flanked a mahogany accent table in front of the desk for John's clients.

Her studio lay at the other end of the sunny room, a simple setup with a couple easels, stools and a drawing table. Clarice glanced to the French door, which opened to the front porch where she sometimes worked. *Hmmm*, today was tempting, but 60° still felt chilly. Anyway, at this hour plenty of light streamed through the east window.

In the walk-in supply closet, which fit a tiny sink and smidge of counter for cleaning her brushes, she chose a brush and tore the plastic wrap off her palette. On the way out, she flicked on the pricey ventilation unit, which somewhat served to make the turpentine odors more bearable. In the studio, she threw open a window for good measure.

Clarice studied her current composition of an elderly couple leaning over the railing of a picturesque arched bridge. Only their backs and slight profile could be seen in the painting, but their positions spoke volumes to her: the man leaning over, his elbows resting on the rail, his hands softly clasped in silent meditation. His partner close enough that their sides touched, her raised arm resting high on his back. Their faces turned in obvious contemplation of the natural scene spread before them. To her they were the picture of contentment, love, and that blessed rest hoped for in one's old age.

She eyed the piece critically, holding the top of her paintbrush to her mouth. The complicated background needed to be more muted; the focus kept on the couple not what they were seeing. The tricky part was painting the background as something at least worthy of all the attention the couple was paying it, but not to allow that beauty to detract from the couple themselves. The scene ahead needed faded tones and shadows... Abruptly, Clarice turned from the painting. Her mood was all wrong for this. Tossing the brush, she strode to the corner and sat at the small drawing table. Her pencil flew frantically across the sketchpad, and savage shapes came to life. In a matter of minutes, three menacing dogs appeared running forward right off the page. Teeth bared and red eyes glaring, there could be no doubt of her fear. Clarice's passion made her draw wildly. She'd have a painting of these ominous mongrels in a matter of days. She recognized the therapeutic release the fevered work was having on her.

"Mom!"

Clarice jumped at the start of Jackson's voice seconds away. She hastily flipped the pad over. "What is it, baby?"

"I talked to Kate at BOCES," he said, crossing the long room and holding out the phone. "She says she misses us. She wants to talk to you."

"Oh honey, is Kate on the phone right now?"

He nodded.

Clarice patted his head, took the phone, and walked toward the kitchen. "Just a sec, Kate,"—she turned to Jackson following— "Jax it's lunch time. Do you want to cook two of those bowls of noodles for us like a big boy?" He nodded and ran to the pantry to get the microwaveable cardboard delights, a favorite of his, barely tolerable for her.

"Kate, I'm sorry. I'm just getting Jax started on lunch. Thanks for calling me back. You have those hooligans corralled?"

"Yup," Kate laughed, "If you call the cafeteria a corral."

Kate proceeded to tell Clarice about her morning of sleuthing. First, she had tried to reach Mrs. Nicestrum's landlord. That was a bit more challenging than she thought. Once she tracked down the right individual, Kate ended up leaving him a message on his answering machine. Next, she called a woman she knows who sometimes drives to Evening Fellowship with Mrs. Nicestrum. Mrs. Sanford told Kate that she had stopped asking Michelle for rides at least a month ago. She felt it was too much for her to drive so far out of her way and told Kate, she was a bit concerned for her too. Apparently, Mrs. Nicestrum had coughed uncontrollably the last time she was at church. Mrs. Sanford told Kate she hadn't seen her lately and assumed she was nursing the cold. A few more phone calls to church friends confirmed Michelle Nicestrum hadn't been to church in weeks. Finally, Kate called the pastor Reverend Vann to see if he knew anything. He checked his hospital list and apologized to Kate, explaining his new assistant had been making the sick calls.

"Sure enough that's where she is, Clarice. Evidently, she's too ill to even call or ask someone to call her friends for her. It breaks my heart to think she's been in there two weeks and we didn't know."

Feeling like she'd just been punched, Clarice scrambled for a piece paper to write the room number in the Cardiac Care unit of Lourdes Hospital.

"I feel awful," Kate said. "I can't make it before tomorrow. My son's dropping the kids off tonight and my husband's useless. Robert wouldn't have a clue how to watch them alone."

"Kate, don't worry about it. I'll see her tonight after dinner and explain why we haven't been there."

"Oh Clarice, will you? Tell her I'm going to contact her prayer group too. Nobody knew. I feel just awful. Tell her I'll try to make it tomorrow afternoon."

"I'll give her your love," she said. Clarice hung up the phone and looked at Jackson slurping long noodles into his mouth. Sometimes he looked so young, and yet... *What goes on inside his head?* She debated for a moment whether to tell him his Nicey was sick. Watching her son's unconcerned head immersed, enjoying his bloated soup noodles, she decided it would be best to see Mrs. Nicestrum first and assess how bad she was before upsetting the little guy.

25

Words that Haunt

Clarice stood in the parking lot outside *The Louisiana Purchase*, an upscale restaurant with a New Orleans' menu. She leaned against her Prelude, tugging the brown suede blazer closer to ward off the crisp evening air. Looking at the two story pink stucco restaurant with its classic French Quarter styling and wrought iron balconies, she thought about her decision not to change from her jeans. At least she'd worn heels and the blazer. She spotted Roxy's yellow punch bug in the parkway, still marveling that anyone would purposefully buy one of those. It fit Roxy, though. Not physically, she noted watching her friend's lengthy frame comically exit the tiny Volkswagen.

Wide beige gauchos and bat-wing sleeves on an orange silk blouse billowed in the breeze like a half-mast sail. Instead of a belt, she wore a giant-polka-dotted silk scarf, its fringe trimmed in dozens of tiny gold trinkets that clinked when she walked. Spindly legs approached in outrageous wooden clogs that she proudly matched with the only wooden purse Clarice had ever seen. The topper to this outfit perched over her short red curls was a brown checked beret.

"Oh Roxy, I have so much to unload on you!" Clarice said as the two friends settled into a small table against the wall of the restaurant.

"Me too, Reece. Let's order first, and I'll yap about all the great stuff you're at work, save the heavy news for later." She plopped her picnic basket purse on the edge of the table almost making Clarice laugh. "I'm starved, takes a butt-load of calories to fill this tower, and I haven't eaten all day." She made a clicking sound out of the corner of her mouth and opened the oversized menu.

Clarice listened to Roxy's office exploits and gossip while they ordered Shrimp Creole for herself, Jambalaya for Roxy, and a bottle of *Blue Nun* to share. Their plates more than half-gone, Clarice could stand no more and reached out to arrest Roxy's animated hand. Roxy stopped rambling mid-sentence about some skank lifting supplies from the storeroom.

"Oh girl, my bad? Tell me everything."

Clarice filled her in right up to this morning's incredible incident.

"These dogs just came outta nowhere?" Roxy cocked her head. "And you say nobody lives for miles on this dirt road of yours?"

"No, it's the top of a mountain, totally undeveloped. It's at least eight miles to the nearest house, and that's at the bottom of the hill." Clarice reached for the wine. "Anyway, there's something about that glen, Rox. Not kidding, I *felt* it heal me, physically and mentally. The cramps in my side disappeared, even the scratches on my legs—" She hesitated, touching her cheek, feeling the miracle—too fantastic to share. "The water, I mean, I could feel my fear leave too..." she trailed off.

"But tell me about Jackson. How did he know about the dogs?" Roxy said and pulled a lipstick out of her wooden picnic basket.

"I didn't say he knew," she grimaced. "He just quoted these verses from the Bible that happen to fit perfectly. It's weird how he's so interested in reading the Bible."

"Happen to fit? Listen to yourself, Reece!" She waved the orange lipstick. "It's like no matter how many signs you get that supernatural stuff is going on, you refuse to admit it." Roxy leaned across the table searching her eyes, challenging her to accept the preternatural happenings. "Besides, you said he mentioned how you would be stronger now and know more. What the heck is that supposed to mean?" Her friend's voice rose to an embarrassing squeak; Clarice became uncomfortably aware of fellow diners. Roxy too noticed the attention and softened her tone.

"Listen, I finally spoke to someone about that woman psychic. I found out her name; it's Harriet Mansfield. She works at *Macromania* practically full time, but she has this gig on the side, you know. This girl I talked to was really impressed with her gifts."

"Gifts?"

"Yeah, from what she said, Mansfield sees people who want help with their jobs or their relatives, gives them advice and whatnot. The girl said she knows stuff about them, things they never told her. She locates lost stuff. And once,—well, I don't know but I heard—she found the body of a murdered child for the police."

Clarice sipped her wine, staring at the floor. Her gut told her to just say no. On the other hand, it would be good if this Harriet could figure out what was going on with Jackson. She was probably a phony anyway. Then again, if she was legit she might know something that would help.

Roxy popped a shrimp in her mouth that she stole off Clarice's plate. "So I thought I could set up a meeting with her for Jackie. I wanted to show her a picture of him, cuz I guess sometimes that helps her see stuff. C'mon, just say yes. It's not like anything bad can happen. And who knows?"

Perhaps it was the wine of which she'd had her share, or this day that would not quit, or maybe it was her friend's whacky persistence, in the end Clarice caved, even handing Roxy a picture from her wallet. They agreed Roxy could approach Harriet Mansfield and show her the picture to see what she would say.

The two caught up a bit more over coffee. Clarice detailed their work on the house and her art show for Roxanne, neither of which her best friend had seen.

"You knoooow Rox, the art show's only there till the end of the month."

"Oh I know, I know," Roxanne said, excited. "How 'bout I find this Bookworm place next Wednesday after work. I can even check out John's office. Then I can come up to the house for the grand tour, visit with you guys. I'll have to think of something great to bring Jackie."

"Sounds good," said Clarice, "but you don't have to get Jax a present."

"Right, like you can stop me," Rox grinned.

The two parted exactly as they'd met in the parking lot with best friend hugs and kisses.

Clarice hopped in the Prelude. *8:03. "Crap!"* her palms smacked the wheel. She'd blown past visiting hours at Lourdes, but there was no way she was going home without seeing Mrs. Nicestrum. She put the car in gear and took off like an Indy driver down the Parkway.

Clarice found a spot in the main lot directly in front of the old hospital. Good thing she knew the room number since visiting hours were over. Last thing she needed was some rule-stickler barring her way. She squared her shoulders, walking with confidence thinking if she looked like she had business there, she might not be caught sneaking in after hours.

In the Cardiac Care section, Clarice breezed past the nurse's station where neither the two nurses nor the aide even looked up from their paperwork. She slipped into Mrs. Nicestrum's room undetected. Except for a lot more equipment and monitors, it looked like any other hospital room. The first bed was empty, and a curtain was drawn around the second bed. Clarice bent to peep underneath for feet. Assured Mrs. Nicestrum was alone, she stepped into the enclosure where the still dignified form lay on her back with eyes closed and arms crossed. Surprisingly none of the fancy equipment was hooked up to her. Good, she thought, Mrs. Nicestrum must be doing much better.

Clarice pulled a nearby chair up to the bedrail and sat, trying not to wake the poor thing. Mrs. Nicestrum looked peaceful and beautiful when the eyes popped open giving Clarice a start.

"Oh, Nicey," she said, "I'm so sorry I woke you." Mrs. Nicestrum gazed at her. "We had no idea you were in the hospital. Couldn't anybody contact us for you?"

"It's not important, dear," the royal voice replied sweetly. "You're here now."

"No, no, we should have been here sooner. I feel so bad." Clarice lent forward and placed her hand on the soft blanket. "I was heartbroken to think of you all alone. I'm going to get us down as your next of kin so this will never happen again. And I'll bring Jackie tomorrow, now that I see you can have visitors. Oh and Kate also said she's —"

"None of that matters. Have no regrets over that. It is very important that you listen to me." She sounded grave.

"Of course, Nicey, of course I'll listen, whatever you want." Clarice's eyes filled with tears at Mrs. Nicestrum so helpless and pale in her hospital gown.

"John is with Jackson now. When he is not, you *must* be with him. Always one or the other until the protector comes. You will know it is the guardian. You must cooperate with him."

"Who? What? Please Nicey, don't tire yourself," Clarice said, a knot forming in her gut. "Jackson's fine. He's fine." She patted the cold arm.

"Listen to me. There is not much time. You have to protect him from the evil one. *He* intends to stop Jackson any way possible."

"Who!?" The hair on the back of Clarice's neck stood on end.

"*He* has already tested you. He may test John, but you mustn't be afraid. It is time for you to face God's plan for you and your son."

"I don't understand. What are you talking about? Nicey, you're not well." Clarice looked toward the door, thinking she should get a nurse. "You just need to calm down." The old woman's arm shot out to grasp her arm and regain her attention. Her touch was positively ice cold.

"Trust only your John, Jackson, and the guardian to come. Cla—rice,—her voice was drawn out and slow—"It is time for you to admit the truth of your own powers. You must not run any longer but turn and face them head on." The freezing grip tightened. "Your gifts will either serve God's purpose or they will lie like buried treasure for which you will be held accountable."

"Gifts... God? Nicey you're scaring me. Let go, let go of my arm. You don't know what you're saying." Clarice stood, that sinking sand feeling coming on.

"Do not be afraid Clarice, my dear little one. I do love you. I have to return now." The old woman's eyes closed as suddenly as they had opened. The icy arm that held her was back on the revered chest as before, leaving Clarice to gape in dumbfounded silence.

Swick-ck-ck. Swick-ck-ck. The shower curtain drape was roughly pushed aside, its metal rings scraping the bar. An attendant wearing blue scrubs and a shocked face looked at Clarice.

"Oh my gosh," he said, "I had no idea family would visit. We had no time, that is... it happened so unexpectedly and on the change of shifts." His apologetic look turned from her to the bed. He stepped past her to the body and pulled the sheet over Mrs. Nicestrum's head. "We would have had her prepared and moved by now, or at least covered. I am *so* sorry you had to find her like this." A face full of pity studied her. "If you'll step outside, I'll get the head nurse immediately to give you the details."

The attendant's words made no sense to Clarice and her mind swam. *Wh-what is he saying?* She looked down at the monitoring machine closest to the bed and noticed the paper hanging from it. *The line is straight. The line is straight. What does that mean?*

"Oh my God," Clarice yelled, immediately needing air. She backed toward the door and bumped into a warm body turning to find a stout looking woman in scrubs. The nurse placed her arm about Clarice's shoulders and led her to a bench in the hallway opposite the nurse's station.

"I'm the head nurse, Alice Jamison. We would have called, but we had no names for next of kin." Her tone was so matter of fact and irritatingly calm. "She went into cardiac arrest around 6:30. The doctors did all they could for her. She was pronounced dead at 7:17. I think the poor dear was just done. There was no more fight in her."

Clarice sat speechless. After a few moments, the nurse spoke again, "Would you like me to call anyone for you?" Clarice shook her head without speaking or looking up. "Do you mind," the nurse continued, "if I ask how you knew Michelle Knee-stroom?" She butchered the name.

Clarice barely offered: "She was our nanny" with a fleeting thought that the nurse might wonder why the family wasn't here for her these past weeks.

"I can walk you to the chapel if you'd like, or we can call your family." The naturally stern face softened a tad and she sounded concerned. At that, Clarice realized she had to snap out of her shock enough to deal with this business-like nurse.

"I'll be alright," she sputtered. "I'll leave you my card. Could I ask you to call us, er me or my husband John? Let us know if we can help with, uh, arrangements or whatever you need. She had no family and I—" Clarice rubbed her temple, "I want to be sure she will be taken care of." She rifled through her small purse for one of the cards she'd printed for the art show. The purse was organized, so why couldn't she see anything? Dang it. Finally, her fingers felt one. *Miller Construction,* but the home number was there.

"Of course, please, don't worry about details tonight, Mrs. Uh... Miller?" she read off the card. "She'll be transferred downstairs to our morgue. She'll be fine there until arrangements are made. We had only a Reverend Vann down for calling. I assume he is her minister. Perhaps he'll know her wishes."

Shaking, Clarice got up to leave and found she had to will herself to move in a controlled manner. She rounded the corner of the unit and out of sight then bolted, like a scared cat down corridors, two flights of stairs, and past the lobby and gift shop. The chill air hit her like a slap in the face. Mrs. Nicestrum dead? Nicey gone? Their Nicey...

"I can't think about all this. I've got to get home first. Home. No thinking. None." She promised herself fumbling for the keys to the Honda.

You must protect him from the evil one. He intends to stop Jackson any way possible. You must protect him from the evil one. He intends to stop Jackson any way possible.

"Stop it. Stop it!" Clarice ordered her brain. Her hands gripped the steering wheel as she struggled to concentrate on the road.

It is time for you admit the truth of your own powers. You must not run any longer.

"No. No, I have no power. I want none of this."

You must be with him, always one or the other until he comes.

"Who comes? What do you mean? And how, how did I hear you? You're dead. You were dead."

You must not be afraid. It is time for you to face His plan for you and your son.

"What plan? No, I'm not thinking about this. Stop it, stop it."

And on and on for the hour drive home.

26

Nicey's Gift

Friday, May 12, 2006

In the First United Methodist Church on Main Street in Endicott lay a beautiful mahogany casket carrying the remains of one Mrs. Michelle Nicestrum. It lay not twenty feet from the first pew. John looked at his wife, her face turned toward Jackson between them. She'd argued against even telling their son, let alone bringing him to the funeral service. Telling him though turned out to be no problem.

That Monday night Clarice had come home without a word to either of them climbed the stairs and went straight to bed. John came up surprised to see her already hunkered down under the covers. He'd called over to Jackson, who was occupied fashioning an elaborate roller coaster of Hot Wheel tracks in the spare room.

"C'mon guy, time to hit the sack."

Jackson retrieved a pair of blue striped PJs from under his pillow. Then he joined John in the hall bathroom where they brushed their teeth together. It was a peaceful bedtime ritual, in wordless looks and smiles, jiggling hands and scrubbing sounds as they bonded over toothpaste and mouthwash. Back in the room, Jackson went to his bookshelf. They'd dispensed with storybooks long ago, and instead read chapters from adult classics. At present, they had been reading *Last of the Mohicans* by James Fenimore Cooper. They were at a good part where Magua hurled his tomahawk at Alice's head, and Heyward broke free and attacked a

Huron, who was suddenly shot dead. So John sitting on the bed was surprised when Jackson pulled his new Bible off the shelf and brought it to bed.

"Why the Bible, Bud? I thought we were going to find out what happened to Chingachgook and Magua."

"Nicey said she reads the Bible every night so I thought since she's gone we could read it in her honor."

John scrutinized his son, "In her honor? What do you mean in her honor?"

"She's gone, Dad."

"I know, son but—"

"Gone from this life." Jackson had clarified looking up into his dad's eyes.

"What in the world would make you think that Jax? Cause she hasn't called lately?" Jackson's eyes teared. Poor guy missed her so much. John pulled him into his arms and lifted him to his lap. Jackson cried softly as they sat on the edge of the bed. When his tears subsided, John assured him that Mommy would tell him all about Mrs. Nicestrum and her illness in the morning. John didn't learn of Mrs. Nicestrum's passing until the following day.

In the pew, John looked from Jackson to his tiny wife. She looked great in the little black dress, but her face was strained with worry. Man, Nicey's death had thrown her! For the last three days, she's walked around like a character in *One Flew Over the Cuckoo Nest.* Her face was so pale against the black, the deep-set eyes even deeper. She hadn't even attempted lipstick and blush... Jeez, did she even eat this morning? He reached for her hand while the minister announced yet another hymn.

Mrs. Nicestrum deserved a bigger crowd. John frowned after a quick glance. Knowing Nicey though, she would have only wanted her closest friends anyway. God, they were going to miss her! The minister, Reverend Vann, droned on in a sermon-like eulogy revealing his lack of closeness to the grand lady. Even so, he spoke of how he would miss the peering eyes from her usual seat at service and miss hearing her lilting voice as the ladies in the *Sowers for Christ Club* darned jeans. Aware of her job with them, a few personal comments were directed their way. A soft type, John thought shifting in his seat and studying Mrs. Nicestrum's pastor. Tall and large under his purple robe with a movie-star mop of dark hair. Possibly one of those voluble but congenial men who mean well but see themselves as filling a role or supplying some need... not necessarily living deeply what they so loudly preach. A whiff of Clarice's perfume caused John to look again at her stricken face.

Clarice sat like a shell-shocked draftee in the pew. *What's next?* She kept looking at the casket half expecting the corpse to pop out of it. And how could Jackson have known before she told them? After she'd broken the news to John that following morning, he'd told her about the odd "coincidence" of Jackson's suspicions and she'd almost keeled over. John tried to get her to open up about what was bothering her, but ultimately she convinced him it was only the shock of Nicey's death.

Coincidence, Clarice sighed. *Roxy was right.* How many supernatural signs could she avoid admitting? She looked at John wishing she could talk about it. It was like leading a double life, all this secrecy. He didn't even know half of her. Her heart sank; she wanted them to be close, but there was always this pile of secrets between them.

Jackson inched over; she looked down. Two wet lines streaked his chubby cheeks. Nearly broke her heart. She gave him a reassuring squeeze. He hadn't cried since that night with John. He's either holding it in or in shock. It's healthy for him to cry, she told herself rubbing his arm, but watching real tears from real hurt on her little one was something no mother could bear well. She watched him closely, her disquiet alerting John, who also turned his attention to their son.

Jackson leaned his head, as if listening hard to something. His wet eyes stared fixedly at the glossy casket. His lips moved, and his head nodded in animated conversation, at times still and silent, then moving again. *Oh, my God, tell me he's not talking to her!* Finally, a sweet smile spread over his face, his little hand raised slowly to his lips, and in the gesture so familiar to both Clarice and John, Jax blew a final kiss toward Nicey's casket.

The trio stood for the closing hymn after which Reverend Vann asked those present to accompany him to the gravesite for the internment ceremony. Clarice absently slipped into her black trench and looked at the dozen or so people following the pallbearers from the church, wondering who would join Mrs. Nicestrum for this final ride. She recognized Kate and her husband, Robert Walker. Rob looked good. She hadn't seen him in a while. In his dark suit, his five foot ten looked tallish next to Kate. Retired and golfing practically full time, he was tan and despite the paunch, looked healthy.

The sky was grey and somehow appropriate. In the Miller's car, everyone was quiet while John pulled in line behind the hearse and the Reverend's white Lincoln. The Blazer was third in line, followed by Kate and her husband Robert's Camry. Only two more cars behind that had their lights on and wore the tiny funeral flags—an Oldsmobile, which held four elderly women from the Ladies Guild, and a minivan with several members of Mrs. Nicestrum's Bible Study group. A heavyset black man of about forty drove the minivan and had two lady passengers. The drive was ridiculously long for the tiny funeral procession of six vehicles.

"Maybe we both should have driven," John said.

"Yeah, it would have been one more car," Clarice said, squeezing the wet tissue in her hand, thinking of the last time they were all in the Blazer in suits—the circus of suits.

She watched the hearse ahead, wondering how final was final. She saw Mrs. Nicestrum's soft face, her favorite tweed skirt, her pearl chain holding her glasses. *Oh God*, she would miss everything about her. After working its way through light city traffic, the miniature motorcade wound its way into the nearby hills and countryside of Newark Valley. Their destination was a humble looking graveyard, whose last resident had moved in more than half a century before.

"Why we going so far?" Clarice said.

"I dunno maybe her husband and she used to live out this way." John offered.

"I don't think so." Clarice got a fresh tissue from her purse and crushed the disintegrated one in the ashtray. "Mrs. Nicestrum said he worked at IBM. They lived in town ever since they first married."

"Didn't he die like thirty years ago? Is he buried here?" John said.

"Nicey's mommy and daddy are here." Jax straightened himself in the backseat, shooting the intel forward. "She has to be with them." He sat back and returned to looking out the side window.

"Jackie," Clarice found herself using Nicey's nickname for him. She spoke low, undemanding, "how would you possibly know—"

"Guess we're here," John said, pulling in behind the white Lincoln. All five cars parked in the driveway of the farmhouse. Clarice climbed out smelling freshly cut hay. She helped Jax out of his seat, watching the hearse pass. It turned onto a dirt road and with undignified bumps, made its way up a bare swath of field toward a white fence. An older man came out of the house to greet the cavalcade and exchanged a few words with the Reverend.

"The owner told me he tried to mow a path out there this morning." The Reverend walked, and the handful of mourners followed. "Real nice man, still, I thought we'd best hike this small distance since I'm not sure there'll be room for our cars and the hearse."

"What's the story here?" Kate said. "I thought Michelle would be buried at Riverside with her husband Matthew. She and I used to visit his grave sometimes on our way to church."

Reverend Vann explained the odd circumstances while the baker's dozen walked up the mowed road toward the graveyard. John was next to Kate's husband whispering, probably catching up on some game. Since John was cozy with Rob, Clarice joined Kate, staying close to the Reverend to hear the story. The graveyard Mrs. Nicestrum had requested, was no longer in use, but had originally belonged to her mother's family and held the graves of her parents, siblings, and maternal relatives.

"It was one of those family graveyards," Reverend Vann said, "common in farm communities. The original land passed a long time ago from Michael and Emily Prey, both buried here." Clarice's head popped up when she heard the name Prey. She looked over the heads of those around her for John. He heard it too, raising his eyebrows in response to her. So, Nicey was the mysterious Prey who got them the land in Ithaca!

The Reverend went on. "The Prey's daughter, Sara Bard, was Mrs. Nicestrum's mother. The home and land changed hands three times since it left the Preys in 1953.

"Over the years Mrs. Nicestrum and her husband would take care of the graveyard, you know, cutting the grass and cleaning weeds away from the stones. After her husband died, Mrs. Nicestrum continued to visit and do what she could. Mr. Weitzer," Reverend Vann nodded back toward the house, "the man I was talking to, he's the owner. Apparently he developed a bit of a friendship with Michelle helping her care for the graveyard."

The hefty reverend stopped for a breath and pointed out a ditch in the soft ground made by the Bobcat sent by the funeral home to dig the grave. "Watch your step everyone. Let's see," he continued, "Michelle came to see Mr. and Mrs. Weitzer months ago and asked if they would allow her to be buried on the site next to her parents if she could make arrangements. She secured the town's permission and the Weitzer's consent too."

"But Nicey, I mean Mrs. Nicestrum, was just fine months ago," Clarice protested.

"My goodness, of course she was," Kate piped up placing an arm on Clarice's shoulder as they sidestepped a patch of mud. "She probably just wanted to get her affairs in order; that's all."

Jackson sprinted ahead as everyone drew closer to the small fenced area of the old graveyard. A dozen or so moss-covered stones of various sizes marked the family's graves. A few were broken and fallen over but had been respectfully propped back up. The bobcat with a backhoe sat a polite distance beyond the fence.

In the farthest corner of the yard lay the freshly excavated grave. The undertakers moved about busily setting up a platform for the casket.

John read the stones. Some of the others followed suit while a few talked quietly at the gated entrance. Everyone kept out of the way of the undertakers obviously working without the normal means available in a modern cemetery. Jackson planted himself as close to the open grave as possible watching with interest while the men set up the platform.

"Clarice, check it out," John called from the center most plot. "Read that."

"Elisha Prey 1761 to 1797," Clarice read dutifully, as she tied the straps of her trench coat felling a chill.

"That has to be one of the oldest graves I've ever seen," John said.

"In fact," the Reverend sidled up to the two, "it *is* the oldest one found in Newark Valley. It seems the Preys were a founding family of the town."

The couple followed Reverend Vann toward the gleaming casket where they found Jackson holding Kate's hand. The pastor donned a purple stole with gold fringe and held open a slightly worn prayer book. He cleared his throat and recited the comforting prayers of the United Methodist Church. Soon he invited anyone who wished to say something about Michelle to share their memories with the group. The ensuing silence was awkward to say the least. All the mourners looked respectfully down contemplating their shoes, as if the action would help take the pressure off any would-be speakers. Just as Clarice began to question the wisdom of the whole tradition, Kate spoke.

"I will always treasure the gift of Michelle. We had such good talks, and I always felt she was really and truly in God's presence. I felt holier just being near her. I—I" Kate welled up and had trouble continuing. Her husband Robert drew a tan arm around his wife. "I'm... going to miss you, Michelle. You enjoy heaven." Kate managed to finish.

Kate's icebreaker worked. One after another—practically everyone in the group—had a memory to share. Like the time Mrs. Nicestrum came to visit a sick friend and ended up staying with her for two days nursing her back to health, cooking meals, cleaning her house, and running errands. Another told of an all night vigil of a different kind where Mrs. Nicestrum had joined him in prayer for his daughter who was critical after an overdose. The list continued with talk of soup kitchens, volunteer work, and long, long, hours spent in prayer.

John and she had no problem adding to the list, but as they each testified, it was the small things that touched Clarice the most.

". . . the way Mrs. Nicestrum would tuck Jax in," Clarice continued, her throat tightening, "It was always the same. She'd pull the covers over him," Clarice's voice got high and tiny, "kiss his forehead and say. . . 'Sleep tight, don't let the bedbugs bite—'" Clarice could barely go on, tears overflowed her eyes, ran down her cheeks. "Oh God! Nicey...sleep tight." The bittersweet memories too much, she stepped back surprised to see Jackson step forward.

From the faces around her, she wasn't the only one shocked that a child his age would be brave enough to speak alongside the shoe-pondering adults. He stood in front of the handsome brown casket, its gold handles reflecting the sun's rays. Wiping a new tissue over her eyes, Clarice watched her not quite six-year-old son command an audience of adults.

"*Be not forgetful to entertain strangers,*" —Jackson's head was down, his voice clear and mature—"*for thereby some have entertained angels unawares.*" He paused, let the verse hang in the air, then raised his head and his voice.

"*My God has sent His angel and has shut the lion's mouth, that they have not hurt me: For as much as before Him innocence was found in me; and also before you, O King, have I done no wrong.*"

"Well I'll be," the Reverend whispered, "Out of the mouths of babes! It's from the Old Testament...Daniel, six twenty-two, I think!"

Jackson turned to the faces in the semi-circle about the casket, stopping at his mother's and strangling her heart.

"I loved her so much."

His voice, so clear and sonorous a moment ago, had deteriorated to that of a teary child claiming the instant compassion of all.

"She wasn't just my protector; she was my...Nicey."

Clarice made a move intending to rush to him when he shot his hand up in a signal for her to stop. Jackson collected himself, and again scripture poured from his mouth in mature, ringing tones.

"For you are the God of my strength: Why do You cast me off? Why go I mourning because of the oppression of the enemy? O send out Your light and Your truth." The little voice boomed, *"Let them lead me; let them bring me unto Your holy mountain, and to Your tabernacles."*

With this last Psalm, a light glowed at the seams of the casket where the lid closed. To Clarice it looked like someone had placed a spotlight (or three) inside the coffin. Very soon, it surrounded the coffin in a swirling haze. Clarice watched assuming she was the only one seeing it. The swirling light formed a giant ring and spun madly around the casket. It rose slowly till it reached the top; then the spinning light fell in on itself like tub water rushing down a drain. Now the size of a soccer ball—and as round—this intensely bright orb floated forward stopping before Clarice and hovering in front of her face.

The regal voice of Mrs. Michelle Nicestrum rang out one last time.

You will understand your purpose, Clarice. I cannot leave you much, but it may be enough for the flight. I leave you: Bravery, Strength, Unselfish and Ultimate Love.

John and the others gaped at the spectre before them. Clarice was right about something though, for while those around her saw the radiating manifestation, they had not heard Mrs. Nicestrum's voice as she had.

Without warning, the light smashed into Clarice's chest. The impetus knocked her tiny body right off her feet, hurling her backward into John's arms. Everyone let out an audible and almost unified gasp. She lay in a dead faint as John lowered her gently to the ground.

"Mom! Mom!" Jackson rushed to his mom, placed his head of golden curls on her chest, and spoke softly. John heard the words, which in the confusion only registered somewhere in his subconscious. "Nicey gave you her gift, Mom. You have some of her aura. Yer gonna be all right, now. Rest Mom."

Bewildered John looked from his wife and son to the bystanders. Dumbstruck were Reverend Vann, the old ladies, Kate and her husband, as well as the man and women from Mrs. Nicestrum's Bible Study. Then true to the human condition, a sort of awareness crept back to the crowd. After a breath one of them cried, "Oh my God." Others echoed the sentiment, and as is often the case in circumstances that test our faith and the grip we have on reality, the cry was as much a release as it was a sincere invocation.

Reverend Vann was the first to ask after Clarice, but he would be the last to ask what had just happened. Even though dealing with the world unseen was his life's vocation, in truth he preferred not to dwell on the realm beyond the senses. So after 9-1-1 was called and the ambulance arrived for Clarice, the Reverend surrounded by the little troupe of parishioners demanding answers, made his way to his car in complete denial of all he had seen. And at least several others followed his lead pretending the manifestation was merely some odd effect of the sun playing off the metal handle of the casket. Those in denial, including Kate's husband Robert, decided Clarice had merely fainted from the shock of the spectacle.

Gerard on the other hand, the man from Nicey's Bible Study, was completely convinced that he had seen proof of life beyond the grave. He was intently discussing what had occurred with Kate and the women he'd driven. A powerful black man of only 30, who could bench 300 pounds in the morning and feed soup to Alzheimer patients in the afternoon (and did so often), Gerard was held in the highest regard as a prayerful, levelheaded individual of great integrity and compassion.

"I agree with Gerard. There is no use denying what we have seen."

"It was a gift from God," another of the women spoke.

"I don't know why we were allowed to witness it," Gerard said, "or exactly what it means. I do know one thing, that family needs our prayers. I think we should call the prayer line right away."

"How about we meet tonight and try to arrange some sort of special prayer group?" Kate suggested. The four talked animatedly but stopped to hear what the EMT's were saying to John, whose voice had risen.

The technicians had checked all Clarice's vitals, strapped her into a stretcher, and lifted her onto the ambulance. John stood by the doors stubbornly.

"Sir, it's best if you follow the ambulance separately to the hospital. It's against policy for us to carry non-patients."

"That's bull! I want to be with my wife." John's voice rose, but his eyes pleaded for them to give in to his demand.

"Mr. Miller, she's not in any immediate danger. She appears to be in a state of shock. All her vitals are fine."

Robert Walker stepped in to reason with John. "You can drive Jackson and yourself over. It'll be more practical not leaving your car here. And Jackson is certainly upset enough without the extra drama of an ambulance ride or having to ride with someone else." John looked at his son, who on the contrary seemed to have the calmest demeanor of all.

"Look... John," Rob pleaded, "the longer you argue about it, the longer it will be before she gets help."

That was all the convincing John needed. He buckled Jax into the Blazer, the ambulance doors shut, the lights and siren suddenly came to life, and the two vehicles shot into the country road.

Soon the only car remaining in the driveway was Gerard's red minivan.

Mr. Weitzer had been watching all that was going on, but like the funeral workers, who were having coffee in his kitchen when the phenomenon occurred, he was in the dark about what had caused the little young lady to collapse. Weitzer walked up to the open window of Gerard's van as Gerard was preparing to pull out.

"I probably should have been at the grave and all, but I don't take much to funerals and preachers," said Weitzer, explaining his absence. "Just what happened out there anyway? I heard something about a ball of light."

Gerard thought carefully before speaking. Here was a man of unknown faith, who had befriended Michelle, even allowing her to be buried more or less in his backyard. What good could come of scaring him and his wife with stories of ghosts in their backyard, or lights, or a little boy who quotes scripture as if the entire Good Book was written in his head?

"Um, I understand... at least the preacher thinks, er, well it's possible that the sun played tricks on Mrs. Miller and she fainted; that's all," Gerard prevaricated, putting the car in drive.

"Well, if there is anything I can do." Mr. Weitzer offered.

"There is one thing." Gerard smiled kindly. "You could pray. That little family, the Millers, could use prayers."

"Yup, I could do that."

Weitzer was surprised at how easily he responded to Gerard's matter of fact request for something so personal. The van pulled out, and Weitzer turned back toward the graveyard where he could see the workers lowering the casket into the ground. "I can pray for them." He spoke audibly to no one. "I can do that."

27

I Needed the Quiet

I needed the quiet, he drew me aside
Into the shadows where we could confide
Away from the bustle where all the day long
I hurried and worried when active and strong.
I needed the quiet though at first I rebelled
But gently so gently my cross He upheld
And whispered so sweetly of spiritual things
Though weakened in body my spirit took wings
To heights never dreamed of when active and gay
He loved me so greatly He drew me away
Alice Hansche Mortenson © 1944

John listened to Kate recite her favorite poem. She read as much for Clarice as for him as he paced back and forth in the emergency room space of three gurneys separated by curtains. He had been stopped at the front desk on his way in and waylaid with demands for Clarice's information, especially insurance. He was a patient man, but the process had irritated the hell out of him when all he had wanted to do was be with his wife. Jackson had stood dutifully by his dad while John sat in the chair rattling off information wondering where they had put his wife.

Around the corner and still unconscious, Clarice had been dressed in a hospital gown, examined by a doctor, and had a slew of tests taken by the time John reached the room. A nurse taking blood informed him that the doctor would be back momentarily, and that her general practitioner, Dr. Varna had been called. Kate and Robert had arrived moments later. Rob was sent to buy coffee. Jax was on one side of the bed and Kate on the other while John paced, walking to the doorway every thirty seconds to look up and down the hall for the promised doctor.

"John, John..." Clarice's voice sounded weak and far away, but John responded immediately.

"Thank you Jesus. Praise God," Kate said and moved aside.

"Clarice, you alright? How do you feel?" John held her hand and leaned in close to kiss her forehead. "No, don't move."

"I feel strange," she said.

Strange was fast becoming an understatement. She took in her surroundings and the blue hospital gown, but from the moment she opened her eyes she felt *It*. It would be impossible to describe, even if she had any intention of doing so. Something inside her lay in some unseen area of her being. She watched the invader deep inside, keeping it at bay. Like a stubborn child closing her mouth against the bad taste of medicine, she firmly blocked it with her will. John gazed at her, as this battle of wills raged, physically and quickly, draining her energy.

"Clarice, I was mad worried. I don't get what's going on." John lowered his voice so as not to be heard. "Do you know what happened? I mean what was that light. Are you still you?"

"John..." Clarice looked intently into her husband's eyes, even as her spirit stared at the intruder, her arms crossed in petulant protest. It was exhausting, but she was sure if she let up the vigil, this thing, this light would take over. "I'm still me, of course." Yet her eyes pleaded with him for help and understanding, but it was no use. How could they possibly bridge this gulf of secrets between them? No way could she fight this thing and deal with an explanation to John of everything going on inside her. That would involve opening the can of worms of her past, too. No way, but damn it she needed him.

Help me, John! Her eyes screamed into his. *Please help me!*

I'm here Mommy.

Clarice turned from John to find Jackson by her side. She forced a smile.

I'll help you, he said.

Clearly, he said it. It was his voice, wasn't it? But... his lips had not moved. *What? No, I just have to focus.*

You're gonna be alright now, Mommy. His mouth was definitely NOT moving as she heard him speak. His voice was in her head. A shiver ran through her body. John reached over, pulled the sheet higher, and rubbed her arm.

Rest Mommy. You have to stop fighting. Let the light teach you.

Oh God, how could this be? Clarice felt like she would pass out looking into her son's smiling eyes. She couldn't take another second; sure she had lost her mind, when Doctor Varna finally arrived. He was pleased to see his patient awake and asked everyone to leave the room while he examined her.

A few minutes later, the doctor invited the little ensemble back in the room. John had never even met their new doctor, a short, trim man from India with a slight accent. He was handsome with dark hair and skin, a friendly smile, and a pragmatic demeanor. He issued a diagnosis of "total body exhaustion." Was that even real, John wondered?

"We will keep her this night, run the series of tests on her to rule out the cardiac or the neural problems." The doctor stepped toward the door, writing on Clarice's chart. "I am guessing your wife just needs a lot of the rest." He placed the clipboard in the plastic holder on the wall. When he turned back, he found himself face to chest with John, who wanted a private word.

"You sure there's no danger?" John's voice was low and he and the doctor took their conversation to the hall.

"We can't say for certain until we give more of the tests, but all her vitals are strong, the heart looks normal and the Doppler showed no clots." He smiled at John, clasped his forearm assuring,

"We have seen this before. Has Mrs. Miller been under any unusual stress these last months? I am meaning... besides the loss of your er—"

"Our nanny, Mrs. Nicestrum. Well I—I guess our son has problems that worry us both." John stopped there. No sense getting into all that. "We ah, also just moved to Ithaca in the spring. There's a lot of stress with that, I guess."

"Uh-huh,... well, that all sounds like what I am thinking. We will run the tests; but you will see Mrs. Miller needs plenty of the rest. We need to keep her for a few days if you think she will cooperate. The total exhaustion is nothing of fooling around with."

"She'll cooperate. I gotta say I'm relieved that you're keeping her here for a few days. She'll be safe—" John stopped himself mid sentence. They shook hands and parted.

Even though rest wasn't exactly what Clarice needed, the stay in the hospital did allow her to collect her senses as it were, strike a delicate balance between her body and her spirit while she waged a battle with the uninvited guest in her soul. By the time she went home, Clarice had returned to normal—on the outside anyway—and each member of the little Miller family was content to continue their lives ignoring the elephant in the room.

28

HARRIET

JUNE 6, 2006

She remembered driving, driving on and off like a dream—the wheel, the dashboard, pushing the gas pedal, some winding streets, some hills. She remembered feeling strange, coming in and out of consciousness. Seemed normal in the beginning with streets close to home, then it was as if she had slept and slept well. Later she was awake again, driving, driving. *How am I driving again? Still?* The scenery was more wooded, the roads more winding. Then sleep, peaceful sleep—slipping into it as easily as a drugged patient goes under on the operating table—the delicious feeling of it, sinking pleasantly, her body relaxing to that point of restive wavy sleep.... More driving—the open road, green hills and striped fields, but not for long, as she slipped away again.

Harriet continued walking on the path in a forest of bare trees wondering how she got there. *And where... where is here? But of course —the driving.* How long was she driving? It felt like she was only in the car for all of twenty minutes, maybe half an hour. It seemed ridiculous. The memory of sleep was so strong. The memory of actually driving, controlling the car—it seemed so short, minutes at a time really, separated by these pleasant bouts of deep sleep. In fact, Harriet distinctly remembered nodding off at one point. The car had rounded a curve, and she remembered thinking how she *really* shouldn't close her eyes while she was driving... but as soon as she closed them, she was lost in that pleasant aura of sleep.

Dampish earth beneath her shoes, Harriet continued walking and questioning. Where was the car, then? No memory of parking it, no recollection of even pulling in anywhere. She wracked her brain trying to picture anything, anything at all that would give her a grounded feeling of having been involved in coming here. She ducked a dead limb reaching out on the path like an old lady's arm and thought of keys trying to picture taking them out of the ignition, of pressing the button on the remote to lock the car, a habit as engrained in her as breathing—nothing. Her hand flew to her pocket. *Yes indeedy,* right where she always put them. But for the life of her, she couldn't recall placing them there. No good. Keys are too automatic of an activity to trigger any recall. What else? Surely pulling over, stopping the car, getting out... Pointless, she felt no connection. *Nothing.*

Wet leaves crunched underneath her feet, a twiggy branch brushed her arm, and then another scratched her cheek, making her squint inspecting the scenery. The woods looked old and dead, barren of green even though it was summer. Above her, somehow the lifeless trees managed to block daylight, making it dismally dark. Harriet tucked her arms under the macramé poncho for what warmth it could offer. Her loafers seem to be keeping her feet dry, at least for now, but wetness crept over the bottom of her black, cotton slacks weighing them down. She was in her work clothes—the black tee shirt with the Macromania logo on it beneath the thin shawl. Had she come straight from work?

Harriet stopped walking. A man strode on the path ahead, a couple whispered and laughed behind her. She felt a sense of dread, but compelled she continued, her pace even—not wanting to catch up to the man ahead, nor wanting the couple behind to catch up to her. *Why?* Why would she care?... Cause they would think she was crazy. *Don't turn around. Don't look at me.* She continued to walk, keeping her gait slow, steady.

The air was cold and damp, heavy all around her. Huh... it's fog, she realized. Why hadn't she noticed it before? What on earth was wrong with her?

All at once, she thought of running, the thought of it overwhelming her. She could turn right now, right now! Run as hard as she could straight past that giggling couple behind her. *Could follow the path back... back where?* Her car, a parking lot maybe, the road. She wondered why she thought she'd have to run past them. Would they try and stop her? Was she afraid they knew she was unstable, that she had lost her marbles and had no idea where she was or how she'd gotten there? *Not sure.* But, Harriet realized walking along; there was one thing she felt sure of. They were all headed toward something. She was meant to continue... she would continue, and *they* would see to it.

Harriet looked at the man ahead, but before she could study him, he reached his hand up, as though waving to someone and disappeared from view. It was getting darker by the minute... *dusk?* She came to the same clearing where the man had disappeared. A bonfire blazed in the center. All around its perimeter, people milled about, a couple dozen, maybe more. They seemed natural enough, talking in groups of three or four, here or there. A number of loners silently gazed toward the path where she stood. They looked at her, but she couldn't read the expression on their faces. It seemed that for a brief moment everything was dead quiet. Wondering who she was, just examining a newcomer? What did they want? No sooner had they all stopped talking, than they turned back to their individual conversations.

The couple caught up. They stood behind her politely waiting for her to enter the clearing ahead of them. She glanced at them and stepped to the side out of their way, both young, both tall, towering over Harriet's short frame. She couldn't help but notice the girl's knee-length, kinky hair of a shocking whitish blond. They smiled at her; she looked away.

Harriet walked along the clearing's perimeter, keeping her eyes down at first, then stealing looks, but it seemed no one was taking any particular notice of her. More dead branches held out their bare arms like evil sentries penning her in the circle with the assemblage of strangers. Half way around the clearing, she saw another path similar to the one she'd just left. Again, she surveyed the unconcerned group of chatting men and women near her before moving down the path. Not fifty feet from the clearing, she saw a uniformed man. He looked like a guard or official of some sort. Maybe she could ask him a few questions without arousing his suspicion of what she feared was her loss of sanity.

He was six foot, a fair gut pressing against his khaki uniform shirt, a thick neck and one of those square-jawed faces—easily pushing fifty. The uniform looked like a state trooper, but the color and the brown emblem with red letters were all wrong for NY.

"Can you tell me which way I would go to get back to my car?" She stopped a few feet from him.

"Cars are too far out," he said, "you'd miss the opening ceremony. You don't want to come all this way and chance that, now do you?"

Coop looked at her underneath his rimmed hat. He saw a short, stocky middle-aged woman with dyed blond hair, in that kind of nondescript short-curled fashion of so many women over fifty. Her attempt at an earthy look didn't quite cut it with that yarny shawl over practical black pants and shoes. Her skin had that leathery texture acquired from long hours worshipping the sun, her make-up caked, her rouge unblended. He figured she had a penchant for those large hoop earrings, and dangle bracelets. So many of this lot does.

The woman seemed to be studying him as though she'd never seen a state trooper before. She squinted at his badge; then her eyes moved to his emblem. Jeeze, she better not be after his number. It was obvious she was trying to read the badge but probably needed glasses to do so.

"To tell you the truth I, ah, I'm not really sure why I'm here. I mean I don't really know... you see I, ah, I don't think I belong here." The short lady shook as she spoke.

"Well, aren't you gittin all excited." Coop felt sorry for her. "Where y'all from?"

"New York, Binghamton," she said, "I—I drove."

"Say, y'all are a ways from home aren't ya?" He cocked his head trying to see her better, as if that could help him understand her apparent confusion.

"I wasn't driving long. I, uh,"—she hesitated, shifting gears— "What day is it?"

"It's the sixth darlin', June 6, 06." His eyes narrowed. Didn't this date mean something to all these wackos?

"But it was Monday? I remember Monday morning."

"Ah remember it too," he said, adding a good-natured laugh, "like it was yesterday." He tilted his head, "Look, y'all best be heading back. Sun's 'bout down. They'll be looking for you."

He could see her confusion, but he had no intention of dealing with anything beyond his agreement with *them*. Truth was, he was more than a little scared of them, and not at all sure if he was supposed to be talking to this one. He'd had it with this chanting, weirdo group, but they kinda owned him didn't they? How that leader of theirs ever learned of his one slip, he never figured out. Been happily married, more or less, for seventeen years. He beat himself up mentally again for that one night of indiscretion, lousy sex with some twenty dollar whore the night he lost the promotion. One lousy night hadn't been worth all this. First they get him to lie, bend the rules using state land without a permit; then they make him guard the path, so nobody comes and nobody goes. All to protect Jean from the truth of that one night. He half suspected they were behind that tramp throwing herself at him in the first place. How else could they have pictures?

Harriet saw from his stern look he was done with her. Her mind struggled to piece together the fact that apparently she'd driven some huge distance.

"Y'all turn around and head on back, ya hear. They'll, uh... answer your questions."

She turned back in the direction of the clearing, feeling him watch her. Dusk blanketed the woods now leaving them almost completely dark. A few Tiki torches lit the path. Where did those come from? She reached the clearing. Out of nowhere, a bony hand clasped her forearm. Harriet jumped. Except for the black robe, the old woman with neat hair, red lips, and big eyes, looked as harmless as a librarian. Yet, as she pulled Harriet toward the center of the clearing, she seemed about as well intentioned as a terrorist shoe-bomber boarding a plane.

"And where were you go-ing, my dear?" The smoky voice said. "You wouldn't want to miss the be-ginning, would you?"

A huge man, also robed in black, approached them, Harriet's stomach dropped. His size was fearsome; all she could think of was Jaws (Richard Kiel) in *The Spy Who Loved Me*. An ugly raised scar stretched like a segmented earthworm from his chin to his temple. He held a drink in his hand and handed it to the old woman.

"Thank you, Worm." She smiled at him sweetly then held the cup out to Harriet, "Drink this." Her voice was low, unchallenging, yet Harriet was positive the words were a command. Harriet took the cup, dutifully sipped what looked and tasted like water. She noticed the groups she'd seen earlier formed a circle around the blazing fire. In fact, many of them seemed to be wearing robes. They chanted, a low hum filling the air.

Harriet swayed to the chanting. *What are they saying?* She couldn't understand the words. The robed members stepped forward to form a smaller inner circle enclosing Harriet, Worm and the librarian, who stood on either side of her supporting both her elbows. The blaze of the fire intensified in unison with the mesmerizing chant. Harriet's heart raced. They were all waiting for... something unholy.

One of the robed members unbuttoned his cloak, and Harriet was surprised to glimpse nakedness beneath his robe. The old woman lifted her thin arm and flashed him a palm, "Not yet. You will have time for that afterward. None of you must be distracted." The man immediately closed his robe and continued chanting with the others.

288

Louder and louder the chanting rose, inciting the flames to leap higher and hotter. Her head swam in some altered reality. What was in that drink? She only took a sip.

"Don't fight it," the woman's gruff voice prickled her ear. "It's too late for that, you be-long to *him*." Harriet looked at the woman, but everything was wavy. "It's a great, great honor, dear." The stunted words and punchy syllables could not have scared her more. Again, Harriet was overwhelmed with a desire to run, accompanied by despair, so deep and foul, she could taste it. She yanked her arms, tugging against her captors. The huge man's grip tightened on her arm, the woman's stayed the same, but *her* power over Harriet was more than physical. There was no escape from what was coming. Whatever it was, it was coming for her. And somehow, Harriet *knew* she had invited it.

Suddenly, the fire flashed forward. Harriet felt a dual tug on her elbows as the two holding her dropped to their knees. Both their heads went down, but Harriet's stayed glued to the blaze. A fantastic fiery figure formed in the flames. It emerged from the inferno, the outline of its shape burning and dancing with live embers while the inside was pitch black, a black so whole it was the absence of all light. Unbelievably, part of her wanted the fiery thing to hold her, to have her, a realization that ran through her in a tremor of shame. She wanted it; she feared it. The shockwave of desire and revulsion pummeled her psyche. The blackness inches away rose to engulf her.

"No! Noooo..."

"No, no," Harriet heard her own scream and yanked her head up. She was in her car shaking and cold.

"Y'alright, ma'am?" The voice and face seemed familiar, and the look of concern genuine. It was the officer, the state trooper. She could see his badge clearly now: *TN*. Tennessee, there had to be some mistake. She couldn't possibly be in Tennessee.

"You okay?" he said again, leaning over the driver side window and peering in at her.

She seemed to be okay. At least she was safe and back in her car; somehow, that seemed to be all that mattered. Back in her car, back in control even if half her mind was a big, fat blank. She wanted to go home and get away from this place as fast as possible.

"I'm fine. I think... I... No, I'm fine I just want to get home."

He continued to study her. "Y'all need anything. Any help?"

"Uh, no. Um... maybe you could tell me where I could find the nearest gas station?"

Highway Patrol Officer Cooper Reed watched the red Toyota slowly make its way out across the field, which only hours ago had served as a parking lot for that cult group of black-robed weirdoes. Coop felt sorry for the woman, and maybe even a little responsible. She looked awful, like every ounce of color had been drained from her middle-aged face. What did these freaks do to her? And why didn't she seem to know why she was here?

She'd obviously come of her own free will. His conscience should be clear. He didn't drag her here.

But that's it! That's the last time he'd deal with that group, Jean or no Jean. With that, Coop tossed his hat through the window of his trooper's car, shook his head, and followed the Corolla across the open field.

29

That Old Black Magic

Harriet traipsed from her kitchen floor to the tiny living room and back again. She had no idea how she had gotten there, but she recalled every mile of the 17-hour drive home. Direction-wise it hadn't been bad, pretty much a giant backward L: East on 44, and then North on 81, which ends right in Binghamton. But that left and a right comprised over a thousand miles of road. So long! How could she have done it without knowing it? It gave her the willies every time she thought of it. Would have had to fill up numerous times too.

Harriet leaned over the kitchen table in front of her laptop checking her credit card bill online. The days in question filled the screen. Yes indeed, she'd filled up, and up, and up. Tuesday the sixth and... yup, that following Wednesday. Her body jerked resisting an involuntary shudder, as sketchy memories of that night skated past: the trooper, the woods and clearing, the laughing couple, that girl's hair, an earthworm scar, a bony hand with cherry polish, black robes and the fire... Harriet's breathing increased, her thoughts coming closer to *him.*

Stop! She had to be out of her mind. For the hundredth time, Harriet told herself it was all a figment of her imagination, a twisted evil figment, but still just an invention. The product of stress, a little too much kava with her tea, or maybe the result of some toxic poison that slipped into her fairly health conscious diet.

No chance in hell she would consider doing it! Harriet straitened, slapped the laptop closed, and took up her traipsing.

All week she'd been telling herself that she didn't even know the boy. Told herself that meant the whole thing was a dream. She had nothing to worry about, for a whole week. She knew of no little boys, no one named Jackson. That little fact kept her sane. She'd held onto it like a tiny blow-up raft in a sea of doubt.

Then today that brassy, carrot-slurping Walking Stick came in and shoved a full size harpoon in that raft. She was in her line again, sipping an as-yet-unpaid-for health drink. The redhead had seemed a little anxious. Sure enough when her turn came, and Harriet punched in the number for the smoothie, the woman cleared her throat.

"Uh, my name's Roxanne Cassan," she'd said, "Roxy... I'm in here all the time. I'm uh... partial to drinks that match my hair."

"Yeah, I know. You think if I drank more carrot juice, I could turn my gray around?" Harriet had even joked with her.

"I was in here a few months ago, and I heard about how you helped someone with a—ah, unique problem. I was hoping you could help my friend too."

"Do you mean with our products here?" Harriet reached under the counter for some brochures. "Has your friend read anything about macrobiotics?"

"Oh, no," the Roxanne woman protested stretching out a hand to stop her from bothering with the brochures. The moment they touched, Harriet was electrified.

"What is it? What's wrong?" the Stick kept looking at Harriet's face but wouldn't move her damn hand.

In a flash, a flicker really, Harriet had seen a vision of Jackson's face. She knew, same as if the redhead had shown her that picture Harriet knew she had in her ridiculous neon-yellow purse—this was the face of the boy she had seen. Barely disguising her distress, she had finished the transaction, removed her store smock, and called into the register microphone.

"Isabelle, will you come up front please. Isabelle."

Stick woman just stood there flummoxed. Harriet wheeled around after exchanging a word with her relief. "I can't help you. I can't do it." She'd made her face firm. "I have to go now. My—my shift is over." The Stick began to say something but shut her mouth seeing the end run.

Tonight, in her tiny West Side home, Harriet couldn't relax. She flipped the stereo on low on her way to the kitchen. She pulled a chair over to the fridge (the only means she had of reaching that cupboard) retrieved a bottle of Merlot, gracefully aged— not because it would taste better, but because she watched every ounce of every natural, organically grown food that went into her body. Ironic, she thought, how she could be so chubby, being so careful.

After collecting a glass and corkscrew, she sat at the kitchen table looking out at her tiny herb garden where a light rain fell. If this Jackson is real, then it was real. *He* was real. How did this happen? What happened? She thought she knew some of it.

You know, you're just afraid to admit.

Harriet heard a voice in her head, gulped another half glass, and refilled, wondering if the voice was her own.

You and all your psychic abilities—where did you *think* they came from? The voice mocked her. *Came from? Why, they were a gift!* The words of her own thoughts sounded hollow when the voice returned.

You knew, deep down you knew.

It was true, the candles, the seekers, dream-catchers, and umpteen sessions with people and their loved one's objects. Playing with fire, you get burned. But her games and parlor tricks had always seemed harmless. She even felt she helped some of those who came to her. Never mind about the darkness to the power, she never thinks about that. She wasn't religious. Good and evil were just two sides of a coin that gets flipped and lands randomly on one side or the other, for no apparent reason. But what she encountered in Tennessee, that was just pure...

> *The same old witchcraft*
> *when your eyes meet mine*
> *The same old tingle that I feel...*

The phone rang at the very same moment that Harriet noticed NPR was playing *That Old Black Magic.* Between the jarring buzz and Judy Garland's haunting rendition, Harriet knocked over her wineglass. Flustered she grabbed a towel and picked up the phone.

"H-lo," she grunted, sopping up wine with a checkered dishtowel, noticing her bottle of Merlot was nearly spent.

"Miss Mansfield? Hi, this is Roxanne Cassan from earlier today. I... don't want to be a pest really, but I wonder if we could finish our talk. I didn't really get a chance to explain."

"I remember you, but how did you get this number? Doesn't matter. Honestly, I can't help you. There's nothing to discuss."

Say yes, tell her yes. This time the voice in her head was so distinct. Harriet ignored it wanting only to get rid of this woman.

"It's my friend. She's experiencing paranormal activity," Cassan said.

"What kind of activity?" Harriet caught herself too late.

> *Down and down I go,*
> *Round and round I go*

Cassan talked quickly, obviously buoyed by Harriet's almost ingrained response while Harriet heard only Judy Garland.

> *I should stay away but what can I do*
> *I hear your name, and I'm aflame*

"... sees things that others can't," The stick voice said. "She's had out-of-body experiences, like she flies or something, and her son is very different." Harriet was listening again. "I think he has powers. He's really the one who needs help. Oh, I'm going too fast. I'm sure I'm not making any sense to you. We need you to meet with him. I mean... maybe you can tell if he's like possessed, or—I don't know."

With every intention that the next words out of her mouth would be a firm "No," Harriet doubled over in pain. A piercing pain ran straight through her temple, as if an unseen attacker had suddenly thrust a bayonet through her skull.

You will agree to see her and the boy. You will NOT see the boy's mother. He must be brought to you alone. No mother.

Harriet gripped the table and struggled under the pain. It was obvious the pain was directly connected to her intended rejection of this woman's plea. She entertained the thought of at least seeing the boy. Maybe she could help him. The pain eased as quickly as the admission formulated.

"Are you there?"

"Yes, I'm all right."

"Well, whoever said you weren't?" Cassan said, an irritating cheer in her voice. "Will you do it? At least meet with Clarice and her son Jackson?"

"I'm not sure I—" The attacker thrust again. Blinded and doubled over, she kicked herself for testing it and hurried to think, 'Yes.'

Yes, say yes. Alone, tell her alone.

"Uh, I can meet with the boy,"—immediate respite—"but I can't promise that I will be able to help."

Alone, the voice insisted, accompanied by a subtle pain—the attacker holding the bayonet against her temple and pressing inward. *Tell her NOW!*

"I need to see the boy alone." Harriet's knuckles whitened. "I have to insist on this one condition." She felt sweet relief a second later.

When Roxanne Cassan asked why, Harriet was able to give a coherent, albeit convoluted excuse about mothers blocking psychic energy with their tendency toward over-protectiveness, or some such nonsense. They briefly discussed a possible time and place, Harriet hung up the phone. She slammed down the remainder of the wine. Sobbing she buried her head in her arm on the table as Judy Garland serenaded.

> *Baby down and down I go,*
> *All around I go*
> *In a spin, loving the spin that I'm in*
> *Under that old black magic....*

30

Gabe in Boston

The darkness descended, devouring, enveloping. Swirling blackness, pure evil, conquering and laughing. Vileness insulted every one of his senses. An incredible stench overpowered him. He sank hopeless while putrid slime enclosed him, and he held on to—to what? To WHAT!? All that was good and right? Let go; give in No, I can't... can't let go. Have to finish it, have to win.... *You can't win; you are nothing.* Let go. L E T GO!

"No. Noooo!"

Gabe jerked awake. "Oy Gevult!" He was drenched again.

He slid his feet to the floor, sat on the edge of his bed pushing his fingers through the mass of curls. He squeezed his head between his hands. *Please Adonai, not another migraine.* Cursed nightmares! Why did he have them? Everything else seemed normal. No, it wasn't; it was getting worse: the feelings of anxiety, the nagging sensation he had something important to do, somewhere to be. Agonizing over it was sure to bring that migraine on full speed ahead. The throbbing in his temples sharpened, Gabe willed his mind to go blank, pushing it into neutral. He gave his head one last good squeeze.

"Modeh ani li-fa-ne-cha Melech...," he said in Hebrew, giving thanks for the morning's restoration of his soul. He reached for the glass pitcher next to his bed and ritually washed his hands three times. "Baruch att Ado Elo-hai-nu Melach..."—the English translation of the Hebrew played in his head—*Blessed are you, Lord our God, King of the universe, who has sanctified us with His commandments.* Gabe finished and wondered how many faithful Jews still performed the ritual hand washing or Netilat Yadayim upon waking. For him it would be easier to chop off his hands than to take ten steps away from his bed before performing it.

Still sweating, he wrenched open the fifth-story window for air and maybe relief. The rusty fire escape swayed a little as Gabe planted his feet on the cool iron. Yesterday had been stinking hot, but overnight the temperature had dropped a good ten degrees. Could be the heat wave was letting up.

Usually teeming with life, the streets were much quieter this early. He looked for the top of Fenway Park, wondering when he'd get to another game. A month ago, he'd gone with Sol and his son-in-law, Dan, who he hadn't seen for a year since that sailing trip to the Vineyard. The knife-wielding girl had gone into rehab, but months later, the DA called and said she killed herself. Definitely didn't want to think about that.

Gabe's eyes scanned the street. A man pushed a large food cart below, probably pretzels. He looked like Al, Jewish. *Aaach.* How does someone look Jewish anyway? Why did he always categorize people, Jewish or non-Jewish? It bothered him that he was probably prejudiced in some way. Anyway, the cart pusher did remind him of his cousin Al. He had called last night. They'd been able to talk rationally for a whole fifteen minutes. He loved him; he missed him. It's just this idea you can be both Christian and Jew; it's too much. Al debated like any lawyer, which made the whole thing even more irritating. He insisted he was still a faithful Jew, going to temple every Saturday, worshipping in Hebrew, following Mosaic Law, celebrating Pesach, Sukkot, Shavuot, and every Jewish feast. Al claimed he was more faithful than most of their relatives. That really ticked Gabe off. It sure as hell wasn't true of him! *Oh Hashem, let Al be a headache for another day.*

Gabe climbed back in, headed for the bathroom where Imitrix beckoned like a silent dog whistle. He practically ripped the cap off. He popped the Imitrix and two Advil for good measure, stepped into the shower. By the time he shaved and dressed, the meds had staved off the migraine.

He donned his kippah or yarmulke, which Gabe wore all day, and his prayer shawl to offer his Morning Prayer service. He concluded his prayers with the beautiful Aleinu, praising God for allowing the Jewish people to serve Him, and he expressed hope that the whole world would recognize the one true God and abandon idolatry. All the prayers were in Hebrew and many were sung. Finally, he tucked his prayer shawl and book in his briefcase and headed for the door locking it behind him.

Gabe passed the elevator, opened the stairwell door, and descended five flights, already feeling the heat. Walking down the narrow flights, Gabe felt closed-in this morning. The sensation increased until the walls felt as tight as the elevator would have, and a darkness, darker than it should have been, enclosed him.

"A brokh!"

His curse echoed in the stairwell. Last night's dream really got to him. Gabe stopped on the next landing, clutching the rail for support while his mind swam in the blackness. The same fear gripped him, and tiny specks of sweat popped to life on his chest and face. He closed his eyes against the shrinking walls, but the darkness behind the lids was even more immobilizing. He thought of what he must look like frozen to this handrail, sweating and shaking. What if someone came down? He took a cavernous breath and renewed his descent, fairly bursting through the heavy metal door and onto the street hearing it clang the cement wall behind him.

Hashem, when will this torture end? Was he losing his mind? Why would Adonai torment him with these nightmares? In seconds, he regretted his tone. "Who am I to question you? You know all things Holy One." Nightmares weren't the only dreams he had. Gabe pictured the boy in the forest. The child meant something. He was important.

It was late July; the heat wave had been stretching across the whole country for a weeks. By noon, the city of Boston would be stifling. Already his shirt stuck to his chest under his grey suit coat.

He'd lose the tie and jacket after his first meeting. Even in the heat though, the walk to the museum was pleasant. The tree-lined paths that cut through the Back Bay Fens would land him practically at the museum's back door. This place was easily the best-kept secret in Boston, a tourist-free green oasis of sloping lawns, reedy ponds, picturesque bridges, and gardens with paths to wander and enjoy wildlife. Despite his history there, he loved the community feel. Besides, it was nothing of the unsafe park of the seventies. People lounged on benches or the grass reading, talking, or sleeping in the peaceful nooks of the wild Fens. Gabe smiled at the strains of a violin and a clarinet, which filled the air, compliments of a pair of Berklee Music students. He was almost disappointed when he exited the path to reenter civilization.

Nearing the museum, Gabe hurried his step. Like a nomad gaining an oasis, he entered the side door and enjoyed that rush of cool air. Passing a glass case depicting an archeological dig, Gabe felt humbled. The temporary collection of Jewish antiquities excavated over the last century was complete after more than a year of coordination, hand-holding diplomacy, travel, and well, kissing more behinds than he cared to remember. His job now entailed seeing that the Hebrew Antiquities Collection was handled properly in Boston.

In no time, Gabe breezed through the West wing of the museum, past the handsome collections on permanent display, through the lower rotunda, past the elevator, to the stairs, which led to the third-floor Egyptian Galleries. This floor also held rooms for classes, lectures, and conferences. Even hurrying toward his meeting, he couldn't resist leaning into a classroom for a peek.

A dozen art students scratched their pads, heads down or popping up to glance at an arrangement of a rusty bucket and ladle perched atop a linen covered table at the front of the room. Professor Holmes wove in and out of the sketchers with obvious dedication. Pulling himself out of the room visually, Gabe noted the young man nearest the door. His sketch, rather noncommittal, nonetheless showed a promising level of skill. The guy seemed almost bored, his hand passing lightly over his pad. Typical looking kid with blond hair poking up like he just rolled out of bed, long Hawaiian shirt and Bermuda shorts that screamed vacation in flowered yellows and greens. Gabe's eyes sank to the clunky Velcro strap sandals, then the man's huge brown knapsack, and finally onto a small stack of loose photos on the floor.

Stung, he gaped at the photo on top. It was the woman in his dream, the one with the flying spirit that always thrilled him at first. He'd swear to it. The photo, obviously of a painting, a diaphanous woman stretched out in joyful free flight, looked exactly the same way he'd dreamed it so many times. But who painted it? How could I have dreamed of it? Gabe stepped into the classroom door for a closer look when a hand clasped his left elbow.

"There you are Rabbi. We were worried that we'd have to begin without you." Gabe turned to see a smiling red-faced, freckled man of about thirty-five—Andrew Cafferty, Special Events Development Officer and a bundle of in-bred nerves.

"Of course I don't have to tell you how important this meeting is. Of course, everyone's in there, everyone." Cafferty raced on without a breath, counting them off on his fingers. "Perry Sanders, the Director of Purchasing, the Exhibition Design Manager, and his draftsman, the Preparation Collection Care Management team. Oh, and the Finance Supervisor."

Cafferty, a nervous little fellow, led Rabbi Katz away from the classroom door, down the corridor toward the conference room. All Gabe could think about as he allowed himself to be led was the kid's photo of the spirit from his own dreams!

31

Seth's Photo

Seth Edwards was occupied in the studio classroom sketching one last shadow on the rusty bucket. He was tired of the monkey work, dying to create something from his gut. How many months since he left Ithaca? He used to crank them out there. He thought of Ken and *Bookworm Joes* remembering the photos Ken had sent him of the show that took his place. Some new artist, or new to Ithaca anyway. He tried to remember her name.

Seth put his charcoal down, leaned over his stool, and hoisted his book bag from the floor. He rifled through pockets till his fingers felt the glossy four by five photos. He flipped the first photo to read Ken's chicken scratch on the other side.

> *Seth — here are the snapshots I promised you of*
> *Clarice Miller's work. They lack that prehistoric*
> *edge of your caveman art. LOL. Seriously, her*
> *stuff's not bad. Huh? Hope all is well and you're*
> *painting Boston red — pun intended. Send us*
> *some pics of your new work. Dibs on anything I*
> *love. Don't forget us here, we discovered you long*
> *before BMFA did! Take her easy,*
> *Ken and all at BJ's*

Seth went through the photos stopping at his favorite of the flying nymph. She's really good, he thought, nice lines, ethereal feel. Seth caught a glimpse of Mrs. Holmes out of the corner of his eye. Not wanting to look as disinterested as he felt in this class, he made a pretense of extracting a fresh pastel from his bag, stretched his long arm to the floor, and allowed the photos to plop in a pile by his book bag. He took up his charcoal again and renewed his effort at the rust colored tins.

Minutes later, there was a small buzz at the front of the class. Professor Holmes was explaining that they were heading out to the gallery of European Masters to examine two still lifes by Jean Simeon Chardin circa 1700. He knew a bit about Chardin's perfectionism, his re-working of his paintings, especially "The Kitchen," and was anxious to see it again. The teacher would lecture about the composition, lighting, and in general, point out all the impossible perfection they were expected to imitate when they returned. Seth sighed, looked doubtfully at his heavy book bag. Should leave it. Pain in the butt to carry it all that way and then all the way back again. He pushed the sack under his chair before following the rest of the class out the door.

Time slid by in the gallery for the art students and their stoked teacher. They'd been on the second floor where the museum boasted the finest and largest collection of European masterpieces found in America. Chardin's still lifes were dutifully studied and commented on. Then they were allowed to visit favorites like Monet or Rembrandt.

The three-hour class, which began at nine, usually finished up in the classroom by noon. Today however since time had apparently "worn Nike's" as Holmes put it, she dismissed them fifteen minutes early from the gallery.

Seth swore looking at his watch. He'd have to head back to the third floor to get his bag. Dang, he could have made the noon train easily and made it to Faneuil Hall by twelve thirty to meet Joe. They had hoped to make a few extra bucks doing sidewalk sketches and caricatures in the Commons. He could still make it if he really booked. With that, Seth tore toward the stairs. He reached the empty classroom in record time and grabbed his sack. In the hall, the elevator door stood invitingly open, and Seth jumped in.

Gabe had exited the conference room, a fidgety Andrew Cafferty glued to his elbow when he glimpsed a flash of flower shirt as the elevator door closed. Flipping pages on a clipboard, Cafferty droned on about endless details already covered in the meeting.

When Cafferty next looked up barely pausing in his itemized monologue, he found Gabe had moved across the hall to one of the studios. Puzzled but not deterred, he hurried after his runaway audience.

Gabe immediately noticed the pile of forgotten photographs under the chair and bent over to pick them up. Again, the photo on top took his breath away. *No doubt about it,* this was the woman in his dreams, but who painted it? Where was the kid? Oblivious to the freckled annoyance, who'd followed him and unbelievably not broken stride in his one-man confabulation, Gabe turned to Cafferty, his face full of questions.

"Where are the students? When did this class let out?" he demanded.

"I—I don't understand," Andrew sputtered, no clue how the conversation had changed. "Do you mean Ms. Holmes' class?" he said. "Her class is in session from nine to twelve." Gabe looked at his watch, 11:50.

"Sometimes she dismisses them from the gallery," Cafferty added.

Gabe's mind raced, trying to puzzle something together. The missing piece fell into place remembering the elevator door had been closing when he and Cafferty had entered the hall a moment ago. Could that have been the kid?

"I've got to go," Gabe said, forcing his way past a still dazed Cafferty. He shot toward the stairs, hoping to catch the Bermuda clad artist.

Seth looked up at the few numbers, willing the elevator to go straight past two, so he wouldn't lose any time in his run for the noon E Train. He glanced at his watch: 11:50. He looked back at the numbers. Still a good chance he could make it. *Shoot,* he cringed as the number two lit up.

The doors opened and a tall, heavyset woman outside of them immediately held her hand out to ensure they would remain open. She smiled at Seth then looked behind her.

"C'mon now, Nona. There's still a lot to see." Beyond the immense matron, Seth saw two huge gray wheels and a pair of feet in orthopedic oxfords sitting on the two metal footrests.

"I don't know. I don't know," the crumpled figure in a wheelchair mumbled. The wheelchair was decidedly not 'coming on' as it had been told to do.

The sturdy caretaker, who Seth decided should be called Olga, spoke in a loud but caring voice, "What's the problem, Nona?" Seth, one second away from rushing past the pair to fly toward the main stairs, couldn't care less what the problem was. The big woman smiled at him.

"Would you hold the door?" *Trapped.* He forced a nod and grudgingly took over the post as door holder.

"I don't know. I don't know," the ancient one continued to babble and shook her head violently.

"What don't you know, Nona? Whatsa matter, honey?"

Who gives a rat's patoot what she knows, thought Seth, getting more and more irritated. Olga stepped away from the door and leaned over looking in the old lady's face, patting the paper-thin skin on the boney forearm. Seth had half a mind to let the door go and pictured himself giving a "whoops" expression. Instead, he tapped his foot and shifted the weight of his heavy bag.

The wrinkled arms on the wheels of her chair moved feebly but definitely in a forward motion. *C'mon Nona, you old bag,* Seth screamed in his mind.

"Oh Nona, your brakes are on!" the matron squealed. "Look at you trying your little heart out to move this thing," she tittered, "and I had the brakes on all along." Olga went behind the chair, kicked the metal brake up on each wheel.

Nona's crinkly arms inched the vehicle forward while Seth willed the silly matron to push it for her. No such luck. By the time the three reached the main floor, it was eleven fifty four. Seth had six minutes to make the E train to Haymarket station. From there, he'd still have to walk the four blocks to Quincy Market.

It's eleven fifty, Gabe reasoned going down the marble stairs. Still a good chance, the young man was in class or at least in the building. Two flights later, he headed toward the main lobby where Isaac Schmidt, a security guard, leaned over the inner counter of the round Visitor Center desk reading his copy of the *Boston Globe*. A half-finished caramel-colored brew, long cold, sat beside him.

Isaac glanced up at Gabe over the reading glasses perched on the end of his bulbous nose. Graying and pushing sixty, his short but solid frame still looked strong and tan from earlier years of hard labor.

"Rabbi Gavri'el! I hear you mile away. What hurry you are in?" Isaac queried in his Lithuanian accent.

"Isaac, I'm glad you're available. I wondered if—"

"I vunder something also. I am sorry to... how do I say... beat the punch, but I am needing to know something from you for longest time."

The normally open face looked worried. Gabe, knowing Isaac's penchant for treating him like his personal rabbi and occasionally plunging them into an in-depth theological discussions, blocked the punch beater.

"I promise you Isaac, I'll try to help you with anything that is bothering you but—"

"Rabbi Gavri'el, I bring prayer book with Mincha unt Maariv prayers," Isaac animatedly patted his chest where he apparently carried the little prayer book. "I keep here close to my heart." Gabe noticed tears welling in the old eyes. Silently he prayed to God for the patience and charity to put his own need aside and help his friend. But please Holy One, Gabe begged, may he be served quickly.

"I make accident. . . mistake," Isaac looked at the rabbi for confirmation of his choice of words, "I bring book to restroom. I do not remember to remove my coat." The guard's brow furrowed with worry and guilt. For a Jew, a holy book, or any book with holy words, should never be in a bathroom.

"It's alright, my friend," Gabe said, relieved over the simplicity of the man's dilemma. "The prayer book was covered while in your pocket. In the future it would be better if you should place the book in a packet so that it would have a second cover." The security guard's head nodded in evident relief of his delicate conscience.

"I will get another cover if ever I should forget again. I do not mean to do this thing, Rabbi Gavri'el. Always I would leave my coat in the coatroom."

"I understand, Isaac. He who knows your heart, He also understands." The rabbi patted Schmidt on the back. Snapping his eyes to his watch, he said, "Isaac, listen please, I have no time to chat." Gabe placed both hands on the man's arms to get his full attention. "I need to know if the art teacher, Miss Holmes has finished class."

Isaac honked his nose into his handkerchief while shaking his head. "Now, the class is going. Patricia is done today already."

"Yes, but I'm looking for one young man in particular. He has blond hair, wearing a yellow Hawaiian shirt. You know, big flowers on it." As Gabe spoke, his back was to the stairs and entrance facing the guard's desk.

Just then, Seth exited the elevator, made his way down the stairs, and crossed the near empty lobby toward the glass doors of the main entrance.

"He has a big brown book bag," Gabe continued. "I need to know if you've seen him leave the building."

"But jes, jes, I have seen him," Isaac smiled big, glad to be of some help to the man who had relieved him of his guilt. "Unt, I am seeing him now."

The security guard pointed toward the open door where a second earlier, he'd seen the young man in question pass. When Gabe looked, all he saw was a slew of uniformed schoolchildren, all uniformly short, making their way into the building under the supervision of three chaperones and at least two tag-along mothers with even smaller children in strollers.

The third-grade class of the Immaculate Conception School entered the museum, and from the noise level it was a sure thing, the chaperones would have their hands full. Isaac Schmidt straightened himself and prepared for the onslaught of visitors while Gabe bolted for the door.

Making his way past the blue-plaid munchkins, Gabe burst through the outermost glass door like a deep-sea diver coming up for air. He ran down the curving sidewalk and looked up and down Huntington Ave. In the distance, he spotted the spiky blond head and a glimpse of yellow flower in a small crowd heading to the subway station. Gabe followed but saw at once he'd have to do a light jog just to keep Don Ho in sight.

Crowds were thick this time of day, but a two-buck ride downtown to the best food in Boston was worth it to people who wanted lunch with atmosphere. And Seth, who'd only been in Boston a few months, took every opportunity to see more of it. Intent on reaching the noon train, he had his pass ready, entered the turnstile, quickly sliced it through the machine. Here she blows, he thought, and me with thirty seconds to spare. The subway car was almost full, but Seth managed to find a seat.

Out of breath, Gabe reached the station platform as Seth entered the first car of the subway train some fifty yards ahead of him. Quickly he had to decide if he should chance running to that first car so he could finally catch the nameless kid. The possibility of the doors closing before he could get there was real. He checked his watch: 12:01. No way, it was now or never. He jumped through the open door of the car directly to his left. Good thing too, as the train door immediately closed behind him. Gabe made his way to the front of the car feeling hot and sticky. He got as close as he could to the window, locating the spiky hair and Hawaiian shirt some two cars ahead. Reassured, he sat down keeping the head in view, only to stand again a moment later, determined to stay vigilant in case the kid should exit quickly. The car jerked pulling him off balance. Gabe clutched the metal bar under the window, the familiar rattle caressing him like surround sound. He felt a tiny trail of sweat trickle down his chest, grateful the AC vent was over his head.

How in the world did something he dreamed of come to be painted so vividly? Gabe spread his legs and braced himself against the glass, reaching in his pocket for the half dozen photos. The spirit one was on top, the gossamer woman exactly like the one in his dream. That dream always began beautifully, the euphoric feeling of flying so intense, sharing the woman's elation. It always ended the same, a black vile force overtaking her and plunging her offspring to earth. The same evil force was in this morning's nightmare. Something was curiously similar between all the dreams. They were each connected, as though he were supposed to be getting a message from them.

While he thought, Gabe's head unconsciously dropped when out of the corner of his eye, he saw the flowered back of Aloha Don stand. Next stop: Haymarket. The guy could be going anywhere, but this close to lunch he was likely going to Faneuil Hall. Working his way around the knees and bags of commuters, he positioned himself near the door and held the pole. He peered back to the window but could no longer see the boy who he hoped was similarly poised to exit. The subway made a soft screeching sound, so different from the subways of his youth. Gabe was the second guy out the door, instantly swallowed in a sea of people. Oblivious of the crush and the stifling air, his eyes searched for the kid's stick-up coif.

Boom there it was. Figures, he thought, the guy couldn't be headed toward me. He hurried to the exit but was quickly stuck behind some lumbering fellow who seemed to be having a problem with his feet. Gabe was losing sight of his prey, who was bounding up the exit stairs two at a time. "Oh to be that young again," Gabe grieved, weaving in and out of the crowd around him.

The air felt fresher but wickedly hot after the cooler subway ride. The kid was definitely headed for the Marketplace. Faneuil Hall was only a short walk from Boston's subway system, but Gabe had to run to keep the guy in view.

The Marketplace, as old as Boston itself, was a phenomenal blend of past and present. Modern additions of shops respectfully mingled with three 19th century buildings sporting Greek and Neoclassic architecture. With almost 50 shops, as many pushcarts, dozens of restaurants, and food stalls, Faneuil Hall in the heart of Boston teamed with life and vitality. Over the cobblestones, Gabe hurried past street performers, artisans, and craftsmen showing off their talent and skills. Lost on Gabe were the delicious smells from every kind of ethnic food, tickling the appetites of Market shoppers. Lost too were the restaurants and pubs interspersed with outdoor cafes where tired shoppers watched the busy thoroughfare.

The flat bull atop Quincy Market's weathervane looked down on the out of breath rabbi and the flowered shirt while overseeing the comings and goings in the square as it had since 1826. Dozens of wooden pushcarts pedaled their wares, a juggler twirled something on fire, and a singer belted out "Oh Danny Boy" at the top of his lungs. The kid too ignored it all weaving in and out of the noon crowd, looking nonchalant, but still outstripping Gabe by 50 yards, headed directly for Faneuil Hall.

Gabe pushed himself even harder. Once the lanky youth went through those doors, he'd be lost in the Hall's lunch throng. Finally, at the foot of the steps he stopped and yelled in desperation toward the kid.

"Hello, you there in the Hawaiian shirt!" Gabe called, his burning lungs ready to explode. The kid halted and turned around. Gabe saw the suspicious look on his face and hurriedly reached in his pocket for the snapshots, waving them. "It's these. You left them at the museum."

"Whoa, Dude," he said, taking a half step down in Gabe's direction, *and thank Hashem,* stopping. "Did you follow me all the way from the museum just to give me those?" His mouth curled in amusement while one eyebrow lifted in disbelief. "They aren't that important, guy,"—he added reaching for the photos and noting Gabe's red face—"You okay, there?"

"Listen, would *huff, huff* you *huff* mind speaking with me for a few moments?" Gabe gestured toward a nearby park bench.

The kid checked his watch, looked toward Faneuil Hall then shrugged. "Sure," he said and followed Gabe, who collapsed on the bench.

"You gave me a run for my money. I've had quite a time keeping up with you." His voice came a little easier and he caught his breath, hardly believing how out of shape he was.

"Why come all this way to give me these? Ya coulda left 'em with Lost and Found."

"Yes, but I have questions about them." Gabe stuck his hand out. "I'm Gabe Katz. I'm working at the Museum."

"Seth Edwards," Seth met Gabe's grip, then with one more look toward the Hall, he joined Gabe sitting on the bench.

Gabe speculated where to begin, how much to divulge. "I wondered if you were the artist? I'm interested in one in particular."

"Yeah, they're hot, but sorry to disappoint, guy. I'm not the artist." Seth sat back his long hairy legs stretching out on the sidewalk, looking at the photos. "I've never even met her."

"But what can you tell me about them?" Gabe got a handkerchief out and swiped his forehead. It's the heat, he thought, not old age.

Seth outlined his time in Ithaca and his connection to *Bookworm Joe's*. "So like I guess the artist lives there. Ken would know her." Seth turned the photos over and flipped through them backside up, stopping on one with writing. "Yeah, here it is. Ken wrote her name in the not —Clarice Miller."

"May I?" Gabe asked taking the stack of photos from Seth and locating the flying spirit. "Do you know anything about this picture?"

"Ah that's bet, man," Seth nodded in agreement as Gabe wondered what he meant. "Look at the flow and the feeling. Totally fresh."

"SETH," a young voice called from across the Commons.

Seth waved back to his friend and stuck up a one-minute finger. "That's Joe,"—he turned back to Gabe—We're up for some freelance caricatures from the lunch crowd."

"Oh, I see. Listen I'm sorry I've kept you— "

"No worries, guy. It's all good."

"May I have this?" Gabe tapped the photo of the flying nymph. "I'd be happy to mail it back to you."

"Naw, it's yours." Seth rose, shoving the other pictures in his sack. "Got to go. Peace out."

As Seth joined his friend, Gabe yanked a pen out of his pocket and wrote what he knew so far: *Artist: Clarice Miller—Ken @ Bookworm Joe's, Cayuga St., Ithaca, NY.* He pulled out his Blackberry, hit Travelocity, and searched for flights to Ithaca while figuring out how much time to take off from work, and what he'd say when he told Sol this one.

32

Going... going... Gone!

Harriet Mansfield stood transfixed, her eyes on the baby. Baby?

It was cold and dark in here. Only two bulbs lit the soaring cavernous space. The hundreds of candles were supposed to supply the rest, but each one seemed to do the exact opposite of shedding light. Still she could see the baby plain enough.

Baby... where did it come from? But of course, she knew. It came from one of those girls, his livestock *he* called them. Everyone knew the storie —she'd seen for herself on her first trip to the ranch. The girls were kept in the two stone barns. Caged in stables, they lived like wild dogs, treated worse than animals. Girls *he* had had kidnapped, usually street whores, ones no one would miss. His purpose was simple—impregnation. *He* would rape them periodically, sometimes even allow favored minions the same sick pleasure. Then they were tested daily. When one was found to be pregnant, she was moved from the rat infested, urine soaked hellhole *he* kept them in to the main house where at least in comparison to the barn, she would be treated like a queen.

Harriet listened to the chanting build around her. It was mollifying, but wasn't that the purpose—help her reach that point of no return? She pushed short fingers through her crunchy hair. Too much hairspray; it needed a wash....

Baby?

Think of something... think....

What else? The rooms he kept the pregnant ones up at the main house—they got TV, books, their own bathroom, three full meals a day, vitamins, exercise, even doctor visits—only the doctor came to them and belonged to *him*. Everything to ensure the girl delivers a perfect, healthy baby. Like... this one.

Harriet shifted her weight from side to side. There was still time; the chorus of chants droned on. *Think of something else, dammit, anything. What else, what else?*

The mothers stayed with their infant until the time of ritual. If the mother was still healthy (able to produce) she was thrown back into the rancid barn with the other women-animals where she'd have to fight for food and water where she'd be hosed off weekly by his laughing pigs, and where she'd wait to be chosen again by him for sadistic torture and brutal rape. The smart ones knew a year out of Hades was worth it. Pregnancy was their only hope—aside from death. They fought to be chosen, even lured the laughing pigs—whose only job was to hose them off, throw food on the dirt floor, and shovel their waste-infested hay—taunting and teasing their keepers into taking them behind his back and without his permission.

Except the guards had seen what happens to those who dare—like the last one who was caught with his hand in the goody jar. *He* made Harriet watch too. Indeed, everyone who was at the ranch that day was made to watch. They chained his limbs to four vehicles, which inched outward—his cries, would she ever forget his cries? She'd managed to squeeze her eyes shut, but a sharp jab in her ribs made her watch... the bleeding torso giving up life as its own heart pumped it dry. The trunk was left to rot for nearly a week before he would allow it to be burned. A tremor ran through Harriet leaving behind it the distinct impression she was no longer human.

Ha-Uuumm... Ha-Uuumm...

The chanting changed, thrumming like a living pulse, tickling the sweat on her bare arms. Harriet couldn't see them, but at least 30 or more had come for her initiation. *A great honor, wasn't it?* She forced herself to look at the pink, pudgy perfection sleeping before her. The ax was dull, she noted, running her hand absent-minded along the edge. *That had to be on purpose, that sick bastard.*

Can't do this, CANNOT DO THIS! Has to be—has to be done. Nothing sacrificed, nothing gained. Shut up, shut up, shut up! Think—think of it as something else. Think! damn you.

Dolls, the dolls in the CPR class she'd taken years ago for work. The instructor said the dolls were made of some sort of gel that had the same density as flesh and muscle. Yes, it's a doll, she thought studying the naked form laying face down on the stone, lying so still, she hoped it was at least drugged. Now the PBS show she'd seen about Samurai popped into her head, sword-wielding students taking turns trying to deliver the blow that would sever the heavy wax torso in two. How hard it had been for them!

"Oh God," Harriet cried still fingering the dull blade.

"Are you serious? Are you actually calling upon Him?" *His* mocking voice prickled her ear. How long had he been behind her? "He has nothing for you, I promise you, only damnation." He moved to put his black mouth even closer to her ear. She shivered at how cold and dead his breath felt. "You should curse Him. You *will* curse Him."

She knew *he* was right, no turning back, no redemption, not for Harriet. Probably never was. Look at her pathetic, lonely life. The only meaning she found was in the power *he* gave her! What had an invisible God ever done for her? Made her a nobody, whom nobody loved. She was an ignored reject until *he* made her somebody. *Yes, Yes, somebody, somebody new. Think of the power.* The power, how delicious, how new. How important it made her.

Ha-Ruuum… Ha-Ruuum…

The chanting hummed louder and louder. Power must be purchased. It MUST be paid for… but—but… this is a… this….

This is NOTHING, nothing to you—nothing but a means to prove yourself worthy, willing.

Ha-Ruuum… Ha-ruuum… Ha-Ruuum…

Ha-ruuum… Ha-Ruuum…

The humming rose, a buzzing unified thunder of power, her heart sped in unison, the black oneness calling to her soul. She belonged to the power; the power belonged TO HER! With that Harriet's resolve returned, and with it her determination to seal her own fate. No more thinking. Get it over with. Wild-eyed Harriet Mansfield lifted the ax far above her head.

Just then, the baby squirmed in its sleep, its innocent humanity stomping her resolve. A trick by God to try and stop her, a dirty, cheap trick. Sudden boiling anger raged. *I will not be Yours, and I won't be tricked.* Swift before the body could wiggle again, she brought the heavy tool down on the white flesh. The first whack was horribly unsuccessful for the blow had barely broken through the skin, and felt more like bludgeoning something with a bat. She screamed at the horror of what she was doing, and unable to end it any other way, she immediately raised the ax again. The baby screamed, a scream so human, so alive and so fundamental, it had to come from the baby's very soul begging for mercy.

The scream only incited her. The first blood ran immediately down both sides of the gashed back. It looked so wrong, so impossible that this perfect form should have this huge gaping wound, and the crying was pathetic. It must be silenced. She had to deal a successful blow this time. The third whack had every ounce of Harriet's strength in it, and went straight across the first wound mercifully deep enough to separate the baby's spinal cord.

Whether the baby was dead or not, Harriet didn't know. She *did* know her part was over; her fate sealed. Dropping the ax, she turned, walked down four steps, heard three more ceremonial whacks of dismemberment, and retched all over her shoes.

33

Confessions

In the stillness of the wooded hermitage, Father Simeon heard the tinkle of the first bell warning the monks of Mount Charbel that Mass would begin in fifteen minutes. The monks in the monastery rose at four forty five AM, said their morning offering, Liturgy of the Hours, and completed an hour of meditation before leaving the main house and heading up the hill to the chapel for six thirty Mass.

The aged priest had no need to rise since he'd only occupied his bed in the hut that the monks called prayer shelters for three hours that night. He slept from about midnight to three when an inner clock caused him to rise, kneel by his bed, and pray. And so he'd been for hours. But such was typical of Father Simeon, who had returned to the very hermitage he had founded and built, nearly fifty years ago. Despite his aging condition and health problems, Simeon gained permission of his Franciscan order to retire at the Mount for as long as he desired, residing in one of the twelve isolated huts.

Simeon proceeded to stand, hearing the bones of his knees whine in brazen insolence of the long hours spent on the plank floor. He went to the corner and bent over the bucket of water he'd filled the night before. He splashed his face and neck with the ice-cold stuff trying to dodge his Van Winkle beard then climbed out of the woolen habit and underclothing. Using an old rag and a bar of lye soap, he washed his long limbs. As he washed, he prayed to God that his faults and sins be similarly cleansed. For a moment, so fleeting, shaking with cold, Simeon thought of others his age, sitting on some park bench in sunny Florida, comfortably wrapped in cozy oversized sweaters, tossing seed to greedy pigeons.

"Such a thought, me in Florida," he tsk'd while drying his head of white hair. "I'm as balmy as a palm tree, Lord. You best hurry up and reveal him to me, or I may not recognize him." Simeon's eyes glistened looking up, the lined face as expectant as a child on Christmas Eve.

Over fresh undergarments, the same brown habit was pulled back on, a simple rope tied at the waist, and his weathered feet slid into sandals. Simeon straightened the skimpy blanket over the thin mattress on the plank bed and retrieved his tattered breviary off the small log table. Tucking it under his arm, he latched the slatted pine door behind him, claimed his walking stick, and struck out on the dirt path toward the chapel.

Father Tom sat in the log chapel listening to industrious birds make a musical racket outside the chapel window while all manner of woodsy odor filled his nose. What a place *The Hermitage* was, so private, pastoral. No wonder some of his parishioners loved to come here. Beyond the simple monastery, lay a dozen footpaths through the woods, leading to chapels and hidden lakes, stone-clad shrines, covered bridges and huge outdoor Stations of the Cross.

Father Tom left Saint Elizabeth's at dawn coming early to meditate before Mass. Normally as pastor, he would say Mass at his parish, but a visiting priest was available to fill in, and Tom needed to see Father Simeon.

The chapel door opened again, and Father Tom looked over his shoulder for Father Simeon, but instead saw another Marionite brother who entered flinging his grey cowl back and genuflecting. Tom turned his attention back to the tabernacle. He hoped Father was okay. The old priest was cutting it kind of close for morning Mass.

Usually he met Simeon for confession and spiritual direction, but today Tom came to tell him about the little Miller boy. He'd avoided John Miller twice already, merely nodding when he saw him at Mass. Sitting on the log pew, Father Tom could barely say his prayers, his mind playing over the events he'd come to tell his mentor.

The walk was longish, Simeon's hut being the last on the private path that ran in front of the thirteen prayer shelters. It assured him absolute solitude though, even from passing retreatants. Through the woods, he saw the outline of Saint Francis Pond and passed a grove of trees. He recognized the spot he and Doc Holmes had been chopping wood back in eighty-three when he refused to bide any of Ed's warnings.... Then again, maybe this order of Marionites, so perfect for this place, would not have found the Mount if he had not contracted Lyme disease.

"Your ways are so mysterious, Lord."

Mysterious, indeed! What of the biggest mystery of his life? He saw him so clearly in his visions; he was sure that he'd know him. How much longer would he wait? It had been exactly six years since his first jolting vision, praying in the tiny garden of the Sister Servants of Mary in the Bronx. And last month, he had another glimpse of the Preparer. He saw the boy in a church, big glasses on a round face framed by a halo of blond curls. The child was kneeling in prayer and obvious rapture; his arms were spread wide, his upturned face bright with pure love. Usually he saw him in a fantastic forest setting, enormous ancient trees, a brook as crystal as flowing diamonds, green moss and flora almost pre-historic, the sanctuary to be sure. Yet he still had no idea where it was, nor who the boy was. When would God's plan involve him?

"When?"

"When what, Father?"

Young Brother Angelo seemed to come out of nowhere and joined him on the walkway outside the chapel.

Father squinted at Brother Angelo, tilting his head sideways to peer at him. "Whennn... will skippy monks stop invading the lofty thoughts of their superiors?" He tugged the brother's cowl further over his forehead while the young man respectfully held the chapel door.

Mass felt a bit crowded to Tom with all three rows of wooden benches filled with monks and a half dozen lay people. Father Simeon and Brother Angelo entered with barely a minute to spare. Mass was starkly different with Latin prayers, an old-fashioned tinkle of bells, and the Gregorian chant of the monks. Laced with a transcendental quality rather appropriate he thought, here where people come to withdraw from the world. The closing hymn was beautiful, dominated by the practiced, low voices of the monks.

The chapel emptied rather slowly as each participant stayed behind to say his own thanksgiving. Finally, he and Father Simeon were completely alone. Tom moved to sit in the pew with Simeon. The old monk stopped scratching his long, wooly beard and raised his hand to begin the sacrament of Reconciliation. At first, Tom thought to stop him and explain that he'd come for a different reason today. Instead, having examined his conscience last night, he felt compunction and unloaded himself easily in the sacrament.

Father Simeon sat quietly, eyes closed and arms crossed while Tom completed his prayers of penance. Father Tom reached out, lightly tapping Simeon's forearm.

"Father, I have something that—well, I believe it's miraculous, to tell you."

"You believe, Thomas?"

"No, I know…. I mean yes, I'm sure," Tom stuttered under Simeon's analytical gaze and not a thousand percent sure he wasn't crazy. "It was a few months ago before Mass one Sunday, I was bringing out the gifts and this child, he—" Tom stopped thinking he better start at the beginning. "Wait, the night before I was polishing the wood, the wood in our chapel, the wooden tabernacle, that is. I was using a special chemical." Tom searched for the right order of events. "So, of course I had removed Our Lord first. I wouldn't, well, you know I, ah, placed the Hosts in one of the old side tabernacles." Simeon held his hand up halting the sputtering. Tom took a deep breath, aware that his excitement would quickly exasperate the old man, whose nature was much calmer than his.

Then without a word, Father Simeon rose, entered the short aisle, slowly genuflected, and turned to leave the chapel. Tom followed imitating the priest's dignity, willing himself to calm down. Outside the fresh air and walking did the trick; Father Tom related all the facts of the Miller encounter. They reached a favored spot, the covered bridge between the thirteenth and fourteenth station. It was a small structure with narrow benches built into each side. The two priests leaned over the railing peering into the trickling streambed below. Tom was silent waiting for the measured words of the sage priest.

"Describe the child, Tom."

"He's about six years old with blond hair, sort of has a wavy curl to it. His eyes are the most startling hazel... or green I think. He wears glasses, you see." Father Tom noticed the old man's hands gripping the railing with whitened knuckles.

Simeon turned toward him his eyes almost merry. "Tom, do you realize, do you have any idea," he said then stopped. "No, I'm getting ahead of myself. I have to meet this child and his family, Thomas. It is very important."

Confused by the priest's reaction, Tom searched Simeon's face for signs that this holy priest, on whose discernment throngs of followers would stake their lives, that this, his spiritual director actually believed the incredulous tale of the floating Host.

"Do you believe me then, Father?"

"It must be investigated of course." Simeon said, absently stroking his beard. "Thomas, I've known you since you were in Seminary, been your spiritual advisor for years. In all these years I've never found you unstable." Simeon sat down heavily on the log bench, and Tom continued leaning over the rail.

"Oh man! I mean I'm relieved to hear you say it. You know you're not the easiest person to read." Simeon tilted his head up to Tom and raised one fluffy eyebrow waiting. "Well, you're not," Tom said, "Sometimes, I feel like a kindergartner sent to the principal's office when we meet."

"Come now, Thomas, I'm not that intimidating." Simeon's eyes sparkled up at him with mischief. It was Tom's favorite side of him, when he let anyone see it. "I want you to immediately contact, er..."

"John Miller?"

"Miller," he repeated with a more serious air, "fine. Good then. Arrange a day and place for us to meet his family. You need to handle this carefully, my boy. They may not understand what they are dealing with, and if they do, they may not trust just anyone."

"I..." Tom started to formulate a question but then thought better of it watching the wrinkled countenance. Father Simeon lingered on the bridge sitting on the chilly pine bench, his thoughts a mystery to Tom, who stood there a moment not sure if they were through. The leathery face and bright eyes looked up at him one last time.

"Tom, if this is the child who I suspect, I fear how much our Lord will ask of us in protecting him."

Simeon opened his breviary and bent his head to the daily Office, and Tom knew he'd been dismissed. He had no idea what Father Simeon suspected, or why there would be an *us*, nor why the child would need protecting. Nevertheless, Tom thought walking back to his car, he knew his spiritual director; Simeon would tell him all he needed to know—and no more than he needed to know—and not *until* he needed to know it.

34

John's Dream

"No, never. Never!" John's voice rose — a crescendo erupting from his dream, spilling like lava into his conscious world. His nightmare had reached an unbearable climax, and he woke feeling clammy. Clarice rubbed his back mumbling, "You all right?" then fell back into the deep sleep John had disturbed.

He peeled the sheet off then lay back trying to recall details of the dream while the feeling was so strong. It had begun in Jackson's bedroom where Jax was taking a nap—at least it seemed like a nap, something blurred in his mind about the way the light filled the room with the blue curtain billowing…. Someone was shaking Jax awake, pulling him out of bed. Jax was complaining, a sleepy whine, "No, no, I don't wanna."

A woman spoke. John knew the voice but couldn't place it. It waved in front of him, familiar, yet untouchable.

"It's alright, Jax." The voice was soft and convincing.

Jackson whimpered, but the voice wouldn't listen.

John struggled to make sense of the dread he had felt, however the mind awake and the mind of the subconscious speak two different languages. He strained to remember left with a confusing impression of a scene unfolding like a horror movie, his dread mounting like phantom music playing in the background. He remembered a growing fear over where the woman intended to bring his son. Why couldn't he place the voice? Why! It was familiar. Someone he knows... or maybe someone Clarice knows.

This is stupid; it's just a nightmare. John punched his pillow and attempted to cram into a more comfortable position. He gave up, swung out of bed. *Was the AC working or what?* He put his hands on his sore back and gave it a stretch backward automatically looking for stars in the skylight. Thirsty, he walked toward the bathroom but then changed his mind and crept to the kitchen instead. He got a tumbler, shot ice cubes in it from the fridge door, then topped it off with Jack Daniel's.

Sipping from the glass, John strolled toward the living room, not bothering with lights, the soft glow from a couple nightlights preferable at this ungodly hour. It felt cooler down here. He swirled his ice, looking at the gargantuan stone fireplace. It would have dominated the room if it hadn't been for the soaring cathedral ceilings, he thought randomly. He strained to see out the sliding glass doors, but it was pitch black. No street lights, no neighbor's porch light—that takes getting used to. There'd been so many changes living here, he thought, mostly good.... Things felt off, though. Clarice had been acting weird ever since Nicey's funeral. She was hiding something from him; he was sure. Why are we always so reserved? *God, I love you Reece, but damn if I can figure you out.*

John sank down on the couch, took another slug, realizing it was the last. He remembered what woke him and tried again to recapture the dream, closing his eyes. It seemed the woman, the voice, had no idea that she was taking Jax to something bad. Why couldn't he see her face or place her voice? Why?! The tension built as tension does in nightmares. He heard the woman gaining ground in her quest to get Jackson to go with her. John was desperate to stop them. Jax should NOT go. The fuzzy confusion of a typical dream spun as John's whiskey glass rolled from his hand.

The woman and Jax were in a car together. They were talking, even laughing when without warning, the scene changed. They were still driving... only now the woman behind the wheel was no longer the one John knew or the voice he should know. This one was older, her voice different, unfamiliar. John saw Jax in the backseat, crying, curled up in a ball. His tiny legs and hands cruelly strapped with some sort of cellophane tape. Like a fricking UPS box! John's throat tightened till it physically hurt. Impotent, he watched the unfolding events as the car sped and sped toward some great darkness, an evil waiting for Jax. He could do nothing! Knew he wasn't even present. Could do nothing but scream, "No, no." The tension built till John's mind could no longer face the horror over which he had no control. His conscious mind released him, and he awoke on the couch, glancing down at the empty glass on the floor.

A dream... no, a warning from God. He believed it with every fiber of his being. He just knew. Hadn't he been warned last year, in church on Jackson's birthday? Jax needed to be protected, guarded. No matter how crazy it sounds, John thought resolving to be vigilant. The evil was real, and it wanted to destroy his son. *God, just show me how; help me to protect him.*

35

Simeon's Canticle

At the fridge, Clarice gathered celery, a red and a green pepper, a bag of baby carrots, and for the fifth time considered changing her outfit. Her blue suit skirt was long enough—she hoped. What about the cut, the slight flounce at the bottom, did that look flirty? *Oh, this is ridiculous.* She chopped celery, cutting neat finger-length pieces. *I don't even know them!* John's pastor, Father Tom had called John and awkwardly invited himself and a priest friend to their new house in Ithaca. Apparently, he had nosed about trying to ensure that Jackson and she would be there wanting to meet John's whole family. *Weird,* but the two priests were coming.

What's with John anyway? He sometimes invites work friends or clients over with little or no warning, but a priest? He usually kept his religion pretty much to himself. She moved onto the peppers, slicing them in half and removing the seeds half-wondering though if these priests with their built-in belief in the supernatural would believe any of her stories.... It would be a relief, she admitted, to unload this stuff on an expert of some sort.

"Should be a psychiatrist," she mumbled munching a celery stick and arranging the uniform strips of pepper on the platter. The deep weight inside her always pressuring to come out pushed. It was relentless... never stopping, she'd been living with it—ha, fighting it—since the funeral.

"What is it with you?" She spoke to the ball of light. "Lay off, wouldja, I've got company coming."

Clarice wrestled an avocado out of the grocery bag on the counter while summoning her will to keep the light at bay. She concentrated ridiculously hard on the task. Paring knife in a firm grip, slicing the bumpy rind lengthwise all around the pit, a simple twist, separate the halves... *That's it Reece, focus.* It was working. The task at hand would be enough to squelch the encroaching power, which seemed only to have the upper hand when she allowed herself to dwell on it.

The visit would be simple, "horse-doovers," as John called them and drinks. They'd wondered if priests drink and if so, what? In the end they decided on being sure the bar, really just a high cupboard, was loaded and ready to serve any request. Clarice held the to-do list: coffee, water for tea, lemonade and iced tea, cheese and cracker plate, shrimp & scallop number. The house was spotless for the nickel tour, and the bathrooms scoured. She reached in the junk drawer for a pen, literally scratched off the last items, and retired the list.

John came around the corner shaking his head and grinning. He always made fun of her list making.

"Ta-do list isn't ta-done till you check it all off," she said, shutting the junk drawer with her hip, "everyone knows that."

"Hey, you okay with this?" He rubbed her shoulders.

"Yeah, I guess." She patted his hand as the doorbell rang. Half past four as promised. "What am I supposed to call them?" She picked up the tray.

"Easy," he called as he left, "they all answer to Father."

She carried the last tray into the family room and joined John at the front door. She was surprised to see one so young and the other so old. The old one held her hand slightly longer than needed, his strong, sparkly eyes searching her face. He was very tall and thin with a wiry strength, not the fragility expected of his obvious years. She decided she liked the Gandalf quality, wanting to sketch the creamy swirls of his beard, full nose, and thick brow.

"I guess my directions weren't so bad," John said, breaking the odd connection between Clarice and the priest.

"Yeah, actually we did make one wrong turn, but boy, how remote is this," the younger one said as they walked to the great room. "Beautiful drive, though."

"What can I get you, padres," John said as the two guests chose the leather couch opposite the stone fireplace.

When both men gave a blank look, Clarice offered, "Let's see, we have lemonade, iced tea, coffee, or uh, the bar is stocked if you'd prefer a mixed drink." She moved the shrimp and scallop tray closer to them, handed them each a napkin, and sat on the edge of a nearby chair.

"I'm having Sam Adams if that helps," John said.

"Bourbon on the rocks if you have it," the old one said with barely a pause. John turned to the young one, who rocked forward with a child-like grin, his legs crossed, and his hands laced over one knee.

"Oh, I, uh…I don't know, I—"

"Have a drink if you want one, Tom" the old priest snipped, a tad of irritation in his voice.

"Oh, it's not that," he said with a timid laugh, "I'm driving after all. Iced tea sounds great, thanks." He reached for a scallop nodding his approval.

Clarice was surprised that the old one drank and guessed it must not be against their rules. She rose to help John, opting for an iced tea herself, more to keep the priest company, but thinking she could do with something stronger. The ball of light had been virtually pulsing since she greeted the priests. Despite her nerves, she resisted the temptation. They returned, John carrying the tray of drinks and Clarice distributing

"And (cough) where is your young son?" the old priest named Simeon asked, placing his drink on the coffee table.

"Oh he's upstairs," Clarice said, "playing in his bedroom. We thought we'd leave him play while we got acquainted and made our drinks," Clarice got up from the fireplace chair. "If you'd like, we can show you the house and make our way up to him."

"We'd love to, right Father?" Father Tom said. "It looks grand, John. Did you build it yourself?"

"Not with my bare hands," John cracked, "Actually, Clarice and I designed it together."

"No, you don't," Clarice slapped John's arm. "John is the mastermind behind this beauty, and he's nothing if not humble about it."

The four continued talking as they left the family room, listening to John describe the work involved in making the fireplace to a very interested Simeon. They continued to the east wing and stood in John's office. As John and his pastor talked about the construction business, Simeon wandered over to Clarice's studio on the other side of the room. She watched him with the natural curiosity of an artist over the reception of their work. He passed a few hung pictures, pausing more than politely. Tom and John strolled over to join them.

Simeon arrived at the easel holding her recent composition. Taking one look at the dogs, his legs collapsed beneath him. Clarice made a grab for his arm as he slid to the floor. Tom hastened forward grabbing his other side. John scooped Simeon out of their arms and carried him to one of the tapestry chairs in front of his desk.

"A glass of water," Father Tom said, his voice demanding.

Clarice jumped to fulfill the request, bringing a wet towel as well. She patted the thin skin of Simeon's high forehead above his closed eyes. His lips murmured between the snowy mustache and beard. She caught only one word and it sent a chill across her chest: *Evil*. Simeon revived immediately brushing her and the priest away.

"I'm all right! Give a man some air, just a silly old man's confusion."

"Your heart, is it all right?" The priest's boyish face was grave. "I shouldn't have brought you all this way, shouldn't have involved you."

The young priest's words lit a fire under Father Simeon, who righted himself and determinedly launched from the chair. "Nonsense," he said, "stop fawning over me like a bunch of nursing-home nuns." He straightened his black suit coat. "In any case, we're all involved, whether we want to be or not." This last comment was accompanied by a personal look into each of their eyes, ending with Clarice. He searched her face uncomfortably long as he had at the door. "Now then," he barked, "we will see the rest of this magnificent house you have built." Tom continued to hold Simeon's arm, who shrugged the doting hands aside.

The tour continued, passing quickly through the undersized dining room to the curving stairway. Everyone it seemed, except Father Simeon, was concerned about his taking the stairs. In answer to their unspoken fears, the old man not only led the way but at a good pace. Standing at the top, he peered down at them with grinning eyes. "Bad heart, bah." She heard him grumble under his breath when Father Tom passed.

They explored the upstairs briefly, and soon the quartet was poised outside Jackson's room. Clarice knocked gently.

"Jackie, we have visitors who'd like to meet you. May we come in?"

"Sure Mom."

Clarice and John entered first followed by Father Tom, who hurried forward with an extended hand. Jackson sat on the floor holding an old Rubik's cube that Nicey gave him and surrounded by a pile of nature magazines and the newspaper.

John and his pastor blocked Simeon's view of Jackson, and she watched the old priest's eyes land on the newly finished mural. The Glen filled the wall in a remarkably vibrant scene of giant rocks beside a crystal stream, flora, and mossy carpet, and the ancient trunks of the mammoth trees. With an expression of childlike joy, Father's arm went up, slowly tracing the objects. She was just thinking this landscape was somehow familiar to Simeon when the adults blocking the view of her little boy parted like the Red Sea. Simeon looked faint for the second time today. Transfixed he stared at Jackson.

"How long! How long I have waited," he said in a drawn out sigh.

Jackson stood. All eyes were on the bright face of the old priest. The room was pregnant with anticipation. Simeon moved forward enraptured. Lightly he held both of Jackson's forearms and looked up toward heaven.

"Finally Lord, You have shown me your messenger! Your mercy endures for all ages, for You have not abandoned your children but sent new hope. You have sent a new voice to cry out from the wilderness and call your people to Your Son—For the Groom draws near, and the bridesmaids are unaware. May your name be praised always and your mercy be sung for endless days."

Simeon's face shone. He continued to hold Jackson's arms, gently turning him to face the others in the room.

"This child in your midst, this son of yours, shall be great in the eyes of the Lord. He shall drink no alcohol, nor live as we do. He is filled with the Holy Spirit, and he will turn people's hearts to Christ. Like a trumpet blast, he will awaken souls to prepare for the Lord's return, for he has the spirit of John. Jack-son, even his name bears witness—son of John the Baptist! He will bear light for the Light of the World. He will shine this light on the people in darkness and those in the shadow of death, guiding their feet to the Prince of Peace. He will call to the peoples of this age: '*Make straight your ways and prepare for His return.*'"

The power and veracity in Simeon's voice was undeniable. His words rang like musical notes in a heavenly love song. The import of his declaration filled the room with profound truth. The unseen words burst in the air and hung there like the fizzled trails of a fireworks display. Clarice watched shimmering lights emanate from Jackson and radiate to the edges of the room like ripples in a pond. The light pulsing outward seemed to mix with the unseen words of Simeon's canticle. Clarice labored to understand even one iota of what was spoken... and then it ceased to matter.

Jackson had gone catatonic. Clarice sprang forward gathering him in her arms. She laid him on the bed and sat on its edge stroking his wayward lock. The others in the room came alive after Clarice's move—John shifted his weight, Simeon scratched his beard and only Father Tom seemed flummoxed over Jackson's condition. Naturally, she and John knew nothing would bring Jax out of this state (save some mysterious divine clock); Father Simeon too, appeared to accept the situation whereas Tom was clearly agitated.

"What's wrong? Oh, my Jesus," Father Tom cried, scurrying to the other side of the bed. "Jackson, Jackson." The priest bent over Jax patting his stiff hand to rouse him. His confusion, both over Jax's state and the relative composure of the others was interrupted when Father Simeon stepped in. He led both him and Clarice out of the room. John followed, and they all met in the hall, looking to Simeon, who merely crooked a long finger toward himself beckoning the group to follow. Only to Clarice did he direct a comment as she passed.

"He is safe, as you know. Surely you saw the angelic aura as I did."

Back in the family room, Simeon stayed in control. "John, there is much to discuss. It might be best if you refresh our drinks before we begin." John dutifully left to renew the previous drink orders.

"I don't understand," Father Tom said, looking backward. "Shouldn't we call—"

"Sit down, Tom," Simeon said, indicating the couch. "Please."

Clarice joined him on the couch facing Simeon who stood opposite the coffee table. "It's all right Tom, er Father at least we hope so," Clarice said. "He's been doing this since he was at least four. Nothing we do brings him out of it. We've been to our physician, and he doesn't believe it's serious. I won't say it hasn't worried us. I mean I..." Clarice choked. The harder she worked to suppress her fears, the more she felt that incredible hurt rise to the surface screaming for release, for sympathy, for answers. "I don't know what to do, how to help him. He goes stiff as a board, white as a sheet, staring into space. I can't... I... he—" Clarice broke down into quiet sobs. Her release, once begun, could not be stopped, anymore than a hand could hold back a wave.

Father Tom placed his hand lightly on her shoulder and shyly patted her, all of three times. She could feel his sympathy, yet he had this proprietary reserve, some line a priest can't cross she guessed. She lifted her teary eyes to find John hurrying over with the drinks. He put the tray on the coffee table, nudging the platter of shrimp hors d'oeuvres aside. He then sat on the arm of the couch.

"Everything okay?" John said, placing his arm around her shoulder and giving a squeeze. Clarice was sure he knew exactly what caused her melt down. She felt stupid, these cursed spells of Jackson's! She always hid her worry from John. They both did, trying to be brave for each other. Still she hadn't been the same since the funeral. Even now, that stinking invader sapped all her energy, even the energy to put on a brave face.

Father Simeon reached for his bourbon on the tray and held it out to Clarice. "Come, come my dear. Drink this, and we'll talk. There is so much to explain. Perhaps I can shed some light on these ecstasies of the little one."

Ecstasies? She never heard them called that. Wasn't it some religious term? What was he saying? Clarice clutched the drink and rolled the idea around that this man may have some answers for her. She took a slow sip then a gagging gulp, forcing her emotions down with it.

"Your son is special as you know. You are too." Father Simeon looked into Clarice's upraised eyes. "You were destined from childhood for this task. Remember the hand?"

Hand? Oh my God, did he just say hand!?

"What task?" John interjected sounding angry. "I mean what is it you people know about our son? What is this visit really all about?" John let go of Clarice's shoulder and looked to both men with their black shirts and imposing white collars; then he stopped himself, his respect for them plain.

Simeon calmly bent over the drink tray and chose the glass of iced tea. He ambled across the room to sit in the high-backed leather chair by the fireplace. All eyes focused on the weathered face. The tall, dignified figure sat upright and managed to look relaxed, exuding an air of cool authority. He took a long draw on his drink then ran a hand down the length of his beard. Finally, he addressed them. "I believe Father Tom has something to relate before I share my thoughts."

Father Tom looked at each of them, like he'd been put on the spot. Getting up from the couch, he faced John.

"Remember the first time we met, uh, Jackson's accidental communion? It... wasn't what it appeared." Tom ran fingers through his straight brown hair. "Nothing was accidental about that day." He recounted what had really transpired the first Sunday in May. Clarice listened, shyly interrupting twice to ask the meaning of 'Host' and 'tabernacle'.

"What do you mean?" John said, "Are you saying you gave Jackson Holy Communion *on purpose*?"

"Quite the opposite. I swear to you, I saw the Host of its own accord fly through the air and land on your son's tongue."

Next to her, Clarice felt John stiffen. She studied his stony profile while his pastor finished the fantastic tale. Father Tom moved to stand by the fireplace near Simeon. Just like that, John's look changed, like a light turned on. She was suddenly sure that not only did he believe it, but that it answered some sort of question he had. That was the day of the show; the day they'd been late.

Clarice experienced a bizarre mix of suspicion and relief. She thought of most of their belief system as mumbo-jumbo. Yet,... if these priests and John believed that something this supernatural could occur, they might believe her story. And the old one said something at the top of the stairs about her seeing angelic auras, which of course she had. Although it was only subconsciously that she had ever thought of those auras as angelic or demonic.

"This child of yours is a gift of extraordinary mercy for these end times," Simeon said, "God has shown me great things involving this child. These ecstasies are given to him by God. During them, your son is instructed and grows in grace. He is already being trained for his task; even now a place has been prepared in the wilderness for him to complete this training in safety. He will live entirely alone, in complete solitude. Only in the Silva Templum will he be protected from evil and those who seek his death." Simeon gazed across the room at her hurt. His voice lowered, "You know this place, for you have painted its image in detail on his wall. The time draws near when he will be taken there by his protector. For now, away from either of you, he is not safe."

He stopped. Clarice let the words, so similar to Nicey's in the hospital sink in. *How did this wizard priest know about the Glen? What did he say about ecstasies and a protector?*

Just then, the ball of light inside Clarice pushed, forcing her to abandon her thoughts and redirect her energy to control *It*.

Next to his wife, John was lost in his own thoughts. The mural, hearing it talked about that way, like some secret she had kept from him. She held so much of herself back from him. He never pressed her, never begged her to reveal her secrets to him. Now for both their sakes, he wished he hadn't left her privacy so sacrosanct.

John stood from the arm of the couch, towering over the group. He paced, questions flying out in no logical order.

"What danger are you talking about? Who's trying to harm our son? And what do you mean 'live in the wilderness?' What kind of training?" His voice rose with each frustrated query, "And what do you know of all this?" He wheeled around to her. "Why did you paint his room that way? What was with the picture of the dogs?" John snapped his attention back to Simeon. "I know that was what made you faint."

"Father Simeon, *is* that what made you faint?" Father Tom joined the action.

Simeon, his elbows on the arms of the chair, slowly drew his hands together and made a tent with his fingers—his calmness, a counterbalance to the frantic questions in the room. "Indeed John, although it was not the scene per se, more the evil your wife managed to capture in her painting." Then to Clarice, "I suspect you have seen and experienced whatever you paint." Clarice looked flabbergasted.

"He's right isn't he?" John immediately accused her. "You do paint what you've experienced. Those dogs, Jackson's room, oh my God, that picture of the flying spirit. What does that mean? Is that... you?" John's suspicions poured out aimed at her. He was full of hurt, feeling betrayal in every question. Here was another area of her life she'd hid from him.

"I do—I did," Clarice blurted in release, "I was chased by those dogs. They tried to kill me. I don't know where they came from. I ran and I ran. And then I was in the Glen and everything was... but then at home Jax knew. He knew. He said—" her words choked, she couldn't go on.

Clarice was hanging by an emotional thread. She felt trapped, John and these men demanding she open up to them. And she was not ready for that! It would mean sharing secrets she'd carried and protected all her life. Confessing these things out loud, it would be like admitting they were real. Keeping it inside, there was a chance it was all in her imagination. A ridiculous idea after all she had seen, yet the human mind can do literal gymnastics to deny truths that simply confound it. Like a cornered animal, instead of acquiescing, Clarice lashed back pushing herself up from the couch and slamming her half-finished whiskey on the coffee table for effect.

"I've had enough, I tell you. I'll go crazy. All this talk of flying wafers, auras and evil, it's nonsense. I can't believe we're sitting here listening to this. John, please. Please, make them stop. Make it go away." She pleaded with him for help, to put a stop to this spiraling conversation. Meanwhile inside, the intruder, that damnable ball of light was acting up, besieging her psyche. Trapped inside and out, she locked her gaze on John's face, tears brimming, and desperately begged her husband with her eyes.

Perhaps he was thinking of her hospitalization, afraid of risking her health. Perhaps he was afraid, like her, or maybe it was her desperate pleas as his wife. Whatever the reason, John finally, stepped in to protect her.

"I think I have to ask you gentlemen to leave."

From the chair, Simeon's gaze followed Clarice as she retreated to a corner of the room. Father Tom nodded, agreeing with John.

"I think it would be best if we leave for Mrs. Miller's sake. Perhaps some other—"

"There's so much more to discuss," Simeon protested, rising from the chair and coming toward her. "Clarice you must listen to me."

This set her off again. She'd never felt this out of control, certainly John had never seen her like this.

"No. I won't hear another word," Clarice screamed. "Get out. I mean it! Get out! Just go away." She sounded like a crazed mental patient. "You leave, b-both of you! Leave me—leave me alone." Listening to herself, she thought anyone could see there would be no reasoning with her, yet the old man wouldn't let go.

"I tell you it is of the utmost importance that you speak with us. I have to find out from where the danger will come. I must learn if his new protector is aware of their part." He stood before her, an impressive figure even in old age. For a moment, she felt a huge power beneath his ancient look reaching toward that ball of light. It was all too much.

Clarice screamed again, shrieking, "No. Stop it. Stop, I can't take any more." She held her hands over her ears, "I can't fight any more—you and *It*." She pleaded with her husband, "John, please. John, help me."

Seeing his wife cowering in the corner, her hands pathetically clapped over her ears and the unbelievable pain in her face was more than John could stand. In righteous anger, he placed his bulk between her tiny frame and the tall priest.

"You will accompany me to the door," he bellowed, "now Father!"

Simeon looked at the virile strength and determined face before him, and John literally watched the light go out of the priest's bright eyes before he turned away. Father Tom readily took his arm, feeling, if not understanding, his defeat. Together they walked toward the hallway to the front door. John followed directly behind them, no longer threatening, instead feeling awful about his treatment of the two.

Father Tom broke the uncomfortable silence trying to interject a breath of humor. "Out the door we came in, eh John? Isn't that the Irish rule?"

"Uh, yes... I mean I don't know. Is it?"

"I just thought a name like Miller might be Irish, and you might know the old superstition for good luck."

"Never mind all that," Simeon broke in on the banal exchange. "You will speak to her John about seeing us again. You must begin to understand what is happening. I fear our time is short. You and your wife may be the key."

"Listen Father, I mean no disrespect, but I'm totally lost here. This is sounding very far-fetched. I don't even know what you're talking about. I think my wife and I have things to discuss between ourselves, and right now my only concern is Clarice and Jackson."

"Naturally, naturally," Simeon agreed, scratching his chin under his beard. "Tom, have you one of those little cards with the church's number on it?"

Father Tom searched his wallet, retrieving a card. "John it has my personal cell phone number on it too. I can reach Father Simeon if you—"

"No, no," Simeon snagged the card. "There's a phone at the Hermitage. Uh Tom, a pen?" He waved his hand.

Tom reached in his shirt pocket, pulled out a handsome Cross pen. After a moment of watching Father Simeon trying to click down on the top of the pen, which had no such mechanism, he reclaimed the instrument and twisted the end to make the point appear. "Here you go, Father."

"Highfalutin contraption," Simeon grunted, taking the pen. He laid the card in his left palm. With his right hand, he wrote a shaky phone number and signature in that slanted script of his generation. Handing the card to John, Simeon searched his eyes, "Certainly if you cannot reach me for some reason call Father Tom. After you get things figured out—when things are clearer to you and your wife—you may—you *will* need our help."

John felt the probing eyes of the priest and saw the unmistakable sincerity. He stood at the end of the front porch, watching the men descend the stairs to their blue Ford Taurus. He was eager to return to Clarice and check on Jackson. Father Tom opened the passenger door for Father Simeon, who unexpectedly turned calling up to John.

"I will pray for strength for each of you to finish your task. You too must pray, John Miller and do not cease."

"Okay, Father," was all John could manage. Persistent old bugger, John thought, but slipped inside mumbling the Lord's Prayer in his head"

Tom buckled, formulating his first question of many and choosing carefully incase Father Simeon shut him down right out of the box. Deciding to start with the most distressing he said, "Father, what you said in there, up in Jackson Miller's room, about John the Baptist...surely you don't mean to suggest the child is a new prophet?"

Simeon fiddled with his seat belt seeming to ignore Tom, pulling it out from the holder, stretching it across his lap, finding it too short, and then repeating the process: pull, stretch, release. Following his third attempt, using the same ill-fated, jerking motion, he let it snap back into itself with an indignant huff. "What's that?" he said, "prophet?" The old priest made a snicking sound. "Nonsense, I don't have to tell you, do I, Tom, that John the Baptist was the last of the prophets."

Tom was aware of course of the Church's clear teaching on the matter. The prophetic line of the Old Covenant up to the New had ended with John the Baptist. Even if Luke 16:16 had not confirmed this, it would have made sense to him. The Old Testament prophets told of the coming of Christ right up until John, who as the precursor to Christ, not only prophesied the Messiah's coming but was able to point Christ out saying: "*Behold, the Lamb of God....*" Indeed, all Divine Revelation ended with the arrival of Christ, who was the fulfillment of all prophecies. All the Scriptures—the Law, the Prophets, and the Psalm —are fulfilled in Christ.

Simeon closed his eyes and was silent as Tom continued to navigate the rough road leaving the Miller property, hoping his spiritual advisor would say more without being prodded. When he didn't, Tom cleared his throat, leaving the "a-hem" hang in the air. The elderly priest finally spoke, his eyes remaining closed and his big knuckled fingers laced over his chest. "*God, who in different portions and diverse ways, spoke in times past to the fathers by the prophets, last of all, in these days has spoken to us in His Son…*" His voice quoting Hebrews was soft and far away. "The Father spoke the Word; the Word was made Flesh, and there is nothing more that needs to be said."

"Of course," Tom nodded, keeping his eyes peeled for signs leading out of downtown Ithaca.

"Do you remember Elijah, Tom and the request of his successor Elisha?"

Tom brought to mind Elijah, who was perhaps the greatest prophet of the Old Testament. The prophet came on the scene from nowhere in 9 BC, a powerful voice from God, challenging the Israelites who were worshipping the false god Baal. Elijah confronted King Ahab, and he cursed the wicked Queen, Jezebel. In a showdown with the Baalim priests, he called for a contest between Baal and God to see whose god could light the fire for his own sacrifice. After a day of the priests praying, sacrificing, and even drawing their own blood and getting nothing, Elijah gathered wood, ordered it doused with four jugs of water, and called on God to light the fire. At Elijah's prayer, fire came forth from heaven consuming "*the burnt offering and the wood and the stones and the dust, and licked up the water that was in the trench.*" Much revered by Jews, Muslims and Christians alike, Elijah was taken up by a fiery chariot, and it is supposed he never saw death.

Father Tom answered, "I remember before Elijah was taken up, Elisha asked him for a double portion of his spirit."

"Which—he—received," Simeon finished. "And you recall in the Gospel of Luke that John was to go forth in the 'spirit and power of Elijah?'" Tom nodded again. "Well, God in His wisdom has seen fit to bestow a portion of that same spirit of Elijah and of Saint John the Baptist on young Jackson Miller for his great mission."

Feeling hot, Tom fiddled with the AC as he asked, "What mission?"

"Enough questions for now, Thomas." The priest said pulling his rosary, kissing the large crucifix, and blessing himself. He began the rosary in a loud voice saying, "I believe in God, the Father Almighty, Creator of heaven and earth…"

Tom gave up on the AC and on more answers to his questions—at least for the time being. He cracked his window, and joined Father Simeon reciting the Apostles' Creed.

36

Master of the Ranch

Flying over the rolling hills of NY, Gabe would never have guessed the secrets those mountains held. For him, as the plane flew closer to the ground, on its way west to Ithaca Tompkins County Airport, the landscape was merely a kaleidoscope of rich greens, blue lakes, and undulating hills. He certainly had no idea why a cold shiver ran through his body as the plane flew over a certain area past Albany.

As the plane passed Cobleskill NY, Rabbi Katz leaned forward straining to see out his window. Enormous white letters made of painted rocks and carved into the hillside read "Howe Caverns." He thought about what he knew of caverns, underground caves formed over millions of years in the natural limestone of the land.

In reality, it was not Howe Caverns that caused Gabe to shudder but a little known property some twenty miles east of there, known to its visitors only as *The Ranch*. Nearly 95 acres, the ranch stretched over a mountain quite similar in nature to Howe's Caves. Unlike the tourist attraction however, only a certain elite of the most devoted coven members were privileged to know of its existence.

It was a private property, guarded and cordoned off with miles of barbed wire and signage warning trespassers of their unwanted presence. *The Ranch*, once a working dairy farm owned by a German settler in the early 1900's, had two long stone barns housing livestock of a different sort today. Besides the barns and sheds, there was the main house, which lay apart from the rest and slightly higher on the hillside.

In this house, *he* sat on his faux throne, looking up into the sky as US Air Flight 1034 from Boston passed over. *He* hissed, a foul odor escaping his lips, his head bowed in thought.

Thud!

His fist slammed into the armchair. "Not yet," he yelled, rising to full height. "You will not find him yet. My plan will be accomplished."

He paced the room struggling for composure, then strode back to his royal seat, calmly lifted the receiver of the phone, dialed and waited.

"There can be no more delay," he said.

On the other end, he saw Harriet Mansfield working in the Health Food store. He spoke as the voice of her master, for master he now was. She said nothing.

"You will make two phone calls. You will call both the father and Roxanne Cassan. To both, you will sound exactly like the boy's mother. I will time everything."

No answer.

Harriet was dead inside, he knew. She had ceased caring. About now in her conversion she was thinking, 'What's the difference?'

She would obey him, he felt sure as he hung up the phone, catching a glimpse of himself in the full-length mirror across the room, a dark figure of unnatural height and bony frame. Little flesh and slightly sunken cheeks only emphasized his high cheekbones and forehead. Despite his great age, his look was distinguished, certainly handsome, undeniably compelling. Nonetheless, long ago his physical features ceased to matter to him. *No*, he stepped toward the mirror. What he looked for would never look back at him. Every once in a while, he searched this way, searched for his soul, or looked to see if something had replaced it.... The windows of his black eyes showed him nothing.

Enough!

This frustration coupled with his anger over the arrival of the new protector, who was surely meant to deliver the boy to the sanctuary, threatened his equanimity—a feeling he abhorred.

He exited the room in search of release. In the foyer, behind a puny unadorned desk, sat a wrinkled woman of about 60. She boldly followed him with her eyes, ready for any order. Ignoring her, he turned toward the door and made his way across the weed-infested yard. On the porch, half-asleep in a chair, Mark came to attention and followed his master at a respectful distance.

On the right, *he* passed the small bunkhouse where his workers slept, ate or watched TV, and followed the dirt driveway to the first stone barn. Mark snapped his fingers at a worker outside and pointed for the minion to follow the master. No need for Mark to go any further. Let the barn worker suffer the stink and serve *him* in there.

He felt mad. This wasn't a waste, he told himself. He needed it. It would be for the master too, a sign of the triumph to come. His plan would *not* fail. It would not be allowed to fail.

When *he* entered the stone structure, the fetid smell of human feces accosted his nostrils. Long past were the days when such things could trouble his senses. He had been training his body since he was six to pay no attention to corporal irritants that vex lesser souls. Not so for the minion, who silently followed him, awaiting a command, anxious to be away from the stink. *He* walked down the corridor between the stalls waiting for the first pathetic creature to make a move. Usually he would not honor such a one, preferring the ones who cower. This time however, he violently captured the outstretched arm and yanked the girl toward the iron bars.

"This one," he said. The greasy haired worker unlocked the cage, and the chosen girl sprang forward. He grabbed her by her snarled blond hair and pushed her ahead of him, watching her fall to the ground. "Let the games begin," he sneered. Outside, he signaled Mark not to follow. The bodyguard could keep watch from a distance.

He recognized the girl, an experienced one. Impregnated twice, her prospects of being chosen again were slim, so despite any fear, she'd acted thrilled at another chance. Willingly, she followed him across the yard, her eyes squinting in the sunlight hoping for pregnancy and the yearlong counterfeit freedom it offered. They reached the cave entrance, a four-foot wide hole completely hidden from view.

The opening led to a winding tunnel cut into solid rock. The steep descent under low overhanging rock forced them to bend at the waist. Here only one body at a time could make its way into or out of the limestone cave. He pulled her behind him. After about 200 yards, the tunnel widened and the ceiling rose, till they could walk upright and abreast. The air was clean, cool, and moist compared to the stifling stench of the barn and she looked this way and that, in awe of the natural surroundings where stalactites hung like icicles from the ceiling and odd formations of stalagmites encrusted the floors. He yanked her hair harder, like tugging a dog on a leash, not so much to ensure compliance as to begin inflicting pain.

Crude electric fixtures lit the path. Along the cave wall, were holders where gaslights had hung in earlier years. He saw her looking at the strung bulbs and tugged cruelly causing her to walk in a crouched position to ease the strain.

"This cavern has been used for generations of worshippers. It was I who equipped it with electricity," he said, as if she'd be the least bit impressed. "Not all of the tunnels are outfitted as yet, still the more important chambers are lit, and the rest have gas."

She didn't bother to ask what he and his followers worshipped. Surely, the hell she and her tortured inmates lived answered that. He could see her growing apprehension, her steps slowed, becoming slightly less cooperative. The other rapes for her had occurred either in the barn or at the main house. The cave was new to her. Still she knew the violence of the act, and he guessed she'd be bracing herself for what was to come, hoping only to be impregnated, or at least die easily.

They came to a brusque stop. Here the scene expanded dramatically. The ceiling swept up over thirty feet; calcite-dripping walls surrounded a roundish space, nearly twice as wide as it was high. In the very center, a series of cascading rock steps led to a stone table, which could only be understood as an altar. Beneath it lay two golden basins. Red stained everything, and a faint smell of dried blood hung in the damp air.

From the ledge beside him, he chose a blade and length of rope, watching her eyes pop wide in sudden miserable understanding. Violently she squirmed to free her scrawny arm from his iron grip. She kicked and screamed while he dragged her toward the altar table with an unnatural strength for his age.

"You have wished for this release many times," he said over the sound of her begging. "Why fight now?"

A thick punch in the face had an immobilizing effect giving him the minute he needed to restrain her legs, roping them together, three times round then up to her arms—hog-tied like a calf on the farm in Tennessee. Ignoring her crying pleas, he threw her on the altar stone, raised the gleaming metal high, and executed the delicious slashing with controlled cuts as accurate as any surgeon. His ability to maim while inflicting excruciating pain fell shy short of causing enough shock to make her faint. The screams and struggles of the wretched creature excited him almost as much as the glorious flow of her rich, red blood, which he offered his glorious master. By the time, her sanity and threshold for pain had been breached to the point that her body finally escaped to unconsciousness, he was satisfied and ready to deal the mortal blow. He slashed twice more—quickly, expertly—then plunged his hand in ripping the still beating heart from her chest.

"For you! All for you, my all."

37

Harriet Calling

Harriet hung up the phone and looked at the wall clock in the small office off the kitchen of *Macromania*. She had been chopping herbs when she got *his* call. It was 2:15. The store would close at five o'clock.

I will time everything.

"Whatever," she sassed back at the voice in her head. She didn't care anymore, going back to the long stainless steel counter in the kitchen. She'd do whatever *he* asked.

Harriet played with the butcher knife rocking it lazily over the flat leaf parsley. It occurred to her that she had no phone numbers for this Roxy Cassan or John Miller. No sooner had she thought it, than a phone number popped into her head. It was Cassan's — she knew it was, and she knew *he* put it there. It was disturbing how he could do that, and she wondered if he could read all her thoughts.

Her blood ran cold. She walked back to the empty office, picked up the phone and dialed.

"Hello?"

"Hi Rox, it's me, Clarice." *Better not say anymore,* Harriet thought, *see if the woman can tell that it's not really her friend's voice.*

"Oh honey, how've you been? Everything all right? We've hardly spoken since your collapse after Mrs. Nicestrum's funeral."

Harriet had no idea what the woman was babbling about. She continued, "I know, I'm sorry."

"Oh sweetie, don't be sorry. I knew you needed rest so I gave you lots of space. So are you okay? How do you feel?"

"Uh, I feel fine, but I need a big favor," came Clarice's voice over the line. "I spoke to that Harriet Mansfield. She called me, and we talked about Jackson for a long time."

"You're kidding, she called you? I don't even remember giving her your number or anything."

Crap, Harriet thought not answering her. M*eant to say that Clarice had done the calling. Now what, Red?*

"Hmm... wow, I'm not even sure," Cassan said, "like maybe I did tell her your name. Course if I didn't that just shows what a good psychic she must be! Oh Reece, guess what Hannah did to..."

Ha! The Stick took care of the faux pas herself. The woman hardly breathed between words. Harriet grew annoyed listening to her.

"Listen Roxy, it's important." Harriet cut her off. "There isn't much time. Can you possibly take a drive up here and pick up Jackson from our house? Miss Mansfield has arranged to meet him at *Macromania* after it closes."

"So you're not going?" The Stick sounded surprised. "But I thought you said—"

"No, no, I did but..." Harriet poked the knife she was holding in a stack of papers on the desk and rolled it around on the tip. "I get it now. Ms. Mansfield explained it all. I would just mess up the reading with my... uh, energy or whatever." The papers now had a lovely gouged out hole. "Listen Roxy, I'm out doing errands, and I couldn't possibly be home in time to meet you when you get to the house. John's working in the shed on the ATV, and Jackson's taking a nap. Just go upstairs and get Jackie yourself and bring him to *Macromania*."

"Reece, you want me to just let myself in and go upstairs and get him?" the Walking Stick sounded skeptical. Harriet could hear her thoughts too. She was wondering why Clarice called him Jackie like the nanny (*whoever that is*) used to do. Cassan continued, "I mean wouldn't it be better if John—"

"No!" fake Clarice cut her off, then quickly laughed, sounding light. "Ha ha! John's like a bear when he's working on vehicles. Besides he knows you're coming and all, and Jackie knows his

Aunt Roxy." *Shit, called him Jackie again,* must be Cassan called him that.

A few more minutes went by discussing John's negativity toward the psychic idea. Counterfeit Clarice explained a slight subterfuge of telling John she was bringing Jax to the Ithaca Children's Fair downtown. "So it's best if you don't get into a full fledged visit. You don't want to have to answer a lot of unnecessary questions. I mean... we don't have time for all that. Just wave to him from the drive if you see him in the shed."

Harriet hung up the phone and left the office. *The last bit about the shed seemed to come out of abso-frickin nowhere.* She turned back toward the stainless steel counter and the tofu mess she was creating. At first, she thought she heard her coworker calling then she realized it was *his* voice again.

Wait now; I will time everything.

Harriet returned to work finding reasons to stay in the kitchen and let the other employee run the sole register up front. More than an hour went by when out of the blue the number for John Miller popped into her head. Must be time, she thought, heading to the office. Here goes nothing. Harriet lifted the phone and dialed.

"Yeah?" A deep voice answered stunted and businesslike.

"John, hi." Again Harriet had a pause of anticipation. *C'mon Johnny boy, you buying too?*

"Hi babe," the voice softened. "You getting a lot done or done getting a lot?" John Miller laughed at his own corny joke. "Did you remember my contract?"

"Yeah, I got it," Harriet answered not missing a beat. *Amazing.* She heard only her own voice while Miller definitely heard his wife. "Listen I ran into Roxy here. She's doing something or other for the paper. She suggested we take Jax to the children's fair going on at Dewitt Park. We're on our way home to get him."

"He's still napping. Do you want me to get him up and dress him?"

"Oh, no!" fake Clarice said, "Let him sleep. We'll get him up when we get there. He'll have more fun if he's fully rested." Harriet played with the papers she'd gouged sticking her finger through the hole. "Besides I need you to do something else for me."

"What?" John said.

"I meant to say something before, but I forgot. I think there's something wrong with the ATV in the shed. I turned it on yesterday, cuz... I was gonna take Jax for a ride. It definitely sounded funny, and there were weird fumes coming out of the exhaust."

"Seemed fine to me last time I used it," John argued.

"Aw, I was hoping you'd look into it. You know, today, so we'll be able to keep working the paths tomorrow." Clarice and John had been using the all terrain vehicle, cutting a few paths through the woods, to make it easier for walks, and to cart stones from the creek for rock walls. *I know all about you, Johnny boy — it's freaking amaaazing.*

"Yeah okay, I guess I could look at it," John said.

"Pay no attention to us. We'll be in too big a hurry to chat. Besides, the Fair ends at six."

The phone call finished as easily as the first. Harriet looked at the damaged papers, one of which was the schedule.

Well done. Complete your task; your reward will be great.

"I can hardly wait," Harriet snipped and returned to her chopping.

38

Gabe in Ithaca

Gabe's plane landed in the small airport of Tompkins County. Despite its size, the airport was nonetheless modern and airy. He crossed an impressive terrazzo tile floor in dark slacks and polo shirt, a linen sport coat over his arm and an overhead bag in hand. Gabe blew past the baggage claim sign without the slightest idea where he was going. He circled and stopped in the center of the open space, indecisive. The Avis and Hearst counters stood opposite him. Through the glass doors, he saw a couple Yellow Cabs outside.

"May I help you, sir?" The curly-haired Avis employee smiled at him over the counter. "Welcome to Ithaca," she said, grinning like she and he shared a secret. "It's nice to see the Yarmulke. My family is Jewish, but I hardly ever see any of my relatives wear one." Gabe walked toward the neat package of a girl in the smart red jacket.

"I suppose some traditions are hard to keep for many people," he said and put his bag down. "Anyway, don't get me started on the benefits of wearing a kippah. You wouldn't have time for a poor rabbi's opinion." She looked genuinely interested, so he went on. "I make no judgments on others, but for myself I ask, isn't it always true that He is above me?" Pointing his index finger upward and tapping his black wool kippah, he added, "Why shouldn't I want this helpful reminder?"

The Avis girl heartily agreed, her curly brown ponytail bobbing up and down with her head. She set about discussing Gabe's stay and his renting a car versus using taxis.

"I'm not really sure where I'm going," Gabe said.

"The GPS system is great in these cars, and parking in Ithaca is a cinch, at least compared to Boston, I guess."

Twenty minutes later, Gabe was outfitted with a blue Pontiac G6 and some helpful advice for finding *Bookworm Joe's*, parking, and a Holiday Inn. It took three weeks to clear his schedule and get here. He was anxious to figure this thing out, so he decided to skip the hotel for now. Using the GPS, Gabe easily made his way to downtown Ithaca and managed to find Ken's shop on Cayuga Street. Driving by though, there was no parking out front, so he circled the block till he found a spot on a side street. Once parked, he retrieved his jacket from the trunk where he'd thrown his luggage. He locked the car and walked toward the café cutting through the Commons and slipping into the wheat-colored sport coat.

Around the corner from John's office, Clarice was glad August had been so mild, and today was no exception. August 15, it wouldn't be long, she thought, till the leaves would change and colder weather settle in. Today was a breezy, 72 degrees, a little cloudy perhaps, still, cheerful. She felt pretty in her soft pink sweater and white skirt, out doing errands, normal activities— shopping, ticking things off the list on the pretty blue paper in her purse —and all of it keeping her mind, always fighting for control, away from *it*. She'd saved her favorite shop on the Commons for last, (well almost last). John asked her to pick up a contract for him at the office. That was the only thing she had left to do before heading home, she thought stepping into *Katy's Art Supplies*.

Gabe stepped into *Bookworm Joe's* and looked around. The café had all the right ingredients for a young crowd to enjoy coffee, art, books, and conversation. At present though, the place was close to empty. A pair of summer students sat on one of two plush couches, tiny Espresso cups on the low table in front of them. Dark bookshelves and hanging watercolors stood opposite a diner-style counter. A man in an apron and woman discussed one of the pieces at the end of the shop. Gabe guessed the man might be owner Ken Willis, the one who wrote the note on the back of the snapshot that he carried in his coat pocket. The man was very tall, wore his grey hair in a ponytail, and looked absorbed with his face unnaturally close to hers. Not wanting to be rude, Gabe sat on one of the stools at the counter waiting for them to finish their discussion.

Clarice, one block away, left the art shop intending to head to the office when outside she was approached by an oddly matched couple. The young girl had her slender arm linked with that of an enormously large middle-aged man. It was nearly impossible to ignore the scar that stretched across his face like a fat earthworm. The girl's bright blonde head lying on his solid chest, her fingers playing on his suit coat, her youth, her lank, his age and girth—they looked immediately wrong together.

The leggy girl freed her arm reaching out to Clarice, her kinky platinum locks swinging to life as she lifted her head from his side. Clarice took in the shocking length of hair nearly to her knees.

"Hi there," the girl said, tossing hair behind her shoulder. "We saw you inside and thought we'd say hello." The two smiled while Clarice searched their faces for some morsel of recognition. A ridiculous effort. They could have doubled for Lurch and Morticia's sister, Ophelia on the Adam's family. *No way I could forget these two.*

"I'm sorry. Do I know you?" Clarice said.

"Well, not exactly," the girl answered. "We saw you at your art show back in the spring at Bookworm Joe's."

They asked about her art then how she liked the area. They went on to *Miller Construction*, and Clarice shifted her weight and her bags standing on the sidewalk, feeling the heat and remaining polite as they continued to talk. Actually, the huge man never spoke. He nodded and grinned agreeing with everything being said while not one syllable passed his lips. Mute, she guessed. Every time Clarice was ready to end the conversation with these total strangers, the girl asked her another question.

"So let me get this straight," Ken said, "you're a rabbi all the way from Boston and came just to meet this artist, just cuz you like saw a picture of one of her paintings?" He seemed incredulous, (who wouldn't be?) closing the register and handing change to the young man, who had been sitting at the couch. He gave a nod to the couple as they left the shop. "Man, you gotta be some aficionado."

"Not quite. It's kind of a long story... I'd ah, appreciate any information you could give me to find her." Gabe met the affable eyes.

Ken Willis reached beneath the counter, pulled out a tan plastic index box, and thumbed through it.

"Thing is, Mr. Katz, er Rabbi, Mrs. Miller's husband rents the space right next to me, *Miller Construction*. You passed it on the way here. Only I know he's not there. It's Friday, John works from home on Fridays." Ken continued to flip through the cards shaking his head. "Got to get this stuff organized someday... meant to move it to the computer... haven't really made the time." He placed a finger to his temple, "Wouldn't you know it? Wouldn't you just know it?" he said. "All I had was John's business card, but I remember now I gave it to a guy who was looking to build a new house."

"Do you have their number or know where they live?" Gabe said.

Ken plopped a yellow phone book on the counter and flipped through it. After a few minutes and one wrong number, both men gave up, deciding that perhaps the Millers were too new to be listed.

"Tell you what though Rabbi, John goes to church a lot. I mean even like every day, sometimes. Saint Elizabeth's up on the hill. I bet that Pastor would help you. You know, one clergyman to another."

Gabe turned to leave, and Ken called after him. "Still can't get over you meeting Seth like that. Do me a favor; tell that SOB, he owes me a letter or at least an email... If you see him anyway."

Outside on the sidewalk Gabe pressed his nose to the glass window of *Miller Construction* his hands cupping his eyes. He looked around the small space. There, hanging over the desk was the original portrait that began his odyssey. Even from this poor angle, it stole his breath. The phone number for the business was on the window, Gabe pulled out his cell. Inside on a desk, the phone rang. When the answering machine picked up, he left a quick message, snapped his phone closed, and walked back toward his car.

On the sidewalk, Clarice had the uncomfortable feeling that this couple wished to delay her in some way. Something felt wrong and dark about them. Plus that stupid ball of light in her chest was jumping like mad. It was all she could do to carry on a civil conversation and keep it at bay. She told herself she was being stupid as the woman went on about local politics in Ithaca. Why on earth would these complete strangers want to keep her here? The huge man, looking more like a bodyguard than a boyfriend, looked from his stringy mate to her to passers-by. Clarice's ungrounded suspicions grew, making her feel more and more uneasy.

She had just decided she would have to check her watch and make an excuse when, just like that, the couple let her go wishing her goodbye and good luck. Clarice felt strange and wanted to get home to Jackson and John as soon as possible. She passed a Pontiac G6 and turned the corner.

That same instant, Gabe turned the corner in the other direction. Their faces, mere inches apart, the two barely missed bumping into each other head-on. The near miss wasn't close enough to require any apology, so each continued on their way. Gabe felt a strong surge of energy from the small attractive woman while Clarice felt a similar electric surge and a powerful aura all around the Jewish man. A millisecond later, both turned back to catch a glimpse of the other as each figure disappeared around the corner.

Back in his car, Gabe turned on the GPS and searched for Saint Elizabeth's in Ithaca. The computer came up with an address and phone number. He quickly ruled out a phone call, assuming that he wasn't likely to get such information about a parishioner over the phone. He put the car in gear, and followed the pretty female voice directing him to Saint Elizabeth's Church.

Clarice opened the door to her husband's business and saw the flashing light on the answering machine. Pressing it, she snagged a pencil to make a note of the message.

"Uh, my name is Gabriel Katz. I'm trying to reach a Clarice Miller regarding her art. My number is 617-555-8203."

The man on the street! It was him. She could still see him and his aura. The voice on the machine was the protector.

The information about the man wasn't exactly her own. What the heck, that ball of energy was at it again.

Go home, now. NOW! It insisted.

The sense of urgency overwhelmed her and Clarice's motherly instincts felt on fire. She quickly looked for the contract John wanted, locked the office, and ran unabashedly all the way to the outdoor parking ramp where she'd parked three hours ago.

39

Tzaddik

Father Tom wasn't exactly busy when Leo, the church sexton, came into his office apologizing for interrupting. A venerable lay worker, Leo had been serving Saint Elizabeth's for nearly thirty years.

"Father, I'm sorry to disturb your work,"—Leo bowed more like a butler than a sexton—"but there is a gentleman in the nave, or more precisely a rabbi, asking to speak with the pastor of the church. He says it is urgent. Would you have time for him?"

Father coyly folded his hands over the, ahem, 'work'—cartoon doodles he was toying with for the bulletin....

"I'm not too busy. I can see him."

"Shall I show him in, Father?"

"Hmm... no, I don't think so. He may be interested in seeing the church. I'll go to him."

From the sacristy door, Tom peeped out at a good-looking man in a tan sport coat in the first pew, who was admiring the architecture of the old structure. His rich black hair showed beneath a skullcap. Tom tried to think what those were called. From this distance, the rabbi looked young and fit. Father Tom made quick advances, crossing the Sanctuary. The man in the pew smiled at him and stood.

"Such grand spaces your Catholic churches have. Probably very peaceful for prayer." The rabbi said as he shook Tom's extended hand.

"It's quiet now, but it gets hopping on Sunday. I'm Father Tom O'Donnell, pastor of Saint Elizabeth's. You're a rabbi I understand?"

"Yeah, I'm Rabbi Gabriel Katz from Boston. I'm looking for a parishioner of yours. I wondered if you could help me. Her name is Clarice Miller. I was told her husband John may be your parishioner.

The hairs on the back of Tom's neck came to attention. "Uh... just what is your business with the Millers?" He saw wheels of hesitation spinning in the handsome rabbi's face, which now that he was close, he guessed to be about 45. What could he have to say that would cause this much doubt? Tom smiled hoping to put him at ease. "How about a tour of the church?"

They walked the aisles taking in the fourteen hand-sculpted Stations of the Cross, the floor to ceiling stained glass windows, and the impressive buttress work of the century old church. Father Tom explained the history of Saint Elizabeth's with pride and stories. Stories about how the immigrant founders gave up lunches for a year to build the outdoor shrine and how once, in the middle of the night no less, they ran a pastor out who tried to remove too many statues. That was in the sixties, Tom explained. In the back of the church, they stopped at the marble baptismal font in front of a huge stained glass window of John the Baptist pouring water over Jesus. From there, they wandered into the modern confessional room.

"I guess I pictured this differently," Gabe tapped the arms of the comfortable chair, looking about the clean space that felt like a sitting room.

"Oh you mean face to face. Yeah, I guess Hollywood still portrays the sacrament as some spooky event. Whispers murmured into grates, heavy velvet drapes and all that." Tom grinned, sitting in the chair. Rabbi Katz sat in the other. "I prefer this. So do most of my parishioners. We talk more naturally, get to the heart of what's troubling them."

"Like a good counselor?" Gabe said.

"Some see it like that." He looked pensively at the floor then back up. "It's certainly effective for unloading. Got to be at least part of what God had in mind. For the believer though, a sacrament involves grace and faith. In Penance, every sin confessed is not only forgiven, but strength to avoid it is gained by supernatural grace—Oh,"—Tom waved his hand in a gnat swatting motion—"You didn't come all this way to hear about Catholic theology. Forgive me, Rabbi."

"Ha, that has to be a new one, 'Forgive me, rabbi', even for these walls, hey Tom."

Both men laughed. The quiet returned and the rabbi crossed his ankle over his knee, holding it comfortably.

"I should explain why I'm here, give you the whole spiel. My story is hard to describe exactly, but I guess that was partly what made me fly all the way out here rather than try to connect with Clarice Miller by phone. For six years now, I've been having these dreams, very repetitive; same dream over and over. They're different from regular dreams or nightmares." The rabbi looked at Tom's open face and carried on explaining the dream of the flying nymph, the chase in Boston, the information he got from Seth. The rabbi uncrossed his leg and leaned forward holding his hands. "I just have this gut feeling there's some plan or mission I'm meant to fulfill.

"Mission?"

"Yes, I don't understand it, but I think it has something to do with this boy of my dreams."

"Boy, what boy?"

"It's a figure in my dreams. He's young, maybe six or seven, blond curls, big green eyes. I always see him in this idyllic forest setting."

Tom's ears burned. The mural in Jackson Miller's bedroom! That day after visiting the Millers, Father Simeon had told him that the boy's protector might be unaware of his role. He said he felt strongly that the protector would seek out Father Tom, and that if that should happen, anyone searching for the boy or one of the Millers should be brought to him at the Mount directly.

"Rabbi Katz, if I tell you that I don't think you are crazy, will you grant me the same benefit of the doubt?" The man's nodded. "I... uh, I think I know someone who can help you." He shared what he knew of the Miller's and their special child.

"So you believe your priest friend, this Simeon at Mount Charbel has information that will help me understand my dreams?"

"Have you got a car, Rabbi Katz? Mine's in the shop. I think we should go see Simeon."

After a summer of Boston's heat, the country air felt great. The Fens had nothing over the spectacular view and lush woods of the hermitage at Mount Saint Charbel. On their way to see Simeon, Gabe followed Tom down the path, curiously examining the little shacks they passed every fifty yards or so. Tom called them prayer huts—about the plainest little structures he'd ever seen, made of logs, topped with wood shingles and a single chimney pipe. They came to the last one at the end of the path, the same as the others. Tom knocked on the rough-hewn door and called respectfully.

"Father Simeon, it's Tom and a visitor, Rabbi Katz."

They heard a couple steps and the door swung open. A brown clad monk appeared on the stoop, his full-bearded face as lined as the trees.

"Praise God and His Mercy," the monk cried, stretching his arms up. "He has provided the Protector for His voice."

Gabe barely took in the old man and strange greeting before he found himself in a tight embrace. The monk let go and said, "I am Father Simeon. Now let me look at you,... a Jew and a Rabbi even!" Simeon's eyes bore into Gabe's making him feel lightheaded.

"Oh, no! Not here Gabrielus, not here. Come, you must sit down." The old priest was almost tickled leading Gabe to the lone chair in his hut while Tom stood there wondering how Simeon knew the rabbi's name before he told him.

"Remain outside Tom and pray. Oh, and stay close; you'll be needed very soon," Simeon told him before shutting the door. He crossed the floor, and Gabe stood. "Sit, sit, sit." He waved a worn hand and stood before Gabe in the chair. Simeon held the edge of the tiny table while he knelt on one knee in front of Gabe. The monk's beard and mustache fascinated him while the leathery face and sharp eyes struggled with deep emotion.

"You have no idea how long. . ., so many visions and dreams, and here you are...." his almost hidden lips moved behind the snowy tufts. Gabe attempted to ask a question, but the old man flatly ignored him and crossed himself as Catholics do.

"Now you shall see your part," Simeon said. Still kneeling on one leg, he took both Gabe's hands in his. "Relax, try to clear your mind and rest in God's spirit."

This is nuts, he was sitting here holding hands with a Gentile in the woods. The hands, large, tough from work yet thinned with age, held his with an honest grip. *This is crazy.* He could hear Bubbe yell meshugeneh. What in the world was he thinking when he flew here?

You came for answers. Now be still and be silent.

The words sounded firm, distant but clear, and clearly not his. Then he realized what was happening, what must be happening as inexplicable as it seemed. And Gabe was astounded at how quickly he accepted the idea. Linked like this as they were, holding hands, their two powerful souls united. In some mystical whirlwind of merged spirits, Gabe and Simeon shared visions and knowledge. Together they watched the boy in the mystical Glen. Together they saw Clarice flying then streaming images of incidents: Mrs. Nicestrum fighting the black force, demonic dogs chasing Clarice, a crazed man after Jax, Harriet with the ax, the poor women at the ranch, and more. Gabe saw and understood.

As more images swirled in, Gabe heard the old man's voice reciting Latin prayers. Startling himself, he heard his own voice in Hebrew mingle with the monk's. As their souls touched, there was no longer any need of words to communicate the information to Gabe. It was clear to him, his role was to replace the elderly woman and protect the boy. It was clear now that he had been chosen by God to deliver the boy, and that he had been given a special power to do it.

A power lay within him. He was a *Tzaddik*, the righteous one. Tzaddik, the old Jewish word for a completely righteous individual possessing a mystical power for God's glory. He had to get in touch with his gift as Tzaddik.

"See!" Simeon's voice broke through. "See it Tzaddik. Use your power now. What do you see," the old man demanded. "What do you see?"

Gabe concentrated all his effort, calling out to God to reveal the power and purpose of Tzaddik. Instantly, his soul was overwhelmed with new and frightening images. He was literally electrified. Simeon's hands reluctantly flew off Gabe's in an act of self-preservation, and the priest slumped in a heap.

Some minutes later, Gabe awoke slightly dazed, standing in the center of the room. The young priest was hunched over Simeon, who lay on the floor, his back propped against the wood burning stove.

"Is he alright?" Gabe said.

"You tell me," Father Tom yelled at him. "I hear a scream and come in here to find Father collapsed on the floor and you over there not responding... standing there, oblivious."

Simeon stirred, his eyes blinking. He patted Tom's arm.

"Stay calm, Thomas. I'm fine. It was just too powerful for me." He looked over at Gabe, "What are we to do?"

Tom looked confused by Simeon's asking Gabe direction instead of the reverse.

"We have to hurry. There's no time at all." Gabe told them. "I have to reach the boy. I need to be taken to the Miller's immediately."

"Go with him, Tom," Simeon said.

"What? It's a Holy Day. I have Mass tonight for the Feast of the Assumption."

"I will make arrangements for your parish," Simeon said. "Just go. Drive like the wind—no, with the angels and on their wings! And may God remain with you, Tzaddik Gabrielus."

40

Kidnapped

After Clarice's call, John went to check on Jax. He stood in the doorway of Jackson's room, sun peeping behind blue curtains, watching his son sleep peacefully. A funny feeling crept in the pit of his stomach. Déjà vu? He remembered something but couldn't put his finger on it. John was a doer, the kind who never puts anything off, and right now, there was work to be done.

He headed down the stairs and out the kitchen door to the side yard, passing in front of the garage. He continued across the grass to the tool shed, which housed the ride-on mower and the ATV. The twelve by eight shed, like a miniature stable, lay opposite the house facing the side yard. It had only one entrance, a single garage door, which opened with an electronic remote. Small windows across the top faced the curving driveway. John tapped in the code, and the tight spring of the opener contracted to lift the door. It was loud. He looked at the heavy oversized mechanism he'd adapted from commercial parts —more than overkill for the small garage door, but it had saved him money.

He went to the Honda Rancher, and turned it on to give it a test ride. It wasn't new, but a 2003 he found on Craig's List. He thought it'd been performing well hauling rocks and blazing trails. Not sure when the previous owner last changed the oil.... He let it run a few minutes to warm the oil while he went to the garage to retrieve his socket wrench where he'd left it. Returning he switched it off, got the oil pan, a towel and the wrench. He lay underneath it and set to work. When it was done, filter casing and all, he poured two new quarts in and checked the level. John fired the Rancher up again and moved in front of it to listen. As the engine roared, he stood away from the ATV's exhaust with his back to the door.

The noise and his position left him completely unaware that Roxy had pulled up in her Volkswagen Beetle. Turning to clean up the mess, John noticed the car. He almost stopped working to go say hello, then looking at his grease-stained hands the oil pan that needed emptying and remembering what Clarice had said, he went back to work.

"No, no. I don't wanna."

Roxy sat on the bed. Jax rubbed his eyes looking at shocking orange capris and a purple knit shirt.

"It's alright Jax. Mommy said you should come with me. She said you have to, dear." Roxy gently pulled Jax from his bed.

"I don't wannna go."

"It's for your own good honey, to help you. . ., and Mommy too. You want to help Mommy, don't you?"

Putting on his wide glasses, Jax sensed no deception or prevarication in his mother's best friend, and he did want to help his mommy. His mom seemed so confused over Nicey's light, the light that was still trying to help her.

"Your Daddy knows your coming with me."

Again, Jax sensed nothing looking at the cheerful face, the tight red curls and dangling coin earrings. Little by little, it seemed right to his generous heart to go with Auntie Roxy and do what his mother wished. Rox and he picked out navy shorts and a striped golf shirt. Roxanne ran her comb though his messed up hair. Using a little spit for polish, she pronounced him handsome, and the two made their way downstairs to the car.

John rubbed creamy hand-cleaner on his hands, removing the grease with a paper towel. He felt a little miffed over having wasted his time, convinced the Rancher hadn't needed anything. Abruptly, the garage door opener whirred to life. The door lowered. John went over to the control to see why it was malfunctioning. The door ignored all the button pushing and continued closing. Glancing out the window, he saw Roxy and Jax walking down the front steps to the punch bug. He waited a second, still holding the paper towel and rubbing, expecting to see Clarice. Where was she?

Like a lead weight, the truth hit John at once understanding his dream. Jackson was never supposed to be without one or the other of his parents. Clarice was not there. She was not with them. The voice, the woman in the dream, it was Roxy! She was taking him somewhere bad, to something evil. John pushed the controls, nothing. He raced over to the handle, pulled and tugged. The door refused to budge, some diabolical force holding it down. The garage door mechanism above him gave a menacing hum. John banged on the window yelling with all his might, but the shed was too far from them. Roxy looked over at John in the window of the shed. She cheerily waved back to him. He realized too late, that to her, his banging hand must look as if he was waving at them. She was pulling out!

John went nuts. He had to escape the shed. The windows were too high. It would get him nowhere breaking them. The buzzing hum above continued. He decided to break the door. It wasn't even insulated, only thin plywood with a couple of two-by-fours for cross bars. He grabbed a helmet off the shelf, jumped on the ATV, and cranked it up. He revved the engine, put his head down like a charging bull, then rammed the Rancher straight into the shed door. The thin wood gave way as the nose of the Rancher broke through, splintering wood all over the front rack. He flipped the reverse button to go again when the machinery above whined louder making a hideous sound.

SCREE—KA—RANG! The spring that held the door snapped, a heavy metal bar broke loose flying through the air and headed straight for John's middle.

41

Macromania

Roxy and Jax laughed as they pulled into the lot of the health food store in Binghamton. They had been playing the game of Punch bug, which Roxy was surprised to learn Jackson had never played.

"You mean to tell me your Auntie Roxy drives this bright, yellow Volkswagen Beetle, and your momma never taught you how to play Punch bug?" They had been happily engaged trying to spot the little cars and enjoying the lively competition.

"That last one was a tie, you little sneak."

"Nuh, uh. You gotta say Punch bug and punch too. You can't just punch." Jax giggled, "That's four to three. I'm gonna win, Auntie Roxy."

"Says you. Anyway, we're here squirt." Roxy parked the car in the empty lot on the side of the store. "I'll catch up with you on the way home."

"I don't wanna go in," Jackson's eyes grew wide behind his glasses. "You shouldn't go in there."

"Well jeez, honey, there's nothing to be afraid of." Rox saw his fright and guessed his attitude would only worsen if she forced him, so she made a quick decision. "Jax, Auntie Roxy's just going to go in and talk to the nice lady for a minute. Then maybe you would like to meet her." Ignoring his protests, Roxy reached for her gold sequin purse and stepped out of the car. Then she leaned in again.

"Jax, you stay right there and don't touch the door handles. I'm going to lock the car. I'll be right back."

With only a twinge of unrest over leaving him alone, Roxy walked to the storefront. It was closed of course, but she knocked hoping Harriet Mansfield would hear. She did and walked up front, taking off her apron. Dressed in black slacks and a Macromania T-shirt, she yelled through the glass to Roxy. "You have to go around to the side door. I don't have a key." She looked down and noticed Roxy was alone. "Where's the boy?"

"In the car." Roxy answered.

"Okay, that's fine," Harriet said.

The side door was right by Roxy's car, and she waved to Jackson as she passed. He threw himself against the window.

"No, don't go in there. She's bad."

"I'll only be a minute, honey. Calm down." A moment later the heavy metal door on the brick wall opened, and Roxy disappeared inside.

"Wow, what a fuss he's making!" Roxy remarked to Harriet, seeing the knife too late.

Harriet was determined not to prolong this, so she figured she would strike first thing. No games or chitchat. No chance to change her mind. No dull axes either. The butcher knife had been finely sharpened.

Roxy was taken by such surprise that it was impossible to block the first blow. Thanks to some latent skills, gained once upon a self-defense class, she did manage to deflect it from being fatal. Harriet, a good eight inches shorter than the lanky redhead, had been aiming for Roxy's heart, but with the deflection, the blade sliced into her left side under her ribcage. The shock of pain that shot through Roxy necessarily affected her next move. As her left arm instinctively covered the wound, her right arm pushed at Harriet with all her might, and Harriet's pudgy frame fell awkwardly against the metal counter.

"What are you doing?" screamed Roxy in disbelief, blood spilling over her hand, between her fingers and onto her purple sweater.

"No chit chat, Red."

Harriet was on her feet attacking again. This time Roxy kicked her away. Still the knife managed to connect, slicing a deep gash into Roxy's thigh. Bright red blood gushed all over the orange capris.

"Oh, my God!" Roxy's other hand went to her thigh. "Are you insane?" She doubled over in pain nearly to the floor, keeping one eye on her attacker.

"Shut up!" Harriet shouted, ignoring the pain from the well-placed kick, this time throwing her entire body on Roxy. Roxy saw the blade poised above her and reached for the wrist wielding the instrument just as both women fell. The two rolled on the floor with Harriet's wrist locked in Roxy's grasp until for a moment Roxy was atop Harriet. She was determined to stay that way. Ignoring her injuries, she placed her long legs around the thick torso squeezing her knees tight, even as she continued to hold the woman's wrist, keeping the knife back.

For a chunky woman, Harriet had incredible strength. Roxy was losing blood at an alarming rate out of both wounds. Harriet gave a giant heave and toppled Roxy. The two women thrashed again rolling back and forth. Up against the legs of the steel table, Roxy saw an opportunity and slammed the wrist she'd been holding for dear life into the metal, hoping to dislodge the knife. It fell from her grip and skittered under the table.

Harriet immediately scooted under the table to retrieve it. Roxy made for the door half rising and slipping in her own blood. She came down hard just as Harriet reclaimed the blade. Harriet rose up and leapt at Roxy. She swiped with the knife. Roxy managed to throw herself backward and dodge the blow. This caused Harriet to swipe air and the knife moving in a perfect arc ended in her own clavicle.

"You effing bitch," she screamed in pain.

Roxy crawled away, unable to stand, searching for escape. The door lay beyond Harriet on the other side of the room. She felt light-headed and for the first time she realized what all this might mean for Jackie. "Oh God, don't let her hurt Jackie."

Harriet pulled the knife out of her self-inflicted wound.

"That is it, Stick! We are done!"

Ignoring her pain and the blood running down her white shirt, she lunged at Roxy's retreating form. She yanked the red curls, and with one sure move, Harriet dragged the instrument across Roxy's neck, severing her windpipe and trachea. She watched satisfied as the life-blood oozed out of Roxy.

Harriet looked at the pool of blood, red spatters, and streaks. "Great! You stupid, stupid, carrot-slurping whore," she blurted kicking Roxy's lifeless body, "Look at the mess you made. Fat chance I can ever come back here."

She pulled open a metal drawer, retrieved a cloth, and pressed it against the deep gash in her left shoulder. She went to the tiny office and searched for duct tape. None. All Harriet found was a tape gun with clear parcel tape. It would have to do. Wincing, she pulled her left arm out and lifted the wet shirt over her neck. She put a fresh towel on the wound and used the tape to secure it to her shoulder. Just then, an alarm sounded in the parking lot.

"Stinking kid!" He must have set the car alarm off. That was all she needed, someone might hear it from the street or apartments above the stores. Harriet pulled her shirt down over her arm and went back to the dead redhead. She flipped Roxy's body over and rifled for her car keys.

"Dammit Stick, where are they?" She kicked the corpse. Then she remembered the ridiculous shiny purse by the door where she'd first slashed her. Grabbing the purse and carrying the tape, Harriet headed out the side door to gift-wrap the boy for her master at *The Ranch*.

42

Streams of Living Waters

Twenty minutes after leaving Ithaca, Clarice's white Prelude pulled into the stone drive. She'd been anxious the entire drive home and sped the whole way. She parked in front of the house intending to run straight in the front door and up the stairs to check on Jax when on the bottom step of the porch, something caught her peripheral vision. Clarice turned to look toward the shed. Never in all her worry or fretting would she have been prepared for what she saw. She screamed at the ghoulish scene while running to the shed.

The ATV's engine was still on, more than half of it sticking out a ripped opening in the shed door. Through the hole, she saw her husband's large body covered in blood and laying across the back of the vehicle. She flew to him screaming, "John! Oh God, John!"

He was slouched to the side and leaning over the back rack of the Rancher, a thick metal bar impaled in his torso. "John! God, John, John!" She threw pieces of two by four and plywood off him and the ATV when she got a frightening eyeful of the bar running straight through his sternum. It was hexagonal in shape about an inch in diameter and running at least two feet long. Sticking out a foot from his chest, it ran all the way through and ended a good five inches out his back. "John, John..." she whimpered climbing on the front end and reaching in to touch his face. He moved; her heart beat again. He was alive and tried to speak.

"Jackson, she took... Jackson."

"John, John, what? No, don't try to talk. How did this happen?" She flipped the engine off. "My God! Just hold on." Her hands had no idea what to touch and moved gingerly over his face and chest. With Herculean effort, John lifted his head.

"He's gone. They have him," he said before blacking out.

Her heart stopped twice over, first when thinking John was dead and again at his last words of her son being taken. She crawled further into the torn opening, supporting her weight, careful not to touch him, and leaned down as close as she could to his lips to feel for breath. He was still alive! She struggled to control her panic and think of what to do.

"You hang on," Clarice ordered her soul mate. "Do you hear me, John Miller? You hang on and live." She ripped his T-shirt away to get a better look at the bar. Blood oozed from his wound, and even though her first instinct had been to remove the metal bar, any fool could see it acting as a plug for what would be a gaping hole in his chest. She backed out of the ragged opening, shards of wood scraping her side. Climbing off the ATV, she ran across the yard and driveway toward the kitchen door.

Shaking, she snatched the Tracfone off the counter and dialed 9-1-1 while running upstairs to look for Jax. "Jax, Jax!" she screamed, reaching his bedroom and finally noticing the phone she held had no tone. Nothing. *No no. This is not happening.* They never did get the phone line up here, and cell service was good but iffy. Sometimes one cell would work when another wouldn't. Clarice ran to her room shouting one more time, "Jacksuuun!" The phone on John's nightstand gave her nothing. Her cell was still in her purse in the car. She bounded outside convinced Jax was gone as John had said.

"John, John, hold on," she cried, fumbling to work the phone from her car. Her cell was a long shot, and anyway, she hadn't charged it in three days. Nothing. Nothing. *No no no no no!* She tore back to the shed.

"Oh, my God. John! John! What am I supposed to do?" she screamed into the air. She looked through the hole at the giant spring dangling from the garage door opener, and it hit her all at once—the day in November when she was looking for Jackson, the darkness around the machinery parts on the floor. Clarice clenched her fists let out a stream of expletives cursing the opener and shaking with anger.

This was getting her nowhere. What were her options? She had to think. *Think, Clarice, think!* An ambulance would never get there on time. And even if she could get John in the car, he might bleed to death on the way.

"*God! God—*

A small interior light broke through her sobs, as though Nicey were there delivering the message herself:

The Glen!

"Alright, yes. Okay, okay, the Glen." She spoke aloud to the tiny voice. "We can do this John. We can do it. You breathe. You hear me? You hang on."

Clarice looked at the Rancher. It was the only way. If it were possible to be grateful for anything in such a crisis, she felt relieved that John was already on the vehicle because there was no way she could lift him. Besides that, the ATV now had trails on which to make its way toward the Glen.

The vehicle had broken through the door but only part way. After a bare second of trying to push the plywood with her hand, Clarice ran to the garage grabbing an ax off the wall. She came back and hacked and pulled the wood free enlarging the hole. It felt like she was working in slow motion, though as she kept a constant eye on John. Once the hole was big enough, she looked at John's position and the long bar. He was slumped to the side and the bar protruded out over the seat. Clarice hoisted her pink jean skirt and carefully positioned herself in front of her husband's body. The only way she could fit was to drive the thing while standing up. She cranked the engine and lay down over the front handles till they cleared the door. She drove as fast as she dared, tears streaming down her cheeks, and her heart begging a God, whom she'd always denied, to have mercy.

* * *

Father Tom drove the rental car since he knew the way to the Miller's house in Ithaca. From Maine, the back way up made the most sense. They picked up 79 at Richford and raced the winding road toward Ithaca. Tom was still in the dark.

"Just what happened back there?"

Gabe Katz leaned over, cranked the AC. "It's really hard to explain, and I only understand so much myself."

"Try."

"Are you going as fast as you can? It's crucial that I reach the boy." Tom merely looked at him, and back at the speedometer: 85 mph.

"I saw a lot of things with Simeon. It was like we were in each other's minds. The scenes were familiar but new—because I understood more, I think. The Millers were chosen for the boy before he was even born. And the boy has been destined for a very merciful task of our Creator, one that will save untold souls." The rabbi took a deep breath and slowly let it go.

"Ever since I was young, I felt different. Like there was some power I possessed. Honest, except for that feeling and a few weird dreams, I was a normal guy till about five years ago. That's when the dreams started. Well, I uh, I told you all that.... Anyway, I've had the feeling there was something I had to do. An intense feeling, somewhere I had to be, something to accomplish." Gabe paused. "The boy is that something."

Tom concentrating on the road made no comment.

"It's him I'm meant to protect and guide to a sanctuary, so one day he can fulfill his destiny."

Tom dared to take his eyes off the road for a second to peek at Gabe. "Don't get me wrong when I ask this, but... protect him from what, from who?"

"Evil," Gabe said, "pure evil. I saw this black force, okay, not saw, more like felt—Gabe shook his head—No, that doesn't explain it. I—I can't explain that part. With Simeon, I saw this human element threatening the child. I also saw his parents."

"John and Clarice," Tom said.

"I guess so. What's the boy's name then? I might as well know."

"Jackson. He's exceptional, extremely intelligent, and well spoken. His looks are—"

"I know," the rabbi cut him off, "some of what I saw was past, but some, I'm certain was present, or even future. The last thing I saw felt as if it was happening right then. I'm praying not."

"Why? What was the last thing you saw?" Father Tom pointed to a sign for Ithaca.

"It was the father. I saw John Miller. The black force was stopping him from protecting... Jackson?" Tom nodded. "The father was badly injured. He may be dying as we speak. And the boy, Jackson, he's been taken, I think." Gabe reached under his kippah, and rubbed his head.

"Kidnapped?" Tom said and blessed himself. The rabbi's eyes closed, so Tom drove silently, keeping his questions to himself. About fifteen minutes later, they drove onto the Miller's curved stone drive. The damaged shed was the first thing they saw. Father Tom sped over the grass to pull up directly in front of it.

Investigating like the archeologist he was, Gabe noted the blood, the broken spring, and even the missing metal bar.

"He was trying to get out of here." He squatted down, lifted the ax, looked back at the busted door.

"The ax didn't do all this. He drove a small vehicle through here."

Tom pointed to a helmet on the floor of the shed. "ATV?"

"Yeah," Gabe said, looking over at the white Honda then at the SUV in the open garage. "How many cars do the Millers have?"

"Two. The Prelude is Clarice's and John drives the Blazer."

"She may have come here and found him." Gabe pointed to a bloody footprint. "Probably hers. Is Mrs. Miller a very petite woman?"

Both their eyes followed Clarice's prints. "I'll check the house?" Tom said turning.

"Wait." Gabe held his hand up and closed his eyes. "No, no need. It's empty; I feel it." He stood for a moment transfixed, staring in the direction of the woods. "I know where they are."

Gabe hurried toward the forest, twisting backward and calling over his shoulder, "You should stay here. It may be important to watch the house. Wait for Simeon."

With that, Gabe broke into a run, his feet following the path of the ATV's fresh tracks.

Holding the handles tight, Clarice made her way toward the Glen, which called to her as strongly as ever. The path John had blazed ran out some time ago. With difficulty, she'd been maneuvering the vehicle, between trees and undergrowth. Now though, the ATV was stuck good. She pushed the stupid red button and pulled the brake lever—cursing Honda for the design—put it in reverse and then jumped it forward. Same trick she'd been using when the wheels got trapped in roots and ruts. But this time the thing wouldn't move.

She got off moving carefully and checking John. He was still unconscious, his breathing dangerously shallow. Petrified, but striving to remain analytical, Clarice bent to look at the wheel in question. It needed something to grip. She ran around collecting rocks, sticks, anything she could place in front of the wheel. After loading the hole up, she had another go at it. No luck. The wheel spun and spun, shooting the rocks and sticks out. She repeated the attempt gathering more material, laying it down and firing up the motor and whirling the wheels. And again... and once again... Each attempt cost precious minutes. No matter what she did, the wheel refused to move.

She ran her hand over John's beaded forehead. His tanned skin looked white. Desperation surged inside her. She pictured her cheek, how the ripped flesh had repaired itself in the water. The Glen was so close she could feel it, maybe a hundred yards beyond that curve. She was already at the flat part; she could hear the water gurgling. She had to get him to its healing waters before he bled to death. Seconds were precious; her husband's life was slipping away.

Frantically, she tugged his body to get it off the useless ATV. He was so heavy, and she so small. However, what Clarice lacked in physical strength, she made up for in her determination to save him. She inched his torso on its side closer and closer to the edge, afraid of doing more harm than good, but seeing no choice—she gave a giant heave and let herself fall back under his weight, cushioning his fall and turning him so the bar would not be pushed further. They landed with a thud, her backside hitting an ugly root. He lay on his side partly in her arms on the forest floor. Clarice sat there as the hopelessness of the situation overcame her. Hot tears streamed down her face.

"Oh God, oh God. We've come so far. We're so close." She hugged her husband's insensate head to herself, looking up to heaven demanding help. "You have to help us! You have to!" Crying and stroking his face and arm, she stayed like this for she couldn't say how long when she heard—

The water! She carefully released John's head, got up from under him, taking a quick look at the metal piece protruding from the wound.

"John Miller, you hold on," she spluttered, "D—Don't die! You hear me? Don't even think you can leave us!"

Clarice ran with all her might to the Glen. It was even closer than she had thought. Ignoring its beauty, she went directly to the stream and waded in, her sandals slipping on the algae covered rocks. She stripped off her sweater and dunked it in the water. Curling it into a ball, she lifted it from the stream, and ran back to John feeling chilled as the afternoon heat waned.

That was how the Jewish man in the kippah found them with Clarice squeezing water from the shirt over her husband's wound and into his unresponsive mouth. The stranger knelt beside a half-petrified Clarice and whispered, "Oh, Hashem, Hashem!"

When Clarice looked at him, she saw only this tremendous beautiful white light. "Help us! I beg you."

But the water from the Glen seemed to be helping. John was coming to, although delirious. "Jackson, Jackson," he murmured. He lifted himself, his effort giving Clarice an idea.

"If you help us, I think we can get him to the water."

The man didn't even question her. Clarice assumed with his powerful aura, he must feel the force and pull of the Glen, too; it was probably how he found them. Together they hoisted John with the bar sticking out his back and his front between them. The man shouldered most of the weight, although John semi-conscious carried some of his own. They covered the fifty yards to the Glen in silence and helped John into the water. They propped him against a rock so that his entire lower torso was in the brook. She and the man stood on either side of him in water up to their calves. Water soaked his loafers and the bottom of his jeans. His tan suit coat got doused too positioning John. She was oblivious of her own wet skirt and sopping tee. The cold crystal water flowed gently past them, and an unthinkable peace surrounded them. They stayed this way for some time.

"Take it out, please." Clarice begged the man to remove the metal bar as she struggled to keep her footing in her slippery sandals. "I know it will heal if we remove it." The Jewish man furrowed his brow, questioning the request.

"Yes, take it out," John begged. "Out! Now."

He let go of John's arm. Clarice slid herself further in the water to hold John more securely while the stranger placed his hands around the bar. "Brace yourself Mr. Miller. One, two, three—" He pulled hard, and the two-foot piece slid out of the gaping hole. John yelled in pain and passed out.

Clarice watched shocking blood gush from the wound like water from a garden hose. Seconds later, it stopped, and crystal water ran straight through the open cavity, which literally shrunk.

"The voice of the LORD is upon the waters:" the man spoke in a low respectful tone, "Elohim of glory thundereth: the LORD is upon many waters."

No Psalm could have sounded more real to her. Clarice showered John's face with kisses. "Oh John, John, thank you God, thank you," she said repeatedly in a half-cry half-whisper.

They held him some minutes shifting their weight and position watching the miracle continue to shrink the wound. Over her shoulder, Clarice saw the pink sweater balled up and lying about five yards from them on the creek bank. She'd been clutching it in her left hand as they walked John to the Glen and touching it to his face, hoping it would give him added strength. John's eyes remained closed, his face white.

"Can we move him to the moss? He still needs to rest, but I think the waters have done their work," Clarice said.

They dragged his bulk ashore inching the dead weight to the nearest boulder and sat beside him on the mossy carpet. John's eyes closed again.

"Do you know who I am?" the man asked.

Clarice studied his handsome face, as she lowered to the ground with her sore back against the rock. She gently lifted John's head and positioned him in her lap. She recognized him, remembered bumping into him on the sidewalk, and hearing the message on John's machine. Though there was more to his question. "The message said your name was Gabe Katz? Are you the man that left the message at John's office?"

"I am, but I think you know I'm more than that," Gabe told her, sitting on his knees in front of them. "I am the Protector, chosen to help your son... just as you were."

"Oh, but what about Jackson? Where's our son?"

At Jackson's name, John's eyes flew open, and his arm gripped Clarice's. "Roxy took him. You... called, said you were coming... taking him to a—a fair." John fell back weakly, closing his eyes for a second. "But you weren't with her," he wheezed. "I knew she... wasn't su-pposed to take—"

"John, I never called you."

Slowly, painfully, between continued and ignored entreaties for him to rest, the information came out in stuttered words from the phone call to Roxy waving good-bye. John would not give up until she knew what happened.

"But if she waved to you," Clarice reasoned, unconsciously rubbing John's arm, "she couldn't have known what she was doing would be dangerous for Jackson. And if someone called John, pretending to be me, maybe they called Roxy the same way."

"We're obviously dealing with demonic forces. These people work using that power, amazingly cunning," Gabe said. "If your friend was involved unwittingly, can you think where she would bring him? Think; it wouldn't be somewhere you don't know or haven't talked about."

"No, not really... I, uh," Clarice stopped rubbing John's arm, "unless she took him to see that psychic woman. She's been bugging me for months about him being brought to some psychic in Binghamton."

"Where? What's her name? What do you know of her?" Gabe hammered.

"Nothing I—I know she works at a health-food store on Main Street in Binghamton. I've never been there, but Roxy goes all the time. Oh, what's the name of it...?" Clarice patted the moss, and bobbed her foot. "It's a weird name, starts with an M or an S... shoot, I'm sorry that's all I know—Oh wait, that's not true, I remember her first name. It's Harriet."

"Listen, don't ask me how," Gabe said, getting up, "I can't explain anything that's going on. I'm sure your son is alive, only he has to be found soon." Gabe wrestled out of his sport coat, threw it over John.

Clarice knew he was alive too. Somehow, she also knew she couldn't leave John yet—more precisely, she was not supposed to leave the Glen yet. Like the rabbi, she couldn't explain how she knew. She just knew.

With what information he had, Gabe left them at the Glen. He found the stuck ATV. From there he easily traced a path back to the house. Out of breath and running toward the rental car, he saw the two priests approaching him. The old one was now wearing a long black cassock. By some means, he had made it there on his own.

Simeon addressed Gabe holding the car door open, "When you find him, bring him back here. We will be praying for you. Trust God's power, Tzaddik."

Gabe made no comment, nodded and threw the car in gear. As the two priests watched Rabbi Gabriel Katz speed away, Simeon's hand went up making a giant sign of the cross in the air.

43

Just Rewards

The yellow Volkswagen Beetle sped up 88 towards Cobleskill. In the back seat, Jackson Miller, his feet and hands bound with wide cellophane tape, cried. His mouth had been taped too, except the piece that she put on him didn't stay put. He probably licked it with his tongue till it fell off, she thought hearing his voice.

"You don't have to do this. You can change your mind," he said.

"Shut up, kid," she yelled over her shoulder, keeping her eyes on the road.

The kid lay quiet but only for a moment as his voice rang again, annoyingly clear. "No one owns you. Not even *him*. God will forgive you if you just ask for mercy."

"Shut up, damn it!" She yelled again, agitated as much by his beautiful voice as his words—words not meant for her. "YOU don't know anything about it, don't know anything about me." Harriet turned to glance at him when the car careened. So instead, she adjusted her rear-view mirror to glare at him.

"You don't know Jack, kid!"

"It doesn't matter 'bout what you did. It was bad, but it's over, and you don't have to stay bad. God will forgive you if you're sorry." The little boy looked directly at her in the mirror. Innocent eyes behind goofy glasses and that voice pulled at her. What was with his voice?

"What the hell do you know about what *I did*?" Even as she said it, she saw the ax, the blood, the helpless wiggling torso.

"It was really bad about the baby, but you can change." The car swerved, and Harriet regained control. "You're sorry you did it, I know you are. Just tell God you are."

Baby? What was he saying? He knows! How could he know? *Who is this kid? No, I can't listen, I won't.* This was too much to bear. She'd made her choice. Screaming "Shut Up!" at the top of her lungs, Harriet abruptly jerked the steering wheel to the right and pulled the yellow bug off the road. She threw the gearshift into park, practically breaking the Stick's stick. Grabbing the tape gun on the seat, she pushed her door and climbed out. She yanked open the back door, ignoring the pain in her shoulder, and while he begged, "Please don't!" she ran the tape gun around and around his precious head, curls and all. Harriet put her hand to the aching shoulder and drew back bloody fingers. *Bleeding again!*

"You did that, you little brat," she shrieked, raised her leg to kick him, but then she remembered the master's warning: "whole and unmarked." She spit on him instead. Harriet repositioned the towel and re-secured the tape. By the time she next looked at him, he was struggling for air. "Your own fault," she said as she searched the car for something to cut a hole in the tape for him to breathe through. The Stick's car was a stinking pigpen. Her gaudy gold purse was worthless too—nothing in there to use. Jackson was nearly passed out from lack of oxygen when Harriet finally found a pen under a pile of papers and take-out containers on the floor. Roughly, she poked two crude holes through the tape, got back in the driver's seat, and continued to the ranch.

He saw them pull in, standing at the window that looked down the whole yard.

"What an appropriate vehicle," *he* said to the worker in the room, at the same time positioning his foot over a large cricket trapped inside. He brought the foot down in a slow, deliberate movement, noisily crushing the insect.

"Them friggin' bugs are everywhere this year," the worker said.

"See that the boy is brought to the cave," *he* said. "Place him in the fourth antechamber."

"Yes, sir. What about the woman?"

"Send her to me. Be sure the boy is unharmed. Mind,"—he raised a long finger—"he must be whole and unmarked." The man waited. "Go," he yelled.

Listening to a cricket, Harriet entered the stuffy foyer of the house at the ranch, hopeful that he would at least be grateful for her loyalty. She stood by the small desk waiting. In her mind, she rehearsed what she wanted to ask for, like a new location and identity. That just made sense, seeing her prints would be all over that murder scene in Binghamton. The cricket stopped. No way she could go back to *Macromani*a.... A worker came out through the double doors and motioned her to go in. She entered the red and gold of the ornate parlor, wondering if she had time to go back to her house and get some of her personal things, maybe take some cash out of the ATM.

"That won't be necessary." *He* answered her unspoken thoughts sending a prickly rush down her back.

He rose from his chair, smoothing gray hair back from the handsome aged face. Coming around the room, he stood directly behind her. Leaning his height down to accommodate her short frame, he spoke in her ear, his foul breath hissing the words past her hoop earrings. "You did as you were told. You brought us the boy." She felt his bony hand on her shoulder; his long fingers and yellow nails caressed her neck.

"Yes, I did do what I was told. I have... I haven't once defied you." She had neither control over her stuttering, nor every hair on her middle-aged head standing on end.

"Did *I*... tell you to make a mess?" His fingers tightened on her neck. "Did *I* ask you to murder the woman there where she'll be discovered and connections made to you?"

"I didn't think she would fight like that. I didn't know—I thought it would be easier there in the shop. I thought... it—it would be quick." Harriet shifted her weight. She felt her cellophane bandage slip, pain from the stab wound sharpened as air crept under the makeshift dressing.

His silky voice mimicked her, "Oh, you didn't think, you didn't know. You thought it would be easy, thought it would be quick." His fingers moved on her neck, flicked the cellophane, loosening it more. "Well, which is it, Harriet? You didn't think, or you thought?"

She felt utterly petrified when his voice unexpectedly softened.

"Harriet, Harriet, my dear little soothsayer. Oh, how you reveled in the attention you received, taking such credit for borrowed gifts. Tsk, tsk, tsk! That's the sin of pride, don't you know." He moved slightly forward in order to look in her face and his grip loosened. "Oh, it 'tis a long list of sins though isn't it, Harriet? And we haven't time for all that have we? You will be looking for your just rewards won't you? Perhaps, a beach house, a new life, hmm? Want to be a psychic somewhere warm? Malibu, maybe...? What do you say, Harriet?" He played with the tape, making her wince in pain. "Don't be afraid. Tell your master what you want."

She relaxed a little, thinking he understood. He knew she couldn't stay here. They would find her, ask a lot of questions—maybe it would threaten *The Ranch. He* waited for her to speak. "Yeah, yeah,"—she brightened—"that would be good. I would like to live somewhere warm."

"Warm, ha ha ha. Yes, very." His left hand came again to tighten on her neck. His long yellowed nails dug so far into the skin they drew blood. At the same instant, his right hand shot out like a serpent snapping her neck like a chicken.

"I told you tramp, we haven't time for all that."

44

The Light

Clarice sat on the plush carpet of the Glen, her back resting against an enormous boulder. John lay on her chest, his big legs sprawled between hers. She watched her husband sleep, a fresh tear rolled down her cheek. Her fingers lightly passed over his torn T-shirt, revealing the wound, entirely closed like a physician had taped it shut with an invisible bandage. *A miracle!*

In gratitude, Clarice thought of her Creator. Such a long, long time since she allowed herself to talk to Him. When did she first begin shutting God out, blaming Him for what she saw, for her parents, their illnesses, and the loss of them. Everything was different in the light of the Glen. Sitting here holding her peacefully sleeping and whole husband, she experienced a friend in God like never before. HE knew her, HE alone understood her—all of her—all her worries, her grief, her loneliness. He knew, He understood, and He loved her. Oh, how He loved her! Could that be true? Could all of it, her abilities, dad's cancer, mom's mind, everything with Jackson, be part of some huge plan—all of it have a purpose? A hundred understandings washed over Clarice, but one stood out.

She was not alone.... *Oh God,* she never was alone!

You were there. You were with me when I was little, with me when dad died, there when I said goodbye to mom... when her eyes opened one last time and she recognized me— Oh God, that was You, wasn't it? You were there when I held Jackson, the first time. You sent us Nicey.... You—You sent us John! She looked at John, whose beautiful tan color had returned to his face. She stroked the brown hair and lifted his hand to her lips. Clarice cried—if not uncontrollably, certainly un-controlled. Sitting in the Glen holding John, she cried, chest heaving, nose running, shoulder shaking sobs of a lifetime of loneliness, resentment, confusion, abandonment, denial—everything...

Running out of her as freely as the waters rush by in the Glen.

Clarice emptied every speck of her life, past, present and future. She gave it all to God because only He could take it. And like the gentle Creator He is, He had waited for it to be given. God would never take it from his creature; it had to be offered. Clarice Martin Miller offered it now, allowing the hand, the very hand she'd seen a lifetime ago, to hold her.

Inside of Clarice the light, waiting all these months for her consent, spread to her very core, and at last, she reached out to it for answers and help.

She saw many things: parts of her past, of Nicey's and Jackson's, even flashes of John's attack, and of Roxy's murder. She saw God's plan for her son, the part he was meant to play one day, and one special truth that she would share with her husband when the time came—that time couldn't come if neither she nor his protector could find Jackson.

Search in Spirit.

Of Course! The out of body experience she enjoyed when pregnant. At once Clarice knew she would be able to find Jackson if she could fly again. With all her being, where she had spent a lifetime fighting the unique ability within her, she gave herself over to it.

The familiar wave whooshed in her belly, and Clarice watched the Glen fade around her. Thousands of balls of twinkling lights came into focus. Her body grew heavy, sinking down against the rock and ground... down... down... down while her soul, rose and lifted... up... up... up. The two, body and soul, so remarkably like each other, it seemed impossible that they could ever become detached. However, she felt herself willing the separation. In a moment, Clarice was hovering above the scene at the Glen, strangely looking at herself still holding her husband.

She rose higher and higher, as if her spirit needed to clear the treetops and forest. It did, Clarice realized. Perhaps being alive, a creature of body and soul, her spirit was constrained to obey some laws of the physical world. Whether it was true or not, Clarice felt she could no more fly through a solid tree than walk on water.

Clarice hovered high above the dark forest with no idea how to fly. She looked at her spirit arms and hands, transparent (a lot like her painting.) Clarice pushed them forward, did a sort of breaststroke through the air, and moved a discernible foot. She added legs to the mix doing a frog kick and moved slightly farther. *No good.* This wasn't water or air; she was spirit. She moved a foot—exactly how far she envisioned that stroke would take her. This had to be an exercise of the will. How did she sail that first time?

Clarice concentrated. *God, help me.* At once, her spirit surged forward. The rush of air flowed over, around, and through her. Then it stopped and she was hovering. *What happened?* Why did she stop? She tried again. Again she flew. A few more times this way and that, and the process clicked, her mind controlled her speed and direction like driving a car.

Now what? Which way? She had no idea where to look for him.

"Jackson, Jackson," her spirit called to her son in a language and a voice unfamiliar, yet perfectly instinctual. This time instead of bobbing and weaving in the manner of a carefree neophyte, she flew with the intensity and purpose of a hawk in search of prey. Calling his name her spirit hurried away over hill and vale. Spotted areas of houses or buildings held numerous darks and lights of what she now recognized were good and evil energies.

Jackson would emit such a light, and she knew it well. Clarice called to him searching and searching. It felt like a child's game of hot and cold. She sensed his aura. If she strayed away from it, she experienced it becoming weaker. Using this sense of direction, she sailed through the atmosphere. In no time, Clarice was zeroing in on her son, a heat-seeking maternal missile. He was so near that she could hear him calling to her in that same mystical language of the soul. Despite being only intellect and will in this form, Clarice was still aware of the physical world beneath her, farmy hills, very few houses. She suspected it was still the hills of NY and descended to the cold lower earth to find her son. Her spirit flitted this way and that trying to find a way to him. Was he buried alive in this hilltop? What could the cold mean? She couldn't be feeling it physically.

Around and around she flew still seeing no entrance. If she was spirit, Clarice reasoned, she should be able to go through the rock. She slammed herself forward plunging toward the mountain face, but as soon as she got close—saw trees and dirt and rock—she stopped short like a stalled car. She restarted, plunged again with the same result. *Shoot!* There's no time to learn how to walk through walls! So... how was flying possible? Maybe flying, a common dream, something all men dreamed of, was real to her subconscious mind, therefore possible to her spirit. She'd never dreamed she could walk through walls or pass through solid material, so she couldn't.

"Mom," Jackson called again.

There's no time. Clarice looked around. Two dark figures below appeared to enter the mountain. She zoomed in on them and discovered a hole in the rock. Her essence like a string of white light sailed in the opening.

She streamed in effortlessly, maneuvered the short labyrinth of passageways to the fourth chamber. These chambers about three to five feet wide were nothing more than carved out niches along the side-winding passages of a cave. Clarice's spirit was soon united to her son, and with her light so close to his, the two appeared as one.

He sensed something as soon as the essence came near the ranch. *He* went to the window probing the dusk with his eyes. For a split second, he thought he saw a stream of white light near the cave entrance. Concentrating, he felt only the annoying light of the child. Still, he couldn't take any chances. The child had to be sacrificed in the right ritual, in the presence of all the elders, who must watch the boy's destruction. Timing was not nearly as important, but it was after all the eve of her feast day, August 15. And what could be more perfect than to destroy the child tonight with all those insipid rosary mumblers wagging their beads in her honor? The sacrifice of the child would be his ultimate gift for the Master, given on a day usually painful to him.

He called out to the hall where some minion always waited to do his instant bidding. "Check the child," he commanded, "and report back to me if anything is unusual."

What the lackey saw when he reached the cave was Jackson, alone, still wrapped in cellophane tape and quiet as a lamb. His mouth had been uncovered. His screams were meaningless here, except to incite the gathering faithful to greater excitement and anticipation of the sacrifice.

Clarice was there in essence with her son. Both of them saw the young worker, who stood in the doorway for a moment looking at Jackson. He sneered, pointed a finger gun at her son, and pulled the pretend trigger. "Soon kid, soon." Jax ignored the worker, watching instead his mother's spirit hover above him. She wished she had her body to whisk him away. As it was, she was physically incapable of helping him. Though their communication was new to them, Jackson had no trouble following every one of his mother's thoughts. Their spirits embraced and he gave her clear instruction.

"Mom, bring my Protector to me. He'll deliver me from the fiends."

Clarice zipped away so fast that her speeding light force was undetected. She flew off in search of the Protector, Gabe Katz.

"The boy is the same. Nothing has changed." The worker reported.

"So you say. What is there to tell me of the preparations?"

"Some of the elders have arrived and are communing upstairs. A steady stream of lessers has been coming, gathering at the shrine of the sacrificial stone."

"What of the robes and black candles? There can be none unclad tonight."

"Most have come with their own, but we have at least a dozen extra. We put them and the boxes of candles on a table by the entrance."

"And the hounds? They are to be freed before the ceremony." *He* spoke observing the minion's expression. "Oh ye of little faith. They will not harm a black heart such as your own. They will only attack white energy; they will not touch that which has been marked for sacrifice."

The man left, hoping his heart was foul enough to keep him safe from the mongrel beasts.

45

John's Burden

John was engrossed in the deepest, most satisfying slumber of his life. He had fallen asleep in his wife's arms, and as he slept, his body healed. In the glen-induced coma, John dreamt. In his dreams, God enlightened him. He saw Clarice flying, and knew it was her spirit. He understood her ability to see the forces at work in the hidden spiritual world. He saw Simeon and the man who helped him to the water. He felt their powers. He saw his adopted son, and in awe, learned of Jackson's place in God's plan. He was also shown a painful fact, one he would share with Clarice when the time came. Most of all, John felt God's incredible love for him. And all the while he slept, he grew strong again. In a way, he was stronger than he had been before, at total peace with God's will. This new peace would barely be disturbed, except for the filial love he held for his wife and son.

When John awoke, still enclosed in Clarice's embrace, her arms felt cold and her legs stiff. He rolled over, finding her unresponsive and catatonic, much like one of Jackson's ecstasies. Jackson! He had to find him. This time his wife was the helpless one. He wouldn't leave her. Without much debate, John gently lifted his tiny wife into his arms, feeling as strong as a bull, and walked out of the Glen.

He carried her all the way back to the house and entered through the kitchen door. John went directly to the leather couch and laid Clarice down.

"John, what happened?" Father Tom said, startling him. In the doorway of the dining room, he saw both priests. Simeon's long black cassock made him look more wizardly than usual, and made Father Tom's clean-cut brown hair and full face look even younger.

"She's gone stiff, just like Jackson does. I can't get her to respond." Both priests looked at his torn shirt and disheveled appearance, minus the blood since the cold creek water had washed most of it away.

Father Simeon stepped to Clarice's side. Placing his hand over her arm, he closed his eyes and was silent for a full minute.

"She is not entirely here," he said, opening his eyes.

"Bilocation?" Father Tom said.

"No, this is different. She's separated from her body, at least mostly. Her spirit is free somewhere else."

"Where, how?" Father Tom questioned.

"What are you both talking about?" John turned his gaze from Clarice. "What's going on?"

"See, I came here with a man," Tom moved close, "a rabbi from Boston. We saw the shed, and thought you'd been injured. We saw blood and Clarice's tracks; then the rabbi ran to the woods to find you both, but he came out alone. Father Simeon came in a taxi while he was gone."

"John," Simeon placed his weathered hand on John's shoulder, "your son has been taken by *them*." The old hermit spoke gently, "Your wife is trying to find him. His Protector is doing the same. And I have a suspicion,"—he paused, eyes twinkling at him—"you know all of this already in your heart. Whatever healed you also showed you these truths. No?"

John looked in the bright eyes, thinking of all he'd been shown. "Yes," he said, "the rabbi was there in the Glen helping move me. He pulled the metal bar out. I passed out, and while I was asleep... anyhow I'm healed. I think, she uh, passed out or," John's voice dropped "left her body while I was out." He knelt on one knee by Clarice and caressed her cheek. "What can I do?"

"Nothing for her. We've got to prepare ourselves for their return. We'll pray for God's chosen one to be delivered from the enemy, for his protector, his mother, and for our own strength too."

"Tom, my case," Simeon said.

By the door, Father Tom retrieved a tattered brown and yellow checked suitcase and placed it on the coffee table. He unbuckled the leather straps and opened the lid. In it lay candles, crucifixes, stoles, a large bag of salt, and vials of Holy oils and water.

"It's for exorcisms," Tom said to John, who found himself staring fascinated. "Father Simeon is an exorcist."

Tom picked up a handful of candles, and John helped the priests light them and place them around the family room. They set out several crucifixes, too. Next, they sprinkled the room, John, and themselves with Holy Water and blessed salt. Father Tom moved the coffee table against the wall. Finally, they knelt in a tiny circle in front of the couch by Clarice's body, and prayed the rosary.

46

Deliverance

Rosie easily found *Macromania*.

"Nice job, Rosie." Gabe tapped the Pontiac's GPS computer. (Her mechanical voice and bing-bing-bing when announcing turns reminded him of the Jetson's maid.) All he had to do was punch in the words, "health food," "Binghamton" and "Main Street," for Rosie to find it. By the time he reached the store at 7:30, it had long since closed. Like Roxanne before him, Gabe pulled into the side lot, walked around to the front of the store, and peered in the window. The shop was deserted. No phone numbers or names of owners were posted. Only the opening and closing times: Monday through Friday, 10 AM—5 PM. Like Roxy again, Gabe walked the same path back to his car. He was about to get in when a red hand smudge on the gray metal door of the building caught his eye. Moving closer he found the door slightly ajar.

Entering Gabe was entirely unprepared for the homicide scene. Neither was Clarice, whose spirit found Gabe at that same moment. Clarice shrieked in agony. *"Roxy, Roxy, no , no, no!* She swooped down closer to her best friend sprawled in blood on the floor, slashed and bruised. *"Oh Roxy,"* her soul she cried out, *"be alive, be alive,"* her disbelief spilled as she fluttered madly around the body of her dearest friend. Even staring at the slashed throat emptied of pools of blood, some nutty thought of the Glen healing her darted by... but her soul was gone, the body a shell....

Gabe was astonished at the obvious fight the woman had put up against her attacker. "Baruch Dayan Emet," he said, "Blessed is the true judge." Sickened, he looked down at the twisted mass of blood and felt at odds with the thoughts in his head. Gabe was a Kohan, in the direct line of the priesthood since God first set aside the Levites for temple duties in the days of Abraham. Tradition dictated that a Kohan never be defiled by being in the proximate presence of the dead. As a rabbi and faithful Jew, he felt strongly for the woman, who had no one to perform the immediate services for the deceased, such as closing her eyes and mouth, laying her body in a dignified manner. Yet touching the body was out of the question from a religious standpoint—from a secular one too since this was a crime scene.

Crime scene? My prints! They were on the doorknob so far, nowhere else. He had to wipe them off and get out of there. He couldn't leave without finding out more about Harriet, the one who probably killed this poor soul. Gabe figured the redhead on the floor must be the friend that the Millers spoke of, the one who took Jackson. Harriet must have the boy.

On the steel counter was a box of disposable gloves used for food preparation. Pulling on a pair and dodging bloody footprints, Gabe carefully made his way to the office. Killer went this way too, he noted. On top of the desk, he saw a stack of papers with a bizarre hole gouged out of the middle. A schedule lay on top with the name Harriet and hours, but no address. He searched the desk for the name Harriet, found a few memos and messages with her name, but nothing to lead him anywhere.

On the bulletin board behind the desk, there was a master list of the employee's addresses and phone numbers. "Harriet Mansfield, 216 Bentwood Ave. Endicott, NY," he read, committing it to memory. Gabe left, first taking a handkerchief out of his pocket and wiping the door and handle on the way out.

Still reeling from the shock of Roxy's murder, Clarice watched Gabe's light. It was strong, like her son's. Even with Roxy five feet away looking like that, all she could feel was her son's peril. She watched Gabe's translucent form, seeing him rifle through papers on the desk. It occurred to her that he was looking for information about Harriet.

Sure he was headed to the woman's house, Clarice shouted in her mind at the man desperate to communicate. *NO! You are wasting time! It's a waste of time! No! I'll take you to my son.* She sent out the message, over and over, as hard as she could, trying to reach him.

In the parking lot, Gabe noticed the sun had almost set. He turned on the car's ignition, the clock slightly aglow in the dusk read 7:54. He programmed Rosie, punching in Endicott, then the street: Bentwood, and finally the number: 216.

No, No! Clarice's soul screamed without words the location of her son. Waves of telekinetic energy filled the car. Her spirit flitted back and forth in frustration. It seemed Clarice had no way to reach Gabe, but then something happened that surprised them both. Gabe looked at the GPS, which gave its first direction to exit the parking lot and turn left. The top of the screen, displaying the destination, read "Cobleskill." Gabe tapped the screen to change the location, and retyped Harriet's address.

"Proceed 100 feet and enter highway on left," Rosie's voice ordered. Good. Gabe put the car in gear and drove ten feet. Once again, the destination had changed on the tiny GPS screen reading "Stonefield Rd., Cobleskill NY."

"Endicott, you messed up robot," Gabe thumped the box still driving down Main. Once again, he chose "New Destination" and re-entered the information. Once again, the machine changed the destination to Cobleskill.

Immediately, Gabe thought of the black demonic force, afraid it might be trying to keep him from finding the boy. Sensing nothing, he pulled the car over and concentrated, reaching deep down to his gift as Tzaddik. He placed a hand over the GPS screen, closed his eyes, and was quickly convinced the energy affecting the GPS was good. From it, he felt love and concern for the boy.

"It's the mother," he cried. "It's you!" He laughed, looking this way and that in the air. "Okay, take me to him, and may Hashem protect us."

For over an hour, the car sped up 88 toward Cobleskill while Gabe alternately prayed for the boy and talked to the mother in the

GPS, sometimes placing his hand on it and other times straining to look out the windshield, imagining the filmy spirit woman flying before him.

The blue Pontiac pulled onto the long dirt road that led to the ranch, and Gabe's senses throbbed. He was by no means the only traveler heading to this place. He stayed behind the car in front of him trying to keep his wits about him. It was pitch dark out, so he couldn't see much beyond a sea of parked cars in the fields around him. So full in fact, that the car in front of Gabe gave up immediately and parked on the side of the dirt drive instead of looking for a spot in the field. Gabe followed suit and pulled in behind him. The driver and two passengers got out and walked up the hill. Gabe sat a moment letting them get a head start. Getting out of the car, he sensed Jackson right away. The boy was being held somewhere in this place.

A few spotlights shone on posts and buildings. He could make out an old farmhouse at the top of the property, the outline of a one-story structure on the left, and two flat stone buildings ahead on the right. Slowly he followed the three people in front of him, two of whom had on long black robes.

Clarice had flown ahead as soon as Gabe was on the right road. When she joined her son, Jackson was already aware his protector had arrived. On the way in, Clarice had sensed the dogs rather than heard them. She asked Jax if he knew anything about them.

"They're not dogs, even if they look like them. They're demons, although they haven't been allowed to hurt me. They sense my light; they want to tear me to shreds. Mom, they can see our light. If they see my protector's light, they'll kill him."

The dogs petrified her.

"They can't hurt you physically, Mom while you are *spiritus unus*. Only, they will frighten you. The elders are here too. But as long as you're in here with me, they can only sense one light."

"Who are the elders?" she said.

"They're the highest in this evil group. They have some powers. One is to see auras like you. You've seen one before, Mom. Member the doctor?"

She looked at her son wrapped in tape, his little feet and hands dark purple. Time was short. They needed a plan and fast. First, she flew out of the antechamber and through the sinuous passageways to the great hall-like room. There, every manner of minion had gathered. They wore hooded black robes and held lit black candles while they swayed and chanted. Clarice saw a number of them behind the stone altar leading the assembly in a ritual. They looked like versions of the hideous form she had seen so many years ago in math class. Misshapen beasts with slime dripping from tusks that projected from Jackal faces, which stood, even beneath their robes, on cloven feet.

If they hadn't been in such deep reverie, they would have seen her presence right away. Even so, they slowly sensed Clarice's light disturbing the darkness. The creatures at the front stirred, stealing glances toward Clarice. She noticed their awakening awareness, at once realizing she needed to be in the same place with Jax. They could see her light! Quickly she retreated, returning to Jackson.

"Hurry mom" he urged, "my protector is coming near the dogs."

Clarice knew what had to be done but could hardly believe she would be able to face her paralyzing fear of the dogs. She flew outside to find the fiends. She got no further than the cave entrance they now guarded. The beasts had to chase her spirit in order to give Gabe a chance to escape with Jax. She darted out making a show directly in front of them, crisscrossing this way and that, and weaving in between and around them. The dogs went crazy, yelping and barking. After she got them all excited, she shot out, away from the entrance and toward the farmhouse.

Both dogs took the bait and chasing Clarice's light. Jackson had been right, but frightening was a mild word for what they were doing to Clarice. The very bowels of hell lay open before her trying to devour her whole. Thinking only of her son, her spirit kept them occupied and away from the cave.

A fearsome sound bit the night, and Gabe stopped walking hearing an eruption of growls, yelps, and howls. The hellish din went straight to his core—whatever those fiends were they were a threat. Gabe paused at the large box of robes and carton of black candles. He followed the example of the man in front of him and donned a robe. He lit a black candle off the Tiki torch and continued up the dark trail.

The dogs' savage growls receded; at least for now, they were no longer a threat. This dignified pace was killing him drawing nearer to the hole where the three before him had disappeared. His need to reach Jackson and the nearness of the child overpowered him. Coming to the opening Gabe crouched under the low hanging rock as he'd seen the others do and realized at once that he was in the underground world of a pre-historic cave. Soon the narrow descent eased, and Gabe was able to walk upright in the widening corridor. Relieved since there seemed to be no one near him, he slipped away down the side passage. These caves were a confusing labyrinth. Under any other circumstance, they would have crippled Gabe's progress. Yet he and the boy acted as two charged magnets. Turning and winding through the gas lit passages, Gabe found the fourth antechamber. It was completely unguarded, and he saw why.

The poor child was bound head to foot in cellophane tape. Gabe rushed to Jackson's side, placing his finger to his lips. "Shh," he motioned and ripped at the tape freeing Jackson. Lifting the child, he gazed at him. This was the boy of his dreams, the boy he was meant to save! Under glasses too big for the cherub face, Jackson's green eyes met his. He smiled and threw his arms around Gabe's neck, hugging him.

"I waited for you for so long, Gabrielus Vindico," the boy's sweet voice whispered in Gabe's ear. "Will you take me to God's sanctuary prepared for me?"

"Yes Jackson, for this, you and I were born."

Gabe whisked his charge from the chamber.

On the way in, Gabe had found his way easily through the confusing maze of corridors by sensing the child. Now holding Jackson, he had no such magnetic force to guide him. All he had at present were dimly lit channels. Before too long, he was in the slightly wider passageway lit with electric bulbs. Unfortunately,

Gabe turned left instead of right. He and the child found themselves at the mouth of the great hall where vast numbers of Satanists swayed and hummed. Jackson took one look toward the stone altar and the members behind it and buried his innocent face in his protector's shoulder. Gabe hastily retreated, reversing direction toward the cave entrance.

The master of the ranch heard the fiends. *He* was in the farmhouse waiting for every last worshipper to arrive. *He* would not make his appearance until moments before midnight when the ritual would reach its climax, and the child would be sacrificed to satan by him, sealing the fate of so many, many souls.

What's this?

Something disturbed the atmosphere. He went out to the porch to investigate, finding the dogs running crazily about the yard. He knew demons possessed them because he had placed them there himself, but they were acting like senseless dogs, chasing an invisible prey. He grew angry and raised his hand to stop them when he saw it—white energy, flying this way and that. So the dogs had caught an intruder!

Gabe reached the entrance and thought of the swarms of minions in the main hall. There must have been hundreds of them. He felt their black hearts, heard their evil incantations, and he knew they could *not* be allowed to follow. They were—each and every one of them—a threat to his charge. They had to be stopped, but what could he do? Gabe paused hesitating at the opening, turning back toward the interior of the tunnel. He heard the dogs not very far off in the distance. They would tear him and the boy to shreds if they came back this way.

"Gabrielus, you know what to do. You have the power. God wants you to use it right now!"

Jackson was right. He was Tzaddik! He paused a moment, closing his eyes, concentrating on the power within.

Repositioning his charge to his left hip, and with no further hesitation, Gabe raised his free arm, holding it high over his head. Quickly, he pulled it down in the swift motion of a sword. An incredible force of power came forth from him. Like a laser beam, it sliced across the rock opening and cracked it wide. The earth made a great rumbling sound, and the ground beneath them quaked. Gabe stepped backward watching in awe the consummation of his powerful blow. In thunderous tumult, the rocks crashed one upon another, sealing the cave entrance shut. Holding Jackson, Gabe ran with all he had to the car hearing a terrifying scream rip across the yard.

He screamed at that moment. Too late the master understood the ruse, and what it meant. As the dogs ran wild with hatred after Clarice's elusive spirit, *he* screamed again, a shrill and inhuman shriek that followed Gabe and Jackson in the night as they sped down the hill.

* * *

Clarice's spirit couldn't keep this up much longer. She knew they'd won the battle (hardly, the war) as soon as she saw Gabe and Jackson's light escaping down the hill. She also knew she had to return to her body —and fast. She needed to be back by the time Gabe and Jax got there. Clarice saw a tall, black figure enter the yard. Such an ethereal cold arose from his black form that she wondered if he was even human. The creature looked up to the sky and let out a shriek from the depth of its black heart.

"Come!" *he* screamed again, yelling to the dogs.

They obeyed; the relief was immense when the beasts stopped chasing her. Clarice couldn't spend another second in this state. Outrunning the dogs had sapped all her strength. If she waited any longer, she feared she might not be able to return at all.

Soaring back and back, Clarice flew, using her body like true North on a compass. As she flew, she wondered about the creature down there, the damned soul with the blackest entity surrounding him she had ever seen. Who or what was he? Would it follow? Clarice sailed this time, no aura-seeking missile, but using her will and its connection to her own mortal flesh as a guide. Soon she recognized their land, and her light streamed down the great stone chimney of her house.

Hovering in her own living room, she saw her husband and the priests praying in a circle. A beautiful light surrounded them—stronger, different than each of their separate auras. She could see their angelic companions too, joining them in prayer. How stunning they looked, like men made of crystal reflecting a thousand rays of the sun. In an instant, Clarice felt herself sinking, her spirit becoming heavy in a good and familiar way... down... down... down.

She moaned on the couch. John was by her side at once. "Clarice, Clarice," he whispered gently.

"Oh John!" Her arms wrapped his neck and tears sprang to her eyes. They both held tight a full minute before Clarice pushed back, her hand searching his stomach through the rip in his shirt. Feeling the smooth skin and the miracle, she laughed, a crying huff-haw of sweet relief.

"Thank God, John. Oh, thank God,"—she kissed him sitting up—"Jackson's on his way! The Protector has him. I don't know when they'll reach us. Time is different in the spiritual world. Remember the Jewish man who helped us in the Glen? He's the Protector. He's so powerful. I don't know if it's enough."

"It will be enough if we help," Simeon said.

Both priests had been standing at a discreet distance allowing the couple their privacy. John helped Clarice stand, and all eyes turned to the sage hermit.

"All of us have a part to play. Each one must be true to the light within them. Such is the essence of faith."

Clarice looked at all three men, one too old, one too young, and one too innocent, an unlikely group to fight the evil she'd seen. Yet the light and power, the heavenly beings that she saw in this room only a moment ago, gave her hope.

"What do you want us to do?" Clarice said.

"Trust," Simeon said, "and pray. We'll continue until they arrive."

Tom looked at Clarice, the only non-Catholic in the room. "There are many ways to pray. We can pray any way that you're comfortable."

"Comfortable, I can't promise," she said with a nervous laugh, wiping her wet eyes. "I'm pretty new to prayer. I guess you could say I was born-again a few hours ago."

"Reece, wait. What?" John gawked at her, a big surprised grin on his face.

"I'll tell you later." She looked up at him biting her lip and slipping her arm around his waist. He squeezed her and kissed the top of her head. "It's alright, though," Clarice looked at the confused faces. "I saw the power of your prayer before I reentered my body. I think it was so strong because you were praying together."

"Communal prayer has always been recognized as the strongest form," Father Tom said. "Where two or three are gathered in my name, there I am in the midst of you."

"I know the Lord's Prayer. I can join you for that," she said, her eyes still glistening. "Do you have a tissue," she whispered to John. He reached in his back pocket for a handkerchief—her hero to the last. Clarice blew her nose and spoke still wiping, "I think I know the blessing yourself prayer, too."

"The Glory Be?" Tom nodded. "That's great."

The four returned to the center of the living room and held hands. They said the Lord's Prayer and the glory prayer and took turns reciting Psalms. Simeon invoked every saint he knew of in a long litany with everyone answering: "Pray for us." They prayed spontaneously too, praising God and begging for help and mercy. They called on Jesus, asked his mother for aid too. No stone or spiritual help was left unturned by anyone in the room.

* * *

He was mad. His 200 elite and elders were in that cave. A cavern made fortress, ironically by him. He was the one who had ensured there was only one entrance. When he first came to power a half century earlier, he had the coven seal all other exits. The tourist attraction of Howe Caverns, and that ridiculous Hippie element at Secret Caverns, had worried him. He thought that one of the many yet unnavigated passageways of those caves might connect to his cave. So he sealed them, and in a way... those 200 black souls now trapped there.

He was mad but not entirely alone. Someone was always within earshot to do his instant bidding. He still had his bodyguards, two he particularly liked close to him since his control over them was ultimate. Some tiny remnant of his weak humanity admitted that their presence fed his burgeoning pride and made him feel even more important.

He was mad, so he yelled.

And when he regained control over his senses, he yelled words. "Get the car!" By the time Cain pulled the car around from behind the bunkhouse, and *he* had climbed in back and Judas in front with Cain, they were at least fifteen minutes behind the Protector and child.

"What about the cave? Shouldn't we try to save them?"

"Why Judas, is that genuine concern for friends? How incredibly unnatural for you," *he* said. "A waste to be sure,... nevertheless, nothing, nothing is as important as getting that boy back. You will drive like a bat out of hell, Cain."

It seemed the physical world with all its immovable laws could not be controverted by those two cars racing to Ithaca, no matter how righteous, nor how corrupt the commuters. The most those two speeding cars could do was manage to cut the usual two and three-quarter hour drive to just under two hours.

Rabbi Katz was driving about fifteen minutes before he knew they were being chased. So, they hadn't all been trapped in the cave-in. Gabe couldn't *see* who was chasing him; instead, he *felt* the blackness in hot pursuit.

"*He* is coming, and he is not alone." Jackson Miller said, as though answering his thoughts. The boy sounded mature beyond his years.

"What else do you know, Jackson?"

Jackson answered Gabe in many, unexpected ways. They talked about religion, God, and the scriptures. Gabe's heart was moved while he listened to this graced being. Such understanding, he thought, yet still he labored to see the purpose. Jackson answered in Scripture.

"And He will send his angels with a great sound of a trumpet, and they will gather together his elect from the winds, from one end of heaven to the other. Jesus comes, Gabrielus."* Jackson smiled at his protector. "It doesn't matter if you believe that it is His Second or His First Coming because it will be His last." He spoke more of the Messiah, of the judgment to come, and of the mercy of God quoting Isaiah 18.

"Come now, and let us reason together, says the LORD: though your sins be as scarlet, they will be made as white as snow; though they be red like crimson, they will be washed as white as wool."

For two hours, Gabe listened, his heart expanding as never before, his soul buoyed with hope. His determination to safeguard this treasure of God to the sanctuary of the Glen doubled, and Gabe raced through the night.

47

Facing Off

Clarice was the first to know. "They're here," she cried springing up off her knees. She ran out the front door and down the stone steps to the lawn, awaiting Gabe's car mere seconds away. Gabe pulled up directly in front of Clarice, who took hold of the passenger door handle before the car even stopped. Mother and child were in each other's arms, joined a second later by John.

Gabe bound up the steps to the porch to share a few words with Simeon, who came out still wearing the long black robe of a priest. "Something's after us. I don't think we have a minute to spare."

"Yes, I sense them too. We cannot linger."

Gabe wanted to say more though. His heart was on fire, and he wanted to know Simeon better. "I learned... the boy told me so many things... I—" He hesitated and the two exchanged a deep look.

"I know Tzaddik," Simeon's eyes twinkled, "we will all learn much from this child." His long fingers reached out to Gabe's forehead, and the lips mumbled between the whiskers. Gabe realized the priest was blessing him.

Gabe stretched forth his hands in the traditional way of the Kohanim. He held his palms over Simeon with the thumbs linked, and also the first two fingers and the last two on each hand so as to form five spaces—five windows through which God's blessing would flow. He spoke solemnly, "May the Lord Adonai, bless you and guard you."

They both lowered their hands and embraced before Gabe ran down the steps to gather his charge.

"I love you so much, sweetie. We'll help you," Clarice whispered to her son. "We're ready." *Ready but scared.* She moved for John, so he could hug Jax too.

"We have to go," Gabe interrupted. "How are your limbs, child?"

"They feel fine. I can walk."

With that, Gabe reached for his little hand while Clarice held the other. John walked directly behind, and the four of them headed in the direction of the Glen. They had not even reached the stone path between the shed and the garage before the Cadillac Deville arrived. When Father Tom saw the ominous black car, he disappeared in the house to get holy water and a crucifix. The caddy pulled in fast, and all three occupants hurried out of the car.

He pointed a bony finger toward the path and yelled at Cain and Judas. "Get the boy."

Simeon descended the stairs, his walk purposeful, and his eyes on the dark man. He stopped in the front lawn before a giant oak and turned to face him.

"My, my what have we here?" *he* said, not moving his eyes from Simeon's face. He came around the car to confront him. The two stood facing each other about ten yards apart. Such striking similarities! Both men were old, both stood tall and lean. Both knew self-deprivation, training their bodies to submit to their souls. Each had spent at least the last fifty years depriving their bodies of worldly pleasure, spending long hours in communion with the being they worshipped. Lives of fasting and prayer but for such very different masters, and for such very different reasons—one for pride, and the other precisely because of his humility.

Their battle would take place in their wills with whatever powers they could wield or call upon. Like two great wizards they faced -off, the priest in his long black cassock and *he* in a suit as black as his soul.

Meanwhile, Cain and Judas set out to lock horns with the Millers. Clarice sensed the evil that arrived with *him*, the same blackness she had seen in the yard at the ranch. When she turned and saw the two huge men coming for her son, she knew she would not be accompanying Jax. So even though John yelled at her to run and, "Just go!" Clarice stood by her husband's side as Gabe holding Jackson's hand sailed past her, the two of them running as fast as Jax was able.

John wasted no time and slammed his body into the bigger of the two with a crew cut. The other, not much smaller with long dark hair and Italian looks, kept his eye on the prey ignoring John and her. He ran past Clarice, not even considering her a threat worth confronting. But a lioness protecting her cub should never be dismissed. No way was that devil-kissing brute touching her son! She thought quickly as he passed and landed a crude roundhouse kick to his kneecap tripping him.

The big one was knocked off his feet by John's initial move. He jumped up so quickly, John barely caught his own bearings. Fists flew, and each man landed a decent punch on the other's left cheek since neither of them had blocked.

Clarice had learned a few things in a self-defense class once with poor Roxy. Just after she tripped him, she jumped on his back and clawed his face with her hands, hoping her fingers would connect with his eyes. One finger definitely hit a wet eyeball, and she dug it in for all she was worth. He screamed in agony but still had the presence of mind to grab her wrists. Moving himself to a crouched position, he violently flipped Clarice like a rag doll over his head.

She slammed the ground with such force John looked up from his fistfight, and for his trouble caught another one on his chin. The blow dazed him but seeing his wife thrown flat on her back by that lummox, John became even more enraged. He turned back to his foe determined to be done with him. John's next blow knocked him out.

Clarice lay unconscious at the mercy of the Italian hulk, who hovered over her, pulling a switchblade from his jeans. John leapt at the guy, grabbing a fist of black hair and yanking him off his wife. The two wrestled for control of the blade.

Inside, Father Tom was fishing a bottle of holy water out of the checked suitcase. He crossed the room to retrieve the biggest crucifix, leaning on the mantle above the fireplace. Grabbing it too fast, he nicked himself on the pointed end. The crucifix was solid bronze, given to Simeon by Pope John Paul II two decades before, a replica of the top of the papal staff. The end screwed into a handsome base, only Simeon's base had been missing for years. He kept the crucifix in the suitcase. Armed with the heavy cross and holy water, Father Tom appeared on the porch.

He had been engaged in a mind reading battle of wills with Simeon but laughed aloud for Tom's benefit.

"And what do you think you have there, boy? Hmm?" His lips pulled back over yellow teeth. "Water you think is holy because it was blessed by your ridiculous excuse for faith?" The black eyes fell on Tom's hand squeezing the crucifix, and his voice mutated to a high-pitched tenor. "Oh my, am I frightened of that!" The eyes narrowed still staring at the symbol of Tom's faith. The voice fell, deep and guttural, unnaturally loud with the strength of a dozen voices.

"Your crucifix! Tis nothing but ornamentation, window-dressing, decorating your phony belief. You and all your kind with their soft lives of feigned poverty and convenient offerings! When was the last time you imitated him?" A bony finger pointed to the naked figure of the cross. "You worship what you refuse to follow!"

Tom froze on the porch. What a tremendous mind-boggling fear came over him in the presence of this evil creature! He felt puny in comparison and unconsciously clasped the crucifix tighter for support. Images of all sorts assaulted his mind. Impure pictures he had secretly enjoyed, fantasies he'd long forgotten and renounced came flooding in. Words invaded his thoughts too. And every word and image was so clearly a personalized-violation of his privacy that he was dumbstruck, completely unprepared for the power of the onslaught.

"Go back inside Tom!" Simeon ordered, hearing his own desperation betray his fondness for the young priest. The revelation of his fatherly love to the evil before him was immediate.

"Oh I see," *he* said, triumphantly turning his attention back to Simeon, speaking aloud again. The voice was vicious but mortal, telling Simeon this battle would rage, both on a human and demonic level. "You have a thing for this little altar boy, do you?"

"You vile son of Satan, you would not recognize love in any form."

"Son of Satan, is it?" *He* paused calculating, "Not by birth —by choice, which is more than I can say for your kind fed this Catholic crap from your cradle."

In that split second of the admission of his birth, Simeon's mind went back to the first time he saw him after seeing Clarice as a little girl. Simeon pictured him swinging on that swing set, staring up at his mother. Remembering his enemy's weakness, the old hermit dove in like Ahab with a sharpened harpoon.

"Your birth?" Simeon's hand went to his beard and stroked in a familiar way, forcing himself to look casual. "Yes," he spoke slow and controlled, poising the harpoon, "you were born to a very human mother and father."

"What of it, *priest*?" *He* spoke the last word so disdainfully that hatred literally hung in the air.

Simeon's voice rose, and even though it was no match for the prior chilling volume and bestial quality of his adversary, it sang with simple power and resonant truth.

"And those parents, who truly did love you, gave you a Christian name did they not?"

He must have feared where Simeon was headed, the blow to his pride too much to bear, for his black heart contrived to distract the priest with some parlor games instead. *He* glared up at Father Tom on the porch, still frozen with fear. His mouth turned up at one corner, and Father Tom's entire body levitated off the porch floor. Tom yelled no and pathetically threw the holy water toward the evil man His arms were not his own, and the water merely spilled around him.

"Put him down," Simeon bellowed. "You will not harm God's priest." Except Simeon knew *he* would do exactly that.

Tom's body jolted forward like a puppet and smashed into the stone pillar across from him. His face was immediately bloodied, leaving a trail of red as he slid down the column in a heap. In the yard, *He* sneered glancing to enjoy Simeon's distress then back to Tom, who was moaning and attempting to right himself. "Not done yet, Father Thomas O'Donnell? The party is just warming up. How about a game? Ooo, I know London Bridge." Tom's body levitated again. "I loved that game in the schoolyard."

"Take the keys and lock him up....." The body hung limp between the stone pillars, and his voice rose enjoying his own fun while he sang.

"Lock him up, lock him up..."

Tom's body slammed into the opposite pillar and stayed elevated. With a violent jerk, it flew backward again slamming into the first post. The body was on its way to hit the other stone pillar when a shocked Simeon retaliated, desperate to save his friend.

"Your name is permanent," Simeon's voice boomed across the yard. "Even in hell they shall call you by your given name."

"Shut up, priest!" Tom's body fell to the porch floor with a thud.

"The inmate beasts of Hell shall revel in the torture it brings you, in the irony of your name."

"You speak of hell as if it is a bad place,"—*he* hurried to change the subject—"You shovel that manure because it is what you have been fed. You are nothing more than a stable boy shoveling manure for a master who..."

Simeon stopped listening. Humble in his own knowledge of his human weakness, he knew that it was not wise to carry this conversation too long. Father Simeon hurried to deliver the punch, willing his voice to be heard by his rival, the unconscious Father Tom, and even the very woods.

"Your name is CHRISTIAN!"

"Born to Emily and Todd Menger in the month of Our Lady, Queen of Heaven, May 1, in the year of Our Lord Jesus Christ Nineteen and twenty five!"

"Shut up. Shut up," Christian's voice became so very human, Simeon knew he could begin the words of exorcism, thrusting the harpoon across the yard.

"Exorcizo te, omnis spiritus immunde, in nomine Dei ✝"

The priest made the sign of the cross in the air toward Christian. The ancient words of exorcism in Latin rang: "I exorcise thee, every unclean spirit, in the name of God." Christian laughed loudly, but Simeon only continued more forcefully.

"Patris omnipotentis, et in noimine Jesu,✝" (The Father Almighty, and in the name of Jesus) Father made another sign of the cross.

"Christi Filii ejus, Domini et Judicis nostri, et in virtute Spiritus ✝ Sancti";

(Christ, His Son, our Lord and Judge, and in the power of the Holy Spirit)

While the powerful words poured from the lips of this worthy priest, the agitation in Christian's face increased, and the legion of devils possessing him attempted to unleash a hell on earth to stop the holy ritual. Twigs and debris on the ground came alive, and hurled themselves toward the priest, who stood amidst the maelstrom undeterred. A loud crack peeled across the air as a heavy tree branch broke off the ancient oak tree in the yard and came hurtling toward Simeon's side. A blinding light appeared on that same side of the old priest. The enormous branch bounced off the light and fell harmlessly to the ground. Simeon dashed forward, drawing close to Christian, continuing the exorcism using his given name.

"Ut descedas ab hoc plasmate Dei Christian, quod Dominus noster ad templum sanctum suum vocare dignatus est, ut fiat templum Dei vivi, et Spiritus ✝ Sanctus habitet in eo. Per eumdem Christum Dominum nostrum, qui venturus est judicare vivos et mortuos, et saeculum per ignem.

(That thou depart from this creature of God, Christian, which our Lord hath deigned to call unto His holy temple, that it may be made the temple of the living God, and that the Holy ✝ Spirit may dwell therein. Through the same Christ our Lord, who shall come to judge the living and the dead, and the world by fire.)

Simeon's hand touched Christian's face, which was contorted beyond recognition while his once baptized soul fought to remain the body that housed his invited guests. For any other exorcism, these words, and this ancient ritual, may have had to be repeated many times to exercise such evil. However, the demons in Christian's body were subject to their master, Satan, who saw his enemy escaping to the silva templum, the forest sanctuary where the child would then be untouchable. So even as Father Simeon pronounced these last words, the legion was more than willing to flee this house being swept clean.

At the sign of the cross, churning black clouds escaped every orifice of the vessel named Christian, who screamed at their departure. The evil darkness churned and gathered overhead into a magnificent cloud. The writhing black legion raced in the direction of the Glen.

Christian malice burned in eyes fixed on the priest before him. He cared nothing for being free of his guests.

"What have you done?" He screeched. Willingly sealing and claiming his place in Hell, Christian leaped at Simeon, seizing his throat with both hands and choking God's priest.

Simeon felt every inch of his humanity slipping away, his struggle waning, becoming weaker and weaker.

Back on the porch, Father Tom was coming to. As he lifted his head, he saw the man choking Simeon. Still clasping the bronze cross, half-crawling he descended the steps. Trails of blood ran down Tom's face, his fingers tightly curled around the metal stem of the crucifix. He kept his eye on the two figures on the lawn. Father Simeon was on his knees now, eyes bulging in a purple face. The evil creature bent over him, his iron grip squeezing the life from Tom's confessor. The man was oblivious to Tom's presence staggering up behind him, even though Tom's crippled approach was anything but silent. The man's full attention and concentrated hatred was on the murderous strangulation of the priest.

All Tom thought of coming up behind the pair was the need to save Father Simeon's life. Father Tom raised his arm as high as he could, and with all his might, he drove the pointy end of the gold crucifix into Christian's neck. The heavy gold screw pierced the base of the skull having at once the same effect as a broken neck as complete as any beheading. Christian Menger was dead.

In the back yard, John fought the two bodyguards alone as Clarice lay knocked out. She awoke seeing her husband in front of her, battling the two fierce men. She could see John not only holding his own but getting the better of them, a regular John Wayne in the *Quiet Man*. At that moment, she heard a piercing scream from the front yard as the legion of devils quit their possession. Streaking above her a jet stream of black headed toward the Glen.

"Jackson!" she cried, getting up, ignoring the searing pain in her head. Leaving John and thinking only of her baby, Clarice ran—ran as fast as she had ever run—to catch up to Gabe and her son.

48

Thunderclap

Wind howled all around them as they made their way in the ancient forest. Gabe and Jackson both felt the powerful force of the Glen pulling them forward. However, if he and the boy continued at this rate, the black force—that they both realized had just been released—would catch up with them. In that instant, Gabe understood the protective force of the Glen was not meant for him. Gabriel Katz was meant to stand and face the entity with all he had, every ounce of his will. He was Tzaddik. He stopped, and Jax, who was holding his hand, looked up questioning.

"You have to go on without me," Gabe shouted above the roar of the wind. "I have to stay to face it alone."

Jackson shook his blond head and tugged Gabe's hand in the direction of the benevolent force.

"Go! Go!" Gabe yelled as forcefully as he knew how. Jackson, so small in his little navy shorts and blue sneaks, tilted his head and looked pitifully at his guardian, tugging again. Gabe peeled his hand from the little guy's grasp, realizing it would be difficult to move such childlike loyalty.

"Jackson," Gabe bent to his level and held the small elbows, "You must listen to me and do exactly as I say." The boy shook his head. "You feel the pull?" Tears welled in the little one's eyes. "Do you feel it? Do you?" He nodded. "I need you to run toward it, allow it to draw you. I must stay here to protect you. You have to leave me." Jackson fell forward grabbing Gabe's neck, whimpering. Time was short.

He threw his shoulders back and raised himself to full height. His face shone with zeal. He was in earnest now to take on the task that surely was his from the time he was born. *I am Tzaddik!*

"You WILL GO from me," his voice commanded. The command Jackson heard was ultimately divine. "NOW!" he shouted.

Obedient, Jackson let go of Gabe's arm, cast one quick look back, and then ran for all he was worth into the almost sucking wind of the mysterious force.

Gabe had only a second to watch him leave before he turned to square off with it. The horrible blackness reared up in horrific proportions the closer it drew. Gabe held his hand out in the motion of a traffic cop, exactly as he had in his boyhood dreams, exactly as he had in the *Black Dog Café* on the Vineyard—this time with the confidence of God's servant, the confidence of Tzaddik.

"Stop!" his voice rang, a thunderclap in the still forest. "In His name, you will stop!" The blackness directly before him halted. Gabe held his hand steady, looking straight into it while it offended every one of his senses. The thing seemed to laugh at his puniness. Gabe refused to feel small. He set his will firmly, ready to do battle to defend Alohim's chosen one.

The blackness shifted and swayed, writhing before him. Gabe could feel his mystical power wane with his mounting fear. The evil mass pulled back and high, some thirty feet above him. Flashing forward in a roaring wind, it assailed him with the force of a hurricane. Flying backward twenty feet, Gabe slammed against the trunk of a mammoth oak. Incredible pain shot through his back and head. Blood from his smashed skull ran down his neck. He barely registered the warm thick flow between his shoulder blades when he saw the black cloud rear up again.

Gabe hurried to right himself and weakly held out his arm to arrest the force again. *No time.* It pulled him forward whipping him into another huge tree straight ahead of him. Dazed and facing the wide trunk, as though he were hugging it, Gabe took inventory. His face was crushed—his nose broken and pushed to the side, his skin torn in a dozen places by the thorns of a vine that covered the tree. He attempted to turn over to face the thing again when suddenly there was no point. It surrounded him, a tornado spinning around its victim.

The darkness descended, devouring, enveloping him. Its swirling blackness was pure evil, conquering and mocking. Its vileness insulted every one of his senses. The stench overpowered him and while putrid slime enclosed him, Gabe held on.

Hold on to what? To what? The same question, at the same moment, he had always dreamed it. Even so, such mind-blowing fear and hopelessness, he had never felt, nor even imagined, not even in those premonitory night sweats.

... And they spun, he and the blackness.

And as they spun supernaturally downward in a motion that Gabe could only liken to a flushing toilet, Tzaddik engaged the enemy. This truth was lost on Gabriel Katz, for as long as he held on and fought with every ounce of his strength, every evil dot of that malevolent force, that legion of Hell sent to destroy the boy, was engaged instead with Tzaddik Gabrielus, chosen by God for that very task.

But for Gabe spinning in the fetid whirlpool, he saw no escape. What he did see were the bodies of souls, who appeared as transparent embers of fire. They moaned and cried in agony. Their despair was so real, he could taste it. Gabe hurtled toward Hell, sinking in a sea of malodorous quicksand.

"Oh Elohim, by your name save me. By your strength, defend my cause." The words of King David wet a tiny light of hope, like a drop of sweetest water on the driest lips... and Gabe held on. "My heart pounds within me," he prayed feeling that his heart would explode under the evil besieging it. "Death's terrors fall upon me. Fear and trembling overwhelm me."

The holy pleadings fell from his mouth, each one a precious drop dousing the hungry flames licking his soul. Against the winds of the forest still whistling in his ears, Gabe heard something.

Be not afraid.

The message encircled him, piercing the dark with light. And Gabe held on.

Take courage, It is I. Do not be afraid.

"Have Mercy on me, Elohim. My foes turn back when I call on you. This I know; Elohim is on my side."

In the swirling blackness, a hand stretched forth, the same hand that once lay on a little girl's window pane.

And Gabe reached out and held on.

Gabe held the saving hand of his Messiah, and felt himself being pulled, rising against the quicksand from Hell. The darkness lifted.

Gabe felt the flesh of his ripped face against the bark of the oak tree. He lifted his head but only got as far as his chin, which propped itself against the tree. Even the lids on his swollen eyes were hard to lift but finally opened to a fuzzy focus. The brown bark above him had yellow streaks running through it, a pattern... something etched in the trunk. He forced his puffy lids wider and made out the words.

"*Thou win*"

Scratched in childlike letters on this ancient oak were the mysterious words of his youth. The same words scratched in the bottom of his dresser drawer all those years ago. Here they were on this tree at his blood-stained fingertips.

"Thou win!" he yelled while his chest managed only a loud whisper.

He saw it now. Many sinners shall not perish but will repent and prepare for the coming of Christ. Jackson, like a new John, will be a voice crying out in the wilderness for *this* generation. The boy lives, and he will be prepared for the great task God has set before him as a son of John. Even his name made sense now, *Jack's son.* John the Baptist prepared the world for the first coming, and Jackson in his father's spirit will warn the world of the second coming, a thief in the night! How much time is left? How near is the Messiah?

For Gabe, he was nearer than that. His body slid down against the trunk of the massive oak, his hand stretched upward still touching the mysterious words of his life. He closed his eyes, and peace spread across his blood-streaked cheeks. His lips formed the words with awed reverence, "Hashem, Thou win. Thou win."

49

Voice in the Wilderness

*And thou, child, shalt be called the prophet of the
Highest: for thou shalt go before the face of the
Lord to prepare his ways. {Luke 1:76}*

Clarice and Jackson sat in the protective womb of the Glen.
Outside its borders, the blackness had receded, and Jackson knew
that for now at least, the legion of devils that had threatened him
and taken the life of his second protector had returned to Hell.
Nothing would find him here in this Glen, which would disappear
from human sight like the mythical *Brigadoon* of old. Heavenly
angels with flaming swords would guard it, the same way they hid
the Garden of Eden.

He rested in his mother's arms. His mother had valiantly
caught him up just when the black force was about to overtake
him. She swooped in, and on swift and sure feet, she delivered him
to the silva templum.

Back at the house, Father Tom and John worked on reviving
Simeon. The two thugs had given up after sensing their earthly
master was gone. They had run to the car out front, first the Italian
then the bigger one. The Italian stopped at the body, stooped,
yanked the coat flap from under his former master, and retracted a
billfold from the inside coat pocket. The big one took one quick
look at the corpse and spat on it before jumping in the caddy. They
drove off, bruised and beaten, and likely wondering what should
become of them.

Simeon lay on his back as Tom supported his head. He'd given him last rites after John used CPR to revive him. It seemed obvious, Simeon's spirit wished to be released from its temporal work, and begin its ascent to Heaven. He spoke, and John and Father Tom held their breath to hear what he said.

"Lord, now let your servant depart in peace according to your word. For my eyes have seen your salvation, which you have prepared before the face of all people. A light to lighten the Gentiles and the glory of thy people Israel."

"He's quoting Luke's Gospel," Father Tom whispered.

John nodded, his eyes welling as they both watched the light leave Simeon's once twinkling eyes while his spirit met his Savior.

After laying Simeon's body respectfully, Tom stood. Without a word, John and he solemnly headed toward the Glen, the Glen they would never find, and never see again.

Clarice felt her son stir by her side. "Is it time, Jackson. Does it have to be right now?"

"Another minute, Mom, that would be okay." Jackson answered, already following the instruction of the Holy Spirit, which he directly received in the Glen.

"What can I say? You know your poor mother's heart is breaking." She stroked his beautiful beloved curls, tucking that always-naughty lock in place. *Oh, God will I ever see his curls again?* "What about your gl–glasses?" He'd lost them somewhere as they ran through the woods.

"I don't need them here, Mom," he said, his beautiful eyes smiling at her. "Mom, I belong to God. He's with me here." She studied him, silent. "I'm happy, Mom."

"Oh honey b–bear," her voice cracked at the favorite nickname. She prayed for strength and words. "I'll hold onto that thought of your happiness... and God's love for you—ev-everyday," she choked, "every single day you are away from us."

"You have to pray, Mom with dad. Pray for me; pray for the world too, for all the souls. Jesus is so thirsty for souls. We have to help prepare them. Pray mom, pray."

Jackson stood, his action gently inviting his mother to do the same. Clarice looked about the Glen, still so enchanting, with mixed feelings. It was protecting her son; it was also taking him away.

"But... what will you live on, what will you eat?" She straightened his collar and nervously continued to run her hands along it and his tiny shoulders. "Oh my God I don't know if I can do this. How will you... what will you wear?"

"God knows I am flesh and blood, Mom. He knows what I need."

"Oh my baby, my baby. I knew, I... always knew from the time you were a born that you were not really mine. You do belong to God, and I'll think of you being in His arms."

The two embraced again, filled with warmth and beautiful light. And while she held him, (her hands wandering over and over his arms, his neck his precious hair — her kisses not stopping) she wondered how in heaven's name she would let go. How could she do what had been asked of her now that the time had come? *Oh God, I can't — give me strength!*

She cried, he cried, and they held on.

"It's time," he said simply and let go of his Mom. She looked at him — his face calm, his eyes bright with expectation, a serene smile... and even though she knew he was putting on this brave face — both to help her let go and as a truth about the state of his soul — she knew he would be happy here. He would be loved and embraced by God, the angels, and the Glen. And even if she did not see the thousands of twinkling lights, (and she most definitely did), she felt the power of the ancient Glen, supporting her. She firmly let go of her son. *Not mine. I won't call him mine. From here on*, she spoke to God, *I'll call him our son, but You better take care of him* — she shook a mental fist.

He stood there, his collar curling on his little striped shirt, his thin legs poking out of little navy shorts, his red sneakers; she took it all in and especially his serene smile. He seemed happier here than he'd ever seemed; he seemed full.

"Mom."

"I know, honey." She bent to hold his arms. "I love you. I *Will* see you, I will." He just looked and smiled.

One last kiss on the top of his head, gently squeezing his arms and Clarice forced herself to turn from him. Clarice walked out of the Glen, the only way she could, without a single backward glance. She knew the Glen would not be visible anyway.

Clarice knew. She had been shown many things while holding John. She understood her son would be prepared for his work here in the Glen. Her son would not be returning with her to the house. She would never again find this place. It would disappear once again—a mystical Eden, guarded by angels, hidden from man. *The Glen* would no longer call to her spirit as it once had; and unless God wished, her son would not be returned to her—and not as a child. *My God, how can I do this?*

The Glen answered her unspoken question with a zephyr, which brushed her cheek like a mother's lips delivering the softest kiss. She accepted the kiss as she accepted that God would sustain John and her. Their sacrifice would help save souls. Her spirit reached out in consent to her Creator. Clarice agreed to God's plan, giving her miniature fiat as the mother of her Savior had done two millennia ago.

"Let it be done to all of us according to His will. His mercy endures forever." ✿ ✟

430

Meet the Author

Carla Coon has been happily married to her husband Darrell for 25 years, living in Upstate New York and raising their eight children. They are new grandparents to three baby girls. Carla's first novel, *THE GLEN*, was born of a synergy of two great passions: religious studies and the outdoors.

Carla Coon's professional experience includes serving as Editor of *LifeWork*'s for NYSRTLC, where she also contributed a monthly column. Carla wrote in-depth pieces for *National Catholic Register*, and her articles have been published in *New Oxford Review, Catholic Faith & Family, The Catholic Sun* and the *Press & Sun-Bulletin.* In previous positions, she was Program Coordinator for a non-profit group and Director of Religious Education at a large parish.

Once a ballroom dance instructor for *Arthur Murray's,* Carla enjoys music and dance, roaming art museums, and travel with her husband. Her current work involves coordinating the establishment of family support groups in the Syracuse and Binghamton area.

& the Author's Family

(From left to right) Cpl. Gerard Coon, Ellen Coon, Darrell & Carla Coon, Catherine Coon (in front), Angelica & Daniel Coon, Stephanie Coon, Sr. Mary Philomena Coon, OP, Carl Coon and Cpl. Kevin Coon. Two grandparents, three parents, two in high school, one in college, two business professionals, two in the United States Marine Corp, and yes, one Dominican Sister of Mary.

Look for more in this series:

BACK TO THE GLEN, Book II

OUT OF THE GLEN, Book III

www.carlacoon.com

https://twitter.com/CarlaCoonAuthor

http://carlacoon.com/blog/

A Goodreads Author